G.J.

'An exciting, twisty read that had me hooked from the first page . . . a brilliant summer read'
LISA HALL, BESTSELLING AUTHOR OF *BETWEEN YOU AND ME*

'The best kind of mystery novel, a cool and compelling story of secrets within secrets . . . A story that's hard to put down – and hard to forget'
ALISON MACLEOD, BOOKER-LONGLISTED AUTHOR OF *UNEXPLODED*

'I was gripped from page one . . . He approaches a tough subject with remarkable skill and sensitivity. I loved it'
FLEUR SMITHWICK, AUTHOR OF *HOW TO MAKE A FRIEND*

'A gripping read, cleverly weaving multiple narratives and time frames to give a disturbing insight into a troubled childhood and its repercussions . . . heartbreaking'
JULIET WEST, AUTHOR OF *BEFORE THE FALL*

'[G. J. Minett] writes with such assurance and subtlety to produce a gripping puzzle which is also an uplifting story of redemption and recovery'
THE MORNING STAR

'Minett has created a cast of interesting characters and there is satisfaction in watching them discover the untruths and half-truths handed down through generations'
THE IRISH TIMES

'If you are a fan of beautifully written and thought provoking mysteries, look no further . . . a gripping drama, with long kept secrets at its heart'
NORTHERN CRIME REVIEW

'This is o   ot and vivid
character   ed with this'

G.J. Minett studied at Cambridge and then spent many years as a teacher of foreign languages. He studied for an MA in Creative Writing at the University of Chichester, and won the 2010 Chapter One Prize for unpublished novels with the opening chapter of *The Hidden Legacy*.

Also by G.J. Minett

The Hidden Legacy
Lie In Wait

ANYTHING FOR HER

G.J. MINETT

ZAFFRE

First published in Great Britain in 2017 by Zaffre Publishing.

This paperback edition published in 2018 by
ZAFFRE PUBLISHING
80-81 Wimpole St, London W1G 9RE
www.zaffrebooks.co.uk

A CIP catalogue record for this book is
available from the British Library.

ISBN: 978-1-78576-388-5

also available as an ebook

1 3 5 7 9 10 8 6 4 2

Typeset by IDSUK (Data Connection) Ltd
Printed and bound by Clays Ltd, St Ives Plc.

Zaffre Publishing is an imprint of Bonnier Zaffre,
a Bonnier Publishing company
www.bonnierzaffre.co.uk
www.bonnierpublishing.co.uk

This book is dedicated with love and gratitude to
Ruby Julia Minett.
Mum.

PROLOGUE

SATURDAY 25TH JULY 2015

The storm, when it finally arrived, was every bit as impressive as the forecasts had predicted. It was meant to materialise sometime around midday and maybe that was what lulled everyone into a false sense of security because well into the afternoon the skies were still clear and any thoughts of hailstorms and forty to fifty millimetres of rain within the first hour seemed fanciful in the extreme. *Typical Met Office,* was the general consensus. *Haven't got a bloody clue!* Except, of course, they did. Their sense of timing might have been slightly awry, but there was nothing wrong with their assessment of the storm itself. They knew exactly what to expect.

It came almost literally out of the blue. The first warning shot was a stiff breeze which announced itself by ruffling awnings and newspapers, lifting skirts and skimming the dust and litter from the surface of the pavement. Then the clouds came scudding across like locust swarms, treacle black, thick as molasses, chasing the light from the sky and squatting over the West End like some malevolent entity. Nature's literal five o'clock shadow.

People were slow to react at first. There were a few puzzled glances at the shape-shifting skies as everyone tried to work out what had happened to the sun. Then a handful of nervous uh-ohs turned into a collective gasp as the first fat drops of rain began to fall.

The effect on the streets below was electric, casual strollers diving for the nearest available shelter as if their lives depended on it, queues washed away in an instant. The rain and hail sluiced and skidded their way down the streets like mischievous children, puddles forming in seconds and inching their way towards each other to create a series of mini-lakes as the beast of the storm breathed its fury over the scene below.

In the foyer of The Prince of Wales Theatre, where the matinee performance of *The Book of Mormon* had only just finished, there was momentary chaos. Those who had decided to skip the encores and get to the head of the taxi queue had barely staked their claim when the first wave of hailstones swept over. A few resilient souls decided to stand their ground, until a passing van, hugging the kerb too tightly, sent one of the mini-lakes arcing into the air like a rogue wave. This was enough to send them scuttling back to the foyer, where they were met by a solid wall of people coming the other way as more and more members of the audience began to drift out of the auditorium and press forward, unable to understand why nothing seemed to be moving up ahead. Tempers were already beginning to fray at the edges.

Aimi was several rows back and still a good way from the doors but she heard the first crash of thunder all right. If it had been up to her she'd have been happy to go off to the bar and sit this one out. They had plenty of time to get back to the hotel room and change before dinner – a few minutes either way wasn't going to make much difference.

Unfortunately Joe was cut from a different cloth. Joe didn't do patient. To be fair, he also didn't do crowds or confined spaces, but that was no more than incidental here. She'd seen the glint in his eye and knew that his real motivation stemmed from the element of competition, a challenge to the ego he simply couldn't resist. No sooner had he realised that nothing was moving than he started using those broad shoulders of his to break up the impasse in front of him, one hand easing loiterers out of the way and the other clamped firmly around her left wrist as he dragged her along in his wake.

It's fair to say his efforts were not meeting with the general approval of others around them and one woman, having been jostled by him, looked as if she was about to put him straight on a few points of etiquette. Then she caught sight of Aimi and stopped in mid-protest, rearranging her features as best she could to sketch at least an approximation of a smile.

'Oh . . . hello,' she said. 'I almost didn't recognise you.'

Aimi turned to face the woman, struggling to place her.

'I'm sorry?'

'Oh, you probably won't remember me. We met earlier this year . . . Vicky Finn?'

Aimi's uncertain half-smile was strangled almost at birth. Swap the flowery summer dress for a professional dark blue business suit and the tablet she felt obliged to consult every five seconds and the missing pieces slid easily into place. She knew exactly who this woman was . . . and she also knew this was not good. Not good at all. Joe had turned to see what was going on, his interest no more than half-hearted for now, but even half-hearted was unwelcome.

'I'm sorry,' Aimi said. 'You must have the wrong person.'

'No,' the woman persisted, clearly a little slow on the uptake. 'The charity dinner in Brighton – you remember?'

'Actually, my husband and I . . . we're in a bit of a hurry,' Aimi said, and with that she turned her back, urging Joe forward with a new-found sense of purpose. She hoped that would be enough. Surely she'd take the hint now. Even so, she didn't dare to look back in case it was viewed as an invitation to continue the conversation.

As it happened, Joe solved the problem anyway by clicking back into gear. He'd spotted a gap up ahead and decided that offered a possible way forward. And when she *did* finally risk a glance over her shoulder some thirty seconds later, the woman was nowhere to be seen, already swallowed up by the crowd.

Only then did she realise just how fast her heart was beating.

Vicky Finn meanwhile was less than impressed.

'I think I just got snubbed,' she said to her sister.

'You sure you've got the right person?'

'Oh yes,' said Vicky, removing her glasses and slipping them into their case. 'I spent an entire afternoon and the best part of the evening running round after her. I'm not likely to forget Mrs Vedra in a hurry.'

She dropped the case into her bag.

'I'll tell you something else too – the man who was with her?' She smiled.

'That's not Mr Vedra.'

PART ONE

1

FRIDAY 14TH AUGUST 2015

Ashford. Ashford . . . *International.*

There was something about that adjective that always niggled away at Billy, brought out the cynic in him. It came across as just that little bit too desperate to impress, as if seeking to confer upon the place a status, a sense of glamour and mystery which was never entirely warranted by the town itself. Even the positioning of the word felt like an afterthought, almost a pose if you like.

He knew this was unfair, that he wasn't really in a position to offer any informed opinion on Ashford and its merits. Quite apart from anything else, he hadn't actually been into the town centre since he was six or seven years old and plenty of water had passed under that particular bridge. A lot might have changed in twenty years – certainly Mia always spoke highly of the town. She said he ought to try it sometime. It was apparently a pretty place with a real buzz about it on market days. She ought to know – she'd been making that journey into the gallery every day for years.

Even so, he had no memories of Ashford that would raise it above the level of most other towns nestled in that south-eastern corridor. It seemed to him that but for a quirk of geographical location which placed it in a direct line from St. Pancras to the Channel Tunnel, many more appropriate adjectives might just as easily have sprung to mind.

Ashford *Anonymous,* for instance. Or maybe Ashford *Average.* Ashford . . . *Anywhere.*

He picked up his rucksacks and slung one over each shoulder, his mind automatically seeking out other examples of alliteration that might fit the bill.

Ashford *Afterthought*, he decided eventually as he stepped down onto the platform.

A number of passengers had got off the train with him. Some headed for the exit, others were now dotted along the platform, waiting likewise for the connection to Rye. He decided against taking a seat, preferring instead to stretch his legs for a while. Even ten minutes was better than nothing. He'd been sitting all day in the media suite, not to mention several hours at home the previous evening, hunched over laptops, converting graphics into manageable file sizes. Sometimes it felt as if he spent more time using HTML, CSS and JavaScript than English. A bit of gentle exercise would do him good. It might also present a moving target for the sense of despondency that was hovering in the wings, waiting for a chance to settle over him. He knew it was there, knew as well that he'd never outrun that particular cloud, but it went against his instincts just to sit there and give in to it.

He'd done this journey three or four times a year since he first left home, initially for university and then for a variety of jobs in London when his studies didn't work out quite as envisaged. Christmas, he thought, ticking them off mentally. Mia's birthday certainly. His own, of course. Even Matthew's for a while because he knew how important it was for Mia to be able to feed the illusion that they were a family.

Every trip seemed to follow the same template somehow. The early stages always offered plenty in the way of distractions. There was the bustle of St. Pancras for one thing, St. Pancras *International*, a place which more than lived up to the adjective. There was something about the noise, the energy, the excited chatter echoing throughout the station concourse that he found compelling. Thousands of lives all converging at once. So many potential destinations for each of them, so many plans. It fired his imagination, inspired him to believe that the more prosaic Southeastern service he himself was taking might somehow draw upon the magic of its illustrious neighbour. For a short time at least, he was part of this great collective adventure. Paris, Amsterdam, Brussels, Marseille – they were all clamouring for him to reach out and seize an opportunity for himself. The fields rushing past the window in a blur were like some cinematic representation of the life he could be leaving behind. It was so easy to believe that all he had to do was stay in his seat and everything would come to him.

But it was never the Eurostar and as Ashford began to draw near he'd be jolted out of his trance, aware suddenly of a shift in the atmosphere, which took on a physical form. His foot would start tapping, he'd realise he had a crick in his neck from sitting awkwardly with his head pressed against the window. He'd start counting down the minutes, then the fields, the buildings. He'd get up and drag his rucksacks out of the overhead rack and hug them to his chest, trying to squeeze from those final few minutes some last vestige of the fanciful alternative lives that had been distracting him earlier. Then, as the train began to slow before grinding to a halt with an audible groan, he was back to being a poor relation again. Back in the real world.

In Ashford.

Ashford . . . *International.*

And the moment he picked up the rucksacks and stepped down onto the platform he knew this trip was only ever heading one way . . . and it wasn't into the future.

Now, well into the final leg of the journey and only a few minutes out from Rye, he gazed through the window at fields which, to the untutored eye, were not so very different from the earlier ones. But these were not opening the way to a brighter future – instead it felt as if they were rushing past to attack from the rear, suck him in and close the zip behind him. And as the first strands of early evening mist drifted past, he recognised each and every wisp for the fragment of memory it represented.

The past, it seemed, was never going to leave him alone.

And it was never more than a whisper away.

2

JUNE 2002

Thirteen years earlier

The car's there when he arrives home. He can see its roof rack from several yards away, sticking up above the fence that divides their property from the Wilsons' next door. Neither house has a garage, just a small concreted area directly in front of the house and separated from Udimore Road by a narrow strip of pavement.

He pauses for a moment on the front step, digging deep into his bag for the little purse in which he keeps the door key. His mother gave him one of her old ones and makes him take it to school because he's managed to lose three keys in as many months. He's not happy about it 'cos it's gross. It's got flowers on it and looks a bit gay, so he makes sure it stays right at the bottom of his bag where none of his mates will see it. He has to admit, though, that he hasn't lost a key since he started using it.

He's just managed to find it when he hears the phone ringing in the hallway and his first thought is school – they've sussed he's bunking. And it's not like it's his fault. Until the illness – they just call it that now rather than give it a name; that way they can pretend it's not so serious – his mum used to go through his bag every evening. She'd take out his planner and find out what homework he had and then check his timetable to see what lessons he'd got for the following day so she could pack all the right books for him. It's only recently he's had to worry about his PE kit. It's always been there by the front door in his sports bag, waiting for him when he comes downstairs in the morning. Even after they found out what was wrong with her, she was still managing to get up early, sort out breakfast for everyone, do him a packed lunch and make sure he was set up for the day.

But things have been getting a lot worse lately and she can't do half the things she used to. She's getting clumsy and her fingers don't seem to do what she wants them to. His dad's been on at him about how it's time he started thinking for himself instead of expecting everyone else to run around after him. 'You're thirteen, not six. You're not helpless!' *And he doesn't mind that . . . he can see it makes sense. Only it takes some getting used to and sometimes he just forgets, that's all. He doesn't do it deliberately.*

His heart starts hammering inside his chest as he waits there for his dad to come and answer the phone. He's been working from home for a couple of weeks now because he doesn't want to leave her on her own any more than he has to. They both try to make out it's nothing to do with the illness *– they've always planned for this, they say, 'cos he's ten years older than her and getting near retirement anyway, but Billy's not stupid. He knows.*

But no one comes to answer the phone. Instead it carries on ringing and even though he hasn't been counting he knows the answerphone will kick in any second now. And sure enough, to his relief, the ringing falls silent. He can't tell whether they've left a message or just hung up but it feels like a reprieve of sorts, however temporary it might be. Hardly daring to believe his luck, he waits a few more seconds, then cautiously inserts his key in the lock and lets himself in.

The first thing that strikes him is the silence. He can hear the fridge whirring in the kitchen and the slap, slap of his shoes on the tiles in the hallway, but that's it. No TV coming from the front room. No radio playing in the kitchen. Nothing. His first instinct is to call out to ask if anyone's home but he doesn't want to break the spell that seems to be hanging over the house at the moment. Doesn't want to push his luck. He leaves his bag by the front door and walks through to the front room, wondering if his mum has gone to sleep on the settee instead of going through to her room. They've moved their bedroom downstairs now because it's too difficult for her to get up and down the stairs and if she's going to need a wheelchair before long they'll have to get some sort of chairlift installed and his dad says they cost the earth. So he's taken their double bed apart so he could get it out of their bedroom and then reassembled it in what used to be the dining room, having shifted the table into the front room. It's all a bit cramped, but that's not the sort of thing you can complain about really, is it?

She's not in the front room. That means she'll be in the bedroom and he's about to poke his head round the door to let her know he's home before deciding against it. She may not have been in there long and if he disturbs her now it might take her ages to go back off. Instead he starts to climb the stairs, assuming his dad will be in the new study he's created out of their old bedroom, only he's not there either, which is a bit of a puzzle.

He goes back downstairs, noting with some relief that the light on the answerphone isn't flashing. Then he walks through to the kitchen and makes himself a cheese sandwich while he tries to work out what his dad's up to. He can only come up with two possibilities. One is that he's popped out for a couple of minutes, maybe to get a paper or some groceries, but if that was the case he'd have taken the car. He doesn't walk anywhere if he can help it. The other is that he's in the bedroom with her. Maybe he's got one of his migraines and has decided he needs a break from work. Or maybe they're just having a quiet chat together, a bit of privacy, but if that's the case surely he'd have come out to answer the phone?

There's an obvious way to find out, but if there's even the slightest chance his dad's asleep in there, the last thing he wants to do is wake him. He'll be finding things for Billy to do – homework, cleaning, tidying his room. There's always something, as if he can't stand the thought of anyone being able to sit and relax. No . . . better to let him carry on sleeping if that's what he's doing. Maybe it'll put him in a better mood for later.

Billy pours himself a glass of milk, picks up the sandwich and as he's doing so he hears the noise for the first time . . . a scratching sound, half a dozen strokes followed by a plaintive mewling. It's coming from the bedroom opposite. Luna, he realises. He hasn't even thought about her. If she's in when he gets home she usually comes and wraps herself around his legs before he's had a chance to shut the door behind him but they've got a cat flap now so as often as not she's out sunning herself in the garden instead. By the sound of it, she's managed to get herself trapped in the bedroom. If she keeps on making that noise, she'll wake them up and he can kiss goodbye to any chance of having some time to himself. He'll probably get chewed up for making a sandwich without asking and helping himself to a glass of milk as well. He can't let that happen – he needs to get her out of there.

He tiptoes over to the door, turns the handle and opens it as quietly as he possibly can.

3

FRIDAY 14TH AUGUST 2015

When the train pulled into Rye, Billy walked straight through the tiny waiting area and out of the building. There was no sign of Matthew yet but that was no great surprise. Mia had sent a text earlier to say it might be touch and go because he was driving back from a meeting in Hove. He'd do his best but a lot would depend on the traffic. Billy had offered to get a taxi instead but she wouldn't hear of it and he knew better than to insist. She was always quick to pick up on anything like that. Nuances were her speciality, especially where the relationship between her brother and husband was concerned.

He sat on the step immediately outside the building, leaning against one of the pillars, his legs draped across the rucksacks. Much of the heat had gone out of the day but there was enough residual warmth for him to feel comfortable in just T-shirt and cut-offs, even though it was gone seven. He tilted his head back and closed his eyes for a moment, suddenly aware of just how tired he was.

Double whammy, he told himself. Work was manic just now, the only word for it. He was starting to think maybe moving into a flat with Karun and Zak wasn't the smartest thing he'd ever done because although they got on well it was inevitable they'd be taking the job home with them more often than not. It was getting harder and harder to find a clear dividing line between work and downtime. Even so, he felt he'd probably be able to handle the workload and the odd hours if he could just recharge his batteries from time to time, but ever since that first call from Matthew a month or so ago, he'd been going to bed dog-tired and taking an eternity to get to sleep.

The moment he'd heard about Mia, he'd dropped everything and caught the next train back to see her. She spent the whole weekend he was there protesting that her *funny turn* had been blown out of all proportion and he'd done his best to go along with that because that's what she desperately wanted him to believe. But he'd never really bought into it and the moment he was back in London the doubts had begun to eat away at him. He needed answers badly, if only to enable him to settle into some sort of regular sleeping pattern and now, after Matthew had called again last night, it seemed the perfect opportunity had presented itself. This time, he promised himself, he wouldn't be returning to London without the full picture.

He opened his eyes as a white Audi convertible pulled up in front of the station, roof open, Massive Attack playing on the sound system. He was no authority on cars but knew more than enough about the A3 Cabriolet, having had to sit through a ten-minute lecture plus guided tour under the bonnet the last time he came home. Matthew Etheridge sounded the horn even though Billy was already getting to his feet.

'Need a hand with those?' he called out, one arm resting casually on the door frame. He nodded at the rucksacks but showed no signs of unfastening his seat belt. Billy shook his head and hoisted them into the back of the car, draping them across the rear seats. He got in the front and was still pulling the door to as Matthew swung round in a 180-degree turn to rejoin Station Approach.

'Sorry, I'm late,' he said. 'You been waiting long?'

Billy puffed out his cheeks and shook his head. 'Fifteen . . . twenty minutes.'

'Bloody traffic – I tell you, I could never live in Brighton. It's all stop start stop start right the way along the seafront. Nightmare.'

Billy shrugged his shoulders to make it clear it wasn't a problem, then leant back in his seat and closed his eyes. He didn't need to look at the route they were taking. It was imprinted on the inside of his eyelids – Cinque Ports Road, Tower Street, Landgate, then right into Fishmarket Road.

'It's good of you to drop everything like this, mate,' said Matthew, just a hint of the Aussie twang sneaking through as it did from time to time. He'd been here since he was a teenager but had never really lost it completely.

'No problem.'

'Naah, I mean it. Really appreciate it. I'd have given you a bit more warning but the US guys switched dates on us late in the day as usual.'

They'd already been through all this on the phone the previous evening, but this was the way their conversations had tended to go in recent years. Repeating the tried and tested always felt like the safe option.

'When are you off?' asked Billy.

'Wednesday morning. I'm meeting their legal team in Boston on Thursday, then I've got an appointment with the

CEO in New York on Friday and back Saturday. You OK to stay that long? I mean, it's not eating into your leave too much?'

'It's fine.'

'That's good . . . because I didn't mean you to come straight away. You could've left it a few days. I'd feel bad if –'

'It's fine, Matthew.'

'Right.'

Billy opened his eyes as they dropped down to Skinner's Roundabout and turned left onto the A259, heading for Camber.

'So how is she?' he asked, deciding there was no harm in chancing his arm here. There might be some mileage in rehearsing a few questions before they arrived.

'Mia? She's good, she's good. You know what she's like. Always trying to take on more than she should. I've managed to nag her into taking the week off from the gallery so you can spend some time together and she can relax a bit. Do her good – she's really looking forward to it.'

'But she's OK.'

'Sure.'

'So why the summons?'

Matthew laughed. 'It's not a summons, mate.'

'So why the invitation then? It's not like I need one to come and visit my sister. And it's not the first time you've been called away on business either but you've never worried about leaving her on her own before, have you?'

'Well . . . no.'

'So why now? What's so different this time?'

Matthew ran one hand through his number-four buzz cut, one of his more predictable tells whenever he wanted to buy some time before answering.

'Nothing. Not really. It's just . . . look, I thought maybe it would be better to have someone here with her, given what happened . . . you know.'

'But that was just low blood pressure, right? That's what you both told me.'

'Absolutely.'

'And they'll have given her something for that, won't they?'

'Well, I think it's more a question of making a few adjustments to diet and lifestyle actually –'

'So there's no reason we should be worrying about her blood pressure, is there?'

'Well, if you put it like that . . .'

There was a silence which Billy was determined not to break if he could help it. The question was still out there.

'It's just . . . look, it's all a bit isolated out here. I guess I'd be happier knowing someone was with her, you know? Better safe than sorry . . . especially at night. She tell you someone broke into the golf club just last week?'

Billy turned away and looked at the scenery as they drew clear of the town.

'I hope you're more convincing when you're talking to your clients.'

'No, seriously,' said Matthew, risking a glance to his left as if seeking to lend weight to his reasoning. 'There's been a few complaints recently about kids on motorbikes making a nuisance of themselves late at night. I don't like the thought of her being out here on her own, is all.'

Billy turned to look at him more closely. Matthew never seemed to change somehow, physically at any rate. There were a few more worry lines around the forehead and eyes but he was still in really good shape, all those sessions in the gym keeping the years at bay. Billy ran a lot and played football for a Sunday league team so he considered himself to be fitter than most but he guessed Matthew would probably have the edge over him. He'd turned forty a year ago but you'd never know it to look at him.

'It's not just that though, is it?'

'Billy –'

'What's wrong with her?'

Matthew indicated right and turned into Camber Road. There was a pause in the conversation which felt to Billy like a diversionary tactic, as if Matthew was rethinking his strategy.

'Look,' he said eventually, 'I really think this is a conversation you should be having with Mia not me.'

'So there *is* something wrong with her.'

'I didn't say that.'

'You didn't say there isn't either.'

'Tell you what,' he said, reaching out to turn off the music. 'We'll be home any minute now. I'm just going to dash in, grab my kit and head straight back out to the gym so you and Mia will have plenty of time together and you can ask whatever questions you have then, OK?'

'And she'll tell me she's fine, never been better and there's nothing at all to worry about . . . which is why I'm asking you. What's wrong with her?'

The golf club flashed past on the right, Point Farm on the left. Almost there now. Matthew gave a deep sigh.

'She'll tell you, Billy,' he said eventually, turning into the drive as they reached the sandstone house they'd designed themselves. 'It's why you're here, OK? Her idea not mine. She wants to tell you herself rather than have you find out some other way.'

'Shit.' That moment when your worst fears are confirmed. And he'd known all along. He just knew. 'Find out what?'

'Uh-uh . . . no way. You can talk with Mia. But it's not what you think, OK? I'll tell you that much.'

'You don't know what I think.'

'It's not what you think, Billy.'

Matthew pulled on the handbrake and switched off the engine.

She's standing at the kitchen window when they arrive. She goes to the front door and they're still sitting in the car until Matthew looks up and realises she's watching. Then he grabs his brief-case and puts on the big smile he always brings to the fore when there's an audience – the one that never quite joins all the dots – and gives her a quick peck on the cheek on his way into the house to collect his sports bag.

Billy dumps his rucksacks on the doorstep and hugs her.

And hugs a bit longer.

He knows, she thinks to herself, as the embrace continues. *He knows.*

There's a flash of irritation with Matthew for the briefest of moments before she realises this is unfair. He hasn't necessarily said anything. Billy's just very intuitive when it comes to things like that. Despite the age gap of nearly nine years she and Billy have always been so close. He was the miracle baby who came out of nowhere long after their parents had given up all hope of a second child, and she'd thrown herself wholeheartedly into the role of protective older sister. They'd spent so much time in each other's company when he was younger it's hardly surprising that each has this ability to sense when all is not right with the other. Almost telepathic – like twins, their mum always used to say. Matthew likes to imagine he's got a good poker face but the truth is he's more or less transparent and Billy was always going to sniff out the lie of the land before they got here. She should have realised.

So as soon as Matthew has dived back into his latest toy and roared out of the driveway once more, almost burning rubber in his anxiety to leave them to it, she brings through the meal she's prepared for Billy, pours him a glass of his beloved Tizer from the two-litre bottle she managed to track down especially this morning, and sits down opposite him at the dining-room table.

And opens up.

Because there's no point in delaying things with small talk. There's no skirting their way round this particular elephant. He knows why he's here and they're not going to be able to relax and enjoy their time together until they've got this out of their system. So she talks.

And talks.

Eases her way into it because she knows the first priority has to be to allay his fears about ALS. It has absolutely nothing to do with what's been happening lately but that will have been his initial, instinctive assumption. He'll have done his research and will be aware that even though ninety per cent of cases are not inherited, that still leaves ten per cent that are, and a one-in-ten chance won't sit well with him. In that curiously fatalistic way of his, he's been glimpsing shadows and fleshing out worst-case scenarios from the flimsiest of evidence bases for thirteen years now. Logic won't be enough – it's never made even a tiny dent in his conviction. And because these fears are so deep-seated there's no way he's ever going to buy into any feeble evasions such as they've been using till now. It has to be the truth.

So she tells him everything – or everything she feels she can at any rate. She watches his face as she promises him, offering to swear on a stack of bibles, that when she collapsed a month ago it was not in any way related to ALS or any other form of motor neurone disease for that matter. She can see the conflicting responses flickering in his expression, the desperate desire to believe her doing battle with the wariness that comes with embracing hope because they both know from bitter experience that hope's what kills you in the end. She assures him the fainting fit – it's verging on the dramatic to call it a collapse – was down to working too hard and having abnormally low blood pressure, both of which she's put right since he was last here. It has nothing to do with ALS. Nothing at all. It's just that the tests they put her through led to further tests and referrals and . . .

She's been able to carry him with her so far because it's all been true. She's given nothing he can pick up on that infallible radar of his. But from here on in she knows she'll need to be a little more selective as to which truths he needs to be told because she's not sure he can handle the whole of it. She's not sure *she* can.

So she works her way through the sanitised account she's been preparing all day and she can see the shadow fall across his face before she's even touched on the most challenging areas. She reaches across the table and takes his hand, *squeezes* it as if to show him – *look, look at how hard I can squeeze, feel the vitality in there. There's nothing to worry about.* And she's about two or three minutes in before it dawns on her that he hasn't interrupted once to ask a question or to challenge her on some element of the narrative which he finds dubious. She's not sure what she was expecting to see – tears probably, maybe a flash of anger over her decision to keep this from him until now. But this is not the Billy she and Matthew took in and cared for until he was ready to leave home. It's not the obsessive young man who threw himself into his degree course in web design with such total absorption that he burned out two thirds of the way through and had to leave. This is a different Billy – calm, reflective, analytical, as if aware that the balance has shifted to some extent and it's his turn now, at twenty-six, to play the protective, parental role that she's shouldered for so long.

Encouraged, she presses ahead, playing safe, sticking to the facts, embroidering nothing, merely massaging a few percentages and highlighting some factors at the expense of others.

Too close to the optic nerve for surgery to be risk-free – true, but only in the sense that any brain surgery carries an element of risk. Billy doesn't need to know that the specialist certainly wouldn't rule it out as an option.

Even if they do go for surgery, it's unlikely they'd be able to remove all of it. They could, however, have a much better chance if they went in after radiation has reduced the size but again . . . better not to confuse things. She has no intention of putting herself through radiation, chemo or anything else that invasive.

Radiation is possible but there's an eighty per cent risk of further damage to eyes and brain. Partially true at least, but she's plucked that figure out of nowhere in the hope that this will lend weight to her argument.

She knows she's being disingenuous, placing question marks against the one option she really doesn't want to consider because she knows Billy well enough to be sure that's the one on which he'll fixate, the one he'll see as offering hope. She'd rather keep her feet on solid ground, can't bring herself to try anything that might result in her losing her sight because that's the one outcome that terrifies her more than anything else. She hopes in time he'll understand this. He knows how important her work at the gallery is to her. Take that away from her and she's not sure what the point is anymore.

As a final clinching argument she throws in her one out-and-out lie of the evening, telling him that the specialist feels there's a realistic chance she'll be fine without any treatment. It might be years before her condition worsens. He's known several cases where the tumour hasn't grown or moved and the patient has gone on to lead a happy and successful life. This is what she wants to try, what she chooses for herself.

Billy doesn't look happy about this. She wonders if she's over-egged it and would have been better off just sticking with the facts. But he says nothing for now. He goes back to his meal, chewing over every morsel of what she's just said.

Nothing's won just yet.

But it's a start at least.

4

JUNE 2002

Thirteen years earlier

The moment he opens the door, there's a scramble at his feet as Luna seizes her chance, squeezes through the gap and hares off into the kitchen. He hears the crash as she flings herself at the cat flap and disappears into the garden. Having freed her, Billy starts to pull the door to as quietly as possible, then decides to risk a quick peep to make sure neither of them has been disturbed.

The curtains are closed but they're only flimsy net ones and the late afternoon sun is allowing enough light into the room for him to see that they're both lying side by side on the bed. Neither has stirred and already it's obvious that something's not quite right. In fact, two things. One, they're lying on top of the bed rather than in it. And two, they're both fully dressed ... and that's what's niggling away at him more than anything else. His dad might not bother undressing and getting under the quilt if he's just having a quick nap, but his mum hardly ever gets dressed at all nowadays. She's having problems with her fingers now as well as her legs and doesn't like to trouble his dad any more than she has to, so she spends most of the day in a nightdress and maybe an old housecoat if she starts to feel the cold. Yet here she is, all dressed up in one of her smartest outfits, what she calls her posh frock. Billy knows his dad must have dressed her – she'd never have managed herself – and the dress is going to get all creased, scrunched up under her like that.

He takes a closer look and realises his dad is wearing his best suit – not one of the grey ones he wears to work each day, but the dark blue one that's always saved for special occasions like weddings. His photo suit, he calls it. They're both dressed as if they were going to go to church. And he's got his shoes on, which is what really gives the game away, because there's no way she'd let him do that, even if they're polished so you can see your face in them. She has this thing about what they might have trodden in.

He steps further into the room, his eyes now fully adjusted to the light, his mind less so but playing catch-up with every passing second. His mother is on the side of the bed nearest to the door and he reaches out. Touches her shoulder. When she doesn't stir, he grips it more firmly. Gives her a shake. Still no response. He pats her cheek and is startled by how cold it is to the touch. Chilled. Like she's been in the fridge.

Later he'll be asked several times if this was the moment when he first realised and he'll say yes each time – of course he will. What else is he going to say? He's not stupid. She didn't even feel like his mother. The moment his fingers came into contact with her cheek, it was like stroking one of the dolls Mia took with her when she moved in with Matthew. Unless you've got a few tiles loose, as his dad likes to say, you'd have to know, wouldn't you? Have to.

But the truth is he's not really thinking anything at all. Whatever the rational part of his mind is trying to tell him, it's not *getting through. Instead he's all instinct – and the first thought that comes into his head at that precise moment is,* why hasn't she got her hot-water bottle? *It may be June and with the windows shut all day it's really quite stuffy in there but his instinctive reaction is to wonder whether he ought to go into the kitchen and make her one, like he's been doing all week because she's been feeling the cold so much lately. Every time he brings her a hottie she smiles and tells him that feels so much better. It would be nice to see her open her eyes and smile right now.*

And then he catches sight of her medication on the bedside table, the boxes and packets that are usually kept in the bathroom cabinet. He picks up each box in turn and they're all empty. He looks across to his dad's side of the bed and the table there has another pile of empty packets along with a two-litre bottle of water that only has a small amount left in the bottom. Deep down he knows what this means but it's not near enough to the surface to inform what he does next. When he reaches across her and grabs his dad by the hand it still comes as a shock to discover how cold he is. He pinches the skin at the end of one of the fingers just to be sure, but there's no response at all. Not even a twitch.

He gets to his feet and tiptoes across to the window, where he opens the curtains as quietly as possible. Then he comes around to his dad's side of the bed to read what it says on the boxes. They're paracetamol and something called ibuprofen. He practises saying it a few times, putting the stress on different syllables to see which sounds best. He's whispering at first till he realises there's no point in doing it quietly anymore. There's no one to hear him. So he tries it in a normal voice, then a slightly louder one, then louder still until by the time he feels he's got the emphasis right he's more or less yelling it . . . just because he can.

I-BU-PRO-FEN.
I-BU-PRO-FEN.
I-BU-PRO-FEN.

Such a stupid word. Where do they get them from?

He looks down at his dad for a moment and imagines him suddenly opening his eyes and asking what in God's name he thinks he's doing, yelling his head off like that, and bites back on a nervous giggle as an idea occurs to him. He takes a tissue from the box on the bedside table and tears it into small strips, before taking two of them and sticking one in each of his dad's ears. He sits back and nods to himself – that should do it. Not going to hear anything now. Then, as an afterthought, he takes two more strips and pushes one into each nostril, then shoves what's left into the mouth which is hanging conveniently open.

Now he can make as much noise as he likes. Who's going to hear him?

5

SATURDAY 15TH AUGUST 2015

Shreddies . . . Shredded Wheat . . . Rice Krispies . . .

Billy kicked the rear left wheel of the shopping trolley to line it up properly as he continued to make his way along the cereal aisle, eyes glued to the shelves in search of Alpen. There seemed to be some unwritten law which guaranteed that every time he picked a trolley from the rack it would be the one with a mind of its own. None of the wheels seemed particularly keen to head in a straight line, so what should have been a gentle stroll around Tesco was fast turning into a wrestling match with an unwieldy heap of metal, a contest he seemed to be losing hands down.

Not even a recalcitrant trolley could dampen his spirits though. This was like a trip down memory lane for him – not so much *this* store because the way he remembered it they'd always gone somewhere nearer than Tenterden to do their shopping in the past. But they'd always made a bit of an adventure out of their Saturday mornings – himself, Mia and their mother. He could remember even as far back as when he was a toddler and they used to sit him in the trolley's foldaway seat with his legs sticking through the gap. Mia would push him around the store, taking things off the shelves and asking him to put them in the trolley for her and his job was to stick his arms out to indicate which way they were going next.

Then, when he was old enough, they used to send him off to track down specific items that were deemed to be his responsibility – things like crisps, fizzy drinks and biscuits – and he got to choose. It was almost like being a grown-up.

On the way home from whichever store it was – Mia would know, he'd have to ask her – they'd always stop at a café and have a mid-morning snack and he'd sit there reading his copy of the *Beano* or *Shoot*, totally oblivious to what was going on around him. It was a family occasion but not one his dad ever embraced. Men didn't shop for groceries – they washed cars, mended fences, pottered around in sheds. Maybe that's why Saturday mornings were so precious.

He'd slept in till ten that morning. Tired as he'd been after the journey, he'd still lain there for at least an hour the previous night, trawling back through his conversation with Mia before finally drifting off to sleep. He might well have dozed on until midday if she hadn't come in to wake him, but the moment she said she was going to the supermarket and wanted to know if he fancied going with her, he'd leapt at it.

Matthew had a golf match scheduled for midday and was happy to leave them to it. He offered to give them a lift to Tenterden, suggesting they could get a taxi home. Mia's Fiat was sitting there in the driveway and Billy wondered why they didn't just take that. As if reading his mind, she launched into an obviously pre-rehearsed spiel about the brakes being a little unreliable lately and how she wouldn't feel comfortable using it until she'd had them checked over. It sounded shaky, her swift glance at

Matthew not lending any conviction to it whatsoever and it was difficult to escape the conclusion that the real problem was the prospect of Mia being behind the wheel. He thought of offering to drive instead but didn't want to make her feel any more uncomfortable than she already was.

He found the Alpen halfway down the aisle, pondered over it for a few seconds and then opted for the Original rather than the No Added Sugar variety. Sod's law said it would be the wrong one but he'd try to remember to check with her before they got to the checkout – always assuming he could find her in here. She'd gone off to queue at the deli counter ten minutes earlier and he hadn't seen her since. The place was heaving.

He fetched the list out of the trolley and worked his way down it to see where he needed to go next.

'Billy?'

He looked up, half-expecting it to be Mia standing there, although even as he did so it dawned on him that the voice was wrong – familiar, yes ... but not quite right. And the moment he realised who was standing there in front of him, this whole morning's trip down memory lane took on an altogether different perspective. He was dumbstruck for a second or two in a way he'd have been the first to dismiss as a cliché in different circumstances. He stayed rooted to the spot for a moment, uncertain as to what would be the most appropriate way of greeting her, and it was only as she solved the problem for him by stepping forward and giving him a hug that his mouth finally managed to find his voice.

'Aimi?' he said, breathing into her hair.

Mia's on her way back from the deli counter, trying to track down Billy and the trolley. She's just rounded the corner at the far end of the aisle when she catches sight of him, locked in an embrace with someone she doesn't recognise at first. She takes a few steps towards them, but when they break apart and she has a chance to see who it is, she promptly turns on her heel and heads back in the opposite direction, hoping they won't have noticed. All of a sudden, the washing products seem to offer an attractive alternative.

She has no wish to talk to Aimi Bradshaw . . . or Vedra as she is now, always assuming she hasn't moved on already. Probably not, she thinks to herself. The Aimis of this world tend not to turn their noses up at the sort of money and influence that comes from being a member of the Vedra family. She'll have recognised the golden egg the moment it rolled into her path and for as long as the goose keeps on laying, Vedra will be as good a surname as any.

If she doesn't like Aimi very much, she trusts her even less. At the root of it is the seemingly unassailable and, in Mia's estimation, utterly inappropriate place the girl has assumed in Billy's affections. If she could be granted just one wish in whatever time is left available to her, it would be for some miraculous event to rip the blinkers from his eyes and enable him to see the girl as she really is. Failing that, she'd settle for knowing he was in a happy relationship with someone who cares deeply about him, someone who might take the gloss off his warped memories of Aimi that owe more to his feverish imagination than anything else. Their so-called relationship was one of those teenage things, an unfortunate collision of circumstances – for Billy a first crush at a time when his emotional radar was, quite understandably, all over the place and for Aimi a chance to share and revel in some of the attention that settled on him around the time of the inquest.

Although she was relieved at the time, Mia can see now that it was unfortunate that it all came to a sudden and dramatic end when Aimi's parents split up. She went to London to live with her father and Billy was left feeling his soulmate had been ripped from him. Anyone with an ounce of common sense could see it wouldn't have lasted much longer than the six months or so they'd had together anyway. Unfortunately, when it came to Aimi, even that ounce was way beyond Billy's reach.

So yes ... Mia is keen for Billy to move on with his life. For some time now she's been hoping he'll find someone else to obsess about, which is why she's been paying such close attention to his presence on a variety of social media of late. She's resorted to this – almost stalking him online – out of desperation. He's always been good about staying in touch – in fact, ever since he first left home he's made a point of phoning her on a regular basis – but these calls never shed any significant light on his social life. She knows more than enough about his work, even if she still can't remember what a front-end developer actually does on a day-to-day basis, and she can describe in detail the strengths and weaknesses of his techie friends, so effusive is he when it comes to talking about that side of his life. Relationships, however, are another matter altogether and unless she embarrasses them both by asking pointed questions the subject never comes up.

So she's taken to diving into Facebook, Twitter, Instagram, checking photos for faces that crop up on a regular basis. She does the same with names, hoping one will stand out after a while and hint at some sort of attachment. A few months ago she picked up on the fact that a pretty girl with oriental features seemed to be draped around Billy in several photos and the name Nuan started to feature with encouraging regularity. She went as far as googling it and discovered it means *affectionate*, which seemed like an encouraging omen. Then, just as she was starting to get her hopes up, Billy posted photos of a party he and his friends had thrown to say goodbye to Nuan, who had apparently finished her course and was heading back to Jiangsu. Mia had to work hard to keep that particular disappointment in perspective.

Matthew finds her obsessive interest in Billy's social life highly entertaining, although not in an unkind way. He does his best to reassure her, tells her that when he himself was not all that much younger than Billy is now the last thing he was thinking about was narrowing down the field and looking to settle down. He was casting his net as wide as he could until he met her and having a terrific time too. He'd be more concerned if Billy wasn't doing the exact same thing. It's how males are, he tells her. They don't find the idea of monogamy very appealing at that age.

He also thinks she's a bit unfair when it comes to Aimi. He says her assessment is necessarily filtered through a shared history that would make it impossible for anyone to remain objective. He won't come out and say she's always been too close to Billy and resents the idea of anyone else coming between them, just as she's never given voice to her conviction that even an intelligent and perceptive man like Matthew can lose all perspective over a simpering smile and a casual toss of the hair. These are shadows that are tucked away in a dark recess of their relationship, waiting for the right moment to show themselves.

No, when it comes to Aimi, fairness isn't high on her list of priorities. She can remember so clearly that first time when Billy brought home this alarmingly self-possessed girl with the ingratiating smile, the little silver cross at her throat, the dancer's physique which endowed her with an almost feline quality as she moved about the house. It could have been mere coincidence that she appeared on the scene so soon after the delayed inquest and the attendant media interest which plucked Billy from relative anonymity amongst his contemporaries at school. Mia, however, didn't think so for one minute. The girl hadn't been there more than two or three times before the dynamics in their relationship became apparent. It was clear Billy was never going to come anywhere other than second. She told Matthew very early on that she hoped Billy wasn't getting too carried away because Aimi was all wrong for him. He couldn't understand what her problem was, but she was right then and she's right now. The last thing Billy needs is for Aimi suddenly to materialise out of nowhere like this.

She's just about filled her hand basket and needs to get back to him so that she can empty it into the trolley and check to see what else they need. It must be getting on for ten minutes since she left them together. That's going to have to be enough. So she walks back towards where she last saw them and as she does so she sees Aimi in one of the checkout queues. She's taking items from her trolley and placing them on the conveyor belt. At first Mia thinks maybe she can slip past unnoticed, but as Aimi reaches in for the final item she looks up and smiles. Mouths the word *hello.* Waves.

Mia can't quite bring herself to blank her entirely so she offers a grudging nod and walks off to find her brother.

Not while I'm around, she thinks to herself.

They were back in the kitchen, unloading all the shopping, before Mia got around to it.

'Was that Aimi I saw you with earlier?' she asked, reaching up to put the biscuits in the overhead cupboard, her voice light and airy, her back turned to him so that he couldn't see the disingenuous expression on her face.

'Yes.'

He smiled to himself. Most people would have said something right away, but not Mia. He knew she'd seen Aimi – she couldn't have been more than thirty feet away when she turned around abruptly and walked off. But she didn't say anything when she came back to find him or while they finished their shopping. She swapped banalities with the woman at the checkout and joked with the taxi driver who helped to load all the bags into the boot, and during the journey home she talked about anything *but* Aimi.

But he wasn't fooled for one minute. Assaults from Mia, he'd learnt over the years, were never full-frontal. She preferred to ease her way into difficult conversations. She'd pick her moment and sidle into it the way someone with no sense of rhythm takes to the dance floor. He could read her like a book, but that of course worked both ways, which meant there was no point in trying to lie to her. Far better just to keep the answers as short and vague as possible and hope the uncomfortable bits slipped through the cracks.

'I don't see much of her nowadays,' Mia said. 'How is she?'

Nowadays. Pick out the subtext . . . 'now that she's married.'

'She's OK.'

'She looks well.'

'Yes.'

'Pass me the dishwasher tablets, will you? I think they're . . .'

'Got them.'

There was a long pause. He waited, knowing there was no point in trying to anticipate where the conversation would go next, which angle she would choose – but no way was it over just yet. They'd all but finished packing the shopping away before she picked it up again.

'Funny bumping into her like that.'

'Sorry?'

'In Tesco. In Tenterden, of all places.'

'Yeah.'

Another pause.

'You used to play football with one of the Vedras, didn't you?'

Nicely done. Sly little reminder there in case he needed one.

'TJ.'

'TJ?'

'Yeah. Tommy. Wanted everyone to call him TJ 'cos he thought it sounded cool. Mad as a sack of frogs.'

'That's not the one she married though, is it?'

There you go. Nice one, sis.

'No. She married Joe.'

'That's right. I remember now.'

She closed the cupboard and scooped up the hessian shopping bags from the floor. He followed her out of the kitchen and into the lounge where she put them in a basket in the corner. He picked up the *Guardian* from the coffee table and flung himself at the beanbag which he'd always regarded as his own. He'd have taken it with him if there'd been an easy way to get it up to London. It would go well in the flat.

'I wonder if she always does her shopping in Tenterden,' Mia said, disappearing back into the kitchen.

'Don't know, sis,' he called out. 'Why don't we ring and ask her?'

She came back through with a damp cloth and flicked it across his face before using it to remove a mark she'd noticed on the coffee table.

'Sarky. Lowest form of wit. And you seem to be forgetting – I'm your big sister so I get to ask as many nosey questions as I like.'

'I noticed.'

'So . . .?'

He looked up from the paper.

'What was the question again?'

She sighed.

'Don't you think it's a bit funny that you're back here for one night and she just happens to bump into you in a supermarket that's about a forty-minute drive away from where she lives?'

'Not if I messaged and arranged to meet her there, no.'

'You *didn't*,' said Mia, standing in front of him with one hand on her hip.

'No. I'm yanking your chain, sis. Apart from anything else, how would that work exactly? I didn't even know we were doing the food shop till you dragged me out of bed, let alone where we were going, remember? And even if I'd managed to guess, you think she'd just drop everything and come running when we haven't even seen each other since we were kids . . . eh?' he challenged her when she failed to respond immediately.

'So it's just a coincidence then?'

'It happens. That's why there's a word for it.'

Mia walked behind the settee and back into the kitchen where he heard the click of the switch as she turned on the coffee maker.

She called through to ask if he wanted one and he said no. Next thing he knew, she was leaning over the back of the settee and resting her chin against the top of his head.

'Sorry,' she murmured. 'It's just me. You know what I'm like.'

He reached up to pat her face but was a moment too late as she straightened and retreated into the kitchen.

'So how is she anyway?' she called out to a background of cupboard doors being opened and shut.

'She's still fine. No real change in the last three minutes.'

'I asked that already, didn't I? I'll shut up.'

'Sounds like a plan.'

Even as the words left his mouth, he wondered if maybe they sounded a little on the sharp side, which hadn't been his intention. He left it a few seconds, then got up and stood in the doorway.

'She's fine,' he said in a voice he hoped would sound as conciliatory as possible. He didn't want to argue with Mia . . . not this week. Not ever. He started ticking off the bits of information like items on the shopping list they'd just discarded.

'Busy busy since they moved to Winchelsea. Still settling in – says it doesn't feel like home yet. She's had to give up any real thoughts about a career in dancing. Says her cruciate wouldn't hold up – she's had real problems with it since a bad fall a couple of years ago. Spends a lot of time choreographing now instead with a dance group in Brighton and she's also doing a bit of teaching part-time at a dance school over that way. Other than that . . .' He spread his arms to suggest that there was nothing more he could recall from the conversation.

Mia looked at him for several seconds, opened her mouth as if to say something, then closed it again. Their conversations were always like this whenever Aimi was the subject. Mia seemed to feel the need to weigh the merits of every sentence before speaking. All she had to offer this time was a fairly feeble 'Well, it's good to know she's all right,' which was almost embarrassingly transparent. What she really meant was, *are you OK?* She wanted to know how he felt after bumping into her like that, to tell him he could talk to her any time he liked if there was something bothering him, because that's how she was – always there for him. And above all else, she wanted to urge him to be careful. Nothing so crass as *stay away from her* because she knew how counter-productive that sort of approach would be, but she'd be anxious to reinforce the idea that any contact with Aimi Bradshaw was not a good idea. And contact with Aimi Vedra would be even worse.

He knew all this . . . which is why he *didn't* tell her that before they went their separate ways in the supermarket, they'd updated phone numbers.

Or that they'd agreed they'd meet up sometime soon for a coffee in town or a drink one evening so that they could really catch up.

It felt like the last thing Mia needed to know right now.

6

JUNE 2002

Thirteen years earlier

Somewhere in the middle of all this it occurs to him that he ought to be phoning someone. Ambulance? The doctors' surgery? There doesn't seem much point in either of those. Mia maybe? He checks the clock on the dressing table and can see it's only just gone half four. She doesn't like it when people phone her at work and even though he's pretty sure this would count as special circumstances, he thinks it might be better to wait till she's at least left the gallery. She can take over then – she'll know what to do.

He goes back round to his mum's side of the bed and sits next to her while he's waiting. He takes the hand nearest to him and rubs it between his own to see if that will warm it up a little. Then he looks closely at her face, which he can see more clearly with the curtains open, and he's struck by how pale she is. He knows how much she'd hate that.

Once Mia's here, strangers are going to be traipsing through not just the house but this bedroom specifically. It's bad enough that they probably won't have taken their shoes off at the door but they're going to be looking at her. Bending over and staring straight into her face. She must have thought about the visitors 'cos he can't come up with any other reason why she'd have put the posh frock on, but she obviously hasn't thought about her face and how plain she'll look. She's always been a pretty lady for her age – everyone says so. His dad likes to pretend he's angry when she makes them late because she always needs one last look in the mirror, which usually turns into five or six minutes, but they all know it's not a serious moan. It's more like their private joke and you can tell he's proud of the way she looks.

They'd both like him to believe she'll get better but if there's one thing that gives the game away it's the fact that she's not taken much care over her appearance for a while now . . . as if she's given up. And if strangers are going to come in and stare at her, the least he can do is make sure she's ready for them. That would mean more to her than a hottie.

On the dressing table is a purple case which his dad calls her magic box. He says that's where she keeps all those potions that turn Cinderella into a princess. Billy carries it back over to the bed where he perches at his mother's side. He starts to take things out, lining them up along the bedspread and trying to work out what he's supposed to do with each of them.

He used to watch her doing this a lot when he was small but hasn't done it for so long now that nothing looks even vaguely familiar. He's sure she didn't have half this stuff back then. There are pencils, brushes, a sponge, small balls of cotton wool, various tubes, bottles and jars and a small tin which, when he opens it, looks like an artist's palette with lots of different colours. He decides which items he'll use and puts the rest back in the case, *including a bottle which says 'cleanser'. She won't need that – her face isn't dirty.*

He starts with her eyes, tentatively at first, trying to remember what she used to do. He takes one of the brushes, swirls it around in the eyeshadow, then sweeps it across each eyelid from the start of the lashes to the eyebrow. He picks up and rejects the eyeliner – he's not sure what he's meant to do with that – and even though he knows what mascara is, that still presents him with a bit of a problem 'cos he doesn't see how he can do that with her eyes closed. He has no intention of propping them open with his free hand so it's a real struggle to use it without leaving black smudges everywhere. There's a pencil though, which he's pretty sure was for making her eyebrows look thicker than they were and he plays with that for a while until he's more or less satisfied with the way it's turned out.

He spends about a quarter of an hour in total on the rest of her face, dabbing it with a variety of powders, swishing the brush back and forth to try to make it all spread evenly. He wants to make her look warmer so he tries something called 'blusher', using a brush to sweep the powder across her cheeks. Then he chooses a bright red lipstick and tries to keep his hand steady as he aims to stay inside the lines, just like he used to do in his picture books when he was at primary school. And finally, to round it off, he takes her hairbrush and lifts her head from the pillow so that he can brush it out properly. It feels greasy to the touch and he's not convinced it looks much better once he's finished but at least he's done his best. He thinks she'd be pleased he's made the effort at least.

He sits back and turns on the overhead light to get a better idea of how she looks. And he's disappointed. The lips are ragged where he's slipped outside the lines. The eyelids are not bad but they don't have the sharpness they always used to have when she did them – something's missing there, a bit of sparkle. As for the face, it's certainly not pale anymore, you can at least say that much. But the cheeks look silly with these two pink blobs. He's going to have to do something about that.

What he really needs, he thinks to himself, is someone else to practise on.

7

SUNDAY 16TH AUGUST 2015

The first text came in around one in the morning. He was lucky he was struggling to get to sleep again, otherwise he might well have missed it. His first guess when he heard the beep was either Karun or Zak who had only the haziest, weed-fuelled concept of time. This meant their working hours were as random as their lifestyle and they tended to assume everyone else operated in the same way. When he checked though, the name *Aimi* beamed back at him. At least, *beamed* was how it felt.

u awake?
Yep.
Still fancy meeting up? Need to talk to someone I can trust.

Interesting. He wondered what that meant exactly.

Sure. When?
Tomorrow pm maybe? I mean today. Just realised the time.
Where?
Walking Suki on Camber Sands. U up for it? Say 2ish?

He thought about this. He'd have felt happier saying yes if he'd had a chance to check with Mia what her plans for the afternoon might be. He knew she'd be going to church in the morning. When she was younger she used to go in for that sort of thing in a big way – Sunday school, confirmation classes, communion – and kept it going right up until she moved in with Matthew. Billy knew she'd dropped off for a good while after that, presumably because Matthew was totally dismissive of the whole thing, so it wasn't something they'd ever been able to share. Now she seemed to have rediscovered religion. Billy didn't like to look too closely at why that might be.

He felt the same way as Matthew and had kicked like mad against going to Sunday school. He hadn't given religion any thought since the age of about ten, but when Mia mentioned it before going to bed and asked if he'd like to come along and keep her company, he'd swallowed whatever principles were tied up in all this and said yes. He'd be happy just to sit there with her as long as he didn't have to worry about any of the God bits. She'd smiled and kissed him on the cheek and he knew he'd made the right decision.

So he knows what they'll be doing in the morning and has already said he'll help her with the Sunday lunch. He's got no idea whether she's got anything arranged for the afternoon though. If he knows Matthew, he'll be off to the gym the moment his lunch has gone down and Billy doesn't want to leave Mia on her own . . . but neither does he want to say no to Aimi. She may assume he's not interested and not ask again.

And if she needs to talk to someone, he *really* does want to listen.

You still there?

Yep. Just thinking. Bit later maybe? Say . . . 2.30?

Great. Car park. Outside the Oasis. Will explain then.

Got to go.

OK.

He turned off the screen and flopped back onto his pillow

Need to talk to someone I can trust.

Those eight words, he suspected, were going to keep him awake for a good while yet.

He left the house around quarter past two, a sense of guilty exhilaration tempting him almost to skip down the drive. He'd spent most of the morning worrying about what excuse he might give for disappearing for half the afternoon. It was silly really – it's not like he was a kid anymore. He didn't need to explain or justify himself. If he wanted to spend a couple of hours catching up with an old friend that was his affair. He'd spent his entire childhood looking forward to the day when his every decision wouldn't be picked over by adults and here he was, in his mid-twenties, still unable to please himself without feeling guilty.

But if Mia knew he was meeting Aimi, he'd never hear the end of it. He hated not being straight with her but her tendency to get certain things out of all proportion pretty much took the honesty option away from him. Yesterday morning had been bad enough and that was just a chance meeting and a five-minute conversation in a crowded supermarket. If she knew Aimi had texted in the early hours of the morning to arrange to meet up for a walk along Camber Sands, she'd freak.

But then, to his intense relief, she'd decided over lunch that she felt tired and thought a couple of hours in bed would probably do her the world of good, if no one had any objection. Matthew said it was fine by him – he was going to need most of the afternoon to work on the various papers he'd be presenting during his trip to the States. She asked Billy if he'd be OK and he did his best not to let his relief show. Two problems had been solved at a stroke. Mia wouldn't be offering to come with him and he wouldn't be leaving her there on her own. He could meet up with Aimi with a clear conscience.

Or almost clear.

He told her he'd probably go for a long walk on the beach so that he could give some serious thought to the work he'd brought with him and not even looked at yet. He also needed to phone Karun to let him know he was a bit behind schedule so he could kill two birds with one stone and then get stuck into the work when he got back, feeling refreshed. He worried for a moment that his explanation might have been a little too elaborate, but if she was at all suspicious, she gave no sign of it.

The moment they'd finished stacking the dishwasher and washing up the remaining odds and ends that wouldn't fit, she took her leave and went upstairs. Two minutes later he was turning left out of the drive and picking up the footpath which skirted the road. Just beyond the entrance to Camber itself, he crossed over and walked through a wooden gate into a large grassed area with a gravel path running alongside it. Up ahead he could see a flagpole in the distance with the Union Jack flapping in desultory fashion in a breeze that was barely noticeable until you came this close to the sea. From there, he knew, a path led up through the dunes and then dropped away to the beach, but he'd arranged to meet Aimi at the Oasis Beach Shop which had been a favourite haunt of theirs on warm summer days. He remembered how they used to sit there and pool whatever coins they had before deciding what they might have as an afternoon snack. That presumably wasn't something she needed to worry about anymore.

He arrived a few minutes early and was surprised to see her waiting there already, wearing a white thigh-length kaftan dress and white beach shoes with rip-tape straps across the foot and heel. She had her dog on a lead, a deep-chested, long-legged animal which looked a lot like a greyhound. He'd heard the name of the breed before but was struggling to remember it until Aimi said: *Meet Suki – Suki the saluki. Joe's idea not mine.* She stepped forward and gave him a hug and he made a clumsy attempt to kiss her on the cheek at the exact moment she stooped to stroke the dog's ears.

'Thanks for coming,' she said. 'You didn't mind, did you?'

'No.'

'I felt so embarrassed afterwards. I had no idea what time it was or I'd have waited till this morning.'

'It wasn't a problem. I was awake anyway.'

She smiled and patted his arm.

'I'd forgotten how considerate you are. Remember all those times I was late and kept you standing around waiting for ages? I don't think you complained once.'

He was unsure what to say to this. He didn't remember her ever being late for him. Was she getting him confused with someone else, or was his memory playing tricks on him again? He certainly hadn't forgotten anything else about her. The blonde hair was shorter – she'd worn it loose back in the day and he remembered how it used to whip back and forth across her face when she danced. Now she went for a pixie cut which accentuated her cheekbones and showed off the slender neck to good effect. But she was just as willowy as he remembered and carried herself with a sylphlike poise and confidence that made her look taller than she actually was, even in flat beach shoes. As for the smile, there was no change there either – it still served its intended purpose of sucking you in before the wide green eyes slammed the gate shut behind you. Yesterday's encounter had been too brief, too rushed, so there'd been no time really to shake off the initial shock of seeing her again like that. Now he was able to look more closely at her and take stock, drink in the memories. He was aware of the pull already.

'Oh hell – the ball launcher,' she said suddenly, 'how stupid can you get!'

She'd left it in the boot of the car and couldn't possibly go for a walk on the beach without it. Suki could sulk for England, she said. Her car was in the Gallivant car park on the other side of the road. She asked if he'd mind holding Suki's lead while she went back to fetch it but he offered to go instead. She told him it was in a Tesco bag in the boot along with her cardigan, and asked if he could just bring the bag as it was. She said she might need the cardigan if the breeze got up later. He glanced at the flag again, seriously doubting she'd actually need it.

'It's the yellow Lexus,' she said, handing over the keys. 'I'll take Suki up onto the beach rather than wait here, if that's OK. Let her stretch her legs a bit. See you there?'

He nodded and jogged past the Oasis on his way out of the car park. The hotel restaurant was directly opposite and although he couldn't see her car immediately he eventually found it over to the right of the parking area, tucked almost out of sight. It looked new . . . and expensive. *Probably another present from Joe*, he found himself thinking, aware of a stab of resentment. *A bit more impressive than the occasional portion of chips at the Oasis.*

He snatched up the bag from the boot and jogged back past where he'd left her. The sandy path tugged at his calf muscles as he climbed the dunes, the ground continually slipping away beneath him with every step. When he reached the top, he could see Aimi down below, removing her shoes. It wasn't low tide yet but it was still a fair old walk across the broad stretch of sand to get to the water's edge. Suki had clearly decided she for one was not going to wait for the ball launcher and was already some way off, stretching her legs and moving with a freedom and an effortless grace that made him think of Aimi herself. He remembered watching her at Sports Day, the panther-like quality in her movements as she stretched ahead of the other girls in the sprint events. Suki seemed like a good choice of companion for her.

He stood at the top of the dunes and called out to her, waving her cardigan and when she waved back he floated all the way down to her.

The beach was divided into lettered zones. They'd joined it at D and were approaching G before she managed to broach the subject. They'd walked right out to the water's edge and then followed the shoreline eastwards, keeping one eye on the expanse of sand behind them. The tides here were notoriously treacherous and had the disconcerting habit of sneaking round behind unsuspecting strollers, cutting them off from the dunes unless they were careful.

Suki had done enough ball chasing for now and was content to strut alongside them, enjoying the relatively warm water in the sun-streaked shallows. Billy and Aimi paddled side by side, carrying their shoes and the ball launcher. Her cardigan, which she hadn't needed so far, was draped across her shoulders because it was easier to carry that way. They'd pretty much exhausted small talk and he was starting to wonder if she'd ever come out and say whatever it was she wanted to tell him. When she finally blurted it out, it came as a surprise, apropos of nothing they'd been talking about moments earlier.

'I've got to tell someone,' she said, a cloud passing over her features, 'I can't do this on my own. I need someone to tell me I'm doing the right thing or I'll never go through with it. Only it can't get back to Joe or his family, you know?'

A flock of seagulls scattered as they approached, no doubt unnerved by Suki's skittish presence. They flew off with a plaintive cry that seemed to synchronise perfectly with the change of mood.

'I'd have done it before now only I need someone I can trust,' she continued. 'I mean, all the friends I've got right now . . . they're Joe's friends really. They knew him long before we got together and even though some of them are sociable enough, I'm not kidding myself. I couldn't trust them to keep something like this to themselves if they knew. They'd have to tell him.'

'Tell him what?'

She stooped to pick up a shell which she examined closely for several seconds. She turned it over and over, as if looking for some sort of inspiration. Then she dropped it back into the shallows and gave a huge sigh.

'I saw you at the supermarket yesterday,' she said, turning to face him and squinting into the sun, 'and it felt like fate, you know? I thought maybe you might be able to help because you're only here to visit your sister. I mean, you'll be disappearing off back to London in a few days so there'd be no reason for anyone to think you had anything to do with it. Now though . . . I'm not so sure. Even meeting you here today was reckless. If anyone sees us together . . .'

'What if they do?' he asked, working to keep his exasperation under control. 'What does it matter if we're seen together? We could have just bumped into each other by chance . . . like yesterday.'

'You don't understand –'

'No. I don't. How am I supposed to unless you tell me?'

She broke off as another couple drew near. They smiled and nodded as they passed and she waited till she was sure they were out of earshot before continuing, which struck him as a little unnecessary. Then again, Aimi had always been one for ramping up the drama. It was one of the things he loved about her, the way she tried to suck every millilitre of excitement out of a situation. She was never more alive than when she occupied centre stage.

'If my life wasn't such a total . . . *fucking* . . . mess right now, I wouldn't have turned to someone I haven't seen since we were kids. I don't even know you anymore, for Christ's sake.'

'Of course you know me.' It stung a little that she could say such a thing. In the eleven years they'd been away from each other, hardly a week had gone by when he hadn't thought about her, imagined where she was, what she was doing, *who she was with*. Even during the dark years when she seemed to have disappeared off the face of the earth, she was always there. What did she think – that he'd just given up on her? Lost all interest?

'No, I don't,' she said. 'The Billy I knew was fifteen and he'd have walked through walls for me, I know that. But I haven't seen you for such a long time. People change.'

'I haven't changed.'

'Of course you have. We both have.'

'I . . . haven't . . . changed.'

The sharpness in his tone drew her up short. The intensity of her gaze was something he'd never experienced before, as if she was trying to blaze a path through to his innermost thoughts. He sensed this wasn't a time he could afford to look away.

'Tell me,' he insisted.

Aimi was the first to break eye contact. She stopped where she was, watching the water trickle over and between her toes. She wiggled them, trying to bury them in the wet sand, lost in her own thoughts.

'Aimi?'

When she looked up, he could see her eyes had lost some of their fire. Instead they were starting to mist over.

'If I do that,' she said eventually, '. . . *if* I do that, I need you to promise me, *swear* to me, that you won't tell anyone else.'

'You know I won't.'

'And I mean *anyone*.'

'OK.'

'Not Joe or his family, not Mia . . .'

'OK.'

'Not even the police if it comes to that.'

'The police?' He tried to come across as unconcerned but this had come out of nowhere. What did the police have to do with anything?

'If anyone's seen us together, they're going to want to talk to you at some stage, Billy – you might as well know it now. And you'd probably have to lie to them and that could land you in all sorts of trouble if it all came out. It's a lot for me to ask of you.'

'OK.'

'Are you sure you can handle that?'

'I'm sure,' he said with all the conviction he could muster, because that was what he sensed she needed right then.

'You know what his family are like, what reach his dad's got. He plays golf with the chief constable, has half the council in his pocket. If they get the slightest inkling you're tied up in this in some way . . .'

'They won't.'

Suki was hovering, ready for more exercise, so she sent the ball flying off into the distance. It provided just enough of a distraction for her to gather her thoughts.

'OK . . . look,' she said, as they both watched Suki gliding across the sand in pursuit. 'We'll do it this way. I can't just tell you bits of this because you won't make any sense of it. It's all or nothing. So I'll tell you everything, OK – but on one condition.'

'Which is . . .?'

'When you've heard it all and understand exactly what it is I'm going to be asking of you, I want you to take as long as you need to think about whether you still want to get involved. And if you decide I'm asking too much, I promise I won't hold it against you, OK?'

'OK.'

'Provided you just walk away from it and say nothing, I won't let it affect our friendship. I'll figure out some other way, do it on my own if all else fails, and you can just forget I said anything. But if you tell anyone, *anyone* at all about it, I'll never forgive you, Billy. Never. It'll destroy me. Do you understand what I'm saying?'

'Yes.'

'Just the two of us.'

'Just the two of us.'

'Swear.'

'I swear.'

'Cross your heart.'

And just like that eleven years roll away and they're sitting in Mason's Field. He's fastening something around her wrist, a simple rope bracelet with an A and a B etched on either side of the clasp. He shows her the identical one on his own wrist and she kisses him gently on the lips, whispering promises about how she'll write, she'll phone every evening. First thing she'll do when she gets to London is ask her dad if he can come and stay with them one weekend . . . soon. He wants to ask her not to leave. Just 'cos her parents have split up, he doesn't see why he and Aimi have to as well. If she's got to choose which one to live with, why can't she stay here with her mother? He knows the dance school is the real reason and wishes she could put him first for once but doesn't have the words to express how he feels without whingeing and spoiling the moment. And when he asks her to swear that she'll come back to him some day, that she won't forget him and go off with someone else the moment she gets to London, she does so without even thinking about it.

'And hope to die,' he says now.

Just as she'd done eleven years earlier.

She decided to start with the anniversary – their sixth. Not because this was when things began to go wrong, she was quick to add. If you spend that long living with someone, especially if he's as headstrong and used to getting his own way as you are, there are bound to be bumps in the road. But she'd decided to start there because, in her mind at least, it represented a water-shed. She'd found a way of coping with everything until that evening. She'd been struggling just to get through the days ever since.

They'd come off the beach and taken seats outside the Marina Café. Aimi was gasping for something to drink and he was just pleased to be under a sunshade for a while, having made his usual mistake of coming out without having creamed up. He wasn't one for sitting around in the sun and his skin never needed much of an excuse to start burning. The back of his neck already felt sore.

Aimi took a long sip from her sparkling water and as she sloshed the ice around inside the glass with the straw, she told him about the weekend in London that Jack, her father-in-law, had sprung on them as a surprise anniversary present. Two nights in the Brompton Suite at the Kensington Hotel. Theatre tickets for *The Book of Mormon* at The Prince of Wales Theatre, an especially nice touch because he knew how much she wanted to see it.

The problem was, this apparently kind gesture was tainted by ulterior motives as far as she was concerned because he knew, they *all* knew, how gutted she was that the plans she'd been working on for nearly four years to build her own dance school were going to have to be shelved. She didn't go into any details as to why, though he sensed there was more to it than she was letting on. She preferred to focus instead on the way that decision had affected their relationship. She'd felt let down and made her feelings clear at every opportunity so things had been tense between her and Joe for a week or so. The whole weekend had felt like an attempt to buy her off in some way, win her round – and she wasn't about to let him off the hook that easily.

The theatre trip had been magical – she'd worked with a couple of the dancers in the chorus before and even though there was more than a touch of frustration that her own dance career had been cut short before she'd had the chance to get that far, she'd sat back and lost herself in the performance unfolding in front of her. Her enjoyment of the meal later that evening, however, was trammelled by thoughts of what would happen when they got back to the hotel. She knew Joe would be expecting sex to be on the agenda, given that it was their anniversary, but it was the last thing she wanted. While she'd loved the whole theatre experience, she felt that if they made love to round off the evening it would be like signing off on an agreement that everything was OK now and back to normal. And it was far from that.

So she'd tried to fob him off with what even she recognised as one feeble excuse after another, and he'd pushed it and pushed it until eventually she'd snapped and told him the real reason why. And they'd argued. And he'd lost it. Really lost it. He'd hit her, the first blow a slap with the open hand but still powerful enough to knock her across the bed and stun her for a second or two. He'd never done that before, however fiery their rows might have been, and they'd certainly had their fair share of those. But there was always a line there and he'd shouted, stormed off a couple of times, but he'd never crossed it. But now he had. And then he did it a second time, drawing a trickle of blood from the corner of her mouth.

And then . . .

She bit her lip, broke off here and took another sip from her drink. Then, after a quick look to make sure no one was watching, she caught hold of the hem of her dress and lifted one side of it, sliding it up her legs, past the bikini bottoms, then higher still until it was above her waist. He was startled at first, unsure what she was doing . . . and then he saw the bruising around the ribcage, a swirl of deep purple and livid red with a tinge of blue around the edges. It covered an area roughly the size of a saucer and his instinctive reaction was to reach across the table and try to touch it. She let go of the hem and the kaftan fell back into place.

'He did that?' Billy had never felt so helpless in his life. Surely there was something he should be doing now other than sitting there and asking stupid questions, but his mind couldn't let go of the enormity of what he'd just seen.

'Two days ago,' she said, and there was something about the matter-of-fact way in which she said this that stoked the fires raging inside him even more. 'Last week it was the other side. Never the face or anything that's on show, apart from that first night of course. We had to come up with an excuse for that one, but since then he's been much more careful. Pretty colours, aren't they? You get red first because that's the fresh blood leaking into the tissue. Then the blood gets darker after a few hours as it loses the oxygen it was carrying, which is why it goes blue or purple.'

'Aimi . . .'

'You know it's getting better when it goes yellow or green,' she continued, her voice almost expressionless. 'That's the haemoglobin taking effect. I'm getting to be quite an expert on . . .'

'Aimi – stop it.' He reached across the table and grabbed her hand. With her free one she slid the sunglasses down from the top of her head so that her eyes were covered and they sat there in silence for a moment, contemplating the enormity of what she'd just told him.

He asked her why she hadn't done something about this. This wasn't the 1950s. There were people she could turn to nowadays, agencies which specialised in this sort of thing. Why hadn't she reported him? She shook her head, asked him if he'd been listening earlier when she was warning him about Jack Vedra and the extent of his influence in the area. She told him the Vedra family liked to keep things in-house. She'd tried to stand up to Joe once, threatened to go to Jack and tell him how his precious son chose to settle arguments with his wife. Joe had just laughed. Asked her if she really believed he'd give a shit. Did she walk around with her eyes shut? How did she imagine his father settled matters when things got out of hand in his own marriage?

Then he'd grabbed her by the front of her blouse, snapping off a button as he pushed her up against the wall. Warned her that if she ever breathed a word about this, she'd regret it. They'd all rally round and make sure no one believed her because that's what family did. The bruises proved nothing – they could have come from anywhere. Everyone thought she was just a common gold-digger anyway. It would look like she was simply moving on to the next stage of a plan that was several years in the making, one where she seduces then fleeces him for everything she can get – 'not so far from the truth, is it?' She'd be a laughing stock, he'd told her. They'd make sure of it.

Bottom line – she'd made her bed and she'd lie in it till he decided it was time for her to get out. She should thank her lucky stars she was easy on the eye and brought a bit of glamour to proceedings because it meant she still had her uses as long as she looked good on his arm. And if she thought closing her legs was going to change anything, she could forget it, he'd go elsewhere – did she really think he'd be struggling for volunteers?

He told her she could play this any way she liked. She could do as she was told and keep the lavish lifestyle with the designer clothes and flash cars and even her precious dance school because that could be back on the table eventually if she learned how to behave herself. And if she couldn't, well . . . she could go ahead, try to stir up as much trouble as she liked, but she needed to understand that the moment it looked like there would be blowback on the family, she really would wish she hadn't.

He hadn't gone into detail.

'I'm scared out of my wits, Billy,' she said as she brought her explanation to a close. 'I'm not sleeping properly. I'm tiptoeing around the house whenever he's there, although that's not so often nowadays, thank God. He's away with Jack and TJ on a business stroke golfing trip in the Algarve for a few days, otherwise I'd have had to explain where I was going this afternoon and why. He's determined to keep squeezing like this till I see sense. I honestly think he believes I'll come round eventually, he's that deluded. But I can't carry on like this, Billy. I've got to do something.'

He rubbed the back of her hand and tried to look beyond the shaded lenses. He reached out to take them off but she pulled her head and hand away and sat back in her seat.

'So,' she said with a sigh. 'You said you wanted me to tell you. Well, I've told you.'

'What do you want me to do?'

She looked away, then reached down and stroked Suki who was lying on the floor next to them.

'I want you to go away and think about what I said earlier. If you decide this is just too big and you don't want . . .'

'What do you want me to do?' he repeated, his eyes locking onto hers.

She opened her mouth as if to argue, then closed it again, recognising that there would be no point. No amount of reflection was going to change his mind.

'I want you to help me fake my own death,' she said.

8

JUNE 2002

Thirteen years earlier

He goes round to his dad's side of the bed again, taking just the lipstick with him for now. He fishes the bits of tissue out of his mouth and drops them on the floor. Then he sits down next to him and gets to work, concentrating hard on keeping inside the lines this time. It's quite handy that he has his mouth open because it makes it easier to see where one lip ends and the other starts. He does the top one first and is pleased with the way it's worked out – much more accurate than the job he did on his mum. He's just about to turn his attention to the bottom one when a thought comes into his mind and he knows right away that he's not going to be able to ignore it. It's not his fault. If his dad didn't look so funny wearing lipstick, it would never have occurred to him but now that it has he just knows he's going to have to try it and see what it looks like.

So he puts the lipstick at one corner of the mouth and instead of filling in the bottom half of the picture, he draws a line outwards, just a couple of inches or so with a slight upward curve. He leans back and has a good look, then moves to the other corner and does the same thing there, trying to match the exact length and angle of the other curve. And the fit of giggles is back because he used to watch Batman a lot when he was younger and he'd recognise the Joker anywhere, and yes, his dad's got better teeth and there's no crazy grin but the lips themselves are just perfect . . . all he needs to do is colour in the bottom one.

And that's when his dad twitches.

He screams, drops the lipstick and in his panic he slaps his dad's face – not hard, just a glancing blow, but a slap nonetheless, even if it is just a reflex. He leaps off the bed and scoots over to the window, where he stands for a moment, pulse racing, trying to make sense of what's just happened. He didn't imagine it, did he? It was a twitch – he's sure it was. And yet his dad's hand was freezing when he touched it a while ago. How's that even possible?

The frantic pounding in his chest is beginning to slow as the initial panic subsides. He hasn't taken his eyes off his dad since it happened. He's watching his hand to see if it moves again . . . that and the bedclothes covering his chest 'cos if they suddenly start to rise and fall he's out of there and he'll keep going till he can't run any further.

But even though he watches for what feels like several minutes, there's no sign of movement. Nothing. He starts to wonder if it was just his imagination playing tricks after all because that would be the most logical explanation. He catches sight of his mum's hand mirror on the dressing table and that's when he realises what he needs to do. He has to be sure. Picking up his hand like that obviously isn't enough. He's seen films where they hold a mirror up against a person's mouth to see if it goes all foggy. That's what he should have done in the first place – made absolutely certain.

As he picks up the mirror, he notices the A4 envelope lying next to it – Mia/Billy, it says, in his mother's neat handwriting. He ignores it for now and somehow finds the courage to edge his way around to his dad's side of the bed. Holding the mirror over his mouth for a good ten seconds takes every ounce of determination he has but he forces himself to do it, counting them off slowly – ten, nine, eight. It feels like an eternity.

When he reaches zero he takes it over to the window so he can see more clearly and there's nothing. No fog, not the tiniest bit of misting on the surface of the glass, so whatever that was just now, it can't have been his dad breathing. And instantly he feels stupid. He's lucky none of his mates from school were there to see it – they'd have wet themselves laughing, and he'd never have heard the end of it. As for his dad, he'd have been merciless. You big girl! Scared of your own shadow! And even though there's no one there to pass on what's just happened, he knows. He feels humiliated.

So he goes back to the bed, fired up with a new sense of purpose.

The first slap was a reflex, that's all. He'd lashed out in shock as much as anything. But it was nothing – a girlie slap.

The second one now is more controlled – not hard enough to hurt but certainly enough to wake you if you were just asleep or pretending. When there's still no response, he knows for sure there's not going to be any comeback from his dad.

And the third one? He's not sure what that one's all about. Maybe it's payback for giving the tablets to his mum, 'cos if he's clear about anything at all in this confused state, it's the fact that she'd never have been able to do it herself. She hasn't been able to go into the bathroom on her own for a week now and would never have managed to get the tablets out of the boxes.

Or maybe it's because he's had enough of tiptoeing around the place and keeping out of his dad's way for fear of saying or doing the wrong thing. Maybe it's even simpler than that and he does it just because he can.

He can't say for sure because when he thinks back over these few seconds in the years to come he won't even remember hitting him for a third time, let alone why he might have done it.

He won't even remember that he closed his fist.

9

SUNDAY 16TH AUGUST 2015

Billy's very quiet. He seems a bit preoccupied and has done since he came back from his walk along the beach. Mia assumes it's something to do with this work he's brought with him. Then again, maybe that's not it. She asked him when he came in if he'd managed to get hold of Karun and there was just a moment of blankness before he said yes. He does that when his real focus is elsewhere, as if he needs a few seconds for his mind to select the right gear. He didn't elaborate though.

It wasn't till she checked whether he had anything planned for this evening that he seemed to snap out of it. He draped an arm over her shoulder and said no, he was all hers as long as it didn't involve board games, which was a friendly dig at her because she didn't consider Christmas Day to be complete unless they'd spent the entire afternoon playing one game after another. He said he had work to do but if she fancied watching TV he'd be happy to leave it till she's gone to bed and spend the evening just chilling with her. *And Matthew*, he added. That was exactly what she wanted to hear but there's a slightly fuzzy hue to his manner which she finds a little disconcerting.

When you're on the lookout for such things, you tend not to miss them.

The moment dinner's out of the way the three of them sit down to watch reruns of *The Office*, which takes her right back to when Billy first moved in with them. She's never particularly liked the programme, can never relax because David Brent sets her teeth on edge, makes her squirm with embarrassment. She accepts she's in a minority of one – where she sees caricature and cruelty, Matthew sees brilliant observation, insisting he's met the law office equivalent of just about all these characters at some time or other. As for Billy, back when the series was first shown he used to have a thing for the girl who played the receptionist, which she found quite endearing.

She's downloaded the whole of series two, happy to sit through every episode if necessary. She'll only be half-watching it anyway. What matters is they'll be spending the evening together as a family. And yet for some reason the plan's not working out quite the way she's envisaged. Matthew watches the first episode and part of the second before excusing himself and disappearing upstairs, saying he needs to get some more work done on his presentation. He seems anxious about this trip to the States, which is unlike him. He's told her there's a lot riding on it but can't go into any detail, not that she'd be much help if he could. Legal arguments tend to fly over her head without even waving hello.

As for Billy, she wonders whether Matthew has made him feel he ought to be working too. He won't say so because he knows she's been looking forward to this evening, but he's barely reacting to lines that would have creased him up not so long ago. She can't help but feel it's all falling a bit flat.

They start watching a third episode and partway through she asks if he fancies a hot chocolate – she's making one for herself anyway. She heads for the kitchen, telling him not to pause the programme on her account, while she sorts out the drinks and throws in a pack of Hobnobs. Billy's over by the window when she gets back, watching the last of the sun disappear. The programme's still playing to an audience that mentally at least has packed up and gone home. He comes across and sits next to her on the settee and doesn't protest when she picks up the remote and switches off the TV.

'If you want to start work now, don't feel you need to keep me company,' she says, opening the packet and taking out a couple of biscuits for each of them. 'I'm not an invalid.'

He smiles and tells her he knows she's not and he's fine. He'll work better if he leaves it till later – it's what he's used to. She knows this is true. She doesn't know how he exists on so little sleep but somehow four or five hours is all he's ever needed to recharge the batteries and throw himself into his work again, feeling refreshed. From what he's told her, his flatmates in London are much the same. She could never do it. It makes her feel old. On the slide at thirty-five. And no way of knowing for sure how much more sliding she has in her.

They talk about his work for a while. He's described so many times what it is a front-end developer does and she's still not one hundred per cent certain she's got her head round it. As she understands it, if she goes to any website, what she sees there is down to people like him and the way they've interpreted the data given to them. Everything she sees, clicks, all the design layout, the content, images, links, the options for navigating around the page – they're all the work of the front-end developer.

However shaky her understanding of what he does may be, she has no doubts at all about one thing. This job has been the making of him. When he had his meltdown at university at the end of his second year and had to leave the course, she'd been worried sick. She'd driven straight to Southampton and brought him back to Rye where she knew she'd be able to look after him, nurse him back to health. Make her fractured baby brother whole again – for the second time. She'd hoped against hope that he would stay and find work in the area, knowing at the same time it would never happen. The breakdown may have been caused by working too hard but the roots of that kind of obsession go deep and spread wide. She knew from the outset that he wouldn't be staying.

At least London was a compromise she felt she could live with. She was worried at first about the size and impersonal nature of the city, the ease with which he could hide away, but the moment he started floating the idea of maybe moving to California where his IT skills might be put to better use, London suddenly seemed an eminently sensible option. Just far enough away to give him the space he required and close enough for her to get to him within a couple of hours if she needed to.

He'd hooked up initially with a few friends and spent a year or so working in whatever jobs happened to come up – bar work, stacking shelves at Asda, pizza deliveries, washing cars in car parks – and in the early hours he made three times as much with a variety of online services he'd set up. It was these activities – IT access for pensioners, Instant Network Solutions for small businesses, website design for the terminally clueless, as he often referred to them – that first brought him into contact with Zak, who shared his passion for innovative ideas and madcap schemes, for stretching the boundaries of what they could do. And through Zak, Billy had met the third musketeer, Karun. He was the go-to guy for business nous, the only son of a successful entrepreneur who'd made his millions in sports retail. He provided the capital they needed to get KBZ IT Solutions off the ground. He'd let them have office space in one of his warehouses south of the Thames until such time as they could afford premises of their own.

She'd worried for the first few months but had to admit that unless Billy was exaggerating and going out of his way to accentuate only the positive – not such an unlikely scenario – they really did seem to know what they were doing. Even so, the way he'd suddenly imploded at university, when everything seemed to be going his way at last, was never very far from her thoughts and the strange hours he kept made her anxious that history might repeat itself at some stage if he were to push himself too hard. He can tell her as often as he likes that he loves what he's doing, that there *is* no pressure. He even told her once that he wakes every day with a genuine sense of anticipation, which is amazing when you consider what he's come through. It's reassuring that he can speak so positively about his work that a glow comes over him when he does so, but she's constantly on the lookout for any hint that he may be extending his emotional overdraft beyond his ability to cover it.

And there's something about his demeanour this evening that's giving her cause for concern.

Something's not quite right.

She can feel it.

*

'So how is Karun?' she asks.

He smiles. 'I'm good, sis.'

'That's not what I asked.'

'Well . . . we both know it is, actually. I'm just trying to save us a bit of time here. Cut out some of the foreplay.'

She slaps his arm. Love-fifteen. She'll need to do better than that.

'OK, smart-arse. Humour me. Define *good*. You taking your meds?'

'Yep.'

'Honestly?'

'Nope.' He shrugs his shoulders at her instinctive look of dismay. 'Well, what d'you *want* me to say, sis? You don't want me to lie, don't ask me.'

'Why aren't you taking them?'

'I don't need them.'

'Says who?'

'Says me.'

Which is not an answer, but it's all the explanation that's needed as far as he's concerned. How to get past that one?

'So how long have you been off them?'

'Dunno, exactly.'

'OK. Ballpark figure.'

He picks up part of the biscuit that's broken off and fallen into his lap. Pops it into his mouth. Rubs distractedly at the mark that it's left on his trousers.

'Five . . . maybe six months now.'

'That long?' She's genuinely shocked to hear this, does the calculation. 'So you were off them last time you came back here for my birthday?'

He nods his head.

'And you didn't even realise, did you?' he says with a look which suggests an *I told you so* won't be far behind.

'So how come you didn't tell me?'

'Hmmm . . . why didn't I tell you?' he says, staring at a spot on the ceiling in a parody of reflection. 'Lighten up, sis – I haven't shot the pope. I've chucked a few tablets in the bin. In fact, I haven't even done that. They're still in a drawer back home. I just don't need them, that's all. I feel good – have done ever since I came off the things. Doubtless you'll tell me those two facts are unrelated.'

He dips the Hobnob into his hot chocolate and stoops to make sure he gets it into his mouth this time before it breaks off. Mia holds her own cup in both hands, taps it against her front teeth as she takes this in and considers the best way to respond to this level of conviction.

'You think you're the best judge of that?'

'Do I think I'm better qualified than those quacks I've had to put up with over the years?' He's smiling the whole time and clearly wants to suggest this is still light-hearted banter but she's been here before. It won't take much for it to spill over into something more adversarial. The more she pushes, the harder he'll push back.

'So who are you seeing right now?' she asks.

'You want me to talk about my sex life?'

'You know that's not what I'm asking.'

He sighs, the first touch of mild exasperation. He wants to keep it light but she's not playing along.

'I'm not seeing anyone,' he says at length. 'There's no point, sis. I get nothing out of those sessions.'

'Nothing?'

'Zilch. And that's not me having a pop at them for the sake of it 'cos I know they all mean well. It's just they're so . . . unimaginative, you know?'

'Are they meant to be imaginative, then?'

'It might help. They're all so *terribly* earnest and they follow the textbook so closely I swear I can hear them turning the pages under the desk when they think I'm not looking. It wouldn't be so bad if I came out just once feeling like there's been this great flash of insight, that suddenly unlocks all these feelings I'm supposed to have been suppressing, only there's nothing. We just sit there week after week and go over the same old ground while they nudge their theories across the table for me to pick up and swallow and it's all crap. Leading nowhere. Sorry, but someone has to say it.'

She's not sure what she can come up with to counter this. The patient may not be the best person to decide whether therapy is serving any purpose but, if Billy's adamant it's not, the whole thing will just turn into a self-fulfilling prophecy. He has one of the sharpest minds she's ever come across, has this ability to pick out the flaw in any argument and tug at the loose thread until the whole tapestry falls apart. Some of his teachers rated his analytical skills as borderline genius, others just found him insolent at best, threatening even. Their father never did work out how to handle him and the frustration engendered by his feelings of inadequacy frequently led him to resort to the *because I said so* school of reasoning. If Billy has made up his mind about these sessions, there's little point in prolonging the argument.

'You think you're OK?' she asks again.

'You tell me. I spent three days here back in June and you didn't even know I was off them. How did I seem to you?'

It's hard to argue with that . . . but it doesn't mean he's right.

'I'll admit, you seemed fine. I just worry, that's all. You're very good at holding things back.'

He laughs, purses his lips.

'Ah yes,' he says, 'holding things back. You sure you want to go down that road, sis? Hmm? You show me yours and I'll show you mine?'

He's doing it again, twisting things round so that she's off balance. Another thirty seconds and she'll be the one on the defensive, having to justify herself and she'll never find a way back to where they are right now. And it doesn't help matters that he has a point.

'Thought not,' he says, taking her silence as confirmation. 'Not how we operate, is it? Much better to parcel up the truth and dole out the bits we think we can handle. Taught by the best, weren't we? The good old Orr family pragmatism.'

And he's right, of course. He usually is, even when he's so maddeningly, blatantly wrong. Billy's always right, which is why he and their father were always at loggerheads, because their dad didn't have the mental acuity to settle any argument with reason. His only recourse when the arguments ran dry were to shout louder than his son, and that did more harm than good.

She knows where they are now. She can feel him starting to crackle, the energy coming off him like sparks. This is the time to back away. If she presses him still further, she'll be upping the ante with no way of knowing where it will take them. She can't rewind the last five minutes but she *can* turn the TV back on and pick up *The Office* where they left off in the hope that this will take some of the tension out of the air, let them slip back into their respective corners without having lost too much face.

But for some reason she persists.

'They put you on meds for a reason, Billy.'

'Yes. They did.'

'If they hadn't . . .'

'I was thirteen,' he reminds her, getting to his feet and walking over to the window. He looks out over the fields at the rear of the house, his back to her. 'You're right – at thirteen I needed them. I'll be twenty-seven in February. I don't need them now.'

'And what if you're wrong?'

He's wrapping the cord of the window blinds tightly around his fingers. The moment he runs out of cord, he starts to reverse the process, leaning his forehead against the window, which will be cool to the touch this late in the evening.

'If I'm wrong, I know where the meds are, don't I? And you can say I told you so.'

'You think that's what this is all about?' she says, determined not to let him shrug her off that easily. 'This isn't about scoring points, Billy. I'm worried about you. We both know what you're like without them – you lose all perspective.'

'What I *was* like without them,' he corrects her.

'You imagine things that haven't happened and blot out things that have. You attribute importance to people they don't deserve and take it personally when they don't match up to your standards. We've been here before. I don't want to go there again.'

Her voice falters on the last three words and she bites her lip, blinking rapidly. She feels bad about this. Every single drop of emotion that's gone into what she said was genuine and yet she feels like a fraud. Can't win the argument? Play the sympathy card. Why not play on the illness while you're at it?

There's a creak and the sound of a door closing above them, followed by the dull thud of Matthew's footsteps on the stairs. A few painfully silent seconds later, he pokes his head round the door and asks if anyone's going to need the bathroom in the next few minutes. The work is giving him a headache and he wonders if maybe a shower might help. He goes through to the kitchen, takes a couple of paracetamol and then heads back upstairs. He'd have to be slow-witted in the extreme not to have noticed the atmosphere in the room but he says nothing on his way through.

But his intervention has broken the flow. They both stay where they are, each waiting for the other to speak, presumably because neither is sure where to go from here. In the end it's Billy who makes the first move, stepping away from the window and heading towards the ground-floor bedroom which they use as a spare when he's not here. He says he needs to make a start on his work and just for a moment she thinks he's actually going to leave things the way they are.

At the last moment, however, he pauses in the doorway and comes back over to her. Stoops and kisses the top of her head. Picks up his mobile which is on the coffee table. Says goodnight. And is gone.

And she's left feeling the way she always feels whenever she pushes things just that little bit too far – wondering exactly what that has achieved.

Wishing she'd had the sense to leave well alone.

Billy did three things the moment he'd closed the door to the spare room.

First on the list was to message Karun and Zak to say he wouldn't be able to start the work just yet. He apologised and made vague reference to 'things being the way they are', confident it would buy him a little time. They both knew the situation with Mia and he felt bad about using her illness in such a fraudulent way but he'd hardly given the program a moment's thought since his arrival and knew how important it was for him to be focused before he tackled it. The last thing anyone wanted was a botched job.

Second was a text to Aimi to say he was up for it. The reply, asking if he was sure, was encouragingly prompt, leading him to wonder if she'd been sitting there waiting, phone in hand. He confirmed and she signed off with two kisses, which made him feel a bit better about things. He'd spent all afternoon and evening weighing up the pros and cons, which was a pointless exercise when you thought about it because he was always going to do it. Aimi needed help – what else was he supposed to do? But pointless or not, it had thrown up solid reasons not to help her that he'd been forced to push to the back of his mind so that the scales might tip in the right direction. The reminder from Aimi that she was relying on him was worth its weight in gold. He knew the moment he heard her voice in the supermarket that eleven years were nothing. He was back there in the time it took her to smile.

And the third thing he did was to switch off the light and sit there fully clothed, his pillow propped vertically against the wall behind him and his legs crossed on the bed in front. He tried to think of something to do and came up short every time. Work he'd already ruled out – he could no more switch on the laptops than write an opera. Reading? He'd brought *The Night Manager* with him, promising himself he'd finish it by the time he got back to London but he was buzzing – his thoughts were all over the place and he knew there was no way he'd be able to settle to it and concentrate. Mia would have been quick to make capital out of this had she known, but this unrest had nothing to do with the fact that he'd stopped taking his meds. He just needed time to take stock.

He did wonder about maybe sneaking out and going for a walk so that the fresh air might clear his head but he'd heard Mia tidying away and getting ready for bed. He didn't see how he could leave the house without being overheard and knew that would worry her, especially after the way they'd left things earlier. He suspected he'd already done enough for one evening to disturb her equanimity. There was always a delicate balance to be maintained in any conversation with Mia and what frustrated him was the fact that he knew exactly where the boundaries were, yet he'd still go blundering into the no-go areas without any thought of the consequences until it was too late. The least he could do now was let her get a decent night's sleep.

So he just stayed where he was, too lethargic to get undressed, too distracted to settle to anything worthwhile, and painfully aware that it would be several hours yet until he'd feel ready for sleep. Instead, he turned his thoughts to what lay ahead, specifically what he'd have to do in the next forty-eight hours. And top of the list was coming up with an excuse for going missing for several hours without worrying Mia or giving her the slightest inkling of what he was really doing.

He kicked off his shoes, shuffled down the bed until he was lying flat and started to sift through the possibilities.

It looked like it was going to be a long night.

10

JUNE 2002

Thirteen years earlier

She pulls up outside the house in Udimore Road just after six. Her parents and Billy don't know anything about her new Golf. Matthew arranged it all as a surprise on their first wedding anniversary three days ago. It's the first car she's ever bought from the showroom. For the past few years, in fact ever since she passed her test, she's been making do with her clapped-out fourth- or fifth-hand mini but it's reached the stage now where running repair costs are getting out of hand and sticking with it is what Matthew calls a false economy. They can afford a decent second car now that he's starting to climb the ladder at the law firm where he works. She's driven it to Ashford every day this week and it's the first chance she's had to call in to see her parents and show it off. She hopes they're not looking out of the window as she gets out of the car. It would be a shame to spoil the surprise.

Matthew's got five-a-side football this evening straight after work so they've agreed he'll skip the drinks afterwards and pick up a takeaway on the way home. That means she'll have a couple of hours at her parents' place, which will hopefully ease some of the guilt she's been experiencing recently. She feels she ought to be round there more often now that the illness is really starting to take hold.

She remembers how her mother knew about it a week before her wedding and how both parents kept it to themselves for a fortnight to avoid taking any of the gloss off her big day and the honeymoon. That makes it twelve months and counting since the initial diagnosis was confirmed and she knows all the figures. Half don't make it past three years and there's only a one-in-ten chance of making it to five. Steady disintegration until the body shuts down completely. She needs to be here as often as possible, especially now that her father has quit his job.

Only Mia knows this. The cover story, as far as both her mother and Billy are concerned, is that he's engineered a way of working from home, but it's not true. He can't bear to be away from his wife, is determined to see it through with her to the bitter and inevitable end. He says he'll worry some other time about whether his old job is still available. Mia offered to quit the gallery instead when he told her what he was planning to do, but he wouldn't hear of it. He's old-fashioned, sees this as a personal thing between himself and his wife.

She walks up to the front door, holding the bunch of flowers she bought in the supermarket on the way here, and uses her own key to let herself in. She calls 'Cooee' as she does so and drops her keys onto the shelf next to the front door. Then she calls them individually. 'Mum! Dad! Billy!' Three-second gap between each. More of a question mark creeping into her voice with each call. Her voice echoes around the obviously empty house and she decides they must be in the garden. Ever since the weather has improved, her

mother likes to sit out there and get the early evening sun. Any ear-
lier in the afternoon it's too much for her to take – 'might get skin
cancer,' she says, her attempt at gallows humour. But once the real
heat has gone from the day and especially if a cool breeze starts to
get up, she likes to sit out there with a shawl around her shoulders
and close her eyes as the shadows start to lengthen.

Mia goes to the back door and is genuinely surprised to see no
one out there. She comes back in and stands at the foot of the
stairs, calling out to her father again even though logic tells her he
can't be in his office. He would never leave her mother on her own.

She can see Billy's been home because his bag is by the front
door and she also remembers squeezing past the car on the fore-
court which means they can't have gone anywhere. That only
leaves the dining room, as she still refers to it, even though her
mother's bed has been in there for the past couple of months or so.
But if they're in there, they'll have heard her calling, won't they?

Won't they?

And even as she pushes the door open, she senses something is
wrong here. Seriously wrong. The curtains are open but the sun
has moved round from its mid-afternoon position and the room
doesn't benefit from it at all which gives everything a slightly shad-
owy hue, the same indistinct vagueness she experiences when driv-
ing at dusk. The first thing she sees is her mother's face on the pillow
nearest to her and it tells her all she needs to know. Just one look
and she knows what it means. Forget the make-up, which is too
grotesque for words. Even if she'd been able to hold the various
cosmetics herself and tried to apply it whilst lying on her back in
the dark, she couldn't have made a mess like that. But more than
that, there's the artificiality of it all. It looks staged, like one of those
awful scenes the Victorians used to set up so that they could take

group photos of dead people at mealtimes with their surviving relatives. All of this she takes in during the first second or two.

Beyond her mother, on the far side of the bed, she can see her father who is fully clothed, his head bent back at an unnatural angle he'd never manage to sustain if he was conscious. His face looks like some sort of Halloween mask, first impressions suggesting someone has run amok with a palette and paintbrush or maybe a trowel.

Even though her eyes and powers of reasoning are working together to tell her one thing, her instincts are set on a different course altogether and she finds herself reaching across her mother's body to take his pulse. As she comes further into the room, she's startled by a shape at the foot of the bed, curled up against her mother's legs in a foetal position, snoring so gently with each intake of breath that the sound hasn't even registered with her until now that she's inside the room. He's clutching something to his chest and she sees it's a hot-water bottle and that realisation alone threatens to break the dam as she tries her level best to keep everything under control. She knows she can't come apart at the seams right now. For Billy's sake, she needs to get to the bottom of this and sort everything out.

She shakes him and he wakes with a start, his eyes frantic for a second or two until he realises who it is. Then he rolls off the foot of the bed and stays where he is, seated on the rug with his head peering over the quilt.

'Are you OK, Billy?'

He holds up the hot-water bottle.

'She was cold,' he says.

She reaches across now and touches her father's cheek. She knows immediately she doesn't need to feel for a pulse and all *manner of thoughts are racing through her mind at the moment – she's having real difficulty assigning levels of priority to each of them. How on earth can she straighten this out? Where the hell is she meant to start?*

With Billy, she decides. Billy is still here and is going to need her.

She comes around the side of the bed and sits on the rug next to him. Puts an arm around his shoulders and draws him into her chest and despite her best intentions she starts to whimper the moment his head makes contact – a gentle shuddering of the shoulders at first, the initial tremors threatening to give way to something more elemental any minute. She struggles to pull herself together, as much for his sake as anything else.

'Billy – who have you called?'

He shakes his head.

'No one.'

'No one? Why not?'

'Didn't want anyone to see her.'

'That's nice . . . but we don't have any choice. You know what's happened here, don't you?'

'Of course.'

'We have to report it. Why didn't you phone the police or a doctor or an ambulance?'

'No point. They couldn't do anything.'

'But you . . .' Her voice trails away. She knows instinctively she mustn't go there, can't afford to put the thought in his head. If there's any chance at all, even the most remote possibility that either of them was merely unconscious and still alive when he first discovered them, it needs to be kept from him. He'll have enough to come to terms with in the next few months without adding to it unnecessarily.

But it's already there, it seems.

'They were dead when I got here,' he tells her.

'I know.'

'She was really cold and so was he.'

'OK.'

'He twitched, sis.'

'He what?'

'He twitched. I mean, he was dead and everything 'cos I held a mirror up against his mouth and there was nothing there.'

She really doesn't want to hear this. She pulls his head into her chest again to keep him quiet as much as anything. He twitched? What does that mean? Was it just something Billy imagined or can dead bodies actually do that? She's sure she's heard something along those lines but this isn't something she wants him to bring up in front of anyone else. It's not significant in the wider scheme of things but it will make a hell of a difference to Billy if others get to hear about it. The pointless speculation. The stupid theories. The what-if merchants. He needs to be protected from that. She knows that would have been her mother's first thought and already she feels it now falls to her.

She tells him that's something he must never say to anyone else. Never – does he understand? He should just tell anyone who asks that they were dead and cold when he got here and stick to that. That's all he knows. He's thirteen. He's not a doctor. Has he got that?

He nods.

'How long have you been here?'

'What time is it?'

He's dry-eyed. He might just as easily have woken from a good night's sleep for all the expression in his voice. Shock, she decides.

'Not sure.' She checks her watch. 'Twenty past six.'

He shrugs.

'Couple of hours.'

'And you've been in here all that time?'

'Didn't like to leave her.'

Her. Not them.

'And were they both . . . like this? When you got here?'

He nods, then qualifies his answer.

'Well . . .'

'Apart from the make-up?'

'Yeah.'

She pauses, wondering whether this is something she should be leaving to someone better qualified, but the elephant in the room is one thing – this one has crapped all over the bed. It's not something she can easily ignore.

'Why did you do it?' she asks.

He shrugs again.

'Dunno. She looked all pale and I didn't want anyone to see her like that – only I made a bit of a mess of it.'

'That doesn't matter. We can wipe it off, tidy her up a bit.'

He puts the hot-water bottle on the floor.

'It's cold now,' he says.

'Billy . . . what about Dad?'

'What about him?'

'Why . . . what made you put make-up on him too?'

He pauses, as if giving some thought to this answer.

'Practice,' he says. And one side of his mouth is lifting in what looks like the beginnings of a smirk before he manages to bring it under control. Or at least, that's how it looks to her. Surely to God she imagined it.

'We need to get him cleaned up too – quickly. Before anyone else gets here.'

Then she makes a mental checklist of what needs to be done. First there's the question of how long he's been here. If anyone asks, he's to say he doesn't know exactly what time he got home but it wasn't long before she got there and they phoned the police together. He's got to remember this, she tells him. It's only a little white lie but it's really important. They're going to think it's pretty strange if he tells them he was here in the room for at least two hours and didn't call anyone. He has to get it straight. She makes him repeat it back to her, which he does in a slightly remote sort of voice which makes her even more convinced he's still in shock.

Next decision: clean up first and then dial 999 or the other way round? She could probably make the call first and then start removing the make-up. How long will she need? Surely no more than ten minutes. If she has everything ready and starts the moment the call's been made, they're not going to get here that quickly, are they? She wants the authorities here as soon as possible – too much of a delay and they'll want to know why he was so late home. In the end though, she decides she can't afford to risk them arriving before she's finished. Not for the sake of a few minutes either way.

She checks what he was doing earlier and sorts out a timeline with him that will have him arriving home a little later. Goes over it with him to make sure he has it right.

Word-perfect.

She gets him to repeat it while she fetches a pack of make-up wipes from her mother's dressing table. Then she sends him to the kitchen to empty the hot-water bottle and tells him to wait in the lounge. The moment he's gone she starts to work away at her mother's face, gently at first until she checks her watch and realises she needs to *scrub harder, struggling to adjust to the idea that there's no way she can be causing her any discomfort. Billy has absolutely caked it on and it's a complete mess so it takes longer than she thought. She's glad now that she's seen to it before making the phone call. She has no idea how she'd have gone about explaining something like this if others had arrived before she was ready.*

When she's finished, she goes round to the other side of the bed and, as she did just now with her mother, she strokes her father's hair and places a tender kiss on his forehead to say goodbye. It's the only place she can do so because one look at his face tells her he's going to present even more of a challenge than her mother did just now. She straightens his head so that it's at a more natural angle, then sets to work at removing the make-up. She has to scrub away at the layers of foundation, blusher, bronzer, eyeliner – he looks in this light as if his face had been dipped in a pack of Doritos. And once she's removed it all, there are still strange marks around his eye that won't come off, like scuff marks as if he's had an accident recently. She decides eventually that it looks as good as it's going to and goes into the hallway to make the calls.

The first is to Matthew but she gets his mobile and leaves a message. The second is a 999 call and she explains as calmly and methodically as she can what the situation is and asks for advice as to which services she needs. Then, when she's done all this, she heads for the lounge to wait for them to arrive.

And finds Billy's not there.

And the back door is wide open.

He sits on the seat of the bus shelter and examines the flap of the A4 envelope. He's trying to remember how it got from the dressing table in the bedroom and onto the work surface in the kitchen and can only assume it must have been when he went in to fill the hot-water bottle. He doesn't remember picking up the envelope at any stage but that must be what happened because when Mia sent him back in there to empty the hottie, there it was, looking up at him – Mia/Billy on the front in his mother's handwriting.

The moment he saw it he wanted to know what she'd written. He needed to hear from her again and wanted to soak it in without being interrupted, even by Mia. So while she was busy removing all the make-up he slipped quietly out of the back door, through the gate at the end of the garden and cut round the side of their neighbour's house to rejoin Udimore Road. He's not sure how far he's walked from there but when he saw the bus shelter he decided that was as far as he wanted to go. This will do.

He can see, looking at the flap, that someone has already opened it once and then resealed it with Sellotape. The moment he realises there's more than one letter inside, he knows why. He was expecting just a note from her but he should have known his father would muscle in somehow.

He takes them out now and reads his mother's first. It's a goodbye note, not a very long one, almost as if the letter reflects her reaction to the illness itself – she doesn't want to drag it out any longer than she has to. She can't face the idea of making her family sit there for days and months on end, watching her struggle to hold onto something that's starting to mean less and less with every passing day. She hopes they'll understand in time and learn to forgive her, but however much this hurts them they should never doubt how much she loves them and how proud she is of her two darling children. She begs them to remember her as she used to be and assures them she's happier this morning than she's been at any stage in the past twelve months since the illness took hold. She hopes they'll cling to that.

There are a few practical details and as he reads this part there's one thing that gradually becomes crystal clear – she wasn't for one minute expecting him to follow her. He's done it behind her back. She's been assuming all along that he'll be around to look after Billy and instead he's done what he always does and put himself first. He's taken the easy way out the moment it was too late for her to do anything about it and then slipped his own letters inside the same envelope – one for each of them.

Billy reads Mia's first – he doesn't think she'll mind. It says a lot of nice things about her, how special she is and how proud he felt when he walked her down the aisle, even though he was struggling to cope with the secret they'd agreed to keep from her for her sake. He goes on to explain where all the important documents are kept and what she needs to do over the next few days, step-by-step. It's so detailed there's no way he's done this in a few frantic moments this morning. This must have taken hours to put together so that means he's known for some time he was going to do this and didn't even have the guts to tell his own wife. He's sat by the bedside, taken the tablets out of the blister packs, fed them to her and helped her wash them down with a drink, lying all the time about how the kids will be all right, they'll be safe. He'll be there to look after them. And then the moment she starts to go under he jumps ship and follows her. How sick is that?

Billy almost doesn't want to read his own letter. He's pretty sure he knows what to expect. Something brief and to the point – 'be a good boy and do as your sister tells you.' Instead he's surprised to find there's at least as much on this sheet as there was on Mia's. And it's full of the kind of things Billy could have done with hearing at any stage while he was still alive, so how fucking useless is it that he's saying them now – not even saying them but scribbling them *in that stupid spidery scrawl of his, like a few minutes spent putting it down on paper is going to make up for all those years of treating him like some intruder who's somehow managed to worm his way into this perfect family like some fucking . . . fucking . . . CUCKOO or something and if he thinks that's going to make things right and turn the past few years on their head he's got another thing coming 'cos Billy's not stupid – not by a long shot. He knows. He knows. And he doesn't even get two thirds of the way through the letter before he screws it up in a ball. Then he rethinks and smooths it out so that he can tear it into the tiniest pieces imaginable and throw them all into the air for the breeze to carry off into the distance.*

And when the bus stops and the driver asks does he want to get on the bus or doesn't he, he yells back at him and storms off down the road.

Not sure where he's going.

And not giving a shit.

11

MONDAY 17TH AUGUST 2015

The excuse he'd been seeking all evening came to him, as the best ideas usually did, when he'd just about given up looking for it. He'd undressed and was lying in bed, on the verge of falling asleep, when Karun messaged to tell him not to worry about the business lunch – everything was sorted.

It was a measure of just how far removed he was from everything going on in London that he struggled for a minute to work out what he was talking about. Then he remembered the meeting with a potential investor they'd been wooing for several weeks. Until Matthew's phone call had blown everything else out of the water, the plan had been for Billy and Karun to go together. Zak was quite happy to stay well away – he sometimes came across as just a touch too anarchic, a bit of a chancer, and that wasn't necessarily what potential investors were looking for. With Billy now unavailable, the other two had decided it would be best to leave it to Karun on his own, which he was more than capable of doing. *Thank God he's not ill*, Billy had thought to himself, putting the phone on the bedside table and turning out the light.

And there it was. A little bit of artistic licence, an awful lot of flagrant deceit, and the excuse he needed was right there in front of him, served up on a plate. Karun ill, Zak not a viable alternative, *who you gonna call . . .?*

And yes, when he apologised to Mia and told her he'd need to pop back to London for the meeting, it felt like a betrayal on so many levels – of course it did. The reason he'd come back in the first place was to be there for her and here he was, leaving her on her own for the best part of a day. Not only that, he was lying to her face, taking advantage of her good nature, safe in the knowledge that she would swallow her disappointment without kicking up a fuss because that was how she always dealt with setbacks. She'd assume Billy felt bad enough anyway about letting her down and would do anything to avoid making things worse for him.

He felt bad about it but at the same time he couldn't see that he had any real choice. There was no way he could tell her the truth. Just knowing he was spending the day with Aimi would have been bad enough. Add to that the dubious nature of what he might be getting into and he knew he'd never hear the last of it. She'd go into meltdown. She didn't need much of an excuse to start on one of her anti-Aimi tirades and this would be one hell of an excuse.

He promised he'd get the first train back once the lunch was over. Then maybe the three of them could go out to dinner together that evening, she could pick a country pub somewhere and book a table for them. His treat. His way of making it up to her. He didn't have any problem in convincing her about how bad he felt. That was the only genuine part about the whole story.

*

Aimi picked him up outside The Thai House in Tower Street at eleven. He'd suggested the railway station but she was concerned that might be a little too public and increase the chances of being spotted by someone they knew. He'd brought one of his rucksacks with him for the sake of authenticity – he never went to any business meeting without a laptop – and she told him to throw it onto the back seat and get in quickly. Then she drove off, picking up the A21 towards Tonbridge, heading for the M25 and M23 to Gatwick. He'd looked it up the night before, knew it would take an hour and a half each way. Add on another hour or so for some of the other things Aimi had asked him to do and he'd still be back by late afternoon. He promised himself that this evening would be all about Mia to make up for the way he'd short-changed her during the past twenty-four hours.

During the journey Aimi quizzed him on every little detail of the plan, made him go over it again and again, emphasising that she was totally dependent on him. One slip-up and the whole thing would come crashing down around her ears. This would be her one shot at breaking free from the Vedras. Make a mess of it and she'd never get another chance.

He went through it step by step to reassure her that he was on top of things. What he should say when questioned by the police, because she was convinced that would happen. What he should say if he was ever confronted by the Vedras. A separate version for each that he'd had to memorise and pour back out to her. And he was word-perfect.

He liked the fact that she needed his help, understood why she couldn't just get the train from Rye station. It was too small, too local. If anyone got suspicious and decided to ask around, the first place they'd check was the station. If that were to happen, there was every chance someone would remember seeing her – even when dressing down and trying to be anonymous, Aimi wasn't someone who tended to go unnoticed. If, on the other hand, she was driven to Gatwick by someone who'd be able to bring the car back to where it needed to be, no one at the airport was going to know or remember her, not with that volume of traffic. It would mean that even if Plan A didn't work and the search for her got underway, she'd at least have a head start.

And that would be enhanced significantly if she could manage to mislead everyone into looking at the wrong day altogether. Joe was not due back until late Tuesday night so he'd have no way of knowing when she'd actually left. The phone messages would be the key to steering everyone away from Monday afternoon. She had no idea how long that might throw them off the scent, but it stood to reason that every layer of confusion she could introduce would buy her more time and increase her chances of staying off the radar.

Billy asked why Gatwick, and again she seemed to have thought things through carefully. If they managed to track her movements as far as the airport, the initial assumption would hopefully be that she'd left the country. But the rail connection from there to Victoria was quick and easy and provided a perfect launch pad for any number of ways of putting distance between herself and the Vedras. Again – more layers of confusion.

Billy had gone over Aimi's plan carefully, looking for flaws, and thought it was sound. His one great concern in all of this, however, was that she wouldn't tell him where she was going – not yet at least. She apologised, urged him not to take it the wrong way and see it as evidence that she didn't trust him. She knew he'd never deliberately let her down but no one was infallible. If he knew where she was, there was always a chance he might give it away without meaning to. If, on the other hand, he *didn't* know – if nobody knew – it reduced significantly the chances of anyone tracking her down.

He understood, couldn't fault the logic, but still felt uncomfortable at the thought of being in the dark. For one thing, he didn't like the idea of her being out there on her own, looking over her shoulder with no one to lean on. That should be his job and simply driving her to Gatwick and bringing her car back seemed such a paltry contribution – surely there was more he could be doing. And on a more personal level, she'd only just come back into his life after a gap of eleven years. To have her leave for a second time almost immediately felt like history repeating itself and he was only partially appeased by her promises that the moment she felt it was safe, she'd arrange for the two of them to meet up. It all felt so tenuous somehow – so *jam tomorrow*. But in the final analysis it all boiled down to one simple question – did he want her to get away from Joe Vedra and his family or not? The word rhetorical, he decided, was coined for questions such as that.

Aimi drove most of the way but insisted he take the wheel for the last half-hour or so to make sure he was used to the car before they got to Gatwick. The last thing they needed was for him to have an accident or breakdown or to get stopped by a patrol car for some reason on the return journey.

'If something like that happens, walk away,' she told him. 'If you have to run, don't hang around. Just ditch the car, OK? It's no use to me anymore so it's no great loss. But what we can't have is someone putting you and my car together at any stage. Understand?' He nodded and went back to concentrating on getting used to the gears, the clutch, the feel of the car. It was very different from the mini he'd had at Southampton but easy enough after ten minutes or so.

When they got to Gatwick, she directed him to the Departures drop-off zone and he pulled into a space which had just been vacated. He started to get out of the car but she caught hold of his arm and pulled him back in.

'Keep your face well hidden,' she urged him. 'If they do trace me this far you don't want to be picked up by any cameras.' He sat back in the seat and raised a protective hand to shield his face while she went to the boot and removed two suitcases, which surprised him.

'Isn't that a bit iffy?' he called out. She closed the boot and came round to the driver's side window.

'*Iffy* how?'

'You want people to think you're dead, not that you've run away. What if he notices they're missing?'

She put the cases on the ground beside the car and leant in through the window to make sure he was well hidden. She kissed him on the cheek and told him not to worry. She'd bought two cheap cases on Saturday, paying cash. As for the clothes in them, she could hardly start up again with nothing to wear. She'd left plenty in the wardrobe, and besides, Joe was useless when it came to clothes. Ask him to close his eyes and tell her what she was wearing and he wouldn't come close. He'd never know whether anything was missing or not.

She took two mobile phones out of her pocket. One was a cheap pay-as-you-go Nokia, the other was her own rather more upmarket Samsung. The former was to be her way of contacting him. She told him all texts she'd sent to him so far had been done on this phone so that there would be no record of them for anyone to find on her Samsung. As long as he kept it safe and destroyed it when she told him to, he'd be fine. She reminded him she'd ring that evening to reassure him she was OK and let him know when she'd next be in touch. He must keep it somewhere safe – no one should know about it. If the need arose, he should ditch it and the moment she was unable to make contact she'd realise what had happened and find another way of getting in touch. She emphasised repeatedly that no one else must get hold of it under any circumstances.

It had one pre-set number in it, she told him, and that was one he should call in an emergency. She was quite clear what she meant by that. Social calls were out. She didn't want him checking on her every five minutes to find out where she was and how she was doing. Triangulation made it so much easier now to narrow down where a call had been made and he needed to understand that every time he called her, it increased the risk of her being found. Again, he wasn't happy about being unable to contact her as often as he'd like but if it mattered that much to her – and clearly it did – he'd have to live with it.

She told him that from time to time she'd change her own disposable, just to be safe. He needn't worry about that – she'd make sure he always knew how to get in touch. As for her own Samsung, he was to send three texts to Joe at specific times, one that evening, one first thing on Tuesday and the third just after midday when Joe would probably be on his way to the airport in Faro. She'd written out the messages for him on a sheet of paper that he was to burn the moment he'd sent the third message. Joe might possibly reply but it would be little more than an acknowledgement and wouldn't need any follow-up. Joe wasn't big on sentiment, especially when he was away with his father and brother. If for some bizarre reason a reply was expected from her, he should ignore it and Joe would assume she'd turned her phone off.

As for the chances of him actually phoning her from the Algarve, they could be safely discounted. Even when they were a lot closer, it was always Aimi who initiated contact, but given the way things had been between them since the anniversary, it was almost inconceivable that he would ring. Again, if the unthinkable were to happen, Billy must not under any circumstances answer it. In fact, it would be best if he kept it turned off and just checked it every now and then for messages. Did he understand?

He told her to stop worrying. He knew what he had to do and she should trust him. She looked at her watch and pulled him into a clumsy embrace, constrained by the window. She held him for a second or two as she thanked him for being there when she needed him. Then she kissed him again and stooped to pick up the cases, telling him he needed to go – there was a queue of cars hoping for a drop-off space to become available.

He told her to wait, reaching into his pocket and taking out a small package which he held out to her. She put the cases down again and looked at him with a quiet smile as she unwrapped it. She opened the small white box and peeped inside with a puzzled frown.

'You've lost yours,' he said, taking it from the box and undoing the clasp. 'I noticed yesterday that you weren't wearing it. I thought you might like to take mine instead.'

He fitted the rope bracelet around her wrist, the A and the B etched on either side of the clasp faded now but still there if you looked hard enough.

'Billy . . .'

'It's OK. I can get another. You need to look after this one though. It'll bring you luck.'

She looked embarrassed for a moment.

'I haven't got you anything,' she confessed, looking suitably apologetic. 'It's very sweet of you but you didn't need to get me this.'

'Mason's Field,' he said, sensing that she wasn't tuned into the same wavelength just yet. 'Last time you left. You remember?'

'Mason's Field – of course,' she said, although not with any great conviction.

'Cross your heart,' he prompted, hoping to tease from her some indication that she knew what he was referring to.

She smiled, picked up the cases once more and he watched until she disappeared through the doors.

He concentrated hard for the whole of the return journey, making sure he stayed within the speed limit at all times, keeping a safe braking distance between himself and the car in front and also keeping a close eye on any drivers who looked as if they might pose a threat. Aimi had told him to ditch the car if necessary, but he knew that would be a last resort and a very poor outcome. The car needed to be in Camber Sands tomorrow night without fail or Plan A wouldn't make sense.

Once he reached Rye, he drove into the car park in Rope Walk and paid for an overnight ticket. He checked the boot to make sure the small pile of clothing and the note were in there, put the two mobiles in his rucksack for now, locked the car and walked away, keeping an eye open for cameras he'd be better off avoiding.

Once he was on the bus home, he took the three messages out of his pocket and read them again to check the times and make sure he'd be able to improvise if they were to go missing at any stage. It wouldn't be difficult. The content was banal in the extreme. She'd put in one or two affectionate comments, she explained, not because she felt anything for Joe but because that was what she was reduced to in this relationship. Joe expected certain things and she had to fake it or face the consequences. While he was away, he'd be keeping a tally of the various ways she'd let him down; by phoning when it wasn't convenient, not phoning when she should, failing to make him feel as if she was missing him, swarming all over him so that he couldn't breathe – the list was endless, self-contradictory and she'd pay for her indiscretions once he was back, not necessarily physically but she'd pay nevertheless.

The importance of the messages was twofold: she needed to establish that everything at home was normal so that his suspicions would not be aroused. More crucially, however, they would create a timeline that suggested she was still at home, going about her everyday business as late as Tuesday lunchtime, a fiction that would be further strengthened by the appearance of her car in the car park outside The Gallivant late on Tuesday afternoon. Anything that helped to establish that narrative as fact could only improve her chances of getting as far away as possible.

Billy sat back in his seat and relaxed for the first time since Aimi had walked away from the car. He wondered where she was now. Clearly, she wanted him to believe she'd flown out of the country but she could just as easily have taken the train to London. If that was the case she'd be there by now, maybe even setting out on the next leg of her journey. As for her final destination, that was anybody's guess. He remembered the frisson of excitement he always experienced as the train pulled out of St. Pancras, the sense of unlimited possibilities. His was never more than the product of an overactive imagination, but right now Aimi was experiencing it for real. It was his dream as well as hers and he'd have given anything to be sharing it with her. Anything.

One day, he told himself. For now he had a job to do, one which he couldn't afford to get wrong. If the next few days went according to plan that would bring him one step closer to being reunited with her.

She'd promised to send for him when she was ready.

And he would wait till then.

He was good at waiting.

12

WEDNESDAY 20TH APRIL 2016

Portland, Maine, USA

Jeanie Alvares always fancied she could get a decent conversation out of a corpse. It was a gift, she said. Some people were good with their hands, like her husband Richie for instance. Anything mechanical broke down, he'd take the thing apart and have it working again in no time. Her sister Julie? What she couldn't do in the kitchen. She'd been known to rustle up a three-course meal for twelve people at the drop of a hat.

With Jeanie it was people. She just knew how to talk to them and, more to the point, she knew how to listen. Her way of looking at it: deep down we all want to talk about ourselves – we just don't necessarily realise it. Often as not, we need someone to coax it out of us and that's where she came in. *I have one of those faces. People know they can trust me.*

When Richie took the voluntary redundancy package and she'd managed to persuade him that running a guest house was what he'd always wanted to do, the division of responsibilities more or less spoke for itself. Richie would odd-job around the place and keep both the inside and outside of the building in good order, while she was the one who dealt with the guests. She was the one who thought of all the little details that make a visitor's stay just that bit more memorable – fresh flowers in the window, the basket of fruit and bottle of wine in the room when they arrived, the little wrapped chocolate on the pillow each evening alongside the cuddly animals crafted out of hand towels, the regularly updated folders with details of attractions in the Portland area and maps explaining how to get there. She liked to think of herself as the glue that held the whole enterprise together. Nothing was too much trouble.

They had four rooms they made available for rent – The Cherry Orchard, The Seagull, Three Sisters and Uncle Vanya – while she and Richie lived in the annexe. Jeanie cleaned the rooms, saw to the washing, cooked breakfast for the guests, maintained the website and took responsibility for the business side of things. Richie mowed the front lawn every couple of days, changed the occasional light bulb and drove to the hardware store from time to time to stock up and shoot the breeze with Gus and the Nolan boy who worked there, but otherwise he kept out of the way and left it all to her.

It suited her just fine. She loved the interaction with their visitors so much she genuinely believed she had the better end of the deal. The lasting friendships – she didn't think that was too strong a claim – that she'd formed with so many of them over the years meant a great deal to her. They came back again and again, kept up with her on Facebook and sent her cards at Christmas. With some of them she knew intimate family details, which she updated regularly in the big blue notebook she kept in one of the desk drawers in Reception. That way she could ask after children by name, ask relevant questions about whatever line of work each guest was in. It was, she felt, only polite to take an interest.

She could count on the fingers of one hand the occasions when she and Richie had been unlucky with a guest. There was the couple from Wisconsin a while back who'd spent most of the night screaming at each other and then resorted to throwing furniture around the room in the early hours of the morning. That remained the only time in the eleven years they'd been doing this that they'd had to call the authorities out to The Old Theater Guest House.

And there was the strange little Central European man last year who spoke not a word of English and spent the entire weekend in his room, a detail which she found more than a little troubling. They hadn't needed to contact the police about *him* but Jeanie had been worried enough to come close to it on a couple of occasions. She didn't like to think ill of people as a rule but did find his behaviour very odd.

She wasn't sure why the new guest in The Cherry Orchard made her think of Mr Mitrovic. For one thing, there was no language barrier, neither did he show any intention of taking to his room and ignoring what Portland had to offer. He'd been polite enough, if a little désengagé while she walked him through the house, nodding as she explained the various routines, and there was nothing at all in his manner to which she could take exception. It's just that after fifteen to twenty minutes in his company she'd come away with next to nothing she could put in her blue book. She'd asked all the usual questions but somehow the answers had never materialised. It was the oddest thing. He wasn't rude in any way or obviously evasive, but he had this way of deflecting attention somehow, introducing into the conversation random observations which never quite addressed the question she'd actually asked. A little shyness, secrecy even, she could handle, but complete non-sequiturs wrongfooted her entirely.

She knew from the registration book that he was from England. He had a slight accent but that was nothing unusual – England was all accents. His was easy enough to understand but different somehow. She couldn't quite place it.

And that was it really. Family? No idea. Job? Not a clue. She did sense he carried about him an air of melancholy and wondered if the fact he was travelling alone might have something to do with it, but when she asked if anyone would be joining him he didn't answer. Instead he sat down on the bed and started removing his sneakers, throwing her so completely off course that the conversation somehow never managed to find its way to second base.

It was odd, she felt. She didn't like to flatter herself, but most people would have succumbed to her overtures by now and started to open up at least a little. Probably just shy, she decided. Some people simply aren't comfortable with strangers, they need warming up. She'd give him a bit of space for now, let him get unpacked and settled in. At some point though, she'd have another go.

Michael Johnson, she decided, was going to be one of her projects. He'd booked for a couple of nights and she promised herself that by the time he left they'd be like old friends.

And she'd certainly have something worth putting in her blue book.

13

TUESDAY 18TH AUGUST 2015

By the time they'd finished lunch in town, Billy was feeling confident he'd mended enough fences to put his relationship with Mia back where it belonged and even managed to ease his conscience to a certain extent.

The previous evening had certainly helped to pave the way. Matthew had recommended a pub on the A259 with a skittle alley and a half-decent restaurant and the three of them had spent a pleasant, tension-free evening there. Matthew, in the right frame of mind, could be entertaining company, and possibly because he felt bad about leaving Mia for four days, he seemed to be making a special effort to keep things light. Billy, with his own reasons for feeling guilty, was determined to match him stride for stride and between them they'd managed to make both themselves and Mia feel a lot better by the time they got home.

The following morning Matthew had left early for work to make sure everything was in place before he flew out to the States and as soon as they'd had breakfast Billy had bundled Mia into the car – the supposedly iffy brakes had apparently been seen to while he was in London, or so he was meant to believe – and driven her the short distance to Rye Harbour Nature Reserve, just to the south of Rye itself.

The reserve was a large area of shingle ridges formed over the centuries by a combination of the sea and strong winds. They'd come here a few times on Saturday mornings when he was still a teenager, following the network of footpaths and grassy trails, ostensibly on the lookout for the many species of plants and animals that made their home there but in reality taking consolation in each other's company as much as anything else. It became their way of taking refuge from a world that, at the time, seemed to have it in for them.

She'd brought Matthew's digital camera with her and had great fun taking several photos of the wildlife and scenery as well as persuading Billy to pose, something he'd always been reluctant to do. He teased her about the camera, asking why neither of them, with all the money Matthew was earning, had seen fit to buy a better one. It was at least seven years old and had developed a fault from very early on which left all photos with a hazy yellow streak in the top right-hand corner which she and Matthew could never see but which he personally found distracting. Whenever he mentioned it, Mia always laughed and said she was never going to change it for another. *Sentimental value,* she said, as if that explained everything. Mia was big on sentiment.

They had lunch back in Rye at The White Vine House and while they were waiting for their paninis to arrive he told her about the facial and massage he'd booked for her at The Rye Retreat for two o'clock, explaining that he felt bad about having to work all afternoon. This way, she could relax and be pampered for a couple of hours and he'd either take the car and come back for her later or get the bus home and leave the car for her to drive, as long as she thought she'd be up to it.

She offered the predictable token protest but he knew how much she enjoyed this sort of treat and could see in her expression just how touched she was that he'd been so thoughtful. She insisted he take the car, saying she'd get a bus back after the treatments. She gave him a kiss on the cheek as she excused herself to go to the loo and told him he was the best.

He just wished he deserved it.

As soon as he left her in Cinque Ports Street, he headed straight for Rope Walk and the car park where Aimi's Lexus had been sitting for almost twenty-four hours now. Again he took great care not to draw attention to himself, resisting the temptation to open up and see what the car could do once he was outside the town limits. Instead he drove as unobtrusively as possible back to Camber, where he turned left into the car park that served The Gallivant. Ignoring the spaces at the front of the restaurant, he headed off to the right and left the car where he'd found it the other day, as Aimi had asked him to.

'Park up against the white fence alongside the trees, where it won't be so easy to see the car from the hotel itself. I've had a look and don't think there are any cameras but, if there are, the chances are they won't pick you up. Leave the car there and take the keys with you. It wouldn't be a problem if someone drove off with it – might even muddy the waters a bit – but we don't want some do-gooder spotting the keys and reporting it too early, OK?'

He left the clothes in the boot for now as he couldn't exactly risk taking them back to Mia's. He'd see to them later, when he came back after dark to add the final touches to the plan. She'd told him not to walk back out of the main entrance in case she was wrong about the cameras so, following her instructions, he sneaked along the fence and rejoined the road that way. Then he headed back on foot to Mia's house where he made a point of setting up the laptops to make it look as if he'd been working all afternoon before setting out to catch the bus back into town in time to collect Mia's car and bring her home.

Tomorrow, he told himself. Tomorrow it would all be over and he'd be able to give his work his full attention.

As it turned out, he made a start on it earlier than he'd been expecting – just not a very effective one.

After an early dinner, Matthew and Mia decided to go for a stroll to walk off the meal before he set off for Heathrow. With an early flight the following morning, he'd booked a room near the airport rather than get up at some ludicrous hour and run the gauntlet of the M25. Billy turned down their invitation to go with them. He had no way of knowing whether they really wanted his company or were just being polite so he begged off, using his work as an excuse yet again.

With both of them out of the house, he felt it was safe to check the phones just once more. He'd heard from Aimi last night – just a short text message to say she was fine and would ring sometime in the next day or so to check on how things had gone. She'd reminded him for the umpteenth time that he should only contact her in an absolute emergency and ended with a lovely sentence about how lucky she was to have someone like him to rely on. He'd read that message several times today already.

He'd sent his messages for the day and Aimi had been bang on the money. Just the one reply from Joe, a factual one saying he'd be at Gatwick at 8.40 that evening, probably picking the car up around ten so he wasn't likely to be home much before midnight once he'd dropped off the others. No obvious affection expressed, he was pleased to note.

He switched her Samsung on briefly just in case there were any further messages from Joe – predictably there weren't – and then put both phones away in a zip-up compartment of one of his rucksacks, buried under a pile of tissues. Then he sat and looked at the clock.

There were still a couple of hours to go before he was meant to go back to the car so he decided he might as well at least make a start on the work. It occurred to him that if he'd worked the number of hours he'd supposedly devoted to it already, he'd be in pretty good shape to finish by the time he went back to London. As it was, he was going to have to pull out all the stops, so maybe getting a couple of hours out of the way now would at least kick-start the whole process, make it more real.

No chance.

Fine in theory but the work needed his full concentration and that was very much elsewhere. Every so often he'd catch himself thinking ahead to what he'd be doing in a few hours' time or wondering where Aimi was and what she was doing at that very moment or trying to imagine Joe's reaction when he arrived home. He'd be surprised first of all to find all the lights out when he pulled up outside the house. Angry when it was obvious she hadn't waited up for him. Even more so when he realised she wasn't even there. At what point would the anger turn to bewilderment? When would concern take over? How would he go about trying to work out where she was and what was happening? And, best of all, what would be the turning point that made him finally realise she was gone?

It was all too distracting and the work was eventually pushed to one side. Time and a place, he told himself.

Right now, this was his time.

And Aimi's.

Mia went to bed at ten. Billy could sense she was at a bit of a loose end with Matthew having left, so he sat with her for a while, sorting out a problem she was having with her laptop and then watching some American comedy she'd recorded. When she finally went to her room, he said he might possibly go for a walk at some stage to clear his head, so she shouldn't be alarmed if she heard the door. He'd been thinking he'd probably leave it an hour or so but was getting antsy before even fifteen minutes had passed. He couldn't just sit there. He needed to get this done.

He pulled on a sweatshirt and left the house as quietly as possible, retracing the same steps he'd taken just two days earlier. It seemed impossible that it was that recently – so much had happened in the meantime. He wasn't stupid – he knew the implications of what he was about to do, that it could have far-reaching consequences if his involvement ever came to light. Aimi hadn't tried to minimise the dangers and he'd wavered on a couple of occasions before agreeing to help. But when she'd texted last night to say how much it meant to her to have someone like him to turn to and that she really didn't deserve him, all other considerations had flown straight out of the window.

During those difficult years when they'd lost contact, he'd kept her photo in his bedside drawer, the only one he had of the two of them together. He'd shown it to no one, not even mentioned her to Zak or Karun – kept her to himself. And there were times when he'd started to wonder if they'd ever find a way back to each other, especially when he heard she'd flown out to Cyprus with a dance group and even more so when he discovered she had married Joe Vedra. Those had been very bleak, desperate times and he'd thrown himself into his work in an attempt to distract himself from the negative thoughts that were threatening to overwhelm him. But he'd held on . . . and she'd found her way back to him in the end. She needed him, seemed at last to understand that he was the one person in her life she could rely on. So he was in it now and there would be no backing out without letting her down badly.

The path alongside the road was difficult to negotiate in the dark and he was glad when he came alongside a few houses whose lights cast some sort of glow he could see by. When he came to The Gallivant, things were relatively quiet. The restaurant would have shut a while ago so most of the cars in the car park belonged to hotel guests who were already in for the night. He hugged the shadows though, to make sure no one was watching, then approached the car, staying tight to the fence and avoiding the main entrance. He opened the boot and took out the shopping bag that Aimi had put in there the previous day. Then he closed it quietly, locked the car and headed back out of the car park as discreetly as possible.

Crossing the road, he stepped onto the green area in front of the Oasis Beach Shop and picked up the sandy path beyond it that led over the dunes. Even before he reached the beach he could hear voices away to his right, laughter and music and the unmistakable smell of a barbecue coming from a group of people who'd set up an impromptu party on the sand. He headed in the opposite direction, picking his way through the dunes and keeping his eyes and ears peeled for any indication that others were in the vicinity. Down at the shoreline the fringes of the moonlight picked out a man and his dog taking their final walk of the day and fifty yards behind them a couple were walking side by side, staying just out of range of the water. Otherwise – no one.

He stayed where he was for a few moments, stooping so that he wouldn't be seen by anyone else who might have escaped his attention. He looked around and decided that this was as good a spot as any. During the day, always assuming the weather was as hot as it had been recently, the slopes here would be littered with holidaymakers. Eventually someone would realise that the pile of clothes had been there for a long time without anyone coming back from the water to claim them. They'd ask around maybe, wonder whether they'd be better off minding their own business, but there would always be one dependable soul who would alert the authorities ... especially if they'd rummaged through the pile and found the note.

He took everything out of the Tesco bag – light-green blouse, yellow skirt and cardigan, white beach shoes, the note Aimi had written and sealed in a blue envelope, wrapped in a slippery fish to offer a bit of protection. He held the blouse against his face for a moment or two, hoping to pick up a trace of Aimi on the fabric. Then he folded it carefully and put it with the rest of the clothing. He remembered to take her Samsung out of his pocket and added it to the pile, tucking it with the envelope inside the bundle of clothing.

Before sealing it, Aimi had allowed him to see what it said – *Sorry. Can't do this anymore.* His immediate reaction was that it wasn't enough. There was nothing there to explain why she was having to do this. No mention of her husband and the way he'd abused her. Nothing at all in the letter to implicate him in any way other than in the most general terms. It was pretty obvious he hadn't been able to make his wife happy but he might even get some sympathy out of that from some quarters. *Poor Joe – tried so hard but she was obviously unbalanced.* He couldn't understand why she wouldn't want to spell it out before disappearing. That's what he'd have done. He'd already composed the letter for her in his head. In the end though, it was her business. Her marriage, her death. If that was the way she wanted to play it, who was he to argue? Much as it went against the grain, he'd kept his thought to himself.

But squatting down there in the sand dunes, with a cool breeze ruffling his hair and the moonlight shimmying its way across the surface of the water, he found it impossible to ignore the rebellious voices that were urging him on. Joe Vedra should not be allowed just to shrug his shoulders and walk off from this. He should pay for what he'd done. Even if he managed to blag his way out of it somehow, he ought at least to know what Aimi thought of him. And yes, it might be childish. Yes, Aimi would be angry if she knew. But there was no way she would know unless everything went tits up and if that happened one little text message from him would be the least of her worries.

He knew exactly what he wanted to do.

He also knew there was no one there to stop him.

So he rummaged through her clothes for the Samsung, turned it on again and started to type a text message to Joe Vedra. It was brief and to the point . . . and would certainly raise a question or two in the minds of the police when they got hold of the phone.

The message read:

Fuck you . . . and fuck your family

He wiped the phone to clear any prints and replaced it amongst her clothing.

14

WEDNESDAY 20TH APRIL 2016

Peaks Island and the City of Portland, Maine, USA

Kellie Moore watches through the window of the waiting area as the cars and foot passengers disembark from the *Machigonne II*. There aren't many of them at this time of the evening. Tourists may flock over to Peaks Island in their thousands on a baking hot summer's day but most tend to head back late afternoon once they've soaked up as much as they need of the sunshine, the scenery and the apple-pie wholesomeness of the place. That way, they have the whole evening on the mainland to take advantage of what Portland has to offer. The city is rich in bars and restaurants and they are heaving most evenings for a good reason.

The passengers waiting now to cross in the opposite direction are islanders for the most part, plus a handful of tourists who are renting a property on the island and don't want to risk missing the last ferry. She's been here for several months now on a year-long lease with the option to extend, and already she feels on a different level from the day-trippers and fly-by-night merchants who rent for a week or two before rushing off to strike the next place from the wish list. This almost feels like home and she could see herself settling here under different circumstances.

She already knows quite a few of the eight hundred or so permanent residents, if *knows* is the right word for it. She's grown accustomed to seeing the same faces when she crosses in the morning to go to the Academy and is now on nodding terms with most of them. Some are happy to strike up a conversation but no one will press her without some indication that she'd welcome that level of interest. This is what she really likes about the islanders, she's decided. They place a high premium on privacy which makes them the perfect neighbours as far as she's concerned – there if she needs them, but not remotely intrusive. It doesn't feel like they're looking over her shoulder every five minutes.

She'd have taken an earlier ferry but a few of the company had decided to go out for the evening. They'd been urging her to come with them for a while so she'd agreed to go along for the meal, just to ward off any undue curiosity her persistent refusals might generate. Then she'd made her apologies, leaving plenty of time to catch the penultimate ferry. The others were all heading back to Evie's. She knows someone would have offered her a bed for the night if she'd wanted to stay over – Hobie would have been at the head of the queue, she thinks to herself with a smile – but she'd rather get a decent night's sleep. The Academy sets a lot of store by professional standards and she's not about to blot her copybook by turning up tomorrow looking like a train wreck.

They're ready to let foot passengers board now so she joins the queue and shows her monthly pass to a crew member in cut-offs and a yellow dayglo life jacket. Most passengers head for the covered areas on the boat because regulars know the breeze will be distinctly sharp once they're out in the middle of the bay. She imagines the open areas on the top deck will be lovely a couple of months from now, but even though the crossing takes no more than seventeen minutes, that's more than long enough on an April evening.

She squeezes onto the end of a row meant for four people which a middle-aged couple have taken over with their various belongings. They exchange a few friendly words until the boat starts its journey across Casco Bay. Then she closes her eyes as they pass Bug Light on the tip of South Portland, skirting Fort Scammel before heading for Jones Landing on the western coast of Peaks Island. Next thing she knows, someone's tapping her on the shoulder to say they're docking already. She's surprised she dropped off so easily – obviously the early night was a wise decision on her part. She's sitting in on auditions tomorrow morning and she'll need to be at her sharpest.

She gets to her feet and waits with the other passengers while the crew go through their familiar preparations for disembarkation. And it's just as everyone's starting to move forward onto the pontoon that she hears a man's voice calling out, from somewhere behind her.

'Aimi!'

She's so startled she actually flinches, ducks her head down as if hoping to take herself out of his line of sight. She hasn't dared to risk a look to see who it might be. She's seized by the irrational conviction that if she can just avoid making eye contact, the danger will somehow be averted. Then she hears him call out again.

'Aimi – to your left a bit, hon. I want to get a shot of you with the sign lit up in the background.'

And she heaves a sigh of relief, working hard to bring her heart rate back down. It's the third time this has happened and if the Albanians were here right now she'd make sure they knew all about it. First thing she said when they presented her with the documents was, *why not keep the same Christian name?* Every film or TV show she's ever seen where someone takes on a new identity, they always stick to the same first name because that's what you react to instinctively and it takes years to get used to a different one. It's a no-brainer. Works both ways too. Only last week Evie called out to her twice before she realised she was the *Kellie* who was meant to be answering. Little details like that matter. They make all the difference.

When she queried the name on the documents, they turned shitty on her. Didn't take too kindly to a woman who clearly didn't know her place. Reminded her that she'd come to *them*, not the other way round. Asked if she knew who she was dealing with here. Did she want the documents or not? They knew as well as she did that the answer had to be yes – where else was she going to go that late in the day?

So she'd taken them, telling herself she'd get used to it in time. Practised saying it over and over.

Kellie Moore.

Kellie Moore.

How hard could it be?

PART TWO

15

THURSDAY 20TH AUGUST 2015

The week-long spell of fine weather has come to an end. It broke in the night and Mia opened the curtains first thing this morning to a seamless blanket of cloud cover which seemed to have settled in for the long haul. Despite the overnight rain, most of the puddles have already drained away into the parched soil by mid-morning and that's enough to send her to the shed in search of rubber gloves, secateurs and a trowel before laziness can get the better of her.

The garden's been gasping for attention for a while now and, what with everything else that's been happening, she's let it get away from her. When Matthew persuaded her to take a week off work, it did occur to her she might be able to use some of that time to do a few odd jobs around the place, but while the sun's been blazing down she's found it so difficult to motivate herself. Now, judging by the total absence of blue overhead, that constraint has been lifted. Unless the rain decides to pay a return visit, she's going to have to look elsewhere for excuses.

Billy has been doing his best to provide one after another ever since he arrived. You'd think he had nothing better to do but she knows that's far from the case. He's brought a lot of work with him but seems hell-bent on pushing it to one side to make sure she's on her own as little as possible. It's making her feel bad. He dragged her out for a walk on the beach before lunch yesterday, once Matthew had rung from Heathrow to say he was about to board his flight, and last night he watched TV with her for ages while she waited for a text to confirm he'd landed safely at Logan Airport. It's very sweet of him to be so solicitous but she suspects, from the vacant look that comes over him every so often, that he's fallen well off the pace and knows it. She's not comfortable with the idea that she's the reason he's behind with his work, so she pre-empted him at breakfast this morning by making it very clear that she'll be gardening pretty much all day so he can safely spend the entire day playing catch-up if he wants to.

She's been in a couple of times already to check if he needs anything and he seems to have got the message at last. She loves watching him when he's lost in his work, switching between laptops, strange text sprawling across the screens. Gobbledygook as far as she's concerned – forward slashes, equals signs, underscores and those funny little arrowhead brackets, whatever they're called. She knows this is HTML or JavaScript or one of those sets of initials she can never quite remember. He calls them *languages* but they're not like any language she's ever seen and she still has no real idea how they work and what you can do with them.

One thing's for certain though – he's found his true niche in life. She remembers all those evenings when he used to shut himself away in his room with only his laptop for company, peering at the screen well into the small hours. She always worried it was unhealthy, felt she was failing in the parental duties that had unexpectedly come her way. She used to long for the time when he would get out more and find some sort of social life. It feels good to see him making a success now of what felt at the time like wasted years, to know it wasn't all for nothing.

With Billy set up for the day, she's made a start on weeding the path at the side of the house which seems to stay free of infestation for as long as it takes her to clear it and not a day longer. The Forth Bridge of gardening, she tells herself with a rueful smile. All the same, she can't just leave it to strengthen its grip on the property. She can do this, she tells herself. She's not an invalid.

She's worked her way about halfway down the path when she hears a car draw to a halt outside the front entrance and the sound of doors closing. There's no reason for anyone to stop out here unless they're calling to visit, so she comes round the side of the building to see two men enter the driveway. One of them is peering at the number on the open gate, the other is checking his phone for messages. When they catch sight of her, the taller of the two smiles and asks if she's Mrs Etheridge. His face looks familiar – someone she's seen on TV, she thinks – but she can't work out who it is.

When she nods her head, they both reach into their pockets and take out ID cards. They say their names but she doesn't catch them. She's too busy trying to come up with a reason why they might be here and doesn't like any of the ones that spring to mind. As far as she's aware, if two CID officers from Hastings turn up on your doorstep, it's not likely to be good news. Her thoughts instantly turn to Matthew in Boston and her heart gives a sudden lurch.

'We have reason to believe your brother is staying here,' the taller man continues. 'William?'

'Billy,' she corrects him, immediately transferring her concern from one to the other. 'Yes, he is. Is something wrong?'

'Do you think we might go inside?' he asks. The other detective doesn't seem to be paying much attention to the exchange. He finishes whatever he's doing with his phone and puts it in his pocket.

'Why?' she asks. 'What's this about?'

'Please don't concern yourself.' Mobile phone man this time. 'We just need to ask him a few questions to see if he can help us out . . . only it *would* be better if we could go inside.' There's something about the way he carries himself that suggests he may be the senior of the two, although there doesn't appear to be much separating them in terms of age.

Mia nods and leads the way to the side door which she's left unlocked. She goes in first and waits while they both scrupulously wipe their feet on the doormat before showing them into the lounge. Billy has apparently heard the voices through his window because he's already in there as they come in. She studies his expression from across the room, looking for some indication that he's been expecting this, but he's giving her nothing. She draws some comfort from the fact that he looks more intrigued than concerned.

The two officers cross the room and shake hands with him. This time she does manage to hear the names: DI Naylor and DS Barclay. She asks them to take a seat and shapes as if to do the same.

'Actually,' says Naylor, 'if it's all the same to you, we'd like a few words with Mr Orr on his own first. We may want to check a few details with you afterwards.'

She pauses in the act of sitting and asks why. Naylor gives her a reassuring smile.

'There's nothing to worry about. It's purely routine. We'll be out of your hair in no time.'

They would say that, wouldn't they? She's not terribly happy about this. Until she knows exactly what's prompted this visit, she'd rather not leave Billy in there on his own with them. She wishes Matthew was here – he'd have a better idea of what they ought to be doing, even though criminal law isn't his area of expertise. As it is, she doesn't see how she can refuse without making it look as if she thinks he might have something to hide.

And, of course, that's precisely what she *does* think – or what she fears at any rate. Her first thought is of Zak and Karun and the business the three of them have been putting together. She knows Zak is a bit of a loose cannon. A genius with computers, yes – Billy's always raving about the things he can do. She remembers now how he joked one evening that Zak had spent a whole week trying to hack his way into the emails of one of the tabloids involved in the phone-hacking scandal – *just for a laugh*, he'd said. *Give them a taste of their own medicine.* She prays they've not got too clever for their own good and done something stupid, but the longer she stands there arguing with herself, the longer it will be before she finds out what this is all about.

She gives in gracefully and asks if she can make them a drink. Both go for coffee – black with no sugar for Naylor, white with two for his subordinate. Feeling a little like a naughty schoolgirl who's been asked to wait outside the Head Teacher's office, she goes to the kitchen and closes the door behind her, hoping their voices will carry through from next door.

They don't.

While she makes the drinks and adds a packet of digestives from the snacks cupboard to the tray, she tries to imagine what on earth they're here for. *Purely routine,* they'd said. She tries to draw comfort from that. If that's all it is, there's nothing to worry about. If she knew what it was they were investigating and could come up with a sensible explanation as to why they think Billy might be able to help them, she might be able to relax a little.

But she doesn't. And she can't.

So as soon as she's finished making the coffees, she goes back into the room and the conversation – or interview, call it what you will – comes to a temporary halt almost immediately. She takes her time handing out the drinks and offering biscuits in the hope that they might start up again while she's still in there.

Again, they don't.

Billy was ready for this. They had Aimi's phone left in amongst her clothing, her car left overnight in an otherwise deserted car park, so he's not surprised they've come up with her identity already. Added to that, Joe would have been expecting her to be there waiting for him when he came back from Portugal and would have been bound to raise some sort of alarm. Maybe it was a little surprising that he himself had come onto their radar quite so quickly but there could be any number of reasons for that.

He wondered how they'd play this. If TV dramas were anything to go by, they'd almost certainly keep specific details to themselves. His guess was they'd make no mention of the note.

Or the phone, maybe. He'd need to keep his wits about him and have a clear picture in his head of everything they *did* say. And he'd need to make sure his reactions came across as natural, not forced in any way. It would be so easy to overcook it, especially when they told him Aimi was missing, presumed dead. How the hell were you expected to react to hearing something like that? Was there such a thing as a normal response? Some sort of middle ground was presumably safest – shocked but not too shocked. No histrionics. Focus was everything because you could bet your life they'd be well versed in the art of picking up on any discordant note.

Disappearance was the word they were using, he noticed. No mention of any presumed suicide but that was probably just another instance of them keeping their cards close to their chest. He didn't see how they could have ruled it out conclusively at such an early stage of the investigation. Aimi was certainly hoping the plan would buy her more than just a couple of days for the trail to go cold.

It was the tall guy who looked like a younger Arsène Wenger – same angular features – who was doing most of the talking, while his boss sat back in the settee with his arms folded, legs crossed at the ankle and lips pursed, listening carefully and chipping in only when the need arose. He didn't look like the sort who would miss much.

And Billy had been right about them not giving away any more than they needed to. No reference to any mobile. No suggestion of a note. *Remember,* he warned himself. All they mentioned was the pile of clothing found on the beach the previous morning. It was spotted early on by a local woman who made a point of going for a dip in the sea before the holidaymakers arrived in their droves – every day of the year, she'd told them, come rain or shine or severe Arctic blast. She'd left her towel and sandals on the dunes, spotted the clothes as she made her way down to the water and assumed it was someone else with similar masochistic tendencies. But she hadn't seen anyone at all during her swim, which she estimated as having lasted around a quarter of an hour, and it had bothered her enough to persuade her to return to the beach an hour or so later, just to put her mind at rest. When she saw the same pile of clothing still there, she phoned the police. Better safe than sorry.

'I understand you and Mrs Vedra are quite close,' said Wenger. 'Would you say that's the case?'

Are close. Interesting choice of tense, Billy thought. Should he read anything into it?

'Who told you that?'

'Are you saying you're not?'

'It depends how precise you want me to be with the answer. I was very close at one time to Aimi Bradshaw but that was eleven years ago. We were both teenagers. I'd never spoken to Aimi Vedra or even had any contact with her until last weekend, so I'd say describing us as close would be a bit of a stretch.'

'But you say you saw her at the weekend?'

'Yes.'

'And where was that?'

'In Tenterden.'

'And was that something you'd arranged?'

'I told you, we hadn't had any contact, so I'm not sure how that would have been possible.'

The DI on the settee smiled and nodded as if to say *touché* and it served as a timely wake-up call. Don't do it! Billy loved the cut and thrust of repartee, was quick with the one-liners and too easily seduced by them. If he wasn't careful he'd find himself drawn into a battle of wits and put-downs and that was the last thing he or Aimi needed here. He'd promised himself he wouldn't go down the point-scoring route and here he was, almost falling at the first hurdle.

'I'm sorry,' he said, raising a hand to acknowledge he was out of order. 'I'm just . . . I'm having a bit of trouble processing this.' He ran his fingers through his hair and grimaced, aiming for a blend of anxiety and bewilderment, which had looked convincing enough when rehearsed in the mirror earlier.

'That's OK,' Wenger told him. 'All of this must be very distressing for you. So this . . . chance meeting. How did it come about exactly?'

'I was in Tesco – with Mia. My sister. Aimi just happened to be there at the same time.'

'And she lives in Winchelsea, doesn't she?'

'So I believe.'

'That's a fair old drive, isn't it? For a bit of food shopping? You'd have thought she'd have gone somewhere more local.'

Billy waited. He was still weighing up the chance-meeting remark, wringing the sarcasm out of it. He didn't much care for this guy. Too many loaded statements. He was one of those people who go for the sly dig rather than saying what's really on their mind.

'I've no idea – I didn't ask,' he said. 'Look, are you absolutely sure there's no mistake here? They're definitely Aimi's clothes?'

'I'm afraid so.'

As an expression of sympathy, it might have carried more weight if Wenger had allowed the moment to linger for a second or two. Instead he went straight back to the supermarket and asked what they'd talked about. Billy scratched his head and told them it had only been five or ten minutes so they hadn't really had much time to talk about anything of note. No more than catching up really. He made a show of trying to remember the details, gave them the same version he'd churned out for Mia's benefit after they'd arrived back home from Tesco.

'So how did she seem to you?' asked Wenger.

'How did she seem?'

'Did you pick up on anything that suggested she was about to do something so . . . dramatic?'

'No. Like I said, we only talked for a few minutes.'

'And you haven't heard from her since then?'

So here it was. The million-dollar question.

He and Aimi had talked during the drive to Gatwick about what he should say when asked this. She was adamant he should come clean about their walk on Camber Sands. They'd been there all afternoon, walking down on the shoreline, then deep in conversation at the Marina Café. They could easily have been recognised by someone and, even if they hadn't, there were so many other people on the beach that someone was bound to remember a saluki and the young couple locked deep in conversation. It would come out at some stage and, when it did, it needed to come from him.

But he wasn't fooled. He knew she wanted more from him than that – needed more. She was looking to protect him from any possible fallout but the problem was that trying to cover all the bases for him served only to leave her exposed instead. It was like a sheet that's too small – one solid tug in one direction and the other half of the bed is left uncovered. A chance meeting in the supermarket was one thing. It was a coincidence, nothing more. But arranging to meet the following day and spending three hours together – that was different. Anyone with half a brain would be bound to wonder why.

The moment the notion of a possible conspiracy started to gain some sort of traction, the search for a body would be scaled down and the focus would switch instead to working out where she might have gone. He and Aimi had gone to a lot of trouble to buy her as much time as possible because she was going to need it.

He wasn't in any doubt as to which answer would serve her interests more effectively.

'No,' he said, 'I wish I had.'

No histrionics.

No discordant note.

Safe in the middle ground.

Mia watches them drive off, then goes back inside to find Billy. He's at work again on the laptops when she opens the door. When she doesn't say anything, he tears his attention away from the screens and looks over his shoulder.

'Are they done with you?' he asks, waving his hand distractedly at a fly which is mesmerised by the brightness of the screens.

'Yes.'

She stays where she is, leaning against the door jamb, arms folded and legs crossed at the ankle.

'They'll be back,' he says.

'You think so?'

He nods. 'They can't get past the fact that Aimi and I happened to bump into each other on Saturday. I don't think the concept of coincidence plays a very big part in their thinking, which is pretty ironic when you think about it 'cos there's no way I could have set it up. You know that, right?'

'Right.'

'I think they're hung up on the idea that she's done a runner and figure I must know something on the strength of a ten-minute conversation in a crowded supermarket. I mean, why wouldn't she confide in someone she hasn't even spoken to in eleven years? Makes perfect sense, I don't think.'

He turns back to face the screens and she knows exactly where he is right now. She's seen it so many times before. Disappointments he can cope with but anything more than that, certainly something as momentous as this, sends him scuttling back to the fortress. The drawbridge is up, the archers are at the parapets and no one – *no* one – is getting in. She waits a moment, then steps forward and comes up behind him, resting her hands on his shoulders.

'You OK?'

He nods once more. 'Yeah, sis – I'm good.'

'I'm sorry,' she says, kissing the top of his head. 'About Aimi, I mean.'

He hangs his head for a moment, then reaches up and pats one of her hands on his shoulder.

'Yeah.'

'I hope she's OK.'

She says this but knows deep down that what she really feels is relief. The moment they identified themselves, her mind had immediately made the link between Matthew, downtown Boston at night and the crime statistics she'd looked up online before he left. She can laugh at herself now but even though she's had plenty of opportunities to adjust to him travelling on business, she still worries about him the whole time he's away. Planes do crash. Terrorists have got to attack somewhere. Muggers are always on the lookout for tourists who are regarded as easy prey. She can't help herself. He's flying to New York tonight – all her neurotic ducks lined up in a row. The last thing she needed was a surprise visit from CID.

And then, when it was clear it was Billy they wanted to talk to, she switched the point of her panic attack in a matter of seconds. Seamless. Why Billy? What do they think he's done? What are they asking him in there? Why don't they want me to hear it? Are they looking to trip him up for some reason? She wishes she'd been blessed with equanimity, a sense of proportion that would give her an easier ride through life, but she's resigned herself to the idea that if she hasn't developed some sort of balance by now, she never will. She supposes there are worse things in life than caring too much, but it's not exactly a stroll in the park.

And as far as Aimi goes, she's somewhat conflicted here. On the one hand this is terrible, the sort of thing you wouldn't wish on your worst enemy. If Aimi has gone for a late-night swim, got into difficulties and drowned, that is a tragedy, no two ways about it. But she's not one for shedding crocodile tears – she's not going to be destroyed by this. She and Aimi have never been close, in fact she can't even say she likes the girl that much, so it would be hypocritical to make too much emotional capital out of her disappearance. It's very sad but if she's brutally honest with herself she's more concerned about what this will do to Billy than anything else. She herself is over it already.

But they've mentioned suicide as one of the active lines of enquiry they're pursuing and there's a part of her, a part of which she's not terribly proud, that simply doesn't believe it. Not for one moment. Suicide is for people who are suffering, who have reached the end of their tether and just cannot see any other way out. She knows from first-hand experience. It's crossed her mind once or twice since the initial diagnosis was confirmed and she's instantly dismissed it out of hand each time. It hasn't even gained the slightest semblance of a foothold. She's determined to make the most of the time she has rather than just throw it away.

Aimi Vedra, she'd be prepared to bet, has never suffered in her life – not *really*. The odd trip to the hairdressing salon may not have turned out quite the way she'd hoped and she's probably missed out on a few leading roles she'd have *died* for, but suffering? Really? She doesn't know the meaning of the word. She's manoeuvred her way into a lifestyle she always aspired to and whatever frustrations it might bring from time to time, they're never going to outweigh all the positives that seem to run after people like her. And no way would they bring on anything approaching suicidal tendencies. The idea is laughable.

No, if it's accidental drowning or suicide, she knows where her money would go.

'Yeah. Me too,' he says.

And there's nothing there – no way in. There may be a time – later – when he'll come to her and say whatever he wants to get off his chest but it will be at a time and place of his own choosing. She'll never drag him there.

'I'll let you get back to your work,' she says. 'If I can get you anything, you let me know, OK?'

She gives his shoulder a squeeze, then turns as if to leave the room. She's pulling the door to when she changes her mind and pushes it open again.

'Billy?'

'Uh-huh?'

She takes a deep breath and remembers the other evening when she pushed and kept pushing long after he'd made it clear she needed to back off.

'Nothing.'

'No,' he says, still facing the screens. 'Go on.'

'Doesn't matter.'

'The answer's no, sis. I don't know where she is.'

Except that's not what she was going to ask . . . not quite. And she suspects he knows it. Billy likes to fall back on a variety of avoidance tactics and this business of not quite answering the question she wants to ask has always been one of his favourites. He has a way of making her feel intrusive if she insists on taking it further.

'You would tell me, wouldn't you?'

'You know I would.'

'And this isn't all just some elaborate scheme you and Aimi have cooked up between you?'

This time he turns round to face her and she's aware of an intensity in his gaze that almost makes her feel uncomfortable. He maintains eye contact as the silence between them stretches to six, seven, eight seconds. Whatever else might be at play here, it's clear he desperately wants her to believe him.

'No, it's not.'

'OK.'

She offers up the reassuring smile she knows he needs at present.

'I'll be in the garden,' she says as she pulls the door to.

And wonders exactly what it is that Aimi has dragged him into.

Because she knows he's lying.

16

THURSDAY 21ST APRIL 2016

Peaks Island, Maine, USA

'Arantxa!'

Mary-Jo Lassiter groans in frustration as her brindle shih-tzu takes advantage of a momentary lapse in concentration and scuttles off down the sidewalk, her leash trailing along behind her. They're not far from Brackett Point which is pretty much the half-way mark for today's morning walk. It's one of a dozen Mary-Jo's mapped out around Peaks Island, all starting from and ending at her traditional post-and-beam cottage in Central Avenue. This one takes her to the south-western tip and they've just reached Torrington Avenue, when Arantxa decides to have a few seconds to herself.

Usually Mary-Jo loops the leash round her hand while she uses the pooper-scooper but an incoming message on her cellphone distracted her and the silly dog was off before she realised what was happening. She calls out to her because that's generally all it takes for Arantxa to come back looking extremely sheepish, only this time she keeps going, clearly full of the joys of spring, so there's nothing for it but to head off after her.

Shih Tzus may be lapdogs essentially but their little legs can scamper fast enough over a short distance if they choose to and Mary-Jo finds herself having to break into an uncomfortable jog just to maintain the gap and keep her in sight. They've walked so many times to Brackett Point that Arantxa is familiar with the route so there's no great concern for her safety, more embarrassment at how out of shape she herself is. Chugging along after a dog that would fit comfortably inside her tote bag and struggling to gain ground on her is not something she could ever have imagined back in the day when she used to cope with three gruelling sets of tennis, often with no more than a twenty-four-hour recovery period between matches. Surprising what a difference thirty years can make, she thinks. Maybe less so when you factor in the extra fifty pounds or so that come with them.

She's not sure whether to be relieved or horrified when a man steps out of the shadows in front of one of the rental properties in Torrington Avenue and takes hold of the leash, yanking the dog off her feet as she scuttles past. There's this momentary concern for Arantxa's welfare which is quickly swept away as she realises he means the dog no harm. The fact that he's rather good-looking helps her decide she's grateful for the intervention.

'Thank you so much,' she gasps, patting her chest with one hand and scooping up the errant Shih Tzu with the other. 'Wow.' She gives what she hopes isn't too flirtatious a chuckle as she struggles to get her breath back.

'No problem,' he says. Clean shaven. Broad shoulders. She wonders what his eyes are like behind the mirror sunglasses. Blue would be nice, she thinks.

'She doesn't normally do this. Do you, Arantxa?'

She waits for him to ask. *Arantxa* is quite a mouthful – not much point in calling your dog something that unusual unless people are going to ask why – so she's disappointed when he doesn't take the hint. Just smiles, leaving her to make the introductions.

'Mary-Jo,' she says.

'Michael.'

'Are you just over for the day or visiting someone?' she asks, her glance straying to the white clapboard house, its Essex green shutters firmly closed. The dancer's place. Well, old Seth Hooper's originally, but when he died his daughter in Louisiana chose to use a letting agency and pocket the income rather than sell or up sticks and live here herself. It's been rented for the past few months by this blonde girl – Kellie, she thinks her name is – who works at the Dance Academy over in Portland. Mary-Jo has called on her a couple of times to talk about the Neighborhood Watch scheme but never managed to grab a word with her. She finds herself hoping her rescuer hasn't come over to visit the girl. She seems to be turning enough heads already. Too pretty for her own good or anyone else's, is how most people see it.

'Just for the day,' he says, chucking Arantxa under the chin. 'Thought it would be nice to walk right round the island and soak up the scenery. I was just taking a few photos of this place. Someday I'm going to build myself one of these clapboard houses back home.'

'And where would that be?'

'England.'

And at last she has her foot in the door because now she can tell him all about how she played a tournament in London when she was on the junior satellite tour and how she'd once played Arantxa Sánchez Vicario in a quarter-final, taking her to three sets.

'No great shame in losing to her,' she says, having explained to him that Arantxa went on to win four Grand Slam titles. Conveniently, as happens every time she tells this story, she manages to leave out the fact that the Spaniard was only twelve at the time and that far from taking her to three sets she'd only narrowly avoided the embarrassment of a double bagel, picking up just the one game. Some details, she felt, detracted from the story as a whole.

'Well, have a good day,' he says, which she thinks is a disappointingly low-key reaction to something that impressive. Is he not remotely interested in tennis? She can see she's losing him so as a parting shot she throws out the suggestion that if he's looking for somewhere to eat around lunchtime, she could definitely recommend the Peaks Island House Restaurant. She'll probably be having something to eat there sometime around one. He thanks her for the tip and walks off in the direction she's come from, taking the anticlockwise route around the island. She stands there for a while, willing him to turn around but when he does take a backward glance, it's that damned house he's looking at again.

17

THURSDAY 20TH AUGUST 2015

No Caller ID was how the call announced itself.

It was late afternoon and Billy was still working in his room. He'd stopped for an hour or so at lunchtime, during which he and Mia had resolutely talked about anything but the earlier police visit and all things Aimi-related. Then he'd gone back to his laptops while she went off to the shed to fetch the mower.

Billy took heart from the fact that she hadn't even mentioned an afternoon sleep. He knew she found it difficult to get through the day without feeling drowsy. Today though she seemed revitalised, almost her old self for the first time since he'd been home. As long as she was beavering away outside, he felt able to shut himself away without feeling guilty.

And then his phone started buzzing just after half three. Unknown numbers were something he regarded with deep suspicion at the best of times. Usually they were from call-centre operatives with almost impenetrable Asian accents claiming their name was Kevin or Sarah or whichever name they'd plucked out of the air that morning to add a touch of anglicised authenticity to the call. This time the deep voice with the measured, rounded vowels, asking to speak to Billy Orr, was unmistakably Home Counties.

'This is Jack Vedra.'

'He what?'

She's been finishing off the far corner of the front lawn with her back to the house, unaware that Billy's there until he's a couple of paces from her. If that's startled her, it's nothing compared to the volts passing through her now as he fills her in on the phone call he's just received and the reason for it. She's been doing well all afternoon, making quite a good fist of blotting Aimi's disappearance out of her mind. Neither of them even mentioned it during lunch. Now, just as her anxieties over the whole wretched business have subsided, he seems determined to drag them back to the surface again.

'He wants me to go to his place for tea and cakes,' says Billy, a quiet smile in place, presumably to show her there's nothing to worry about.

'Why?'

Billy shrugs his shoulders.

'Only one way to find out.'

'You're not going, are you?'

'Why not?'

Good question, she says to herself. *Why not indeed?* How about because this is just typical of Jack Vedra and the circles in which he moves? Want to talk to someone? Click your fingers and expect him to come running to you with his tongue hanging out. Need something? Send a minion out to get it. Got a problem? Throw money at it and it'll soon go away. The preening, self-satisfied arrogance of people like him with their sense of entitlement and their dismissive attitude towards others who don't share their grab-it-and-run mentality makes her sick. Just a few months ago one of Vedra's golf club cronies pulled out of buying a set of prints from the gallery the moment he discovered the artist was bisexual. That just about summed them all up for her and when she first heard of Aimi's induction into the Vedra clan, she couldn't help but see that as utterly appropriate, clear evidence that she'd been right about the girl all along. How to explain that to Billy though?

'How are you meant to get there?' she asks, improvising swiftly.

'Chauffeur. He's sending TJ round to fetch me. Says he left ten minutes ago.'

Of course he did. Why wouldn't he assume the answer would be yes? It always is, isn't it?

'But are you OK with this?'

'Why not?' He stoops to retie a lace and looks up as he answers her. 'Free cake. It's no big deal, sis. This was always going to happen sometime – might as well get it over with. Joe's there with him. They'll know already that the police have been round to see me and they'll want to make sure they know anything I do.'

'But how can he know they were here? They only left four hours ago.'

He raises both eyebrows and tilts his head – *really?*

'Jack will have known before they even got here,' he says with a chuckle. 'You don't make millions like the Vedras without building up a few useful contacts.'

'But you haven't got anything to tell him. Didn't you explain that over the phone?'

'He didn't ask. He just said there was something he wanted to discuss with me and he'd really appreciate it if I could spare him an hour or so this afternoon.'

'In other words, he sent for you.'

'Yep. Royal summons. No big deal though. Nothing for you to worry about.'

'I'm coming with you,' she says, reaching down and unplugging the hover mower from the extension lead.

'You're inviting yourself to tea at Jack Vedra's?' he asks, laughing now and she wishes she could get him to take this more seriously. He seems to think he's invulnerable – even with everything that's already happened to him, he wanders through life as if there's no way it can ever land a blow on him. She has no way of knowing exactly why Vedra wants to see him but she remembers the certainty that came over her earlier when Billy promised her he knows nothing at all about Aimi's disappearance – the conviction that he was not telling her the whole truth. Jack Vedra doesn't know him anywhere near as well as she does, but you don't make the money he has without learning a thing or two about how to read people.

'I don't want you to go on your own.'

Billy plugs the mower back into the extension lead and kisses her on the cheek.

'I'll be fine, sis. They're the Vedras, not the Sopranos. I played football with TJ, remember? They used to invite me to his birthday parties when we were at primary school. Jack's used to being able to control any situation he's in and he's not going to sit back and do nothing. He just wants to hear for himself what I told the police this morning. You telling me you wouldn't do exactly the same if anything happened to me?'

And he's right.

She'd do whatever it took.

Which is why she doesn't want him to go.

But even as she thinks this, a large white Mercedes draws up, Eminem blaring out of the window. Billy kisses her on the top of the head like a pet poodle and moves off towards the gates. A big, thickset bull of a man steps out of the driver's side and leans on the roof of the car, biceps straining the sleeves of his T-shirt, a huge grin on his face.

'Billy-Bob,' he calls out. 'Long time no see, bro.'

Billy turns and smiles at her.

Mouths the words *don't worry*.

And is gone.

Tommy 'TJ' Vedra had always been a big lad. He looked as if he'd beefed up even more in the nine years since Billy had last seen him but in all other respects it was as if he'd been frozen in time. He was the same larger-than-life buffoon; loud, insensitive, blessed with the IQ of a freshly squeezed dishcloth. It took Billy no more than three minutes to establish this because in that short space of time he managed to tell an awful joke about an immigrant family, yell abuse at an elderly driver who took too long exiting a roundabout and then rounded things off nicely by inviting Billy to feel his deltoids, check out his abs and hit him in the stomach while he was cruising at seventy mph. It made Billy nostalgic for the company of Zak and Karun and glad that London had given him a break from this sort of provincial boorishness.

When they were younger, they'd both played for the same youth football team, Billy as a central midfielder who was always comfortable on the ball and TJ as a hot-headed central defender who didn't feel he'd done his job effectively unless he'd managed to pick a fight with half the opposition. They'd been teammates rather than friends, which suited Billy just fine because a night out with TJ could easily turn into the social equivalent of a casual stroll through a war zone. TJ never needed much of an excuse – a careless word here, a dismissive roll of the eyes there and sometimes even less than that, were all it took to set him off. He could take offence in a monastery garden for the simple reason that his default position was to find a challenge in every comment or gesture that came his way.

When Billy let the side down by going off to university – *like all the other bumboys, ha ha* – they'd inevitably lost contact, but you'd have to live in a social vacuum not to pick up snippets of information about the Vedra empire, even in exile. In case Billy came into that category, TJ was more than happy to bring him up to speed during the twenty-five-minute journey, talking with obvious pride about the security company he now owned which was picking up new contracts by the day or, in his words, *cleaning up*. He seemed particularly keen to know how much Billy was earning, as if determined to prove a point about the relative merits of going to university or getting out and working for a living. It did occur to Billy that his argument might have held more water if higher education had ever been a realistic proposition for TJ, but unless you really could buy yourself a place at university, that was never going to happen. And his obvious pride in what he was achieving with this new company seemed undiluted by any thoughts that maybe his father's influence was playing a significant role somewhere in the background.

Well, good luck to him was Billy's take on it all. If it kept TJ happy and occupied it was no bad thing because a resentful TJ with too much time on his hands was no one's idea of fun. Stupid on steroids did not make for an appealing combination.

By the time they reached the outskirts of Winchelsea and turned down onto Sea Road, Billy had started to wonder whether there might actually be a little method in the manic stream of chatter coming his way, because they were not far away now and still there had been no mention of the reason for this summons. With anyone else he was sure Aimi's disappearance would have been at least mentioned in passing, if not discussed at great length and it was difficult to escape the impression that TJ was under strict instructions not to indulge in speculation of any kind as to what might have happened to his sister-in-law or whether Billy might be able to shed some light on it. Then again, this was TJ and that fact alone rendered comparison with most norms of social behaviour just about redundant.

They followed the road away from the sea and out into open country. Then they took a right turn into a lane which, after fifty yards or so, was barred off by a set of double gates. TJ, with one eye on Billy's response, pressed a button on the console of the Mercedes and said, *It's me, Henrik.* The gates swung open and they drove through, watched all the way by an imposing-looking guard and a pair of equally impressive dogs. The guard waved as they swept past.

'That's Henrik,' said TJ, in typically redundant fashion. 'South African. Ex-military. He's been with us for a couple of years now.'

'What the hell are those dogs?' asked Billy.

'Belgian Malinois – best guard dogs you can get anywhere. Train them right and they're as faithful as shit, but whatever you do don't piss them off. Can't wait for some silly bastard to try and break in here.'

He grinned and slapped Billy's leg, considerably harder than most people would have deemed necessary.

'No worries, Billy-Bob. You're safe as long as you're with me.'

They entered a long driveway through surrounding woodland and eventually emerged into a paved clearing which led up to the main entrance to the house itself – if *house* was the appropriate word for it. It was more an estate, a collection of buildings constructed in a semicircle around a central block. The exteriors of some of these looked as if they dated back to medieval times, although they'd clearly been renovated often enough since then. It wasn't too difficult to imagine an old manor house in the centre with a collection of barns and servants' quarters nearby but the original building at the centre of all this activity was long gone. It was now a three-storey celebration of glass and white sandstone with unrestricted views over the sweeping gardens on one side, the tennis court and croquet lawn on the other and the sunken courtyard at the front with its huge stone basin and fountains. Architecture and real estate were not exactly Billy's strong point but even to his untutored eye it screamed wealth and a certain grandeur.

TJ parked out front and got out of the car, leaving the keys in the ignition. Billy followed him up the broad steps, through huge front doors that wouldn't have looked out of place in Brideshead and into a vast tiled hallway dominated by a white stone staircase which curved its way up to the corridors and rooms on the upper floors. A smartly dressed man in a light grey suit, whom

Billy initially assumed to be some sort of modern-day butler, greeted them both and told TJ that his father and brother were expecting them in the front room. TJ clapped him on the shoulder and turned towards a room on the right, nodding to Billy to let him know that was where they were heading.

'Meadows,' he whispered out of the side of his mouth. 'The old man's business secretary. You'd need an Uzi to get past him without the old man's say-so.'

He opened the door and they both stepped into a bright, breezy room surrounded on three sides by floor-to-ceiling windows that must have been something like twenty feet high. Billy had no idea what material the heavy curtains, bunched for now in the corners, were made of but they looked very expensive. At the far end of the room, French doors gave onto a substantial terrace with an outdoor table and chairs and a canopy swing sofa, and beyond that Billy could see the lawn sloping down to the edge of the wood and, above the treetops, a thin sliver of sea in the distance.

Joe Vedra was standing by the French doors. He turned and nodded to acknowledge Billy's arrival but made no effort to cross the room and shake his hand. Nor did he smile. But then again, Billy supposed, he didn't really have a great deal to smile about at the moment.

And in an armchair, facing the doors through which TJ and Billy had just entered the room, was Jack Vedra.

There was a story that had become part of Vedra folklore over the years. When he was in his early twenties, Jack had been on a hike with friends in the Lake District when a small single-seater plane skimmed low over a neighbouring field and slammed into an ancient oak tree with enough force to cause one of its wings to shear off. The friends, having initially followed Jack into the field, realised that there was every chance the fuel lines might be ignited any minute and instantly ran off in the opposite direction. Jack, however, took no notice of their shouts and clambered up onto the plane chassis, smashed his way into the cockpit and managed to free the unconscious pilot before carrying him across the field to a position of relative safety. Then he sent one of his friends to the nearby village to phone for an ambulance while he attended to the injured man. The subsequent citation highlighted the opinion of the first ambulance workers to arrive on the scene that the pilot's prospects of a full recovery would have been negligible but for his prompt intervention.

The press made a big thing of it all and Jack was awarded a Queen's Commendation for Bravery which he threatened to return in protest years later when the council turned down an application he'd made to develop several acres of arable land into a new housing development. Whether he did or did not actually return it was immaterial – the publicity engendered by the threat meant it had served its purpose. And the housing development went ahead as near as damn it on schedule.

The story might have been exaggerated but that didn't matter – everything concerning Jack Vedra was built on hyperbole. The important thing was that it contained all the elements needed for one of his bravura performances. It was wild, risky, borderline crazy, selfless, brave – pick your adjective to suit your own agenda. It had also served him very well down the years.

Looking at him now, it was still possible to see traces of the decisive man of action who had raced across the field towards the stricken plane with scant regard for his own personal safety.

Even in his early seventies, he looked as if he might fancy a similar challenge if the opportunity were to present itself. In terms of physique, there was no doubt which of his sons favoured him, although there was something more natural and healthy about his appearance than the pumped-up, injection-fuelled beefiness of TJ. He still had a full head of white hair and the smile he switched on as he rose to greet Billy would not have looked out of place on an American presidential candidate. Neither would the handshake which was firm enough to set the tone from the outset – big man, big deal.

He offered a plush armchair to Billy and took an identical one almost directly opposite. Joe sat to one side on a burgundy sofa while TJ sauntered aimlessly around the room, picking up and replacing decorative objects until a look from his father brought him over to the sofa as well.

'It's good of you to come at such short notice,' said Vedra, moving a magazine a few inches to the right so that it sat flush with the edge of the glass-topped coffee table, which separated Billy from the other three. 'I hope it's not caused you any inconvenience.'

Billy assured him it was OK and went through the expected formalities of expressing his sympathies for the situation in which they all found themselves.

'It must be a very difficult time for you.'

'It is,' said Vedra. 'Indeed it is. Particularly for Joseph, of course.'

He turned to face Joe whose expression was like a mask. He was staring at Billy with a fixed intensity and no semblance of the warm welcome his father had just extended. Billy was pretty sure it wasn't his imagination working overtime. He thought he could sense an element of challenge there which he was tempted to meet head-on. The image of Aimi lifting the kaftan to reveal the layers of bruising around her ribcage was still very much uppermost in his thoughts, but he decided now was neither the time nor the place to go there and switched his attention back to Joe's father.

'I don't know if you were aware,' Vedra continued, 'but we've been away on a golfing holiday, just the three of us. We need a bonding session every so often. Thought it would do us good to have a bit of a break and recharge the batteries. The last thing we expected was to come back to something like this.'

Billy mumbled some platitude that sounded hopelessly inadequate and was relieved when they were interrupted by a knock at the door. A lad around Billy's age appeared in the doorway, dressed formally in white jacket and black trousers. He wheeled in a trolley loaded with a selection of cakes and pastries that wouldn't have shamed a five-star hotel at afternoon tea and the next few minutes were taken up with the usual preliminaries – choice of tea, flavour of jam, butter or low-fat spread to go with the scone. Or maybe a slice of walnut cake or a profiterole?

'Do help yourself,' said Vedra. 'We don't stand on ceremony here.'

Billy rather doubted it. The whole thing came across as some sort of parade designed to impress him. He accepted the tea that was offered to him, looking closely at the white china cup which was decorated with what looked like a shield supporting a medieval jousting helmet. The shield itself was cut diagonally by two red bands each bearing three white escutcheons.

'Family coat of arms,' Vedra explained with an apologetic shrug. 'Not my doing, I hasten to add. Well, the tea service maybe, but the coat of arms goes back to Italy in the Middle Ages.'

Once the flunkey had made sure everyone had everything he needed, he left the room and the four of them sat back in their respective seats. *Preliminaries over*, Billy thought to himself. *Now let's see how much they know.*

'Thomas tells me the two of you are old friends,' said Vedra, taking a sip from his own cup. 'Played together in the same football team, I gather.'

'Long time ago,' said Billy, trying not to smile at TJ's obvious discomfort. Calling him Thomas anywhere but within the sanctity of these four walls would probably earn someone a good kicking.

'This is your first time here though?'

Billy explained how he'd moved away to university, then London. He threw in memories of birthday parties he'd attended when he and TJ were both young but added that they had been in a village hall somewhere with a hired entertainer. Vedra nodded as if he remembered it well, although Billy had no recollection of him being there on any of those occasions. Presumably other matters had taken priority.

Vedra asked what he was doing now in London and as he took him through a very brief potted history of how he, Karun and Zak had come to set up the company, Billy got the very firm impression from some of the questions he was asked that Vedra knew all of this already . . . or if not all then at least a substantial part of it. When he casually threw in the remark that he'd almost certainly come across Karun's father before in some of his business dealings, it felt like more than a conversational aside. There were not many strings a Jack Vedra couldn't pull if he felt so inclined.

'So,' the old man said, putting his cup on the coffee table and nudging the tray of cakes closer to Billy. 'I understand you know Aimi too.'

Billy took a profiterole, partly to give his fingers something to do.

'Yes. We were at school together.'

'And you were quite close at one time, I gather.'

'Yes. I suppose you could say that. We went out together when we were about fifteen. A long time ago,' he said, taking a bite from the choux pastry and using a finger to wipe a small smear of cream away from the corner of his mouth.

'But you've remained friends since then?'

'Not really. She moved away to London and we said we'd keep in touch but you know what these things are like. We were very young and it didn't really turn out that way. I've picked up bits of information about her over the years – knew she'd gone out to Cyprus with a dance group and met Joe while she was out there. And I knew she'd married.'

He looked at Joe again. Same expression or lack of it.

'But you weren't in touch with each other in all those years?'

'No. We bumped into each other this weekend and that was the first time we'd actually spoken in eleven years.'

'Yes. I understand that's what you told the police earlier today.'

Billy nodded, not bothering to ask how he'd come by that information.

'And yet you didn't tell them about your meeting on Sunday?'

'I'm sorry?'

Billy blinked and swallowed the rest of the profiterole, hoping to cover his momentary confusion. Vedra was still smiling but he was steepling his fingers now in front of his chest as he sat back in his chair and there was something about the gesture that unsettled Billy.

'I was wondering why you told them about meeting Aimi in the supermarket in Tenterden but not about your little rendez-vous the following day.'

'I didn't meet her in Tenterden,' said Billy, hoping a little pedantry might put him back on the front foot. 'I had no way of knowing she'd be there. We just happened to arrive at more or less the same time.'

'Possibly. But the following afternoon? Calling that a coincidence would be stretching things a bit far, wouldn't you say?'

'We didn't meet on Sunday afternoon.'

'Really? That's not what I've heard.'

'Then you've been misinformed.'

'Camber Sands? A lengthy stroll along the beach, followed by a cosy little chat in the Marina Café? Perhaps you'd like to start again. Here, do have another profiterole,' Vedra added, pointing to the plate in front of him. 'See if it helps to refresh your memory.'

They were following her? Billy reached across and took another pastry as suggested – anything to buy himself a little time. He threw in a couple of sips of tea for good measure. They had to be following her, didn't they? How else would they know?

He tried to think through other possibilities. Maybe someone had seen them together on the beach, but if that was the case they'd have told the police, surely. And yet the police didn't know – or did they? For the first time it occurred to him that maybe this was one of the details they'd been keeping from him this morning. Were they just playing out a little more rope to see where he'd go with it?

And almost immediately it dawned on him that this was far from the worst-case scenario. If the police *did* know, he'd have some explaining to do but he could just revert to the version Aimi had urged him to use in the first place, hint at how desperate she was because of the abuse she'd been subjected to by her husband. But if the Vedras had been following her, did that mean they knew about the drive to Gatwick as well? And his activities on the Tuesday night?

'I'm pleased to see you're giving this some serious consideration,' said Vedra. 'Do take as long as you need. It's really rather important that you get it right.'

'I'm surprised you bothered to send for me, seeing as you clearly have all the answers,' Billy said, opting for a touch of defiance. Even to his own ears it came across as a little petulant.

'Oh . . . not quite all of them. You see, we think you could still be of considerable assistance to us in filling in a few gaps . . . most notable of which would be where Aimi has gone.'

'I've no idea.'

'And yet only two minutes ago you were telling me with a straight face that you and Aimi didn't even meet up on Sunday afternoon, so you'll understand if I'm inclined to treat what you say with a certain amount of scepticism.'

'You can take it any way you like. It won't change the fact that I don't have the faintest idea where she is right now.'

'Yes . . . you'll excuse me for saying that's not exactly the same thing. If I know my daughter-in-law as well as I think I do, she'll have moved on already from wherever she told you she was going. It's who she is, Billy. You have to understand – it's what she does. And there's always the strong probability that wherever she told you she was going was a far cry from the truth anyway, but we're still at the stage of pooling all our resources and information and have to start somewhere. So I'll ask again – where did she say she was going?'

'She didn't,' said Billy. 'But I'd say the sea would be a good guess.'

There was a movement and a sharp intake of breath from Joe which was halted immediately by a gesture from his father who held out one hand as if stopping traffic. Then he turned back to face Billy.

'You might try to be a little more sensitive with your comments. Nerves are a little raw around here at the moment. We're still trying to make sense of everything and get to the bottom of exactly what Aimi has done and why she chose to do it. There are a number of possibilities and while the sea, as you so indelicately put it, remains one of them, I'd appreciate it if you showed a little more consideration for the feelings of others.'

Billy knew without being told that he'd overstepped the mark but the idea that he needed to tiptoe around Joe Vedra, knowing what he'd been doing to Aimi, bordered on the obscene. And the diversion had served its purpose. By the time he'd offered a grudging apology, he'd managed to work out what he needed to do now.

'So we're agreed that you and Aimi did meet on Sunday afternoon?' asked Vedra.

'Given that you've got someone tailing her . . .'

'I can see why you might think that's what happened but I'm afraid you're wrong. We don't tail each other. We are a family that looks after its own. As it happens, we know about Sunday afternoon because Joseph received a phone call.'

'From?'

'We don't know. It was an unknown number and the caller didn't wish to be identified. But he was more than happy to tell us about the little tryst on the beach. He recognised both you and Aimi and was surprised you were being so intimate with each other –'

'Intimate?' Billy laughed.

'Walking arm in arm along the beach, holding hands across the table in the café – I'd say *intimate* is a fair description. I'm sure the anonymous caller was seeking only to make mischief and find a way of upsetting my son – we do have to put up with more than our fair share of that sort of thing – but he was very free with his thoughts on the matter before Joseph hung up on him.'

'It wasn't anything like that,' said Billy, wondering who on earth it might have been. Pointless speculating, he decided. Could have been anyone at all who was at school with them both. They'd been careless. If he'd known what she was going to tell him, he'd have suggested somewhere a lot more private. She really should have known better.

'I was just trying to help her,' he continued. 'As a friend.'

'So let's go back a little, shall we? Perhaps you could start with whose idea it was to meet up in the first place. Let's start with Tenterden.'

'Oh for . . .' Billy ran a hand through his hair and choked off the imprecation just in time as he slumped back in the chair. 'I keep telling everyone, it wasn't arranged. How could it be? I didn't even know I was going there until a few minutes before we left. It was a last-minute thing. The fact that we bumped into each other was pure chance. I don't know any other way to say it.'

'And the Sunday? Whose idea was that?'

Billy paused before answering and looked across at Joe.

'You sure you want to do this?' he asked.

Joe huffed and folded his arms.

'Just answer the question,' he said.

Billy turned his attention back to Vedra and took a deep breath. There was a way through all this, he knew. He just needed to be careful how he went about it. He wasn't remotely bothered about Joe losing his temper and going for him. TJ would be a different proposition, but if it came to it he was pretty sure the old man would find a way to keep things in order and if he didn't . . . well, Billy had been in his fair share of scraps and taken a few kickings before now.

But he had to take his time and think through the implications of every answer, for Aimi's sake. He reminded himself that the longer he could keep muddying the waters, the more time he'd be buying for her to put distance between herself and this family. That was all that mattered right now. It wasn't about him and his ego.

'It was hers,' he said. 'She texted me that same night . . . the Saturday. Or it might have been early hours of Sunday morning. I can check if you like.'

He took his phone out of his pocket and held it up.

Vedra waved it aside.

'I need you to tell me everything you can remember about that afternoon, Billy. What she said, how she appeared to you, every little detail that springs to mind. Even if it seems relatively trivial and no real concern of ours.'

He reached forward and took a slice of walnut cake from the tray, then sat back and waited.

'OK,' said Billy, 'only remember – I'm just the messenger, right? I'm just telling you what she told me.'

'Understood.'

So Billy trawled back through the memory banks, picked out the version he and Aimi had rehearsed during the journey to Gatwick, and pressed play.

'She told me she needed someone to talk to, someone who wasn't in any way connected to your family. She said she was in a complete mess and couldn't find a way out of it so she wanted to talk it through with someone who she knew would be sympathetic.'

Vedra raised an eyebrow.

'And did she say why? Give any indication as to what this mess was that you've alluded to?'

'No,' said Billy, risking a quick glance to see how Joe was reacting to this. He was sitting forward on the edge of his seat, elbows pressed into his knees and chin resting in his cupped hands. Missing nothing.

'I tried to get her to tell me but she wouldn't. She just kept saying she'd been so stupid and if she could only turn back the clock she'd undo it without even hesitating, but it was too late. I got the impression that whatever it was she'd done, it was something you were all going to find out soon enough and she was afraid you'd go apeshit.'

A strong gust of wind took hold of the open French door and sent it swinging erratically on its hinges. TJ got up and pulled it to. His father didn't even seem to notice the interruption.

'But she must have given you some sort of idea as to what it was, surely. You were talking for several hours. Are you telling me you didn't pick up anything at all?'

'What I picked up was that she was scared out of her wits,' said Billy. 'I spent the whole afternoon trying to calm her down.'

'Scared of what exactly? Us?'

'Yes,' said Billy, holding his open palms in front of his chest. 'Like I said . . . just the messenger.'

Vedra shook his head.

'I must confess, I find that very hard to believe. Aimi has been part of the family for a good while now. We've gone out of our way to make her feel welcome. The idea that she would be afraid of us . . .'

'I've seen the bruises,' said Billy.

Silence.

'I'm sorry?'

Billy turned so that he was facing Joe.

'I said, I've seen the bruises. The ones your son gave her.'

'Bullshit,' said Joe.

'She showed me. Nice grouping by the way, hidden away around the ribcage like that.'

Vedra clearly sensed that Joe was about to dive in and again held up his hand to ward him off.

'Billy has been good enough to come here. Let's hear what he has to say first. You'll have your chance later.'

'There are no bruises,' Joe hissed.

Vedra kept his gaze locked on his elder son until he was sure the message had got through before resuming where they'd left off.

'So you're saying she claimed it was Joseph who gave her these bruises or is that mere conjecture on your part?'

'She said it started in London – some show you'd bought tickets for as an anniversary present.'

'*The Book of Mormon.*'

'Maybe. Yeah, I think so.'

Billy repeated what Aimi had told him – the resentment that she still felt because the dance school which Joe had promised her and which she'd been planning for so long had been taken away from her, her decision to pay him back by refusing to have sex on their anniversary.

'She said that was the night it started, when he first hit her, and it's been happening more and more frequently ever since. She told me she feels like a prisoner in her own home. It's been so bad that when she heard about the golfing holiday the three of you had planned, she was so desperate for it to go ahead. She was worried sick that something might come up with the business that would mean Joe would have to stay behind because she needed time on her own to work out what to do next.'

'And did she share with you what that something might be?'

'No,' said Billy. 'I tried to get her to go to the police and she laughed. She said the police wouldn't do anything because your family is too influential in this area. Joe told her he'd make sure she'd be humiliated and she believed him. So then I told her she should just leave him – there was nothing to keep her here anymore and she burst into tears and said I didn't understand. *No one walks away from a Vedra.* Wherever she went, Joe would find her and bring her back, not because he loved her or even felt anything for her but just to prove a point. Just because he could. She said there was no way out.'

He paused at this point to give Vedra a chance to read between the lines and pick up the implications. The old man drummed his fingers on the armrest of the chair, deep in thought. Then, without taking his eyes off Billy, he told Joe it was now time to hear what he had to say.

'You'll keep a civil tongue in your head, however objectionable you may have found what we've just heard. Do you hear me?'

'Yes, sir.'

'Go ahead.'

Joe took a handkerchief from his pocket and blew his nose loudly. Then he put it away and sat there, staring a hole in his lap. Billy was expecting his voice to be laced with a mixture of suppressed fury and frustration so he was slightly taken aback by the quiet, almost resigned delivery when he finally spoke.

'I did not hit my wife,' he began, as if desperate to make his point from the outset. 'I have never raised my hand to a woman in my life. These bruises – I don't know what that's all about but it has nothing to do with me. I never saw any and I certainly didn't inflict them. Aimi and I have been having a difficult time of it in recent months. I don't intend to discuss our marriage in detail with anyone who comes wandering in off the street but you should know that Aimi has been ill for some time. She has been suffering from what was initially diagnosed as a mild form of depression and has been taking medication for it for several months, not just since the evening you were describing.'

He took the handkerchief out again and blew his nose for a second time, more thoroughly this time.

'Hay fever,' he said. This time he left the handkerchief on his lap. 'You're right about the dance school. The news hit her much harder than I'd expected. It was my fault – I knew it was important to her but I hadn't realised she was clinging to it like a life raft and when I had to break the news to her she took it so badly

I had to take her back to the doctor and arrange for stronger medication.'

He looked up for the first time since he'd started speaking and made sure Billy knew who was being addressed now.

'Aimi is very vulnerable right now. I need to know where she is and that she's all right. Even when vulnerable, she can be very manipulative and convincing so you can be excused for believing what she's told you, and I'll even forgive the spiteful relish with which you've poured this all out in front of my family. But I promise you, I'm not going to forget it if I find out later that you know where she is and have kept it from me so I'll repeat the question my father asked a while ago. Is there anything you can tell us that will help us find her?'

Billy sat on his hands. He felt the need to do so because otherwise he'd find the temptation to start clapping with obvious sarcasm too difficult to resist. This had to be the most hammy, overblown performance he'd sat through in a long time. He wondered if anyone in the room was buying it. TJ might, he supposed – he worshipped his older brother and was blessed with the critical faculties of a meerkat – but surely the old man had too much about him to fall for that pathetic piece of am-dram.

'Billy?' Vedra prompted.

'Like I said,' he replied, meeting Joe's gaze full on. 'I've seen the bruises. And the answer to his question is no. I've told you all I know. There's nothing I can think of that would be of any help.'

'And if you had to guess?'

Billy frowned.

'Guess at what?'

'At what has happened to her. The way I see it, there are four possible explanations for her disappearance. One, she went swimming, got into difficulties and drowned. Two, she went to Camber Sands that night with the express intention of killing herself. Three, that is what she would like us to believe but she has in fact used it to disguise the fact that she has run away. And four . . .' he said, pausing as if to allow Billy to get there first '. . . someone else is responsible for her death and is going to elaborate lengths to make us think she has killed herself. What I'd like, given that you've spoken to her more recently than any of us, is your considered opinion as to which of those four scenarios you think is the most likely.'

The thought came to Billy almost instantly. *He doesn't really want my opinion – he's just testing me. He wants to know if I've got an agenda here.*

'I don't feel qualified to answer that,' he said.

'It's your opinion I'm seeking, Billy . . . not a clinical diagnosis. When the police called this morning to tell you she had disappeared, there must have been an instinctive reaction on your part. I'm curious as to what it was.'

An opportunity, he thought. He ran a quick check for potential damage and couldn't see any problem. *Might as well go for it.*

'There is one thing that would automatically rule out one and four if we knew it exists,' he said, dangling the bait. 'When the police came to see me this morning they were very selective about what they told me. Kept their cards very close to the chest. You may have access to more information than I do . . . in which case, do you happen to know if she left a note at all?'

Vedra paused to think about this.

'I'm sorry. You'll understand, I'm sure, that we're not at liberty to discuss any particulars concerning the case.'

Billy smiled.

'I'll take that as a yes then. If there wasn't a note, you wouldn't have needed to put so much thought into how you phrased the answer. Doesn't matter anyway. If there was, it can only be a choice of suicides – a genuine one or a fake one. If you really want to know, I'd say genuine because the girl I spoke to on the beach was so confused and desperate I couldn't imagine her organising anything on the scale this would have taken. I didn't know anything about the depression or the visits to doctors but now I do it makes some sort of sense. So if there wasn't a note, I'd go for an accident. If there was . . . '

He spread his arms and shrugged his shoulders.

'But hey . . . what do I know?'

Vedra said nothing for a while and all four of them sat there, each lost in his own thoughts. Eventually Vedra seemed to come to a decision.

'In that case, I don't think we need to keep you here any longer,' he said, getting to his feet and stretching out his hand for Billy to shake. 'I'm grateful to you for coming all this way. Thomas here will take you back to your sister's place if that's what you'd prefer.'

Billy thanked him and without saying a word to Joe or even looking in his direction, he followed TJ towards the door by which they'd entered earlier. He'd almost reached it when Vedra cleared his throat.

'Just one more question, if you don't mind,' he said. 'It may not be significant but it puzzles me and I don't like loose ends.'

Billy turned back to face him. 'Ask away.'

'The police,' said Vedra, raising one finger and tapping his chin. 'Aimi is a good friend, or was at any rate. She comes to you with this alarming tale of marital abuse which, in the context of her sudden disappearance, is surely something the police need to know in case it helps them with their investigation, and yet you don't say a word about it. Instead you lie to them and say the meeting on the beach didn't even take place. Now, I have to say I find that very odd.'

Already ahead of you.

'Not really,' said Billy. 'I thought it would be better that way.'

'Better for whom?'

'Better for everyone. For one thing, I know you're a very important person around these parts. You won't be short of enemies who would just love a juicy scandal to make life uncomfortable for you. On a much smaller scale than it would be for you and your family, I've been there myself when my parents died so I know what the media can do when they get their teeth into a story. I didn't see why you should be dragged into the gutter for something that wasn't your fault.'

Vedra smiled.

'That's very altruistic of you. You said *for one thing*, so I'm assuming there's more.'

Billy returned the smile.

'I'll admit there was a touch of self-interest in there as well.'

'In what way?'

'Well, it seemed to me I could either say what I know and make myself very unpopular with you and your family, which would probably be a very poor option for me to take, or I could say nothing and maybe do myself a favour sometime further down the line.'

'And what sort of favour are we talking about here?'

'Absolutely no idea. I hadn't gone so far as to consider anything specific. But you're a successful businessman with an eye for an opportunity. We're a developing company which will need investment if we want to move to the next level. Showing sympathy for the position in which you find yourself at present seems to me like the decent thing to do.'

He half-expected Vedra to chuckle at the cheek of it all. It felt like the perfect answer from his point of view – a touch of arrogance, an element of calculation and self-interest but more importantly another layer of obfuscation for Vedra to peer through.

'And remind me – when was it you first heard that Aimi was missing?'

Billy frowned. 'When the police came to interview me.'

Vedra shook his head.

'And yet within minutes you managed to think through the implications of not being open with them . . . and while being questioned at the same time. That's quite an achievement.'

'I'm a very quick thinker.'

'Yes,' said Vedra. 'I'm sure you think you are.'

TJ was unusually quiet during the journey home. Billy didn't feel particularly talkative either, glad of the chance to sit back and close his eyes for a while, having had to work so hard during the last half-hour or so.

It was only as they drove past the golf club that TJ broke the silence.

'This afternoon was your free shot,' he said, staring straight ahead through the windscreen.

'What's that supposed to mean?'

'It means you get away with it for today because Pops says you do. But you only get so many chances and you just used all yours up, sunshine.'

'You want to try that again in plain English, TJ?'

He pulled up outside Mia's house and as Billy unfastened his seat belt, TJ caught hold of his arm.

'You ever shit on my brother again . . .'

He tightened the grip in a way that made the rest of the sentence perfectly clear. Billy gritted his teeth and tried not to show any discomfort but the pressure was intense. When he finally released it and allowed Billy to get out of the car, he reached across the passenger seat and slammed the door before accelerating away.

For TJ that was as articulate as it gets.

And he couldn't have been any clearer.

18

THURSDAY 21ST APRIL 2016

Peaks Island and the City of Portland, Maine, USA

She's up on top deck this time. It's only late afternoon and it's been a surprisingly mild day in the city with no real breeze to speak of. That's not something you can say about the middle of Casco Bay of course, but she's brought a cardigan with her and she's had Hobie's arm around her waist for most of the journey so she feels she can handle a bit of fresh air.

She's been thinking about this evening, hoping she hasn't made a mistake in bringing him back to her place. In the past, she's shied away from the idea of relationships in the workplace or *shitting on your own doorstep*, as Joe liked to call it. She's always worried about any potential emotional fallout if things go wrong and what it might do to the dynamics of the studio. Then she thought to herself, *fuck it*. She hasn't had sex in ages and Hobie's that fit, she thinks she can be excused if she hangs her principles in the closet for one night. She hopes he's not harbouring any illusions about this evening, like maybe it will amount to something significant, because that's not going to happen. She doesn't have room right now for anything more than a one-off.

He'll be leaving at first light. He doesn't know it yet and will probably gripe about it because in her experience men like to imagine there's something about stale breath and sleep-encrusted eyes and unflexed stomach muscles that makes them irresistible to women, but hey ho. There's no way they're getting off the ferry in Portland tomorrow morning or arriving at the Academy together, cute as he is. And he *is* cute. He's from somewhere in the South, has this deep drawl that could spit insults at you and still sound old-school charming. She's choreographed a couple of dances for him now and marvelled at his flexibility, the lightness of touch whenever she's stepped in to show him what she wants. And she's wondered. She shivers . . . and she's not entirely sure it's all down to the breeze.

There's quite a crowd on the quayside at Peaks Island, waiting to head back to Portland. She and Hobie follow the other passengers as they disembark and he pulls her in close as they walk up the sharp incline towards Peaks Café.

They make a handsome couple, she thinks.

Even if it does come with a limited shelf life.

The figure in the shadows watches. And watches. Takes his time over it because he doesn't want to get it wrong.

It's a well-grooved routine by now – this is either the fifth or sixth ferry that's come in since he himself came over this morning. He has the timetable and wherever he's been on the island he's always made his way back here before each ferry from Portland has docked. Then he takes up a position amongst the hordes of passengers waiting to make the return journey, takes the binoculars out of their case and scans the top deck as the boat comes in, looking to see if she's there.

And this time she is.

Michael Johnson moves deeper into the crowd, tugs at the peak of his baseball cap to cover his forehead and puts on his Ray-Bans. She's not likely to see him from that distance but there's no harm in covering all the bases, so he takes up a position behind a family that looks collectively as if it knows the inside of a KFC bucket pretty intimately. Here he can be reasonably confident that he's not going to be seen. He steps to one side and raises the binoculars again . . . and sees him too.

He can't be sure from this distance whether they're together but then they come off the boat and set off up the hill, each with one arm wrapped around the waist of the other. At one point he leans in and whispers something in her ear and she laughs, pulling away and slapping his shoulder. That's enough to convince him he'll be better off heading back to the guest house now. He could follow them to her place, wait to see if he's getting a ferry back tonight but he somehow doubts it. He doesn't look as if he's here for coffee and a chat.

He still has tonight at The Old Theater Guest House so he might as well take this ferry. He's done everything he set out to do today. Knows where everything is. Can lay his hands on what he needs at a moment's notice. There's nothing to be gained from forcing things. If a plan's worth making in the first place, it's worth sticking to and his plan says *tomorrow*. He can grab a shower, then ask Jeanie, his overly attentive landlady, if she can recommend a decent place to eat. It will make her evening – knowing her, she'll probably have a menu and a set of reviews for every restaurant in Portland. Then he can take his time over dinner and get a good night's sleep.

He suspects he'll need it.

Tomorrow is going to be a big day.

19

THURSDAY 20TH AUGUST 2015

The old alarm clock on the bedside table said ten to midnight. He was sitting fully clothed with the pillow placed vertically behind him to protect his back from the wooden bedstead, Aimi's cheap pay-as-you-go Nokia next to him on the quilt, whispering to him. *Only in an emergency,* she'd said. No social calls, no anxious checks to make sure she was all right or to ask where she was. It was too risky, he reminded himself – automatically increased the chances of her being tracked down.

This wasn't an emergency, however much he'd like to be able to use it as an excuse for getting in touch with her and hearing her voice again. How could it be? She'd told *him* that the police would want to talk to him. She'd predicted that the Vedras were going to want to drag him into it to find out just how much he knew. She'd judged it perfectly so far and he was pretty sure she'd have been proud of him this afternoon, first of all throwing the police off the scent and then drip-feeding her version of events to the Vedras, line by line. At some stage he knew he'd have the opportunity to go over it all with her and she'd understand the lengths he'd gone to in order to buy those precious few days for her and allow the trail to go cold. She'd promised, hadn't she? All he needed to do was sit back and wait. A bit of patience.

But if he phoned now ... how was that helping her? She'd know instantly why he'd called, that it was for his benefit not hers and that he was prepared to jeopardise her chances purely because he missed her and needed the reassurance. She'd trusted him to be adult about this, despite the fact they hadn't seen each other in years. He wasn't about to throw all that away now. But he kept the mobile there next to him on the quilt, staring a hole in it. Willing it to ring.

He knew he should be working – he wouldn't be able to sleep for a good while yet and would be better off making good use of the next couple of hours – but work was a long way from his thoughts. This afternoon, especially the visit to the Vedra house, had been a real high and he didn't feel ready to come down from it just yet. He'd already replayed the conversation several times, every sentence, every nuance. He wanted someone he could share it with and the only person there was Mia, who was just about the last person he could afford to confide in. It made it nigh on impossible for him to focus on the day-to-day mechanics of his work.

As he sat there in the dark, he could see in the crack under the door that the light had come on in the lounge. He hadn't heard Mia moving about downstairs because of the Eric Prydz track he'd been listening to through his headphones but as he peeled them off he heard a tap at the door and it swung open. She blinked, clearly surprised to find him sitting in the dark rather than working.

'Mind if I switch the light on?' she asked.

He reached across and turned on the bedside lamp instead so that the contrast wouldn't be quite so sharp. As he did so he surreptitiously slipped the Nokia under the pillow.

'What's up?' he asked, nodding at the foot of the bed to suggest she come in and sit down. 'Can't sleep?'

'No.' She took him up on his offer, tugging at the cord of her dressing gown to fasten it more tightly.

'Any particular reason?'

'Don't know. I was so tired after all that work in the garden today. Didn't think I'd have any trouble going off.'

'Matthew rung?'

She shook her head.

'Not yet.'

Say no more.

'He said this morning he'd ring sometime around six their time when he got to the hotel but maybe the meeting went on longer than expected and he missed his domestic flight to New York.'

And of course he couldn't send a text to let you know.

'Then again, he doesn't always ring every day when he's away,' she continued. 'Maybe it's just one of his daisy spells.'

'His what?'

She gave a tired smile.

'You know – some daisy does and some daisy can't be bothered.'

Billy returned the grin. He liked these little reminders of the cool big sister he'd always had when he was small. The one all his friends used to fancy. Loved her sense of humour, the ease with which she made him laugh and teased him out of his more sombre moods. There were only occasional glimpses of it nowadays and even though they offered painful reminders of how his mother used to rouse herself to get lunches ready on her better days, it was still good to have his sister back for a while, even if the laughter seemed to have to drive through fog to get there.

'He might still ring,' he suggested, not believing it for one minute.

'Not now. He'll assume I've been asleep for ages – which I should have been, to be fair.'

'Why don't you ring *him*?'

She shook her head.

'Why not?'

'He prefers it if I don't.'

'So?'

'He might be busy or with someone important or . . . I don't know. He just prefers it if I don't.'

She got up from the bed and peeped through the closed curtains for a moment, although Billy wasn't sure what she expected to see out there at midnight. There was a security light that came on every time a cat or fox slunk past the sensor but even that only covered half the front lawn.

'You not working then?' she asked, still looking out into the darkness.

'Planning.'

'Sure you are.'

She let the curtain fall back into place and came back to the bed, this time sitting alongside him.

'How far behind are you?' she asked.

'A bit.'

'Is that *a bit* as in *a lot*?'

'Nothing I can't handle.'

'Is that because you're spending too much time with me?'

'Don't flatter yourself.'

''Cos you don't need to, you know. I keep telling you that.'

She shifted her legs onto the bed and, as she did so, her dressing gown fell away for a moment and he could see her small breasts pushing against the material of her nightdress underneath it. He remembered seeing her naked once – *completely* naked. It was while she was still living at home and he must have been about eleven or so, which would have put her at around nineteen or twenty. He'd walked into her bedroom and she'd just finished towelling herself off after a bath and couldn't grab the towel again quickly enough before he saw everything. *Everything.* Looking back, he wasn't sure which of them had screamed louder but he'd never forgotten the shock of the new, the unfamiliar sensation of looking at his sister as a woman rather than a girl. The memory came back now as clear as a bell. He looked away quickly, hoping she hadn't noticed.

'When is it you're going back to London?' she asked.

'Probably Saturday evening, always assuming Matthew's not delayed.'

'You can stay longer if you like.'

'Naah,' he said. 'You two could probably do with some time on your own.'

She studied her nails for a moment, then bit at the corner of one of them.

'Is it that obvious?' she asked.

'Is what that obvious?'

She shook her head.

'Is what that obvious?' he asked again.

'Doesn't matter,' she said and she rested her head on his shoulder.

More secrets. He put his arm around her and doodled absent-mindedly on her head with his fingers, tucking her hair behind her ears to prevent it from falling across her face. Wondered how it was that secrecy had managed to gain such a firm foothold in their relationship.

Mia snuggles into him, enjoying the sensation of his fingers on her scalp as her head rests in the crook of his neck. They used to have this sort of contact a lot when he was small. She would sit on the settee and he'd stand behind her, brushing her hair back for ages – fifteen, twenty minutes at a time. If she had a headache, he'd do the same with his fingers, easing the pain away from the centre of her forehead and pushing it towards the edges as if with a smoothing iron. They haven't done that for ages but it comes flooding back to her now like a long-lost friend calling out to her.

Maybe it's this reminder of a time when life's certainties were so much clearer that forces her hand but, all of a sudden, she realises just how tired she is of all this tiptoeing around each other that's become their default modus operandi of late. For too long, she's been wrapping Billy up in what she's regarded as cotton wool but which are really layers of deceit, telling herself she needs to do this to protect him from truths he's just not able to handle right now. The problem is, these comfort blankets have hardened over the years into a carapace she can't seem to break through when she needs to get near him. And what makes it worse is he's started to do the exact same thing to her, using her illness as his justification for it. *It's the last thing she needs right now* is becoming something of a mantra, not to mention a convenient way of ducking realities that are unpleasant.

If Matthew had phoned earlier, she'd be asleep right now. But he didn't . . . and that feels like providence. And as she lies there next to Billy, his fingers still working away, untying the knots in her thinking, she knows that if she doesn't ask now, she may never get a better chance.

'You remember at the weekend,' she says tentatively, her eyes closed to help her find the right words. 'When we were talking about you not taking your meds?'

'Uh-huh.'

'I said you were very good at holding things back and you asked me if I wanted to open that particular can of worms, or something like that – I can't remember exactly how you put it.'

'You show me yours and I'll show you mine,' he said.

'That was it.'

She leaves it for a moment, tries a couple of sentences in her head to see how they might sound if she ever dares to say them.

'What about it?'

'Can we turn the clock back?' she asks.

He shifts slightly on the bed and she opens her eyes to find him craning his neck forward so that he can see her face.

'Seriously?' he asks, clearly surprised.

She nods.

'You didn't fancy it on Sunday. What's so different now?'

She thinks about it.

'I don't know. It's just . . . it feels as if we don't really communicate anymore.'

'We don't communicate?'

'Not really. Not about things that matter. The moment we stray off-piste and get into dangerous territory, we either clam up or lie and I hate that.'

'You think I lie to you?'

'I know you lie to me.'

He looks as if he's ready to debate this point but bites back whatever he was going to say and leans against the bedstead once more.

'I prefer to think of it as massaging the truth a little. For a greater good.'

She nods.

'I understand. I do the same. But I'm ready to try something different. Get everything out in the open and see if we can find a better way of dealing with it.'

'O . . . K,' he says, drawing the word out to its maximum length. He takes the vertical pillow from behind him and slides down the bed so that he's lying with his head next to hers. 'So what you're saying is, you want to play the truth game.'

'If that's what you want to call it.'

'No, no,' he corrects her. 'It's an actual game. I used to play it with this friend of mine. She did it every time she wanted to clear the air about something.'

'She?'

'You want to play or not?'

She nods and he explains the rules to her. They're not exactly difficult, she thinks. The clue's in the title. Each gets to ask the other three questions, taking it in turn, and the other person has to tell the truth. *Has to*, he emphasises. You've got to commit to that going in or there's no point. Even if the truth is really embarrassing. Even if it might hurt the person who's asking. There's no judgements here. You ask, you listen, you move on . . . but at least you know. And the only other stipulation is that whatever's said in the game stays in the game. Can't be passed on to someone else. Can't be brought up again in conversation or used in any future argument. It's just out there for context.

He nudges her with his elbow.

'You sure you want to go ahead with something like this?'

'This friend of yours,' she said. 'How often did you play this game with her?'

'Dunno,' he says, looking at the ceiling as if the answer might be printed there. 'Four, maybe five times.'

'And did you always tell her the truth?'

'Nope. I lied every time. Probably why she went back to Jiangsu.'

'But why lie? Wasn't that a bit pointless?'

'I knew she was lying to me.'

'And what makes you so sure I won't?'

'I know you won't because you're such a pussy you'd have to get the hair shirt and whip out for having cheated. I know what you're like. So if you're sure you want to do this, go for it. I promise I'll do it properly.' He waits for some sort of response from her. 'Still want to play?'

An animal shrieks outside the window. A fox probably. Protecting her turf or calling for a mate. Life reduced to a series of instinctive actions. No need for difficult decisions or weighing pros and cons.

'Yes,' she says.

They stay where they are. He reaches across to turn out the bedside light but she stops him. She wants to see his face when he answers.

'So how does this work?' she asks. 'Who goes first?'

'You can, if you like. And that's two of your three questions.'

'No way, I . . .'

'Winding you up, sis. Just keeping things light.'

She takes no notice, forces herself to concentrate. Three questions. She could ask several dozen and barely scratch the surface but if this pushes the door open just a fraction it may lead to other opportunities before he goes back to London. She just needs to make sure she asks the right ones.

'OK,' she says eventually. 'Question number one. What do you know about Aimi's disappearance that you're not telling me?'

There's a silence that lasts five, maybe ten seconds. She can hear him marshalling his thoughts, wondering how best to answer this. Eventually he puffs out his cheeks and exhales noisily as if recovering from a blow to the stomach.

'Pfff,' he says. 'You don't take prisoners, do you? What happened to the foreplay?'

'Simple question,' she says, keeping her eyes locked onto his, looking for any hint of evasion.

'OK. Simple answer. Remember – it doesn't go anywhere else, right?'

'Right.'

'OK. I know she's alive. At least, I know she was when she left. And because I'm feeling generous and you're new to this, I'll save you your follow-up question and tell you for free so you don't get to waste a choice – I don't know where she is now or what her plans are but I do know why she left, in case you want to use up another of your questions.'

She is bursting to follow up on this. *How do you know? Did you meet up again with her? When? Why didn't she just go? Why did she have to drag you into it? Why did you tell the police you never spoke with her after that morning in the supermarket? Don't you realise lying to them in the course of an investigation is a criminal offence? WHY DIDN'T YOU TELL ME?!!!*

But she has only two questions left in this bizarre game of his which, for all its artificiality, is at least offering them a certain amount of protection and encouraging them to open up. She needs to take a deep breath and work out which question to ask next.

First, however, it's her turn under the metaphorical spotlight.

'You know what I'm going to ask,' he tells her. 'I want to know what the prognosis is and what the specialist thinks is the best course of action for you right now.'

'That's two questions,' she says.

'If you like. Take them in whichever order you'd prefer.'

'OK.'

She doesn't need to think – she's prepared this answer well in advance, sensing she was going to have to deliver it sometime this week. What surprises her is how relaxed she feels about it now that the moment has finally arrived.

'It's not good. In fact, it's probably going to kill me eventually.' She reaches for his hand and gives it a squeeze. 'I don't know when. It might be a couple of years. It might be a couple of days. But where it is, pressed up against the optic nerve, they can't operate and remove it without serious risk to my sight which I'm not prepared to lose. I know I told you there was every chance it wouldn't get any worse and I could go on to lead a long and healthy life but the chances of that happening are nowhere near as good as I made them out to be. And as for question two, which I might as well take now, if it was down to the specialist, he'd be in there like a shot. He'd rather have a go and take his chances, except they're not his to take – they're mine. So we agree to disagree and I'm just aiming to see out whatever time I have left with my vision intact and feeling good about myself, rather than go through the sort of invasive and degrading treatments they're so keen to inflict on me. And I'm sorry it's not what you want to hear but this has got to be about what *I* need, OK? I didn't tell you because I wanted to protect you but I keep forgetting you're not a child anymore and you have a right to know. So. Now you know.'

There's a long, long silence now and she waits to hear his reaction. When none is forthcoming, she turns to face him.

'You OK?'

He props himself up on one elbow, his hand cupping his head.

'I'm fine,' he says. 'Thanks for being straight with me.'

'I figured you'd probably worked it out for yourself anyway.'

He shakes his head.

'Didn't need to. I knew.'

'Like I said . . .'

'No,' he insists. 'I already knew. But it's good to have it confirmed that you're playing the game properly.'

She frowns.

'I don't understand.'

'I got Zak to hack into your medical records.'

She pulls away from him, almost flinching.

'You did *what*?'

He shrugs his shoulders.

'You wouldn't tell me the truth. What else was I supposed to do?'

'Billy! You . . . I don't . . .' She can't believe what she's just heard, even though it confirms her fears about his new friends in London and their cavalier attitude towards what they see as legal technicalities.

'Just kidding,' he says with a grin. Only he's not. She can tell. *She can bloody well tell!*

'Your turn,' he says, tapping her on the nose to bring her back on track. 'Question number two – make it a good one.'

She stares at him, wondering how many ways he can find to surprise her . . . or would *appal* be a better choice of word? She can't believe the things he's prepared to do to bend the world into a shape that better accommodates his wishes. She's not sure where the line between immoral and amoral is drawn but the casual way he lobs these grenades into the conversation suggests it's irrelevant.

She has to take a few seconds to remind herself that this was her idea. She mentally shuffles the cards in front of her and picks the one she wants to play. *Forget Aimi*, she tells herself. If what he's told her already is true, and she believes it is, she's history. Long gone. Good riddance. If she can get right away and stay out of Billy's life for good, that's one big positive to come out of all of this. It's the Vedras and the police who worry her now.

'OK,' she says, having reached a decision. 'When you went to the Vedras this afternoon, did you tell them you know she's alive?'

'No.' No hesitation whatsoever.

'Honestly?'

'Is that your third question?'

'No. I'm just making sure you've given the right answer to the second one.'

'OK. No. Honestly. That's pretty much the point of the game, by the way. They don't know for sure she's alive. They know it's a possibility but that's all. I don't think they liked me very much but hey ho. Happy with that?'

She is. Her biggest worry all evening has been that he might have told Jack Vedra something which he hasn't told the police and that it will come back to bite him. She's not at all happy that he's so deeply involved in all this but at least he's managed to be consistent.

'My last question,' he says. 'You sure you want to see it through?'

'I'm sure. I swear this is the weirdest game I've ever played. Did you dream up these rules or did Nuan?'

'She did. Well, they sort of evolved over time, I suppose. And I see I'm not the only one who's been taking a keen interest in someone else's affairs, Mia Etheridge. I don't remember mentioning her name at all.'

'Yeah . . . I hacked into your computer. Go on – last question.'

'You're not going to like it.'

'Do your worst.'

'OK,' he says. 'What's with you and Matthew at the moment?'

She frowns.

'What's that supposed to mean?'

'I said you wouldn't like it.'

'I don't even understand it.'

'Sure you do. Is he seeing someone else?'

'Is he . . .?' She bursts out laughing and slaps his leg. 'Matthew? Where on earth did you get that idea?'

'Very good, sis. Convinced me, that's for sure.' He's maddening when he's like this. So insistent that his view of the world is the only one worth considering. She's often wished he was blessed with a little more tact but never more so than now because this is uncomfortably close to the mark.

'I had four days here before he went off to the States and he was hardly ever around. He spent more time in the gym or in his office upstairs than he did with you, even though he was going away and leaving you for four days.'

'Wrong tree altogether, Billy,' she says. 'Seriously. I'll admit he's been a bit distracted lately but that's work – it's not some other woman, for God's sake. He missed out on a promotion twelve months ago and can't afford to let that happen again. This trip . . . it's really important to him and it's been preying on his mind for about three months now. That's all there is to it.'

'OK.'

'He hasn't got time for *us,* let alone someone else.'

'OK.' That tone of voice that says, *I know you're wrong at best and lying at worst but let's move on.* Maddening. He can't possibly know half the things he's throwing around as facts. And this from someone who's not even sure what's real and what's fantasy in his own life!

'I can't believe you wasted your last question like that,' she says, warning herself that it's time to back off or she'll come across as protesting too much. She very much doubts she's managed to convince him as it is. Billy's not normally one for turning once he's made up his mind about something.

'Speaking of which,' he says. 'You want to get your last one out of the way? I could probably do with getting a couple of hours' work done before I go to bed.'

She tries to remember what she was planning to ask earlier but it's gone, driven out by a thought that's just sprung into her head, seemingly from nowhere. She's not sure she dares to ask him, has never come close before now. Not in all these years.

But she knows if she doesn't get it out into the open now, she never will because it's unlikely there will be another opportunity like this one. And even as she starts to form the words she can't believe she's doing this.

'OK. My third question is: what were those marks on his face, Billy?'

He looks puzzled. For a blessed moment he genuinely doesn't have a clue what she's talking about, probably because he's trying to link her question to more recent events.

'What marks on whose face?'

And there it is – that first flicker of recognition. It's as if he's thinking, *surely she can't mean that?*

'Don't tell me it was make-up or that I probably did it while trying to scrub it all off. Someone caused those scuff marks around his eyes and the bridge of his nose and it wasn't me.'

'Jesus,' he says. 'Is this because I touched a nerve just now about Matthew?'

'No. It's something I should have asked you ages ago and kept backing off from it. I want to know, Billy. Help me to understand what happened.'

He sighs.

'What's the point? It was years ago.'

'Billy.'

'For fuck's sake.' She can tell he's getting irritated because he's not one for effing and blinding, certainly not when she's around. 'Even I don't know after all this time. How am I supposed to explain it to someone else?'

'Not someone else, Billy. Me.'

He huffs, still clearly unhappy that she should be bringing this up and even more so because he recognises that failure to come up with a convincing answer will mean losing face.

'I hit him, OK?' he says eventually. He's trying for a certain air of emotional detachment, as if it's no big thing, but he doesn't quite nail it. 'I didn't mean it the first time. It was just a reflex. He twitched – and Jesus, you should have seen me. I mean, I didn't know anything about dead bodies at that age. I'd just bent over him or something and he twitched and it scared the shit out of me. I was thinking zombies and I just sort of flapped at him and scrambled out of reach. No big deal.'

'You said *the first time*. So what happened then?'

'I sort of slapped him. Not hard. And I was still probably in shock . . . I dunno. My heart was pounding away like mad and it was all his fault so I wanted to give him a slap. At least, I think that's what happened. Like I said, it was a long time ago.'

'And that was it? Two slaps? Are you saying that was enough to make those marks?'

He looks closely at her as if weighing up the pros and cons of answering yet another question. She's just getting ready to argue that this is all part of the same one when he starts speaking again, apparently happy to continue now they've gone this far down the road. In for a penny . . .

'No,' he says. 'I hit him a third time.'

'Why?'

He shrugs his shoulders.

'Because I wanted to.'

'But why?'

He looks at her, his head tilted to one side as if he can't believe he needs to explain.

'Payback? For all the times he did it to me.'

'Oh Billy,' she says, despairing at the thought that he's still peddling the same tired fantasies after all this time. 'He didn't hit you, for heaven's sake.'

'You mean he never did it in front of you.'

'No. I mean he didn't do it.'

'And you'd know, right?'

'Yes . . . I'd know,' she says, staring him out but keeping her tone as calm and conciliatory as possible. Billy responds to conflict, to the energy it generates. He sucks it in and returns it with interest. It's important to give him nothing. 'He didn't hit you because he didn't have it in him. He just wasn't that sort of person. And despite what you seem to think, he loved you, Billy.'

He snorts.

'Sure.'

'He did. God . . .' She sits upright and runs her fingers through her hair to tease it back into some sort of shape. 'I know you felt he was tough on you at times but he was from a different generation. I mean, in his day kids did exactly what they were told the moment they were told to do it. He didn't expect backchat, didn't want to have to explain his decisions or get into arguments with his own son. And you –' she laughs '– you were not the easiest person to have around sometimes. I mean, I love you to death but God, you could be hard work growing up. Looking back, Mum and I probably didn't do Dad any favours by being so soft on you. Maybe if we'd been a bit harder when you stepped out of line, it wouldn't have fallen to him to put you right every time.

He didn't find it easy to adjust to the way things were changing all around him but don't *ever* think he didn't love you. He was so proud of you and what you were going to achieve.'

'So proud he didn't even leave a note.'

'He did.'

'For you, yeah. A nice two-sided letter. He didn't leave one for me.'

And this is where he has her because she can't argue with that. She doesn't understand it ... unless the balance of his mind was disturbed because of what he'd just done and what he knew he was about to do. He should have left a note for each of them. When Billy came back that evening and handed the opened envelope to her and she saw just the letter to her inside, she knew how much that must have hurt him. It had hurt *her*. But she can't have him thinking he wasn't loved. They've been down that road once before.

'I don't have an answer for that,' she admits. 'I've often thought it would have been better if it had been the other way round because I didn't need a letter to convince me of how he felt and you did. But if you think he didn't care, you're wrong.'

He shakes his head.

'I don't know how you do it, sis.'

'Do what?'

'Keep defending him the way you do. He was never the saint you make him out to be.'

'I never said he was. If it comes across that way, it's because I'm always having to compensate for you slagging him off. We're none of us whiter than white, you know.'

'We aren't all killers, though.'

Take a deep breath, she tells herself. *Neutral. Don't take the bait.*

'Is that honestly how you see him?'

'All I know is he's the one who fetched the tablets and the bottle. You think she managed to get them out of the pack on her own?'

'Billy –'

'She couldn't even do up the buttons on her cardigan. If he hadn't helped her, she'd never . . .'

He has to pull out now because there's nowhere he can run with this. She would not still be here. She'd have died an unimaginably awful death which she'd been dreading ever since the initial diagnosis. He's in danger of arguing against himself.

'It's what she wanted, isn't it? You know as well as I do – you've read her letter.'

'Yeah, I've read it. Try reading it again and ask yourself – did it sound to you like she thought he was going to chicken out and go with her? Eh? Or was it more like she was expecting him to stay behind and bring up his kids like any decent father would have done? Which seems more likely to you?'

And here's the essence of what it is that underpins all of this repressed hostility. What it is that's been eating away at him all this time. Only he can't say it. Nothing is going to make him say the words: *what about us?*

'It's OK to be angry,' she tells him. 'Just be honest with your-self and admit what it is you're angry about. He chose to go with her and left us and I can't explain any better than you can how he could possibly do that. I'm not even sure I can justify it. But don't rewrite history, Billy. He wasn't the tyrant you make him out to be. And he didn't go because he didn't love us. He went because he couldn't imagine carrying on without her.'

He's about to come back at her when there's a short ringtone which she struggles to locate at first. It sounds as if it's coming from under the pillow. Billy instinctively reaches towards it, then pulls his hand back and sits there as if transfixed. She wonders why he doesn't just take it out and answer it, then realises that his own is lying on the table on the other side of the bed.

Which begs the question . . .

'I'd better go,' she says. 'I can't pull an all-nighter like I used to.'

He flashes her a look that comes across as part relief but maybe also part gratitude as she swings her legs off the bed and walks over to the door. As she's about to close it she turns to face him again.

'One thing. Big favour to me, OK?'

'What's that?'

'When you get back to London . . . go see someone. Please? And start taking your meds again.'

He turns off the bedside lamp and she can only vaguely make out his shape in the darkness.

'Sure, sis,' he says. 'Meds solve everything, right?'

She rolls her eyes and closes the door.

The moment she'd gone, he grabbed the phone. There was one message, brief and to the point.

Safe for now
Get rid of the phone
Will find another way to get in touch
Soon
x

Four lines, each raising its own question. Safe where? Why get rid of the Nokia – was it compromised in some way? How was she planning to get in touch without it? And how soon was soon?

He could almost hear the laptop sigh as he reached across and closed the lid. Not for the first time, his mind was going to be elsewhere tonight.

20

FRIDAY 22ND APRIL 2016

Peaks Island and the City of Portland, Maine, USA

She takes her time getting ready to leave. Hobie's been gone for at least an hour, and was none too happy about it, either. It's amazing how deluded men can be at times, she reminds herself. You can tell them something and they'll go along with it, assuming you'll be bound to change your mind in the morning, so strong is their faith in their performance in bed. The little lady's always going to be won over in the end.

She kicked him out at six with instructions to make sure he was on the six-fifteen ferry. She said she'd get the next an hour later, but another ten minutes in bed were enough to persuade her she could have a lie-in and get the one after that. She didn't actually manage to go back to sleep but it was pleasant enough to lie there and doze for a while. And remember. Hobie's conversation might be on the limited side but she'd guessed right about everything else. Strictly a one-off, she's promised herself, but a very pleasant one for all that.

As it turns out, she's badly mistimed things and now she's forced to choose between a shower and breakfast if she's going to catch the eight-fifteen ferry. She opts in favour of the former, telling herself she can pick up a snack of some sort on the way in. She's in and out in minutes and the moment she's dressed, she grabs everything she'll need for the day, stuffs it all into a bag and leaves.

As she looks up, she realises Tennis Lady is out for a walk and has heard her coming. She's paused at the gate, her pointless excuse for a pet cradled in her arms. You can't really call it a dog. Dogs are like Suki, bursting with energy, anxious to get off the lead and run their hearts out on the nearest stretch of parkland or beach. This puffball expects to be carried most of the way and looks like it might be whisked away if the wind gets up. Shih-tzu? Shit *dog*, more like.

She feels a sudden pang for Suki. No more than that. And then it's gone.

She and Tennis Lady don't exactly know each other but they've nodded a few times in passing and she's been told by one of the girls in Peaks Café that this woman used to be a handy player in her day. It's hard to imagine now because all she seems to have retained from her playing days are her height and big shoulders, but word has it she can still talk a good game. The unfortunate thing is, she's keen to do so at every opportunity.

If she's angling for a conversation now though, she's out of luck. Even if she had the inclination, she really doesn't have time, so she jogs down the path towards her, returns the cheery 'hi there' and apologises on the run, explaining she's going to have to hurry if she wants to make the eight-fifteen.

'That's OK, hon,' says Tennis Lady. 'You scoot off. I was just wondering if your friend managed to catch up with you yesterday.'

She almost doesn't hear it. Another ten yards further down the road and she certainly wouldn't and that would have allowed her to carry on running without having to agonise over whether she needs to follow up on this. But hear it she did. She slows to a walking pace, keeps moving, because that's the key to getting away from people like this, but walking backwards now as she calls up the road.

'My friend?'

'That's right. Good-looking guy. Nice manners. He caught hold of Arantxa for me when she tried to get away.'

She stands still for a moment. On the alert.

'And he said he was a friend of mine?'

'Well, not in so many words. But he was coming out of your garden when I saw him and I wouldn't have thought anything of it if he hadn't said he was from England.'

She conjures up a smile from somewhere. Pins it in place. Takes a deep breath. Wonders how best to frame a casual enquiry.

'What did he look like?'

Tennis Lady offers a description that's short on specifics but long on innuendo.

'I don't suppose he mentioned a name at all?'

'He did . . . now what was it?' Tennis Lady scratches her head as if trying to work the name free from its moorings. Quick look at the watch – the ferry will be in by now. They'll be unloading the first day visitors before long, then loading up those heading the other way, across to Portland. She doesn't have time for this. In all likelihood it's nothing more than a ploy Tennis Lady's been working on to engage her in conversation.

She points in the direction of the ferry dock and spreads her arms in apology. Is just about to start running again when Tennis Lady says she wonders if the name might have been Michael.

And that gets her attention.

'Michael?' she asks. 'You sure?'

'Pretty much.'

'And you say he was from England?'

'That's what he said.'

'And did he say what he wanted?'

Tennis Lady scratches her head, tries to remember.

'Not really. He was looking at your place. Likes clapboard houses, he said.'

'You didn't pick up on a bit of an accent by any chance?'

Tennis Lady clicks her finger and thumb.

'You know, now you come to mention it . . .'

But she's already off and running because she knows if she doesn't leave now there's every chance the ferry will go without her and she'll have another hour to sit there and fret over what the hell he's playing at. She can't believe it. She honestly thought she'd got through to him last time he was here. Couldn't have been clearer. She really didn't expect him to come sniffing around again despite everything she'd said. Didn't he believe her – was that it? Is this him calling her bluff? Because if it is . . . if it is . . .

'Damn you,' she hisses to herself as she races down the hill. 'Just how stupid are you?'

21

FRIDAY 21ST AUGUST 2015

Billy was woken by a knock at the door and was still trying to make sense of where he was when Mia appeared at his bedside, tapping him on the shoulder and asking if he was awake. He grunted and peered through bleary eyes at the alarm clock which told him it was just gone half-eight. He remembered checking it sometime after three in the morning and wondering if sleep was ever going to come. No wonder his system was calling for back-up right now.

She was full of apologies, she hated to disturb him but there was some sort of emergency at the gallery and she wanted to check it was OK with him if she went in for a few hours. He was fuzzy about the details – she was working her way through a long and convoluted explanation that lost him early on and never seriously threatened to draw him back in. He waited her out before saying it wasn't a problem and offering to drive her there, praying she wouldn't take him up on it. His voice sounded unfamiliar as it struggled to find its normal range. He wondered if he might be coming down with a cold.

She said she was OK – they were sending for a taxi to take her all the way to Ashford and back, which gave some indication as to how desperate they were.

'I feel bad,' she said.

'Why's that?'

'Well . . . you've taken time out to come down and spend the week with me and here I am, leaving you on your own on our last whole day together.'

He told her not to worry. He could get more work done if she wasn't here and they could always do something together this evening. She suggested he pick a decent film to download and she'd cook a chilli for them both, an offer he was quick to accept. Truth was, he'd have gone along with any suggestion that allowed him to duck back under the bedclothes for another precious couple of hours. She leaned over and kissed him on the cheek, then left him in peace.

It felt like no more than five minutes had elapsed before he was cruelly dragged out from under for a second time. When he realised it was a ringtone rather than the alarm, his first thought was *Aimi*. Then it dawned on him that it was his own phone rather than the disposable one she'd given him. He made a couple of ineffectual grabs at it before finally managing to check the number.

No caller ID.

'Hello?' he said, pleased that his voice sounded considerably more recognisable than it did earlier.

'We need to talk.'

No preamble then. Straight down to business. He didn't need to ask who it was. Groggy and sleep-deprived as he was, he recognised the voice instantly. It wasn't even twenty-four hours since they were sitting opposite each other and Billy was listening to him as he conjured up some ridiculous sob story about Aimi in the hope his father wouldn't realise what a top-of-the-range arsehole he had for a son. No prizes for guessing what this was all about.

'Wrong,' he said, not even trying to suppress a yawn as it struck him as appropriate in the circumstances. 'You might need to. I don't.'

'You know The New Inn in Winchelsea? One o'clock. Lunch is on me.'

'You have a hearing problem?'

'One o'clock. I'll meet you there.'

'Fuck you.'

'Yes . . . so you said in your text.'

Shit.

'What text?'

'Be there. One o'clock.'

Some chance, he thought to himself as he finished the call and swung his legs out of bed. Clearly he wasn't meant to get any more sleep, although he was surprised to see it was now getting on for eleven, which meant he'd actually gone back off for much longer than he'd imagined. He considered maybe going for a run before brunch. He lifted one of the curtains to one side and it looked like a perfect day for a few miles along the sands. He hadn't had any real exercise in over a week and wondered whether that might be making it difficult for him to get to sleep before the silly hours. He knew better than to ask Mia what she thought. She'd be sure to link it in some way to the fact that he'd stopped taking his meds – they were some sort of universal panacea in her book.

He still hadn't decided what to do about the run when his phone pinged. This message was even more to the point than Aimi's had been.

You might like to ring your nerdy friends at the office.

The rebel in him bristled at this, urged him to go for that run, wash Mia's car, do *anything* but ring Karun and Zak. With people like the Vedras, you needed to stand up to them every so often and remind them that not everyone was in thrall to them, ready to jump the moment they whistled. If he had his way, Joe would be a long time on his own at The New Inn.

The pragmatist in him knew better. If Joe had told him to phone, it would be for a reason. There was an implicit threat in the follow-up text, a certainty in the tone that was ominous. Billy knew he'd be foolish to ignore it. Taking another wistful look at the sun streaming in through the windows, he called Karun's number.

It rang for a while, then went to voicemail. He tried again with the same outcome, so he tried Zak's mobile instead. He answered on the second ring.

'Hey buddy,' Zak said. 'How are you doing?'

'Oh . . . so-so. You know how these things are.'

'But your sister's OK, right?'

'Yeah, she's good,' he said, putting the phone on speaker while he rummaged around for clean underwear. 'Karun not around? I tried his mobile but he's not answering.'

'Oh, he'll be out most of this morning, I think.'

'Why's that?'

'Oh, nothing in particular. Just being Karun, you know? Busy busy. Anything I can help with?'

Billy told him no, it was nothing urgent. He was just ringing to let them both know he was aiming to be back sometime the next day.

'Not sure when exactly – depends on when my brother-in-law's plane gets in.'

'That's cool – long as you're sure you're ready. You know you can take as long as you need, right? Karun was saying only this morning.'

Billy was more than ready.

'I can't seem to focus on the work while I'm here,' he said. 'It'll be good to get back into some sort of routine with you guys there to keep me on track. How are things, by the way?'

'Cool,' said Zak. 'Yeah . . . we're good. A few ups, a few downs – you know what it's like.'

For Zak it wasn't a bad effort. If Billy hadn't been listening for it, he might have missed the slight hesitancy or written it off as typical Zak. Small talk never was one of his strong points. As for prevarication, that was pretty much beyond him.

'So what's with the downs?'

'Awww . . . nothing really. Nothing we can't handle.'

'You want me to ask again, Zak? See if your next answer makes it off the ground?'

'Ah shit – it's nothing, honestly. We just figured you've got enough on your plate while you're down there. It's nothing that can't wait till you get back. We've got it covered.'

'Good to know. So what is it?'

Zak heaved a sigh.

'If Karun asks, you didn't get it from me, OK? Only it looks like Jerry might be pulling out.'

'Ah shit . . . you're kidding, right?'

Jerry Cullen from Osborne Square Investment Group, the guy Karun had been lunching with on Monday. OSIG had been sniffing around for weeks now and the lunch was meant to set the seal on it. Karun had certainly come away feeling like it was a done deal.

'Well, maybe pulling out is a bit of an exaggeration but he rang this morning to say one or two board members want to hold fire till they've had a chance to look more closely at the business plan.'

'Sounds like bullshit.'

'That's pretty much Karun's take on things too. Jerry reckons they'll maybe have another look at us in November or December but it sounded like *no thank you*, for some reason. Karun says he thinks it's one of two things. Either Jerry's over-reached himself and given commitments he wasn't entitled to give or maybe this is some sort of ploy to see how far we're prepared to bend over, you know? He's gone over there now. Jerry's supposed to be in meetings all day but he's going to jump on him, see if he can get a clearer idea as to what's going on.'

Billy didn't need a clearer picture. He was pretty sure he knew what this was all about but didn't want to say anything just yet in case there was a way of straightening things out. He'd got them into this mess – the least he could do was try to get them back out of it.

'So where do we stand financially if they pull out altogether? Did Karun have a take on this?'

'He's pissed . . . big time. But he says it's not like it's going to fuck us over completely. We've got this far without OSIG and he knows, if it comes to it, his old man can keep us afloat out of his pocket change but . . . you know Karun. It's like some sort of personal crusade he's on to show he can do this with as little help as possible.'

Billy did indeed know Karun. He also knew that while they might be able to ride out the possible withdrawal of OSIG, the same could not be said if others were to follow suit in quick succession. What's more, he was pretty sure there was every chance that would happen if Joe Vedra set his mind to it.

He knew he was going to have to find out what he wanted.

Winchelsea didn't appear to have changed in the fifteen years or so since his last visit. His parents used to bring him and Mia here for walks on a Saturday morning and his father made a pilgrimage to the churchyard each time to look at the grave of Spike Milligan who'd been his comedy hero. Every time they gathered there, he told the same story about how the strange-looking script on the gravestone was in fact Gaelic and read: *I told you I was ill.* Then he used to break out in a fit of giggles and within seconds the other two would be at it as well, leaving Billy standing there on the outside, wondering just what was so hilarious. It's not like it was *that* funny the first time.

The town was set on a hilltop, looking down across the Brede Valley and Walland Marsh. In medieval times, he knew from his father's lectures, it had formed part of the Confederation of Cinque Ports and had been a prosperous town until the silting of its harbours had clogged up the trade routes. Now it was so small it was difficult to see how it even qualified as a town – there was an antiquated charm to the place which hinted far more strongly at village life, albeit of a very affluent nature.

Billy asked the taxi driver to pull up outside the churchyard and walked up the road towards a large, attractive whitewashed building. The New Inn, with its colourful hanging baskets and its sign depicting a medieval ship coming into port, looked down on the rest of Winchelsea from its privileged position at the top of the street.

He walked in through the main entrance and had no trouble picking out Joe Vedra. He'd taken a table by the window and was reading a copy of the *Financial Times*, which he folded and placed on the chair next to him the moment he saw Billy. He offered nothing by way of a handshake or even a smile but pointed to a chair opposite.

'You took my advice then,' he said. 'Let me get you a drink. You look like you could do with one.'

'Not for me. I'm not planning on staying that long.'

'Suit yourself.'

Billy pulled the chair back from the table and slumped down into it, legs extended and crossed at the ankle, hands thrust deep in his pockets.

'Nice pub,' he said, taking a good look around him at the comfortable chairs, exposed wood beams and inglenook fireplace. 'One of yours, I suppose? Oh no – forgot. Daddy's the one with all the money.'

Vedra took a sip from his sparkling water and swished the ice around inside the glass.

'Can't help yourself, can you?' he said without looking up, wiping his mouth with thumb and forefinger. 'Always the attitude, even when the situation calls for a bit of diplomacy. You do realise, if you're here to curry favour, you're going to have to do something about that smart mouth of yours.'

'*Curry favour*? You think that's why I'm here?'

'Well, I'd say it's a pretty safe bet. We both know you're not here by choice, don't we?' Vedra seemed amused by Billy's feeble attempt to put up a front. 'I'm assuming you phoned your friends like I suggested. Call it a reality check, if you like. All that panic this morning was the result of just a two-minute phone call. Imagine the damage I could do with a few more.' He leaned forward with his elbows on the table, interlaced fingers supporting his chin. 'By all accounts, you're brighter than most, if a little impetuous, so how about you stop acting like a tosspot and we'll start again, OK? What can I get you to drink?'

Billy thought about it. He knew where the door was, knew equally well that he wasn't going to be using it any time soon. Not until he knew where he stood and, more specifically, just how much of a threat was hanging over the business. Vedra knew it too so there was no point in banging his head against a brick wall. Maybe backing off might be the better way to go for now, much as it went against the grain.

'I'll have a pint of whatever draught lager they have here,' he said, doing his best to make it look as little like a climbdown as possible.

While Vedra went off to the bar to order the drinks, Billy gave himself a mental slap and reminded himself of the promises he'd made before getting out of the taxi. Vedra was calling the shots for now – any fool could see that. There was no point in winding him up just for the hell of it. Trouble was, there was something about the guy which brought out the worst in him. The moment he'd entered the pub, all rational thought had run off screaming in the opposite direction. *Think,* he urged himself. *Big picture.*

'There, that's better,' said Vedra when he returned moments later. 'So . . . let's start again, shall we? Clearly we got off on the wrong foot yesterday and I'm guessing you're not happy about the little stunt I pulled to get you here but I just needed to get your attention. There's no lasting damage done. It's nothing I can't put right with a single phone call and I'll be happy to see to it once we're sorted here. But I'm going to need a bit more co-operation from you than you've shown so far, OK?'

He paused as if inviting Billy to say something in return.

'I'm listening.'

'Good. OK – I'll go first, shall I? I hope it goes without saying that anything said here in the next few minutes stays here. Nothing leaves this room, OK? If it does, I'll know who's responsible.'

He waited for Billy to respond, which he did with the briefest of nods.

'There are some things you need to know,' Vedra continued. '*Really* need to know before you make a bigger dick of yourself than you already have. At the same time, I'd imagine there are a few things you could be telling me that would save me a great deal of time and effort, so I'd say there's a lot to be said for putting our differences to one side for a few minutes. Maybe if we pool what each of us knows, we can come up with a solution that will actually suit us both.'

A solution that would suit them both. It seemed totally implausible from where Billy was sitting but he didn't allow the thought to distract him.

'Can we clear something up before we get started?' he asked.

'If you like.'

'Just to get it straight in my head so I know where I stand,' said Billy. 'Does your dad know about this meeting?'

Vedra's eyes narrowed.

'Why do you ask?'

'It's just that . . . I know I've only got yesterday to go on but the way he took centre stage, he didn't come across as someone who delegates that much, know what I mean? I got the impression he's used to calling all the shots so it struck me as a bit odd he's not here, is all.'

Vedra picked up a beer mat and rotated it end over end, tapping the table with each edge as he did so.

'No, he doesn't know,' he said eventually. 'And I'm sure I can rely on you to make sure it stays that way.'

Interesting, thought Billy.

'Mind if I ask why?'

'You can ask anything you like. Doesn't mean I'm going to tell you. All you need to know for the purpose of this meeting is that I'd rather deal with you directly for now. I think our chances of coming to some sort of understanding are better without a third party getting involved. I don't like to complicate things unnecessarily.'

'Fair enough,' said Billy, who knew a side-step when he saw one. This felt like a bruise he wanted to prod. 'Can I ask another in that case?'

'You think I brought you here so you could ask *me* questions?'

'Bear with me. At your place yesterday, I told you Aimi and I met up on Sunday afternoon at Camber Sands, right?'

'I think,' said Vedra with a wry smile, 'it might be more accurate to say that we told *you*.'

'OK,' said Billy, waving away the split hairs. 'The point is, you've had this piece of information for getting on for twenty-four hours now. I was just wondering whether you've passed that on to the police.'

'No. We haven't.'

Hmmm.

'I thought not. You see, I spent all yesterday afternoon and last night expecting a knock on the door any minute. Nada. I figured they'd be round like a shot the moment they knew I'd been lying to them, 'cos if half of what I've heard about your dad is true, they must be feeling the pressure for a result on this one. Seems a bit odd to me that you haven't even bothered to pass on a significant piece of evidence like that. You mind if I ask why?'

'As a matter of fact, I do,' said Vedra, letting the beer mat fall to the table. 'For one thing, we're not in the habit of discussing family business in public and for another, like I said, I didn't bring you here so that I could answer your questions. When I said there were things you needed to know, that wasn't an invitation to swap roles and start grilling me.'

'OK,' said Billy. 'Just find it a bit confusing, that's all. I thought you'd want any help you could get from the police and media.' He tilted his head to one side as if inviting Vedra to respond. 'Unless you don't *want* the police involved any more than you can help it, that is.'

Vedra leaned back in his chair and folded his arms.

'Have you finished?' he asked.

Billy held up his hands.

'OK. I know – your ball. Just curious, is all.'

Vedra gazed out of the window, seemingly at nothing in particular, for what must have been fifteen to twenty seconds. Billy would have given a lot to be able to read his mind – he could almost hear it ticking over. Eventually Vedra turned back to face him.

'OK. Let's start by clearing up a few misconceptions that have been muddying the waters a bit, shall we?'

'And what would they be?'

'First things first, you really need to get rid of the fond notion that you have an important role to play in Aimi's future, because the plain and simple truth is . . . you don't. I'm sorry – I'm not saying that because I want to hurt you or mess with your head in any way, but you just don't.'

'And why's that exactly?'

'Because you've nothing to offer her. She's turned to you for help and you've made the mistake of thinking that means something but don't flatter yourself. It doesn't. She'll have done that because she knows a soft touch when she sees one. Once she's got what she needs from you, she'll move on and won't give you a moment's thought. And don't take any of that personally. I'm not being cruel for the sake of it. It's just a statement of fact.'

Billy smiled quietly to himself.

'It's good to see you have such a high opinion of your own wife,' he said.

'I love Aimi very much but that doesn't mean I'm blind to her true nature . . . and in your position you really can't afford to be.'

'Hmmm. You love her very much and yet you don't mind slagging her off at the drop of a hat. I'm just a good friend but you'd never hear me talk about her like that.'

'Well, for one thing, it's not your place to do so. And neither are you remotely qualified to form an opinion. You don't know my wife at all. You think you do, but every time you open your mouth you make it quite clear you're remembering that fifteen-year-old girl who ran off to London all those years ago and left you behind. You're not the only one who's ever had a teenage romance. There's an Aimi tucked away somewhere in everyone's adolescence. Mine? Julie Warren. Dumped me for some flash guy with a Lambretta. Thought it was the end of the world but I got over it because that's what you do when you grow up. You, though –'

He shook his head in exaggerated disbelief.

'You can't let go. You seem determined to cling on to it like some sort of comfort blanket. And you've never really got your head around the fact that Aimi's a very different person now. She's not the fifteen-year-old you've been moping after and probably never was. I'll tell you for a fact, she was already street-wise when I first met her in Cyprus and she's not mellowed or lost any of her sense of entitlement since then.'

He broke off as the girl behind the bar arrived with Billy's pint and another sparkling water with a fresh glass for Vedra. He thanked her as she picked up the used one and the empty bottle and carried them back to the bar. Then he wrestled for a few moments with the screw top, which seemed to be caught on a cross thread, before pouring himself another drink.

'And yet I love my wife very much, despite what she's led you to believe,' he continued. 'What you said yesterday about me beating her – not true. Oh, Aimi can be very convincing when she wants to be – I'd probably have experienced the same level of disgust you so obviously felt if our roles were reversed. But the truth is I've never laid a finger on her. Not once. Couldn't do it. Even when she's provoked me, and God knows she's done her fair share of that in recent weeks, I've taken the bait, snapped back, yelled at her, stormed out. Never touched her though. I'm not going to waste my breath swearing on a stack of bibles because it doesn't really matter to me whether you believe me or not, but I'll tell you this much – if she had bruises, they didn't come from me. And I say *if* because I'll lay whatever odds you like that the ones you saw were fake.'

Billy did his level best not to react to this. In almost any other circumstance the words *you would say that* would have been out before he could stop them, but the thought that stayed uppermost in his mind to the exclusion of all else was that he needed to keep Vedra on board, keep him talking.

'Why would she do that?' he asked.

'To engage your sympathies, why else? To get you onside. Don't take it personally – she won't have meant anything by it. She was probably worried you wouldn't believe her without some sort of evidence, so she simply set about manufacturing her own. The irony is, she misjudged the situation, because I suspect you'd have taken anything she said as gospel as a matter of principle, but I guess she didn't feel she could risk it. She needed to be sure you'd believe her.'

Billy shook his head, not buying this for one moment.

'You forget, I saw them. If they were fakes, they were very impressive.'

'They would have been. She's a dancer – she's been in performing arts since she learned how to crawl. She's around make-up artists all the time. And she's a more than handy actress when the situation calls for it. Wakey, wakey, for God's sake. The only other possible explanation, if they weren't fake, is that they were self-inflicted or she persuaded someone else to do it after I'd left for Portugal and you'd have to know Aimi to realise neither of those is even remotely likely. I don't think I've ever met such a baby when it comes to physical injury. No – unless you're lying for some reason, and as far as the bruises are concerned, my guess is you're not, she was faking the whole thing.'

Billy took a deep breath.

'So where exactly are you going with this?' he asked. 'I mean, I'm not saying I do or don't believe you, but if we take your version of events, why would she go to all that trouble just to make you look bad?'

Vedra linked his hands on the table.

'Aimi's not well. She really isn't. The meds I told you about? They're real. She's not seeing things straight at the moment or she'd never have done what she has.' He lowered his head for a moment. 'And she's angry with me. She's lashing out because she thinks I've let her down.'

'And does she have a point?'

'Yes. Yes, she does.'

It was such a simple and frank admission that it took Billy by surprise. He'd been expecting excuses, more verbal dances to avoid responsibility for his actions, but this was as unequivocal as it gets.

'Taking away the dance school was wrong,' Vedra continued. 'Should never have done it. If there's one thing that triggered all of this and persuaded her that running was the best option, that will be it.'

Billy picked up on it immediately.

'Running,' he said. 'Interesting choice of vocabulary there. Yesterday, I got the impression you were still trying to decide as a family whether she'd drowned, intentionally or otherwise, or faked the whole thing so she could get away. Now you sound as if you've made up your mind.'

'Oh, we have.'

This, Billy decided, was not good news.

'Why?'

Vedra smiled.

'I think we both know the answer to that.'

'Humour me.'

Vedra rearranged the beer mats on the table and picked his words carefully.

'You remember how it was we knew you'd gone for that walk with Aimi on Sunday afternoon?'

Billy nodded. 'Something about an anonymous phone call. Somebody saw us together on the beach.'

'The call wasn't anonymous. My father thinks it was because that's what I chose to tell him and I really do hope for your sake he continues to think that because the only way he'll know anything different is from you. You really don't want to do that.'

'So who was it, then?'

Vedra waved it away.

'Not important. No one you know. Just someone whose services I use from time to time.'

Billy nearly choked on his drink.

'You had someone spy on your own *wife*?'

'That's a rather more negative way of looking at it than I would have chosen, but yes – essentially. I was worried about Aimi's state of mind when we flew out to Portugal and wanted someone to keep an eye on her to make sure she was all right. I prefer to think of it as a supportive measure.'

Billy laughed.

'Oh, I'm sure she'd be bound to see it that way.'

Vedra took out his handkerchief and blew noisily.

'Yes . . . well, if I hadn't done that,' he said, refolding the handkerchief before putting it back in his pocket, 'I doubt if I'd have known about Monday morning. You know – when she picked you up outside The Thai House in Tower Street at eleven o'clock?'

That, it was fair to say, stopped Billy dead in his tracks.

The one thing that Aimi had never factored into her calculations was the possibility her husband might be so paranoid that he'd put a tail on her to track her every movement. This, he knew instantly, was a real game-changer. It put him in an impossible position. He was here because he had no choice. Vedra had questions for him and refusing to answer them was not an option. He had no way of knowing exactly how much he knew and how much was just guesswork so any deliberate attempt on his part to mislead was going to be fraught with danger. But telling the truth, come what may, might do irreparable damage to Aimi's chances of getting far enough away. Not only that, it just felt wrong. Disloyal.

'You seem to have lost some of your spark,' said Vedra, happy to milk the moment for all it was worth. 'You've had such a lot to say for yourself until now. I do hope you're not about to dry up just as it's your turn to provide a few answers.'

'I wasn't aware you'd asked a question.'

'Oh, I'm pretty sure you can work out what the question was. Before we go any further though, just remember what's hanging on the answers you give me. Don't let your protective instincts towards Aimi tempt you into thinking you can lie to me and get away with it. I'll know if you're not being straight with me.'

'I don't need reminding,' said Billy. 'You said yourself, I wouldn't be here if I had any choice. Why don't you ask your questions and get this over with?'

Vedra pushed Billy's pint of lager closer to him. He was going to need it.

It hurt him. Hurt him a lot. Felt like a betrayal. He tried to convince himself that if Aimi had been there, if she'd seen just what an impossible hole he was in right now, she'd have understood that he really had no choice in the matter, but his efforts never brought any real respite from the guilt. Bottom line, he'd promised her he wouldn't tell anyone else under any circumstances, her husband especially, and yet when push came to shove he'd folded like a house of cards. If they tracked her down now, it would be his fault.

If only he could have been sure of exactly what Vedra did and didn't know, he might have had some room for manoeuvre. As it was, there was next to none. If he knew Aimi had picked him up on Monday morning, right down to the time and place where it had happened, that meant he probably knew about Gatwick too. The tail wasn't just going to make a note of it and wave them goodbye, was he? He'd be bound to follow them. If he'd had time to work things through in his mind before answering, he might have managed to come up with something to throw Vedra off the scent but he couldn't take the chance of lying about where he'd dropped her off.

So although it went totally against the grain, he told the truth. About more or less everything. The only sleight of hand he allowed himself was a tactical one. He thought there might be some mileage in presenting himself as a bit of a victim too rather than a co-conspirator because he knew that Vedra would want to believe that – it never hurt to allow your opponent the chance to say I told you so and convince himself he'd been right all along.

He dropped more than a few hints that all was less than rosy in the Aimi/Billy garden, especially in the past few days. He gave voice to a subtle mixture of bewilderment and frustration bordering on anger over the fact that he hadn't heard from her since she disappeared. She'd promised to contact him every night to let him know she was safe, he told Vedra, but there hadn't been any contact at all. Total silence from her end. It did occur to him that if you disregarded one text message late last night on the Nokia, this wasn't so very far from the truth. She *hadn't* been in touch, other than to tell him to destroy the phone. He genuinely did have no idea where she was and maybe his concern for her safety added a certain amount of conviction to his narrative because Vedra didn't seem to have any trouble accepting his version of events. He was just happy to see this as further evidence that maybe Billy didn't know Aimi quite as well as he thought he did. Smugness wrapped itself around the conversation like cling film.

Billy held onto this minor deception but, as victories go, it felt a bit like dining on leftovers. If he was able to take any consolation from it all, it was the fact that whatever he coughed up, he may have been offering only confirmation rather than fresh information. There was Gatwick, but how would that help now? And yes, they now knew for sure she'd disappeared a day earlier than Aimi had hoped they'd assume, but from some of the questions he was asked, Billy got the strong impression that Vedra had already been aware of this too. Apart from anything else, wasn't it the only logical conclusion if they knew he'd driven the car back to Rye and left it in the car park in Rope Walk? Why else would she have asked him to do that and then move it the following afternoon? And as for the 'fuck you' text – well, he'd shot himself in the foot with that moment of madness. It took away any room for manoeuvre he might otherwise have had.

Vedra had quizzed him and pushed and prompted for twenty minutes or more and even though Billy had decided to be honest wherever possible, there were so many questions to which he himself was desperate for answers. He started to worry about what Vedra might do if he saw any holes as evidence that Billy was holding out on him.

And yet when the questioning was over, Vedra seemed less concerned about his patchy grasp of what had happened than with establishing ground rules for the future. If Billy wanted to wipe the slate clean and keep investors with the company rather than losing them in their droves, he was going to have to call on any resources he might have in the search for clues as to where Aimi might have gone.

'All those bright techie boys who work for you,' said Vedra. 'I'm sure they'll be able to come up with a few ideas as to how we can track her down. Best-case scenario, she gets in touch anyway, like she said she would, although I wouldn't sit around waiting if I were you. My guess is she's moved on, but you never know. She's under pressure so there's always a chance she might not be thinking straight. If she *does* contact you, you come up with an excuse, you're talking to the police or something, whatever – you find some way to put her off and get her to call back in a couple of hours or so. Then you ring me straight away on this number, right?'

He took a small silver case from the pocket of his jacket and underlined a phone number on a card he'd taken from it.

'I need to be there the moment she gets in touch with you. You understand?'

He nodded, desperate to get this over with. But Vedra hadn't quite finished.

'And you mentioned my father,' he said, leaning forward as if to lend emphasis to the point he was about to make. 'Let's be quite clear about this. If there's anything he needs to know, I'll be the one to tell him. Everything comes through me. You don't need to concern yourself with the reasons why. And I hope you're not tempted to do something stupid like trying to strike a deal with him and selling me out. He's not going to thank you for it. He won't give a shit about the hole you're in, let alone dig you out of it. He'll show you the door and deal with the whole thing as a family matter, the way he always does. And you'll have put me in a very difficult situation but not half as grievous as the one you'll have dropped yourself in. I promise I'll repay you with interest. I hope I make myself clear.'

Billy nodded again and got to his feet to confirm that he'd got the message. Vedra asked him to sit back down again – he still hadn't finished.

'And just in case that's not enough to persuade you,' he continued, 'you might like to bear this in mind. The main reason I'm keeping things from my father is not because of any rift between us, although I'm sure it might look that way. I'm doing all this for Aimi's sake.'

Billy frowned.

'How exactly does that work?'

The words were out before he could stop them. He didn't want to rise to the bait. All he wanted to do was call a taxi and put as much distance as possible between himself and this place, which was now destined to be labelled in his memory as the moment he proved himself unworthy of Aimi – big time. But the siren call was too strong. All it took was the mention of her name linked to any hint of a threat and he couldn't help himself.

'In case it helps to provide you with a little extra motivation, I'll tell you this much,' Vedra said, twisting the wedding ring round and round on his finger. 'When Aimi disappeared, she took something with her. You don't need to know what – it doesn't concern you. But she shouldn't have done it. It was a bad mistake and it could have serious consequences for her. My father doesn't yet know what she's done. I'm very keen to make sure he never does because if that happens I don't see any way back for Aimi. Ever.'

He paused, as if suddenly realising what he'd been doing with the ring, and picked up his glass again.

'She's not thinking straight. If she imagined for one minute my father would fall for that staged disappearance, she's seriously underestimated him. The only reason he hasn't taken a more proactive role in looking for her is because I've managed to convince him it's a domestic thing, a problem in our relationship that has come to a head because of the business with the dance school. I've told him it needs to be me who finds her and brings her back which is why we have to do so as soon as possible and put it right. If I can have five minutes with her, I know I can convince her to do the right thing. What I need you to do is to help provide me with that opportunity, because for all the differences between us and the thousand and one issues on which we disagree, there's one area of common ground and that's our concern for Aimi and her welfare. Tell me if I'm wrong,' Vedra said, rocking back into his seat.

Billy said nothing. He took a roll of notes from his back pocket, peeled off a ten-pound note and placed it carefully on the table next to his half-empty glass.

Then he turned on his heel and left the pub without a backward glance.

22

FRIDAY 22ND APRIL 2016

Peaks Island, Maine, USA

She's had a tough one. That's the way it goes sometimes. You get days where the gods are all lined up against you and everything you touch turns to crap.

If she's looking for someone to blame, she doesn't need to look any further than Hobie. She was under the impression – no, dammit, she knows for a fact – that she'd made a point of telling him she didn't want anyone else to know about last night. Short of branding it across those impressive quads of his, she couldn't have been any clearer. She could tell, though, the moment she got into work, from the odd whispered conversation here and a few sneaky glances thrown her way there, that word had got around. Could only have come from him. The male ego, she's known for some time, is a thing of wonder, but you'd think someone would have come up with a way of neutering it by now. Or educating it at the very least.

He was a bit off all morning, lots of ostentatious yawns intended, no doubt, to make her feel bad for kicking him out so early. When she took him to one side at lunchtime and set him straight about a few things, the yawns turned to sulks and it felt to her as if everyone there knew and was judging her. She's spent large parts of the day reminding herself that she deserves no better, although not for the reasons they'd have offered. She knew this was how it would turn out. What's she been telling herself for the past few weeks, ever since she and Hobie did that slow duet together for the Open Evening concert? Leave well alone. Sure. She might have been able to stick to it if she'd followed a different career but spending all day watching him wrap himself around a succession of women, usually in dances she's choreographed herself – damn, that's hard. When you're cursed with an artistic temperament and a vivid imagination, what the hell are you supposed to do?

Well, now she knows. It'll blow over soon enough. There's nothing she can do about it except sit and wait it out. What she needs right now, though, is a long soak in a hot bath, a couple of long, cool drinks and maybe a DVD before she goes to bed. No later than ten tonight, she tells herself. Catch-up time.

She fumbles in her purse for the key to the front door and lets herself in. It's not quite dark yet but it's gloomy enough inside for her to turn on the light in the hallway. She stoops to pick up a handful of leaflets from the mat. No mail as such – she doesn't get letters for obvious reasons. She does get flyers though, a variety of them, nothing of any real interest. She flicks casually through them, decides they are all destined for the trash can.

She goes through to the kitchen and takes a soda from the refrigerator and snaps the ring pull. Takes a couple of sips and walks through into the living room, wondering whether to have the bath before she eats or later, before she goes to bed. She reaches for the light switch.

'Hi.'

She shrieks. Not a full-blooded scream as such, just an involuntary expression of shock. She whirls round to where the voice has come from and sees him sitting there in her Adirondack chair. Is pretty sure who it is. Then realises she's wrong.

'Jesus!' she hisses, one hand pressed to her breast as if hoping that might bring her breathing back to something resembling normality. 'What the hell are you doing here?'

PART THREE

23

FRIDAY 8TH APRIL 2016

The moment they arrived back at the house after the funeral, Billy announced that he was going out.

'Anywhere in particular?' Matthew asked.

He shook his head.

'Just to the Sands. For an hour or so. Could do with a walk.'

'In your best clothes?'

Matthew's attempt at humour. A none-too-subtle and absolutely hilarious reference to the fact that Billy had refused point-blank to wear a suit. He'd never owned one. Could have hired one easily enough or even borrowed one of Matthew's dozen or so if he'd wanted to, but that was the point. He didn't. What's more, he was pretty sure Mia wouldn't have wanted him to either. If dressing up like a penguin was going to achieve anything, like maybe bring her back for a few hours, he'd have worn a suit every day for the rest of his life. But it wouldn't. It was just window dressing. End of.

Over the years he'd retained only a vague and confused recollection of his parents' funeral. *Still in shock* was everyone else's considered opinion and maybe they were right, although he had enough about him at the time to pick up a few random details that stayed with him. He remembered the wasp for instance. Kept buzzing around the vicar's head, one of those awful moments when half the people there wanted to laugh but knew they couldn't. His dad would have frowned on it, that's for sure, not that he was in much of a position to object to anything. The wasp finally settled on one of the two coffins, resting side by side on trestles, and he'd wanted to walk out front and smash the thing with his fist but you can't do that sort of thing in a church. Sacrilege. God cares so much about his little creatures, doesn't he? Shame about the bigger ones. He remembered thinking how funny it would be if the vicar actually did that – broke off in mid-prayer and smashed it with his fist. *Got you, you stupid fucking annoying . . . FUCKING LITTLE SHIT.* The image had been so extraordinarily vivid, he'd almost choked trying to prevent himself from giggling and Mia had put her arm round him, mistaking the gurgle that came from his lips for something else.

No wasp today. He'd remembered to check. Just as well because, if there had been, the mood he was in, nothing would have stopped him walking out there and smashing it.

As he set out for the beach, he did his best not to snatch the *For Sale* sign from its position at the end of the drive and smash it against the pavement. He'd exploded when he came back the previous evening and saw it there. Mia hadn't even been dead for a fortnight and Mr Sensitivity was already planning for the future. In fact, things seemed so far advanced already, it was difficult not to imagine he'd made preliminary enquiries and had everything on standby while Mia was still around. Like he was sitting there, waiting for her to get out of the way. They'd rowed about it, then sulked – Matthew taking to his office, Billy watching TV with the volume several levels higher than necessary – and had been tiptoeing around each other ever since like guilty schoolboys.

There were quite a few people at the beach when he got there. The temperature had crept into the low twenties, very pleasant for the second week in April, and the holidaymakers who'd taken a punt on a late Easter break were being well rewarded. Some were using the dunes to set up base camp, others were down on the sand, kicking a ball around or digging channels for when the tide came in. On days like this you could almost believe in summer.

Most weekends, especially if the forecasters were making all the right noises, their numbers were swelled by day-trippers from London with their picnics and sunshades and windbreaks and foldaway chairs, whole families setting out early, determined to make the most of it. The Marina and the Oasis looked as if they'd do good business today.

Billy had changed into T-shirt, beach shorts and espadrilles, the last of which he removed the moment he reached the sandy path leading to the top of the dunes. The tide looked from there as if it was three-quarters of the way out, which left vast areas of damp sand to cross before he reached the edge of the water. The moment he dipped his toes in, he knew the people actually swimming in the water were day-trippers. You had to be making a day of it to contemplate swimming in that.

Last time he'd come down here was just after Christmas, a couple of days before New Year. He hadn't been in T-shirt and shorts then. He'd dragged Mia out for a walk and the wind had taken a good ten degrees off the air temperature, seeking out every patch of skin open to the elements and blast freezing it. They'd managed ten minutes heading eastwards along the sand before giving it up as a bad job and accepting that Matthew had been right all along. His offer to stay behind and have mulled wine and crumpets waiting for them seemed with hindsight to be a very shrewd move.

Billy followed the tracks that had been left in the damp sand by a succession of paddlers. Couples walking arm in arm. Children taking three paces to their parents' two. Each recorded step a futile attempt to leave a lasting imprint on this world. The tide would wash them away in no time. He could search for as long as he liked for a trace of Mia and never find one.

The day after their walk he'd gone back to London. She insisted on not only giving him a lift but coming onto the platform as well to wave goodbye. He hadn't realised at the time just how literally he needed to take that wave. If he'd known, he'd have paid more attention to what was happening, frozen the moment in his mind. Instead he was left with a vague memory of craning his neck so that he could see her through the window as the train pulled away and that was it. Gone. No warning. Nothing to suggest that the next time he'd set eyes on her it would be to say goodbye and switch off the machine. He remembered her telling him it could be any time – years, months, even just days. She hadn't said anything about hours, minutes and seconds. Bang – just like that. Gone.

Matthew had been stoical about the whole thing in true antipodean style which asserts that men are ockers and don't give way to finer feelings. He was the one who had agreed to the request to switch off life support. Despite the evidence of his own eyes, not to mention all medical advice and basic common sense, Billy had argued long and hard with more than a touch of bitterness and a few angry words he'd never be able to take back.

He'd earned her a very brief stay of execution, which was pretty much how he viewed it all, before Matthew had finally broken his resistance with the simple observation that Mia wouldn't have wanted this. She really wouldn't. And he was right – Billy could almost hear her saying it. As the specialist had patiently and sympathetically explained, the moment whatever it was fired off in her brain she was as good as dead before she even hit the floor. Preserving an empty shell wasn't going to serve any purpose and he knew full well Mia had never been the sort to cling onto anything by her fingernails. She was full-on – deeply immersed or not engaged at all.

They'd allowed him an hour at her bedside. Matthew had his ten minutes first and emerged, looking uncharacteristically flustered before bustling through, pausing only to let Billy know he'd be waiting in the car. *Take as long as you need,* he'd said as he brushed past. As if you could. Billy had needed a lifetime – settled for an hour. He talked to her, opened up about every little detail he could think of that he'd kept back from her for any number of reasons over the years, reasons that had seemed so important at the time but which this new perspective revealed to be worthless. He stroked her hair the way she'd always liked, massaged her scalp as if trying to break up and sweep away the blockages and short circuits and whatever else it was that had gone wrong in there and shut her down so suddenly.

He thanked her, told her he loved her and left.

Dry-eyed and moving on.

The Marina Café was doing very nicely. Most of the tables, inside and out, were occupied, including the one where he'd sat with Aimi back in August. Seven, nearly eight months. Hard to believe.

He took a seat next to the one he'd hoped for and waited to see if there was any chance the family of five sitting there might be about to move, but it didn't seem likely. They were still consulting menus and taking their time over it. At one point the mother looked across and frowned slightly – he hadn't realised he was staring quite so much. In the end, he moved to a table inside instead.

Nearly eight months. A long time to go without any contact. The last he'd heard from her had been when she sent that message, urging him to ditch the phone she'd given him. *Will find another way to get in touch,* it had said. *Soon.* That hadn't happened and eight months was plenty long enough to sit there and wonder why. You could drive yourself crazy doing that.

For the first few weeks, he'd found himself checking his phone every couple of hours to see if a message had materialised out of nowhere. Had he turned the sound off and forgotten to turn it back on again? That sort of thing. You can do that for a while. The adrenaline will let you feed off it up to a point. Then, bit by bit, you lose some of the momentum and start looking for explanations as to why it's taking so long.

He'd hit on the two obvious ones right away and discounted both, not because they lacked plausibility but because he refused point-blank to give them airtime. The possibility that something had happened to her might have had its roots in logic, but logic in his opinion was overrated, especially on those occasions when it pointed in a direction he didn't want to contemplate. Nothing had happened to Aimi. She was too smart, too streetwise to allow it – even Joe Vedra had said as much. She'd gone to London at fifteen, gone on her own to work in Cyprus at eighteen. She knew how to look after herself. Besides, he'd lost his mother and now

Mia, two of the rocks that kept the flood tide at bay. He couldn't lose the third as well. Not Aimi.

Neither was he prepared to accept that she might have been using him. He knew this was how others viewed it, including Mia and Joe, and he could see why – he wasn't a fool. He knew that the longer she went without getting in touch, the more appearances were against her. He also knew there were plenty of people who couldn't wait to be proved right about her. Poor Aimi – everyone assumed that looking the way she did was an automatic ticket to a free ride through life and she knew from an early age that wasn't the case. Even at fifteen she'd started to realise that, because of the way she looked, she was held to a different set of standards compared to everyone else and OK, that wasn't the way she'd actually expressed it, but he'd understood immediately what she meant. Look the way she did and the automatic assumptions kicked in. Must be a bitch. Must be calculating. Sure to be angling for fast cars, expensive restaurants, an exclusive apartment. Always one eye open for the main chance, a situation ripe for exploiting. Can't possibly have a kind thought for others. Even Mia had bought into the stereotype and her judgement was usually as sound as a bell.

Well, he trusted Aimi. He had faith. Faith, as he understood it, meant believing in something without demanding proof of its existence. The moment you asked for proof or assurances, your faith in someone else was revealed for what it really was – just so much hot air. A sham. Aimi had said she'd be in touch and she would be. And the moment she called, he'd be there. Waiting. Ready.

So he clung to the third possibility, which was that she still felt it was unsafe. He had no way of knowing what difficulties she faced on a day-to-day basis so he wasn't in a position to second-guess her. If she thought it was right to wait a little longer, then that's what he would do. He wasn't sure how she planned to contact him, now that he'd destroyed the Nokia as instructed. Presumably emails, messages and especially phone calls would be too dangerous, especially since she herself would have no way of knowing what was happening at this end.

But she would find her way back to him.

She just would.

At least Joe Vedra had been as good as his word. If The New Inn summit had been all about demonstrating where the balance of power lay, it had served its purpose because Billy had no doubts at all about his ability to yank the stopcock out of their business any time he felt like it.

For that reason he was anxious in the following weeks about the lack of information he'd be able to pass Vedra's way. As soon as he was back in London, he'd sat down with Zak, explained what had happened and enlisted his help. They'd kept Karun out of it because he tended to be a bit of a pussy about such things. As far as he knew, the problem with the reluctant investor had turned out to be nothing more serious than a simple misunderstanding. He'd have kicked off big time if he'd known the part Billy had played in causing it in the first place. He certainly wouldn't have been happy about the idea Zak might be involved as well, even if it was necessary to keep Vedra sweet.

But good as he was at what he did, Zak couldn't operate in a vacuum. He was happy to hack into anything but he had to know where to look in the first place. The problem here was that no one had the faintest idea in which direction to point him and until more information came their way he wasn't going to be of much use. Billy had done what he could to keep Joe Vedra sweet but the threat was always there that at some point he'd lose patience and decide they were holding out on him.

Fortunately Vedra was an intelligent man, capable of judging a situation on its merits rather than allowing himself to be pushed by frustration and anxiety into knee-jerk reactions. He seemed less amused now by Billy's conviction that Aimi would get in touch eventually. He'd viewed it as naïve at first but, given the dearth of information coming their way, he now seemed to see this as their best chance of moving forward and had settled into a holding pattern, waiting for the opportunity to land.

Eight months, though. Long time to circle up in the clouds.

His thoughts were interrupted by the chirping of his mobile. *Surely not*, he found himself thinking. That would be freaky beyond all measures.

It was Matthew.

'Where are you, mate?'

'I'm in the Marina – the café.'

'I think you'd better get back here pretty sharpish.'

'Why?'

There was a pause before Matthew answered.

'The police are here.'

24

FRIDAY 8TH APRIL 2016

Same two as last time. DI Naylor and the Arsène Wenger looka-like. Matthew was sitting with them in the lounge when Billy walked in. He leapt to his feet and disappeared upstairs, saying he'd be in his office if they needed him. As he passed, he flashed a look at Billy, who had no idea what it was meant to convey but assumed disapproval would be somewhere in the mix. As if it was his fault.

Both officers got to their feet and there was a ritual exchange of handshakes before they all took the same seats as last time. Naylor offered his sympathies and apologised for their unfortunate timing – they hadn't known about Mia and certainly wouldn't have turned up out of the blue if they'd known the funeral was only that morning. If he'd rather they came back another time . . .

Such a pointless exercise in civility, it seemed to Billy. They could be here to bury him, they'd still shake his hand before they reached for the shovels and started digging. He knew sending them away wouldn't serve any purpose. Might as well get it out of the way now since they were here. He asked what this was in aid of. Was he to assume it was a formal interview?

Naylor gave a reassuring smile.

'No. Not at all. Any formal interview would be conducted back at Hastings and videoed. You're being questioned as a witness, not a suspect.'

'I thought I'd already done a witness statement.'

'You have. This is a follow-up, if you like.'

'OK.'

'You were one of the last people to see Aimi Vedra before she disappeared, after all,' explained Naylor. 'Sometimes reinterviewing witnesses and asking them to go over things for a second time can jog their memory, help them to recall some tiny detail that might have escaped their attention first time round. You know the sort of thing.'

'Fine by me,' said Billy, 'although I seriously doubt I'll be able to tell you anything different from last time.'

'It's only natural to think that, but you'd be surprised how many people remember something crucial when they go over it again. It's rarely a total waste of time. If you're sure this is OK, we might as well get started. I have your previous statement here. Do you think we could start with that Saturday morning?'

'In Tenterden?'

'No. Maybe back up a little. Take us back to when you first decided to go shopping. Whose idea was that?'

'My sister's.'

'You hadn't discussed it at all the previous evening?'

Billy cast his mind back to that Friday. His first evening there. Matthew had disappeared off to the gym the moment they'd arrived and Mia had decided that now was the time to tell him about her illness. Lied to him, of course. Well, bent the truth more than just a little – maybe that was a better way of looking at it. He'd been doing the same for as long as he could remember so he wasn't about to hold it against her.

When it was all over and Mia had decided she needed to get to bed, had she said anything then about maybe going shopping the following morning? If she had, he honestly couldn't remember it. In fact, what he *could* remember was how pleased he was when she woke him and suggested it, how much he'd instinctively welcomed the chance to slip back into the comfortable clothing of one of their old routines from years ago. That was the first time any shopping excursion had been mentioned – he was sure of it.

He wondered if they still suspected him of lying about this because they clearly had problems accepting that the meeting with Aimi was a coincidence. Their problem, not his. He was on safe ground here. He told himself they could keep asking the same questions as many times as they liked, it wouldn't change the facts or his answer, because they happened to be one and the same.

For the next few minutes they took him back through that morning, asking more detailed questions than last time. *Did he see anyone he knew in Tesco apart from Aimi? Was there any unusual incident that came to mind? Did anyone seem to be taking a particular interest in the fact that she was there? What was her demeanour like? Did she seem edgy, evasive at all?* He answered patiently and truthfully, comfortable with the way things were going because Tesco in Tenterden presented no threat to him other than in their overworked imaginations.

Co-in-ci-dence, guys. Get over it.

'When you and your sister left the store,' said Naylor, 'did Aimi happen to leave at the same time?'

'I don't know. I don't think so. If she did, I didn't see her. We just loaded all the bags into a taxi and left. Why?'

'So those five minutes in Tesco – that was the only time you saw her before she disappeared?'

'Yes.'

'And she didn't contact you in any other way? Didn't phone or text you, for instance? Social media?'

'No.'

'You're quite sure about that?'

'I think I'd remember.'

'OK.'

Billy folded his arms and sank back into his seat.

'We went through all this before,' he said, looking from one to the other. 'I'm not sure why you're bringing it up again.'

Naylor offered a reassuring smile.

'As we said earlier, it's just a follow-up.'

'But something must have prompted it, surely. You don't honestly think I'm suddenly going to remember some detail from eight months ago.'

Naylor started to speak, then seemed to change his mind. Instead he held out his hand and Wenger took two photos out of a large brown envelope and passed them to him. He looked at them briefly, then laid them out on the coffee table in front of Billy.

'Could I ask you to take a look at these?'

Billy reached out, paused and looked up as if to ask for permission before picking them up and examining them in turn. Two men. One dark-haired, swarthy, stocky build, looked as if he was no stranger to a gym. Not quite a rival to TJ in the pumping iron stakes but neither did he look like someone you'd want to get on the wrong side of. Scar tissue around the eyes. Tattoo sneaking up out of his shirt collar and more evidence of ink just below the throat. The other one was older, with rimless glasses and one of those beards that just follows the jawline without encroaching on the face itself. Shaved head. Neither of them would have had much joy passing themselves off as Jehovah's Witnesses at the front door.

He didn't recognise either of them and was curious as to why their photos were being shown to him.

'When you were in the store or just leaving,' said Naylor, who was monopolising the questioning today, 'did you see either of these two?'

Billy took another look at the photos although he knew it was pointless.

'Not as far as I'm aware.'

'Are you sure? Take another look.'

'Won't make any difference. I'm not saying one hundred per cent they weren't there, but if they were I certainly don't remember seeing either of them. Who are they?'

Naylor and Wenger exchanged looks. It could have been staged, could have been a set-up. It was hard to tell. Eventually Naylor reached forward.

'Ardit Jashari,' he said, tapping the first photo. 'And this one . . . Leka Tahiri.'

'Local boys, then,' said Billy.

'They're from London,' said Naylor, straight-faced, his sense of humour apparently working to rule. 'Albanian, originally.'

'OK. So why are you showing me their photos? What have they got to do with anything?'

'We were hoping you might be able to tell us. Or at least, we were wondering whether you might have seen them hanging around in Tesco that Saturday.'

Billy picked up the photos again for one last look, more to show willing than anything else. It had been heaving in Tesco that morning and even if he'd been on heightened alert he doubted he'd have seen them. He hadn't even noticed Aimi till she was standing right next to him.

'Nope,' he said finally, pushing the photos away. 'Sorry.'

'No problem. It was always a long shot.'

Naylor gathered up the photos and passed them to Wenger, keeping the envelope on his lap.

'I still don't get why you think they might have been there,' said Billy. 'What have they got to do with Aimi?'

Naylor shook his head.

'I'm sorry,' he said. 'We're not at liberty to discuss particulars of the case with you.'

And yet you're happy to show me the photos and tell me their names, he thought to himself. *Interesting.*

'So . . . is that it?' he asked. 'Have you covered everything you'd like to ask me?'

'Not quite.'

He reached into the envelope and took out two more photos, which he placed on the coffee table, face down for a moment.

'We wondered if you'd be so good as to take a look at these.'

'More Albanians?'

Naylor turned them over and Billy peered at them. It took him a couple of seconds to work out exactly what he was looking at. When he realised, he picked them up and took a closer look. This, it would be fair to say, was not at all what he'd been expecting.

In the first, he was crossing the road outside the main car park at Camber Sands, heading for The Gallivant and the parking spaces in front and to the side of it. In the other, apparently taken moments later, he was recrossing the road, this time with a Tesco bag dangling from one hand. It wasn't possible to see what was in the bag but Billy remembered it only too well.

When he first realised he was the subject of the photos and recognised the location, his heart leapt into his mouth because he thought just for a brief moment that they'd been taken on the night he left Aimi's clothes on the beach. For two or three seconds his brain was well and truly scrambled – there were too many questions screaming for attention and no time for him to answer them. Then he realised the obvious – these were taken two days earlier on the Sunday afternoon, when he'd gone back to Aimi's car for her. The ball launcher, that's what was in the bag. That and Aimi's cardigan that she'd asked him to fetch. And never used.

He looked again at the photos of him crossing the road to go to her car. Then him coming back the other way. He looked more closely at the second one.

And then he saw it.

And worked so, so hard to make sure he didn't react in any way that would give them anything to feed off.

'So ... what is this?' he asked, putting the photos carefully down on the table, his mind merely flirting with the question itself. His attention was very much elsewhere.

'We were hoping you might tell us.'

'Do I take it this is where the witness interview changes into something more formal? Shouldn't you be reading me my rights and offering me the duty brief or something?'

Naylor shook his head and started drumming his fingers on the arm of the settee.

'Not at all,' he said. 'I meant what I said earlier. You're not a suspect. We have no intention at this stage of charging you with any offence. We're still actively seeking your co-operation in the hope that you'll be able to help us out here.'

'Oh really. And shoving these photos in front of my face is going to help, you reckon?'

'We hope so – yes.'

'They're not what you think they are,' he insisted, looking from one officer to the other to gauge whether his protests were carrying any conviction. 'It's pretty obvious what they're meant to suggest but someone's yanking your chain here. Who gave them to you?'

'They were sent to us anonymously.'

'Well, there's a surprise!'

'And we weren't born yesterday. We'd have to be pretty dim to take these at face value. Someone obviously wants us to believe that the bag contains the clothes Aimi left on the beach and that you've colluded in some way in her disappearance. But we know that's not what these photos show.'

Billy had been on the point of calling the whole thing to a halt, challenging them to leave or arrest him, in which case he'd bring Matthew in here like a shot. He was intrigued, though – what was it about these photos that made them so certain they were nothing more than a clumsy attempt at a set-up?

'Go on,' he said cautiously.

'Well, for one thing there's this. And this,' said Naylor, pointing first to Billy crossing the road, then to the sign which read 'The Gallivant' and the little wooden posts bordering the entrance. 'See the shadows? Almost vertical, which puts the time somewhere around midday. And of course, someone help-ing her to fake her disappearance *could* have taken the clothes to the dunes and left them there at that time with all those other holidaymakers around but we don't think that's very likely. Why not wait till the evening when there's hardly anyone there to see what you're doing?'

'You said *for one thing*,' said Billy.

'I did,' said Naylor. 'For another, there's this vehicle approaching just as you crossed the road.' He pointed to the rear end of a saloon car which was at the edge of the second photo. 'I know you'll struggle to make out the detail on the licence plate with the naked eye but we've had it enlarged and you can see it more clearly then. We've contacted the driver. He lives in Peasmarsh and says he drove over to pick up his mother and bring her back home for Sunday lunch. Came through here sometime after one-thirty and brought her back later that evening, when the shadows would have been a lot longer. So . . . we know these photos were taken around Sunday lunchtime and we also know that our early-morning swimmer, Mrs . . .' He snapped his fingers.

'Ward,' said Wenger.

'Mrs Ward. We know she found the clothes on Wednesday morning. Now, she's adamant she swims every morning from the same spot and noticed the clothes as she walked down to the water. You think, even if someone was misguided enough to risk leaving the clothes there in broad daylight, they'd stay there undetected for three days? Why would she see them on Wednesday, having walked straight past them on Monday and Tuesday? And even if that's what happened, how come no one else saw the clothes there during all that time?'

'Doesn't make a lot of sense, does it?' said Billy.

'No. It doesn't. But someone clearly wants us to think you're very much involved in Aimi's disappearance. Do you have any idea who that might be?'

'No.'

'No idea at all?'

'No. I agree with you though. Whoever it is, I don't think we're talking Einstein, do you?'

Naylor smiled.

'And you're adamant you've never seen those two men before?'

'I'm adamant I don't recognise either of them, if that's the same thing. Maybe if you were to give me a bit of context, like how they're connected to Aimi in the first place, it might jog my memory.'

'As I said earlier,' Naylor repeated, 'we can't discuss particulars of the case with you.'

'Then I don't see how I can help you.'

Naylor nodded as if to acknowledge this before getting slowly to his feet. Wenger made sure all the photos were back in the envelope before following suit. They both offered their condolences again and Billy thanked them before escorting them to the front door. As they were leaving, Naylor turned to address Billy one more time. His body language had something of the Hail Mary pass about it.

'OK if I put a hypothetical situation to you? Off the record?'

'Sure . . . as long as we remember that's all it is.'

Naylor nodded.

'A friend comes to me and asks for help? I'd probably say yes. If it's someone I'm particularly close to, like my family? Wouldn't even hesitate. I get where you're coming from.'

'Hypothetically.'

'Hypothetically. But people like Ardit Jashari and Leka Tahiri . . . they raise any hypothetical stakes to a whole new level. You need to think hard about whether your current stance is the best option here, OK? For you and for Aimi. You decide there's something you want to say, you know how to get hold of me. Only I wouldn't leave it too long if I were you.'

'I'll be sure to let you know,' said Billy. 'If I want to talk hypothetically.'

Naylor smiled ruefully.

'Take care,' he said and followed Wenger down the driveway.

'So what was that all about?' asked Matthew, appearing at the foot of the stairs the moment Billy closed the front door.

'Like you weren't hanging on every word.'

'Just looking out for you. You going to tell me or not?'

'It's just a witness statement. I don't need a lawyer.'

'How about a brother-in-law?'

Billy reached for the car keys that were hanging from a hook next to the front door. Bit his tongue.

'I'm going out for a drive,' he announced. 'I'll take Mia's car.'

Matthew stood with hands on hips, presumably courtroom body language for disbelief or exasperation. As usual, it was lost in translation.

'So where are you going?'

'Out. Anywhere. For a drive.'

'You sure that's a good idea?'

'Dunno, but I'll be sure to give it a lot of thought.'

He unlocked the car and squeezed into the driver's seat. He had to push it back a few notches before his legs felt comfortable. Another trace of Mia wiped away in a moment's careless gesture. He looked at the front passenger seat of the car. A pair of sunglasses she'd left there. A sheet of paper with a postcode and address. In the tiny compartment under the dashboard, half a packet of Trebor mints and a phone charger. All frozen in time. He started the car and drove off without looking to see whether Matthew was there at the front door.

Thirty seconds later, approaching the golf club, he pulled over and manoeuvred his mobile out of his back pocket. Picked the number out of speed dials and made the call. It rang twice before Joe Vedra answered.

'You know Mason's Field?'

'Mason's what?'

'Google it. I'll meet you there in twenty minutes.'

'I'm in the office. What's this all about?'

'Be there.'

25

FRIDAY 8TH APRIL 2016

He arrived ten minutes late. Billy watched from his vantage point in a corner of Mason's Field as Vedra pulled up on the other side of the road and turned off the engine. He stepped out of the car, tucking his sunglasses into his jacket pocket as he crossed the road. He walked through the small row of wooden posts and a line of trees until he had a clear view of the whole field in front of him. It took him a few seconds to locate Billy who was sitting in the nearest corner, picking daisies and lobbing them distractedly up into a breeze which was making little impression on the heat of the afternoon sun.

Vedra walked over, jacket now slung casually over his shoulder. Suit, shirt, shoes, haircut – fuck it, even his manicure oozed money. Aiming for style. Falling just short somehow, somewhere near poser.

'Couldn't have chosen a pub?' said Vedra, checking the area where Billy was sitting for potential grass stains. 'This had better be worth it, whatever it is.'

Busy man.

Billy ignored him for a few seconds, picked another couple of daisies and used his nail to create a slit in the stem of one before threading the other through the gap and pulling the rest of the flower through as far as its head.

'Daisy chains,' he said. 'I'd forgotten all about them. Used to make them all the time.'

He patted the floor to invite Vedra to take a seat.

'Daisy chains,' Vedra repeated.

'I made her one that last afternoon – right here. At least, I think it was then.'

'Have you been drinking?'

'What? No . . . just reminiscing. I remember we came here after her last day at school and sat for hours right where we are now. Stayed here till long after it got dark. She was moving to her dad's place in London the next day so she wasn't too bothered about pissing her mum off and I knew I was going to get slaughtered when I finally got home but I figured it was probably worth it, you know? Seeing as it was going to be the last time.'

'You said we need to talk. I hope you've got something a bit more interesting than this.'

The lack of empathy seemed to have the desired effect on Billy who put the daisies to one side.

'OK. Try this for interesting. How about you tell me what you know about Ardit Jashari, I think it was, and Leka Somebody-or-other?'

Billy was watching him closely. Saw the flash of recognition and something else too. Surprise, certainly – maybe spiked with a shot of concern?

'Who?'

'Nice try. How many Albanians do you know? Me, I don't know any, but I guess you move in more glamorous circles.'

Vedra folded one leg under the other. Licked his finger and rubbed at a mark on one of his shoes, taking his time. He looked closely at Billy.

'Do you want to tell me what this is about?'

'Funny – I was going to ask you the same thing. OK, I'll go first, shall I? I've just had another interview with the police. Second one, although they're at great pains to make me understand I'm not a suspect and that this is just a follow-up witness interview, whatever the hell that is. Only just got back from burying my sister and they're already there, waiting. They show me a couple of photos of these hairy foreign-looking guys – you know the sort, slugs for eyebrows and nose hair you could use to stuff a sofa. The word *iffy* stamped across their foreheads. Then they want to know if I've seen either of them hanging around lately, especially that Saturday when I was talking with Aimi at the supermarket, the clear implication being there's some sort of link between her and these two. I didn't have to lie for once 'cos I don't know them from Adam but I thought to myself, *I'll bet I know a man who does.*'

'What makes you so sure?' asked Vedra, brushing away an insect that had landed on his shirt sleeve.

'I'd cross *poker* off my list, if I were you,' said Billy. 'The big boys'll see you coming from a mile off. You know exactly who these offcuts are and I could do with a bit of help here, OK? What's going on? Who are they and what have they got to do with Aimi?'

Vedra seemed to weigh things up for a few moments, then he patted his discarded jacket and located his phone. He jabbed and swiped his way through it until he found what he was after. Then he used thumb and forefinger to enlarge the photo and handed it over to Billy, who held it slightly away from himself at arm's length, trying to focus more clearly. It looked like some sort of formal reception, men in dinner jackets, women in expensive-looking dresses. Three couples in the foreground were holding champagne glasses, raising them in a toast to the camera and beaming like lanterns. To the right of them, slightly at one remove, was the man with the jawline beard and shaved head. Unlike the others in the photo, he was not holding a glass and gave the impression that he was watching all the merriment rather than participating.

'Yep,' said Billy, handing back the phone. 'That's one of them – the miserable-looking guy on the end. Can't see the other one though.'

'That's Leka Tahiri,' said Vedra, tucking the phone back into his pocket. 'As you said, Albanian. Ardit Jashari's not there. I'm pretty sure he won't be on any photos I've got.'

'So who are they?'

'Uh-uh,' said Vedra. 'That's as much as you're getting. And I'm only telling you that much because you need to know they're not the sort of people you can afford to be curious about. I've no idea what you might be thinking of doing but if it involves asking questions about them, even showing a passing interest, you need to forget it. You ever hear their name again? Walk away.'

'On your say-so?'

'On my say-so.'

Billy thought about it, even though he'd already decided what to do in this eventuality.

'So you're not going to explain how this ties in with Aimi?'

'None of your business, Billy, I told you – you need to leave it well alone.'

Billy picked up one of the discarded daisies and slipped the stem into the corner of his mouth as he got to his feet.

'Then I'll go and ask someone who *will* tell me.'

'Like who?'

'Like your old man.'

He started to walk off, even though he knew he'd already got Vedra's attention.

'I think you're forgetting something. You go anywhere near my father with any of this and you and your friends can kiss your investors goodbye.'

Billy didn't even pause, let alone stop and turn round.

'Oh, I think we moved way past that the moment these guys showed up.'

He kept walking. Mental fingers crossed.

'What the hell's that supposed to mean?' Vedra called. Billy knew he wouldn't want to get to his feet and come after him because they both understood what that simple gesture would signify. He also knew that if he was wrong in his assumptions he was gambling with not just his own future but that of Karun and Zak as well. But he knew he was right. He'd seen it in Vedra's face. So he kept walking.

'You think I'm bluffing?' said Vedra, having to raise his voice now.

Billy ignored him.

'Hey . . . are you listening to . . . Jesus!'

Still he kept walking, pretty sure now that Vedra was on his feet and coming after him. Ten paces further he felt a hand grab his shoulder and turn him round.

'I swear you are the most . . . *aggravating* person to talk to,' said Vedra. Billy stood where he was, looked pointedly at the hand on his shoulder until it dropped away.

'How would you know? You never tell me anything.'

'I'll tell you this much. Forget about the investors. Think about Aimi instead for one second.'

'What about her?'

'If you care about her half as much as you claim you do, you can't go to my father about this.'

'Because?'

Vedra took a sharp intake of breath, let it out in what sounded almost like a hiss.

'I can't tell you.'

Billy waited. Three seconds, four. And walked off again.

'Billy!'

'Give him a call, Joe!' he called over his shoulder. 'Tell him I'll be there in twenty.'

'I can't tell you, Billy.'

Keep walking.

'Billy!'

Don't look round.

'ALL RIGHT, DAMMIT!'

He stopped. Turned to face Vedra, his head tilted to one side as if inviting him to continue.

I'm listening.

That evening he did two things. First, he rang Karun and Zak to say he was going to have to take a couple of weeks. He toyed very briefly with the idea of using Mia and the funeral as an excuse, claiming he needed to have a complete break and get his head straight before coming back to work, but they deserved better than that. He talked to them for half an hour, told them what had happened. What he knew. And what he suspected to be true. By the end of the call, he'd been proved right. They did deserve better. Miles better.

Then he went back to the house and asked Matthew if it would be OK to stay on for a week or so. He offered his best attempt at a gracious apology for his outburst the previous evening, explaining that the sign had caught him unawares. He'd had a chance while he was on the beach to think about things and realised he was bang out of order. Matthew could do what he liked with the house, of course he could. It was bought primarily with his money. His name was on the deeds and if he decided coping with the memories was going to be too much, it was no one else's business.

But if it was all the same to him, Billy said, he'd like a few days to go through the place and salvage a few mementoes. Also, because there wouldn't be anything to draw him back here with Mia having gone and the house soon to follow, this might well be the last few days he'd spend not just here but in Rye itself and the surrounding area. He fancied spending a week or two revisiting some of his old haunts for one final time. He said he'd understand if Matthew didn't want him around and would stay in a hotel in town.

Matthew accepted the apology with obvious relief and said Billy was welcome to stay for as long as he needed. He launched into a convoluted explanation which he clearly intended to serve as justification for putting the house on the market so quickly. Billy hardly listened, begged him silently, patient smile locked in place, to shut the fuck up and stop picking at the scab. When he'd finished, he forced himself to go over and give him a hug to show just how sorry he was because Billy didn't normally do hugs. And when Matthew suggested they get a takeaway and a few beers, have a night in, drink a toast to Mia and draw a line under any differences they might have had in the past, he smiled and said that sounded like a great idea.

He could do this.

And later he'd get an early night and start planning what he needed to do next.

Because the clock was ticking.

26

SUNDAY 10TH APRIL 2016

'Oh REF-ER-EEEE! NO WAY! Did you see that? He was on his way down long before anyone touched him, for Christ's sake. WHAT'S THE MATTER WITH YOU, REFEREE? Mickey ... MICKEY! Who're you picking up? Big guy in the middle. WHO'S GOT THE BIG GUY?'

Mac threw his hands in the air and looked around in disbelief as the aforementioned *big guy* made an unopposed run to the near post and flashed a glancing header just over the bar. Billy chuckled and put an arm around his shoulder. He remembered being on the receiving end of a few touchline roastings himself when he was younger. He knew the bark was much worse than the bite and that Mac would be the first to buy the offending player a drink after the game.

'How long left?' Mac asked.

Billy looked at his watch.

'Ten minutes or so. Still time.'

Mac shook his head.

'We could stay out here till next Sunday and we'd still be one down. Didn't bring your boots with you by any chance?'

Billy laughed. Apart from the apparently trivial matter that he wasn't even registered with the club anymore, he doubted very much he'd have been able to exert much influence on the game in ten minutes. He also suspected that he'd become a much better player in Mac's memory than he'd ever been on the pitch. Mac had been with the club for years and the eleven playing at any given moment somehow never matched up in his eyes to teams of the past.

'You need TJ out there,' Billy told him. 'The big guy wouldn't be quite so keen to make an impression if he had TJ marking him.'

'TJ.' Two initials drawn out into a long groan.

'He still turn out?'

'Once in a blue moon. Got bigger fish to fry now. Bloody headcase, he was. Kicked everything that moved.' Mac bent down and put a roll of tape back in the first-aid kit. 'Shame about his old man though.'

Billy was watching the keeper take the goal kick and the comment almost didn't register.

'Whose dad? TJ's?'

'Had a stroke last night. I was chatting with the ref before the game. He's a paramedic apparently . . . amongst other things!'

This was news to Billy. The last thing he expected to hear.

'So how serious is it?'

'Serious enough. Not looking too clever, by all accounts.'

'Jesus.'

Billy cast his mind back just a few months to that almost surreal afternoon when he'd had tea with Jack Vedra and his sons. He remembered the tall, imposing man with the toothpaste-ad smile and the handshake that left its mark without trying too hard to impress. It had occurred to him at the time that he looked in remarkably good shape for a man of his advanced years. There had certainly been no intimations of mortality about him – he looked as if he could carry on running his own private fiefdom indefinitely.

He wondered what this would mean for the whole Vedra business empire, whether Joe would automatically step up and take over or whether the succession plan – because there would surely be one with an enterprise as vast and sprawling as that – allowed for a different scenario. He thought about how Joe had handled himself in Mason's Field only two days ago, the way he'd been the first to blink when he should have had the balls to see how far Billy was prepared to take it. Billy would have been the first to admit he was no authority on what it takes to run a multi-million-pound corporation but he suspected whatever it was, Joe didn't have it.

When his mobile rang, he wondered for the briefest of moments whether it was Joe calling to put him in the picture. If his father was as seriously ill as Mac had suggested, it might loosen the reins a little for his eldest son and give him more room for manoeuvre in their joint search for Aimi. As long as he had to keep looking over his shoulder and making sure he left no traces for his father to stumble across, Joe was rowing the boat with one hand tied behind his back. Maybe there was a new conversation to be had here.

But when he checked the screen, he recognised the number as Matthew's.

'Billy!' he said, sounding breathless.

'Yeah, I've heard. Mac's just told me.'

'Heard what? No, forget that. Listen – where are you?'

'Hastings. Watching my old team play, remember?'

'Oh yeah, right. Forgot. Listen, you need to get back here. Right now.'

'Sorry,' he said, putting a finger in the other ear to block out the shouting coming from the touchline as yet another refereeing decision failed to meet with the spectators' approval. 'I thought I told you. I'm having a drink with some of the boys after the game. If this is about lunch, I'll probably grab something in the pub.'

'Forget lunch. We've been turned over.'

Billy frowned.

'We've been what?'

'Burgled, mate. There's been a break-in.'

Matthew was waiting by the open front door when Billy arrived, leaning against the door jamb, arms folded. Billy parked Mia's car in the drive and followed him inside.

They went to Billy's room first. The moment he established that both laptops were no longer where he'd left them, he went straight to the wardrobe and stood on tiptoe to reach the broad top shelf, where a large number of books from his youth were stacked in alphabetical order by author's surname, each one with *Billy Orr* printed inside the front cover, immediately above the date when he'd bought it. He chose the pile with *Catcher In the Rye* on top and pulled those dozen or so novels out of the wardrobe. Then he reached through the space he'd created and groped around behind the next pile of books until his fingers located an object not much bigger than a paperback itself with a glossy black cover.

'6TB external hard drive,' he said, kissing it. 'Always keep everything backed up on here. Losing the laptops is a pain but it could've been a lot worse. How about you? They clean out your office too?'

'Yep.'

'Everything?'

'Pretty much. Desktop, laptop. Whole load of papers and files I was working on. Nothing sensitive, luckily – no work-related documents or I'd have been in deep shit. We're not meant to take home anything that's not encrypted and I tend to be a bit casual about that sort of thing. Never occurred to me anyone might want to break in here.'

'So do we know how they got in?' asked Billy.

Matthew ran his hands three or four times through his buzz cut, massaged his scalp with the tips of his fingers.

'Back door,' he said. 'They must have picked the lock. Moment I got back from the gym, I went through to the kitchen to get a drink and they'd done such a professional job on it, I didn't even notice. There's just this tiny nick there you can hardly see and yet, when it came to my office door, they smashed their way through the bloody thing. Must have brought a sledgehammer with them – nearly took it off its hinges. And the weird thing is, the rest of the place they've left completely undisturbed. I mean, even my wallet. It was on my desk. There's getting on for three hundred quid in there, not to mention all my bank cards. Never touched it.'

'So it was definitely the laptops and your desktop they were after.'

'Don't forget the files. And in broad daylight too – that takes some nerve. I know we're a bit isolated out here but they must have left a vehicle of some sort out front all the time they were in here. We could so easily have come back at any moment.'

'And how did they know we were out, for that matter?' asked Billy. 'I could have been having a Sunday morning lie-in.'

'Like I said. Took some bottle.'

Billy looked around from where he was sitting as if to confirm Matthew's assessment of the way they'd left the rest of the lounge. It certainly didn't look much like a crime scene.

'I take it the police haven't been yet. Did they give any indication as to when we can expect them?'

'Ah,' said Matthew. 'About that.'

Billy put Mia's car keys on the table between them.

'What's that supposed to mean? You have phoned them, haven't you?'

'No.'

'Why not?'

'Well, for one thing, I wanted to get you back here first so you could check what's missing.'

'And for another?'

Matthew paused before walking over to the shelf above the fireplace. He picked up a plain brown A4 envelope and brought it over to where Billy was waiting. Watching.

'They left this on the desk in my office,' he said, holding it out for Billy to take. He looked at it suspiciously.

'What is it?'

'Here. Read it.'

Billy hesitated, then took the envelope from him. He opened the flap and was in the act of taking the sheet of paper from inside when he stopped suddenly.

'What about fingerprints?' he said. 'Shouldn't we put gloves on or something?'

Matthew shook his head.

'Irrelevant. The police aren't going to see it.'

Billy stared at him for a few seconds, then slipped finger and thumb inside the envelope and carefully extracted the single sheet of A4 paper, folded once across the middle. It was short and to the point. Typed. No form of address. Just a few lines, centred text, plain old Times New Roman.

WE ARE BORROWING, NOT STEALING.
DO NOT CONTACT THE POLICE.
YOU WILL GET THEM BACK BEFORE THE END OF THE WEEK.
DO AS WE SAY OR THEY WILL BE DESTROYED.
APOLOGIES FOR THE INCONVENIENCE.

'They've obviously got a sense of humour,' said Billy, folding the note and replacing it in the envelope. 'They must think we were born yesterday. You can't be serious about not contacting the police.'

'I am.'

'I'll phone them, then. It's my laptops too.'

'I'm not sure that's such a good idea.'

'You've got to be kidding me. You're not buying all that crap in the note, are you? You honestly think, after all the risks they took to break in here, they're just going to hand everything back afterwards?'

'Maybe, maybe not,' said Matthew, not sounding too convincing from where Billy was standing. 'But what we do know for sure is if we don't do what they say, we definitely won't see the machines again.'

'So what?' Billy laughed, spreading his arms and shrugging his shoulders. 'Jesus, the insurance will cover the cost of replacing them and even if it doesn't for some reason, neither of us is going to be bankrupt if we have to do it out of our own pockets. They're business expenses. We'll just write it off against tax. What matters is finding out who these morons are and the sooner we get the police involved, the more chance we'll have of that happening. I can't believe we're even having this conversation.'

He waited for some sort of response from Matthew, who was looking at the floor, hands thrust deep into the pockets of his sweatpants. He looked distinctly uncomfortable.

'What?' said Billy.

Still no response.

'OK – what am I missing here?'

Matthew sank into his armchair and started untying the laces of his trainers.

'I . . . look, I think I know who did this.'

'Who?'

'I'm pretty sure it's Joe Vedra.'

Billy burst out laughing.

'Oh yeah – right!'

'I'm serious.'

'Then you need to see someone. Joe Vedra? What the hell would he want with our laptops?'

'He came here three weeks ago.'

'And?'

'He . . . wanted something.'

'Wanted something.'

'I said I couldn't help him – couldn't, not wouldn't. And he wasn't very happy about it.'

'Could you be a little more cryptic, maybe?'

Matthew heaved a sigh as he pulled off the trainers.

'Look, this goes nowhere, right? You can't tell anyone.'

And there you go, thought Billy. You have to be some special kind of stupid to say something like that and expect people to keep their word. Like the other person's going to say, *oh, you'd better not tell me then 'cos I'll just pass it on to the next person who comes into the room.*

'OK,' he said, and took a seat at the end of the sofa as Matthew popped the tab on a can of Pepsi.

'He said he wanted my help. Said he'd heard I'd taken on a . . . particular client and he wanted information I wasn't in a position to give. I mean, I knew the answers because I'd been the only person dealing with this client but I wasn't allowed to say anything. Legal professional privilege. He told me he was sure I could find a way around that sort of problem if I put my mind to it and when I stood my ground he more or less asked me how much I valued my job here. I mean, no outright threat, just a lot of insinuations, hinting at the positives that might come my way if I helped him out as opposed to the grief I might be bringing on myself if I didn't.'

Billy remembered his conversation with Joe Vedra in The New Inn in Winchelsea and how he'd gradually ramped up the pressure. If anyone understood what Matthew was referring to here, he did. It didn't mean he was about to change his opinion though.

'And what did you say?'

'I told him the conversation was over and he should leave.'

'Oh, I bet that went down well.'

'Sure. He suggested I might like to go and talk to my superiors about it and said he hoped to hear from me soon.'

'And did you?' asked Billy.

'What, hear from him?'

'Talk to your superiors.'

'Yes. They backed me. Said I'd done the right thing.'

'Better watch your back then. Isn't a vote of confidence from the chairman usually the kiss of death?'

'I know I'm not out of the woods by a long chalk. I'm not stupid.'

He swore as he managed to spill some of the drink down the front of his exercise top, then realised it was going in the wash anyway and merely dabbed at it with his hand.

'So you think he's hoping he'll find what he needs amongst the stuff he's taken?'

'I can't think of a better explanation for someone breaking in, taking just our laptops and leaving everything else.'

'And will he? Find what he's looking for?'

'No. Those files weren't among the ones I brought home.'

Billy paused for a moment to take stock.

'So who was the client?'

'I can't tell you that any more than I could tell him. It's privileged information.'

'I'm not asking for details of anything you discussed. Just who it was.'

'Same thing. Still can't tell you.'

'So did he say how he knew you'd taken on this client in the first place?'

Matthew sighed.

'Didn't need to. There's this paralegal who used to research and prepare legal documents for us. We had to get rid of her because we suspected she was doing a few deals on the side, selling information to interested parties. Professional misconduct. Automatic grounds for dismissal if not criminal charges. We gave her the choice of leaving immediately or being reported to the authorities and she chose to go, which tells a story, I'd have thought. I think it's pretty clear now where she chose as her first port in a storm.'

'And you can't tell me what it was he wanted to know?'

'No.'

'Even though we both know this client was Aimi?'

Matthew paused and wagged a finger at Billy.

'You don't know anything of the sort.'

'Oh come off it, Matthew – who else is it going to be?'

'You can keep banging on about it as much as you like, I'm not going to start playing twenty questions with you or confirming any wild theories you might come up with. I'm just saying, it's going to be some coincidence if he's sniffing around to try to find out what I know *and* our laptops get stolen – that's all.'

'I thought you said it was three weeks ago. You think Joe Vedra would wait that long?'

'He might if he thought it would look less suspicious.'

Billy thought about continuing the argument but decided there was little point. If Matthew had enough about him to stand up to Joe Vedra when he was trying to be persuasive, he wasn't going to cave in under pressure from his brother-in-law.

He snatched up the car keys from the table and got to his feet.

'OK – let's go pay him a visit.'

'Who – Joe Vedra?' said Matthew, almost choking on his drink. 'Are you kidding? You can't just go barging in there.'

'I can if he's got my laptop.'

'Says who? And do you honestly think it's going to be at his place, even if they let us in? Think, for Christ's sake.'

'So I'm supposed to do what? Sit here and wait till he's finished trawling through our laptops and decides he's ready to hand them back? What makes you so sure he'll do that, anyway? If what you say is true, he's going to be mightily pissed off when he doesn't find what he's expecting to. He'll probably just get rid of them to spite you.'

'If he does, he does,' said Matthew. 'Look, like you said, we can replace them. If that puts you in a difficult position, I'll cover it. You won't be out of pocket – in fact, you can pick your own machines – top of the range. Just give me till this time next week. If he's on the level about what he says, by then we'll have them back. If he's not, I'll go out and replace them. But if we call the police, it's going to cause problems for me on a professional level. You don't drag the Vedra name into some grubby little burglary that the press will make a meal of and get away with it. And if my bosses have to choose between me and the Vedra empire, who do you think is going to get thrown to the wolves?'

Billy started to answer, then stopped himself.

'One week, Billy. That's all I'm asking.'

'And what if you're wrong? What if it's not the Vedras?'

'Really? Who else is it going to be?'

Billy thought about mentioning the Albanians, wondered whether it was the right moment to explore whether Matthew knew anything about their sudden appearance on the scene. Decided against it. Instead he milked the moment for all it was worth, waiting until he felt Matthew had been left floundering for long enough. 'One week,' he said, sending the lifebelt spinning out above the spray and into the water.

Always so much more satisfying when they think you're doing them a favour.

PART FOUR

27

MONDAY 25TH APRIL 2016

Two weeks on.

Four o'clock in the afternoon on the sort of Monday that gives April its reputation for unpredictability. Fragile sunshine which never quite manages to convince. Sudden cloudbursts which mist up car interiors and bring wipers onto double speed, then vanish as suddenly as they came, leaving drivers to contend with the spray from the road surface. Alternating spells of gleaming light reflected off puddles and almost Stygian gloom. In a film the camera would be trained on the rain inching its way down windows. Hazy filter. Subdued lighting. Soundtrack adagio – slow and mournful. Oboes and strings.

And against this backdrop four men separately are contemplating mistakes made, opportunities missed, lives irrevocably altered. Wishing they might be granted the chance to turn back the clock and have the last few months again.

As if things might turn out differently second time around.

As if.

Billy is on the train from St. Pancras, heading for Ashford International. From there he'll take his usual connecting train to Rye and spend the night there. Once he's done everything he's there to do, he'll head back to London, knowing he'll be leaving his old stomping ground – he can't quite bring himself to call it home – for the last time. There won't be anything to draw him back here anymore.

Mother – gone.

Mia – gone.

Matthew – seriously?

Aimi?

If he could turn back the clock . . .

He'd go back to that Saturday morning in Tenterden. If he had carte blanche, he'd go even further, right the way back to that afternoon and evening in Mason's Field and this time he wouldn't hold back. He'd ask her to stay – *beg* her not to go to London. To hell with worrying about spoiling the mood of the moment. He knows now that the mood of the next twelve years is what's at stake here.

But allowing himself carte blanche won't alter the fact that Aimi wouldn't have listened anyway. Her dancing would have come first – he knows that now. Far better to settle for that Saturday meeting in Tesco, or maybe even better the Sunday afternoon on Camber Sands. He'd find a way to persuade her not to go . . . somehow. There were always alternatives – had to be. He hadn't been able to see any first time around because she'd caught him on the hop, shocked him when she showed him the bruises and told him what she'd been subjected to. That had driven from his mind all thoughts other than the certainty that she had to get away from here.

But if he could have the time again, knowing what he does now, he'd be better prepared. That afternoon on the beach was the crucial moment, the point in time when stepping back from the brink was still possible. She'd gone to the Albanians because she was mad as hell and so set on making sure someone would pay that she ended up lashing out and taking everyone else down with her, but it didn't have to be that way. However bad the alternatives might have seemed, he'd have found a way to make her understand that running away was never going to solve anything. The further she ran, the bigger the gulf between the two of them.

Things could have turned out so differently. Now he's left dealing with the fallout.

He's been looking ahead to what he has to do in the next twenty-four hours. He's not sure when exactly – there are too many variables right now. But nothing is unknowable forever. Secrets have a way of sneaking out. Not so long ago he was at the mercy of events, not sure who was telling the truth about what. Now he knows. Everyone was lying. He shouldn't be surprised. The moment something important is at stake, the natural first instinct is to cover yourself, examine where you are vulnerable. Then you patch it up as quickly as you can and hope no one has noticed and if there's no way round it . . . you lie.

He's not about to take the high ground here or feign indignation because he's done the same thing often enough. But he knows now that Joe Vedra has lied, not about the Albanians and their part in this but about the real extent of his involvement. Matthew has lied too, and not just by omission either. Jack Vedra, ironically, has probably played with a straighter bat than most but he's the catalyst in the whole sorry mess so he's not going to come out of it with any great credit. And from what Billy's been hearing, he's pretty much a spent force now anyway.

And Aimi.

He turns away, doesn't want to go there just now.

Can't.

On the connecting train to Rye, he runs his fingers through the fresh haircut, still so unfamiliar to the touch, even though it's been over a week now. He watches out of the window as the fields slide past, the rain zigzagging across the windows and partially obscuring his view. It's not so long ago that they used to make him feel hemmed in, but not any longer. He finds it hard to believe they used to have such a dispiriting effect on him. They're just fields. There are no wisps of early evening mist beckoning him on, luring him in. For years now he's found this journey unsettling at best and verging on debilitating at times and now that he's decided he'll never need to make it again there's nothing. And maybe that's the point, he thinks to himself. Maybe the memories and mental strings that bound him to the place are broken now for good and he can get on with the rest of his life. The next time he takes a train out of St. Pancras International, it won't be the Southeastern service – it could just as easily be the Eurostar and he'll be free to go wherever the mood takes him.

This new-found sense of purpose has its roots in one thing and that's the fact that he now knows everything. And this, he tells himself, is what absolute conviction and clarity can do for a person. There's a freedom that comes from knowledge.

He thinks he might be mumbling from time to time because the girl in the seat opposite got up and moved to a different carriage a few minutes ago, as if not quite sure of him. He doesn't care. He needs to go through it all, time and time again, to make sure he has everything straight in his mind. He can't afford to be derailed tomorrow by the slightest thing. It's got to be word-perfect. Fact-perfect. Pose-perfect.

Just one more nail to hammer home and he can leave for good.

Jack Vedra is lying motionless and silent in his private hospital bed, surrounded by his thoughts. Silent by choice rather than because speech is beyond him. Facial flexibility is returning incrementally. If he pushes himself, he is now up to producing a series of half-formed sentences which at least make some sort of slurred sense and if all else fails he has other ways of getting a message across through sheer force of personality if he can summon up the energy. These attempts take a lot out of him though, and that's a level of self-indulgence he can't afford any longer. Besides, there's something intensely dispiriting about putting yourself through all that effort, just to sound like something that's crawled out of the swamp. The fight, in all honesty, has gone out of him.

They tell him he's *on the mend* but it's a curious definition of the word. The first three to four months, they insist, are the crucial ones because this is when the most rapid recovery takes place. If that's true, it's the most discouraging thing they could have told him because any progress has been painfully slow. It's been two weeks now and there's been enough progress maybe to bring the prospect of a weekend home visit a little nearer, but for all their smiles and encouragement, he knows. He just knows. The stroke has taken from him things that it will never give back. Things that go way beyond the quantifiable by which the specialists and rehab people set so much store. There's something broken inside.

He's doing all they ask of him. The instructions have been crystal clear. The key to any sort of recovery is rest. Rest and therapy. And physio – physio coming out of his ears. Visitors are warned to keep conversations light and undemanding. Anything relating to business is strictly off-limits which, to his way of thinking, rather takes away the point of having a conversation in the first place. He's never been one for small talk – visits, even from his wife and sons, tend to drift off into long spells of awkward silence with each party desperately trying to think of something worthwhile to say that won't overtax him. He's being treated like a four-year-old.

This apparently is how life will be for the foreseeable future. He's going to have to find new interests and adjust to a way of life that's anathema to him, a different *pace* of life, because his days of empire-building are over. He wishes now – of course he does – that he'd been able to hand over the reins in an orderly fashion some time ago. Might possibly have done so if he'd seen even vague hints that Joseph was ready to step up to the mark. He's paying a severe price now for stalling, trying to buy time for his eldest son to develop the kind of aura and charisma needed to carry off a position like his with some conviction. The longer he's delayed, though, the more apparent it's been that he's pushing rocks up a hill. Joseph is bright, has ideas, so many boxes ticked but he lacks the fire, the backbone to make that step up. He's not ruthless or devious enough to be a leader of men. The eternal lieutenant.

Not like that wife of his. She has it in spades – and he uses the word *has* advisedly because he's never believed at any stage that she's committed suicide. He's been happy to persuade the authorities that it's all down to a domestic upset between her and Joseph and put pressure on them to back off because the last thing he needs is for word to get out about the way he's been taken for a ride by his own daughter-in-law. The sharks would soon start circling if they sniffed blood in the water and as for what the media would do with it, it doesn't bear thinking about. He'd be a laughing stock.

First time he met her he knew she had something about her, knew she was going to be more than a match for Joseph. He'd watched her with a sort of amused tolerance instead of taking her seriously and ended up underestimating her as a result. Never thought she'd come up with a stunt like this. Not for one moment.

If he could turn back the clock . . .

He knows he should never have taken on the Liri Group. If he had his time again, he'd work with them, come to some sort of compromise over the Upland Acres development scheme rather than opting for full-frontal assault. The problem was, it was the world's worst-kept secret that they're financed by Albanian money and Jack himself is old-school. Mafias seem to be springing up all over the place in recent years – they'll have one in Norwich next. In the old days you knew exactly who you were doing business with and there might be sharp practice and a few strokes pulled here and there but that was to be expected, even admired. Everyone understood how the game was played and you knew your place. These days you never know exactly who you're talking to or the lengths others might be prepared to go to. The Liri Group were showing just a little too much ambition for his liking and needed slapping down. As far as Jack was concerned, cosying up to them was the thin end of the wedge. Far better to put your foot down from the outset and show them who they're dealing with.

He made the wrong call and they've been scrambling frantically ever since to repair the damage. Wounded pride. An old man's folly. Hubris. Call it what you will but the fact remains his error in judgement is the reason for the mess they're in. Should have seen it coming and didn't. And now he's left a bloody great mess that he ought to be clearing up, not just because he's responsible for what's happened but because he's always been the only one with the experience and the drive and the know-how to do this. Problem is, that's not the case anymore. Experience and know-how, yes. The drive? Two out of three won't cut it and he knows it.

Shouldn't have taken her dream away from her either. He knew how much that bloody dance school meant to her, how much time and money she'd invested in planning for it. If he'd been thinking straight there was probably some other way of getting together the money he needed to see off the Liri Group but he'd been under real pressure at the time and it looked like the perfect quick fix. There had been no problem with any of the properties in his wife's name or Thomas's, but they needed Aimi's too – and she had always been different. Should have known.

Should have known.

Too late now though. It can't be any of his concern anymore. Younger heads are going to have to sort it all out. As soon as he's well enough, he'll cash out and get on with his life, what's left of it. Several years ago, he and his wife bought a condo in St. Pete's, Florida with a view to spending the English winters there. Best-laid plans – she's ended up going on her own more often than not. Always something cropping up that made it impossible for him to spend time there with her. The irony is that he now has all the time in the world and won't be allowed to travel. It's going to be a long time before they'll give him the all-clear for a transatlantic flight but the moment they do he'll make the trip, get some sun, clear his head and maybe try to make sense of what's happened with the benefit of a bit of perspective which distance and the passing of time will bring.

For now, though . . . that seems a very long way off.

He turns and watches the rain as it trickles down the window. Picks one drop and bets himself it will reach the bottom of the window before the others.

He loses again, by quite a margin.

It's a disappointing habit to be picking up at his time of life.

Matthew turns off the in-flight entertainment and tries to find room for his headphones in the storage compartment in front of him. He's two and a half hours into the flight and unable to settle to anything. The film he's been watching is ponderous and trying too hard to be worthy. He could start a different one or listen to some of the extensive music library, or maybe watch a handful of the sitcoms and documentaries that are on offer, but he suspects the result will be the same. Nothing much is going to hold his interest for any length of time and he'd be better off dozing if he thought for one minute that might be possible.

By rights he ought to be able to sleep through the entire flight because he's exhausted, physically and emotionally. His mind is too active though – it's been buzzing ever since he first received the small package by special delivery on Thursday morning containing the disposable phone and the message which was activated the moment he turned it on. The instructions were clear – fly to New York, go to the Archer Hotel on West 44th Street and take the room that was reserved for him. Stay there and do nothing, go nowhere, call no one. Just sit there and wait to be contacted.

He remembers the excitement. The relief. And he's done everything he was asked to do since then but the way things have panned out it feels like a huge waste of a weekend. His body clock is all over the place and he wouldn't mind if he could see the point of it all but it's difficult to escape the conclusion that someone's messing him about. And he'd very much like to know why.

If he could turn back the clock . . .

He'd push the metaphorical one-dollar bill back across the table. He honestly would. He thought he'd developed good instincts that would serve him well when he needed them but they've let him down badly this time. He can't bring himself to feel hard done by because he doesn't deserve any sympathy. A wide-eyed rookie would have given this a wide berth and here he is, not only in the hole but still digging, still failing to learn from his mistakes, still imagining it's all going to work out right in the end. It's too embarrassing for words.

His flight gets in at eight thirty. By the time he's cleared Heathrow, it'll be far too late to put his trust in Southern Rail. He'll grab a room at one of the airport hotels and travel back tomorrow morning. He's not due back in work until Wednesday and by then he hopes he'll have had another message to explain what the hell went wrong. In the meantime, he needs sleep, if he can just find a way to stop his brain from flicking through the possible explanations.

He turns his face towards the window and looks out across a sea of cotton-wool clouds, their edges tinged with orange. He has no awareness of the rain beneath them but it's difficult to avoid the feeling that this is just a taste of what's to come.

A storm is brewing somewhere.

And he's adrift in a rudderless boat.

Joe Vedra carefully lowers the phone and sets it down on the table. He sits back in his chair and closes his eyes. Counts to ten. Tries to compose himself.

But the tears squeeze their way out anyway.

His own personalised rainy-day window.

It's over now. They'll find her eventually. He's been entertaining hopes all this time, against all available evidence and in defiance of any logic, that he'll manage to track her down and bring her back in time to repair the damage she's done, but this latest stunt of hers will flush her out into the open far too early. She's obviously lost it. She's a sharp, incisive thinker who doesn't panic easily and he's been hoping those qualities might be enough to enable her to stay one step ahead of those on her trail but she's been out there, effectively on her own, for so long now and he can only guess at the pressures she must be under. It looks as if they're starting to take their toll.

Once might be OK. Once you might just get away with. *Might*. Twice and you've no chance. There's not a person alive who hasn't heard the story about the kid who cried wolf. She must have known, if she sat down and thought about it, that there was no way people would buy the same vanishing act twice. He can't even imagine what's pushed her into doing this but if she's right and she really has no alternative other than to disappear for a second time, couldn't she at least show a little originality in her choice of method? Drowning? Clothes left on the beach?

He remembers his father a while back when Billy Orr came to the house. *It's who she is,* he'd said. *It's what she does.* Allowing herself to be defined so easily is asking for trouble.

And if she thinks the fact she's in the US – some place off Portland, Maine apparently, although Christ knows how she wound up there – if she thinks that's the safer option, she couldn't be more wrong. It's taken them about five minutes to work out her ID was fake – some girl who'd died aged five in a house fire for Christ's sake – and once they'd gone through the house she'd been renting and taken prints from every room and DNA from her hairbrush in the bathroom and a used glass she'd left on the coffee table and then run them through the system, look how long it took them to come up with a match for an ongoing investigation in the UK. Did she think these people were amateurs?

So she's on the run again. He hasn't known her whereabouts for a long time now. He knows where he *thought* she was – where she was *supposed* to be – but New England is a hell of a long way from Marbella. He can't even take consolation from the fact that at least he's picked up her trail again because so has everyone else. It's so stupid – so unlike her.

If he could turn back the clock . . .

He'd tell her *no*, the moment she came up with the idea. He'd say *no, we'll do it this way*. He'd take her hand, walk into his father's office and stand up to him for once. Tell him, *we'll find another way. There's no way you're taking the dance school off the table.* Aimi didn't create the mess with the Liri Group, so ripping her dream away from her shouldn't have been an option. If he'd had the balls to back her then, things would never have got this far.

He sits there in the armchair and tries to visualise where Aimi might be at this very moment, what her next move might be. He knows it's pointless. He had no idea she was in Maine, so how is he meant to know where she'll go from there. Even so, he closes his eyes and tries to picture her. On a plane, maybe – that would be a result, especially if she's on her way out of the US. From now on, every second she spends there is fraught with danger. He hopes she won't make the mistake of thinking that because it's such a vast country it will be easy for her to hide away until everyone's had enough of searching for her and gives up. That would be almost as misguided as opting for the same disappearing act when so many better alternatives were available to her, especially with all that money at her disposal.

He knows he's lost her.

He knows what she's done.

But that doesn't mean he'll stop looking.

28

TUESDAY 26TH APRIL 2016

Matthew pays the taxi driver and wheels his case down the drive. He's only been gone since Friday and he might have got away with just a rucksack but for all the work he's taken with him. He decided when packing that if there was a strong possibility he was going to be spending the better part of the weekend in his hotel room, he might as well make good use of it.

He takes his keys out of his jacket pocket and lets himself in through the front door. There's a small pile of mail on the mat, most of it junk, and he sorts absent-mindedly through this as he walks into the living room. He drops it onto the coffee table and is about to take his case upstairs when he happens to glance out of the window and sees the sunlounger in the middle of the lawn.

He's startled by this. The loungers have been in the summer house at the end of the garden since last September and who-ever has put the chair there must have known where the key is kept. He's already decided it can only be Billy when he sees him emerge from the summer house with a second lounger under his arm. He's barefoot in a sleeveless T-shirt and shorts, which strikes

Matthew as a little underdressed. It's warmer than some of the weather they've had recently but it's not exactly mid-July.

He bangs on the window to get his attention and Billy waves without looking up as he sets the lounger up next to his own, facing the sun which has seen off the early-morning mist and most of the clouds. He looks different and Matthew realises it's his hair. It's actually a big improvement, he decides. It was always an unruly mess, far too long, most of the time. Made him look like a hangover from the flower-power era. Now he's had it not only pruned but shaved into a buzz cut which resembles his own. The sincerest form of flattery, he thinks.

Quite what Billy is doing here is a mystery. If he's honest, he's not altogether happy to see him. In terms of the demands made on emotional resilience, Billy is high-maintenance. Mia was the glue that held everything together and since she died they've made less of an effort to keep up the pretence that there's something there worth preserving. Billy was her brother, her surrogate son and by extension his, so he worked hard for many years to establish a relationship that's sustainable, keeping friction to a minimum, as much for her sake as anything. He's more than paid his dues. He's never been blinded though to the fact that they are very different individuals, totally dependent on her role as lynchpin.

In most respects they're chalk and cheese. He finds Billy's informal, laid-back approach to life irresponsible. OK, he's not afraid of hard work – he'll give him that much – but it has to be work he enjoys and life just isn't like that. Put anything in front of him that doesn't immediately fire up his imagination and he could procrastinate for England. He's a *mañana* merchant who leaves dirty plates and glasses and clothing lying around for someone else to pick up and dismisses anyone who asks for a little co-operation as anal. In particular, he's always mocked what Matthew does for a living as *establishment arse-licking*, happy as he was for it to pay off his overdrafts during that two-year holiday he had at university. He's sure Billy would have his own list of grievances if they ever went at it, because he's never short of an answer, has always been too quick-witted and sharp-tongued for his own good.

That's why Matthew is both surprised and more than mildly irritated to see him taking over the back garden as if he owned the place. When everything missing after the break-in was returned anonymously a few days later – along with an apologetic note which felt like the ultimate piss-take – Billy had come home from London to collect his laptops, turning up in a rented minibus. He'd proceeded to pile into it everything that belonged to him, along with a number of mementoes and objects of sentimental value, and it felt like the end of an era somehow. The one thing he didn't do, unfortunately, was hand over his keys – Matthew will make sure he does so this time.

Billy looks up now and points to the lounger with a sweep of his right arm. Matthew shrugs his shoulders and mouths the word *what*, so Billy points at him, then at the lounger and finally at his mobile which he's holding up. Matthew decides he might as well get this over with. Maybe Billy's only here for the morning. He can live with that. When he goes this time, it will be for good.

He turns away from the window, takes off his jacket and drapes it over the chair, and heads for the back door. There's a sudden flash of Mia saying, *deep breath, love,* and it stings him as he turns the handle and steps outside.

*

'What's with the haircut then?'

Billy's sitting on one of the loungers with the backrest at an angle of forty-five degrees. He doesn't look up from the mobile into which he's typing at a ridiculous speed.

'Fancied a change,' is all he says.

'It's an improvement anyway.'

Matthew takes the other chair without adjusting the back. He's not planning on staying out here any longer than necessary.

'With you in a moment,' Billy says, putting the finishing touches to whatever it is he's doing. Matthew closes his eyes and allows the sun to work its magic for a minute or two. He slept much better than expected last night at the airport hotel, managing to push all the anxieties and conjecture to one side for long enough for his weary mind to recharge its batteries. He woke up feeling groggy but has grown into the day as the hours have slipped by and he now feels ready for anything. Even Billy.

A couple of minutes elapse while he enjoys the sensation of sun on his face. Billy rests the mobile on the grass next to his chair and lies back as well, eyes hidden behind dark glasses. Most people in Billy's situation would probably offer some sort of explanation at this point as to what they were doing there but Matthew has long since given up on any thought of measuring Billy by the standards of others.

'Surprised to see you here,' he says. 'You back for any reason in particular?'

'Yep.'

Matthew waits but Billy doesn't elaborate. *OK*, he thinks. *One of those moods.* He refuses to rise to it. Keeps his eyes shut and his irritation under control. *Last time*, he says to himself again, clutching the prospect to his chest like a comfort blanket.

'Not trying to get rid of you or anything but any idea how long you're staying this time?'

'Depends.'

'On what?'

'On how straight you are with me.'

'About?'

'About a number of things, actually.'

Matthew opens one eye, the one nearest to Billy.

'Is this going to be one of your clever-sod conversations by any chance? 'Cos if it is, I'm sorry, mate, but I've got better things to do.'

'Suit yourself. I'll just leave the email as it is then and you can have a cosy little chat sometime with the Vedras and the police too – whichever get to you first. My money's on TJ.'

Matthew swings his legs round and sits up slowly. Tries to look casual about it. He has no idea what Billy's up to here but if he's looking for buttons to press he's stumbled on a couple of good ones, that's for sure. He's pretty sure he's about to be subjected to another of Billy's fairy-tale perceptions of reality, a patchwork of speculative theories, cobbled together by a mind that's not quite in sync with the world around it. Still, he needs to hear him out – you never know how close his wildest imaginings might come to what's really been happening.

'And just what's that supposed to mean?' he asks, trying to inject into his expression a touch of ennui – *been here so many times before.*

Billy sits upright, swings his legs round too, so that he's facing him. Then he peels off his sunglasses, slowly. Folds them, places them at the foot of the lounger and looks Matthew in the eye.

'What it means is, I've sent a scheduled email to CID in Hastings, with both Joe and TJ copied in. I'll leave it up to them how much they think the old man should be told.'

'And what email would this be?'

'Just a summary of everything I've managed to find out about you and Aimi. Oh, and the Liri Group and the three point two million and . . . no, that's probably about it, apart from any documentary evidence I've managed to put together. Yep. I think that's it.'

Matthew has been following this with an increasing sense of despair. He wants to believe Billy's bluffing, that he doesn't know half of what he's claiming, merely seeking to wheedle more detail out of him through false pretences. He's pulled this sort of stunt so many times in the past, is very good at it. But it's the mention of the three point two million that's really floored him. Where the hell did he get that figure?

'I've set the time and date for exactly one month from now, which is pretty generous of me under the circumstances,' Billy continues in a normal, everyday tone, as if they were discussing some household transaction, not playing with the rest of Matthew's life.

'I've got a few questions I want to ask you and depending on the answers you give me, I might want to edit some of the detail in there. I can always cancel it altogether if I like what I hear or change the date so that it's sent right now if I think you're taking the proverbial. Up to you, really.'

He tilts his head to invite Matthew to respond. He tries to laugh it off.

'Is this another one of your jokes?'

'Nope. Never been more serious.'

'I haven't got the faintest idea what you're talking about. You're making no sense.'

'Humour me. You going to tell me what I need to know or not?'

'Be my guest,' says Matthew, as if he could care less. 'What do you want to know?'

He has no idea where Billy is going with this but the sooner he reins him back in the better. A china shop is no place to allow someone like him to blunder wildly about.

'OK. You won't like some of these by the way. I thought it only fair to warn you.'

'Ask away.'

'Right then – question number one.'

Billy pauses. There's a vacant look in his eyes. If Matthew didn't know him better, he'd say he was on something. That's half the problem – he should be and almost certainly isn't.

'Did you fuck her?' Billy asks quietly.

Matthew's mouth drops open. Nothing comes out at first. This is the last thing he was expecting to be asked. If this is the starting point, where the hell do they go from here?

'What?' he manages eventually.

'Simple question. Did you fuck her? Yes or no?'

Voice calm, controlled. But something there underneath.

'What sort of a question is that? Did I fuck who?'

'Aimi. Who else?'

'Aimi? No, for God's sake. Are you *mad*? Of course I didn't!'

Billy nods as if confirming something to himself. Makes a mental note.

'OK. A bit unfair not to warn you first, so I'll give you a chance to think again. Meant to say that every time you lie, I'm bringing forward the email schedule by three days. My guess is, once it reaches the Vedras and the authorities, you're going to want to be as far away from here as you can possibly be. TJ gets very upset when he feels someone's dumping on his brother so if I were you I'd be looking to keep those thirty days intact and buy yourself as much time as you possibly can. Do you want to change your answer?'

'Look, mate – I know you've been having a helluva time of it lately. We both have. You look to me like you're not taking the meds again which isn't going to be helping. You're all over the place.'

'I'm not the one who's twitching right now though, am I? I repeat – do you want to change your answer?'

'No. *No!* I didn't . . . and I can't believe you'd even dream of asking me something like that. It's ridiculous.'

'OK, so that's lie number one.'

'It's not a lie, for God's sake.'

'And yet we both know it is, so that takes you down to twenty-seven days. How far through is the house sale? How long till the money's in your account? I'd say you can't afford to lose too many more of those days before you go. Ready for another question yet?'

'No, I'm not ready – what's the point? You're just going to say it's a lie and take another three days off.'

'Not if I think it's the truth. It's up to you to convince me. OK – next one. Why?'

'Why what?'

'Why did you fuck her?'

'No, no, no,' says Matthew, shaking his head. 'We're not doing this. How can I answer that? I've already told you I didn't do it.

What possible reason can I give for doing something I haven't done?'

Billy raises a finger in acknowledgement.

'Yeah, that first lie is going to be a bit of a problem, isn't it? Maybe I ought to let you in on a little secret so we can get it out of the way once and for all. Then you can re-evaluate your tactics so far.'

Matthew eyes him warily. He's been half-expecting him to launch himself out of the lounger and come at him with both arms flailing and he'd actually prefer it if he did because that he can deal with. But there's a composure and certainty about Billy's manner that he finds unsettling. Sometimes when he's off the meds you can tell because he comes across as just that little bit too excitable. *Manic* would be too strong a word for it, but *agitated* certainly. All extremes, no middle ground. There's no trace of that here though. It's a Billy he doesn't really recognise and it's adding to the sense of impending disaster that's creeping over him.

'What secret?'

'The break-in?'

'What about it?'

'It wasn't the Vedras.'

Please, no, he thinks.

'And how would you know that?'

'Because it was me. Or to be strictly accurate it was some friends of mine, but it was my idea. I was watching a football match at the time, if you remember.'

Matthew nods. It makes sense. Doesn't feel like a bluff.

'You arranged for someone to break into *my* house?'

'Yeah, nice line in moral indignation there, Matthew. You might like to save some of that for a more appropriate time, don't you think? And again, to be strictly accurate, they didn't break in. They used a spare key I had cut for them and then left a little nick in the door to make it look that way.'

'They smashed my bloody door to bits.'

'Then you shouldn't have been so tight-fisted and secretive with the keys to your office, should you? I can't get a copy of something I haven't got. Anyway, the point you seem to be missing is that the contents of your desktop are not exactly a secret anymore. I've gone over them so often I'm nearly word-perfect. It took this friend of mine less than twenty-four hours to open up everything I wanted to have a look at, including emails between you and Aimi going back several months which you thought were so safe. Whole load of other interesting documents too, including financial records and transfers. So now we both know where we stand, maybe that'll persuade you to stop pissing about and take this a bit more seriously.'

It does. All of a sudden, he's taking it very seriously indeed. He's been so sure it was the Vedras who were behind the break-in that he hasn't given any consideration at all to possible alternatives. The Liri Group did cross his mind briefly because he knows enough about some of their backers and associates to be sure they're capable of something like that, but he'd discounted them because he couldn't see what they stood to gain. Aimi's plan was something they'd be actively encouraging because it worked entirely in their favour. Why would they put it all at risk by pulling a stunt like that?

No, it had to be the Vedras, even more so after Joe came into his office and tried to pressurise him into talking about his dealings with Aimi. It dawns on him now that it's just as well he was wrong because if Billy's friends really *did* manage to get into the documents with very little effort, there's every chance the Vedras would have done the same. They'd be sure to have access to the same levels of expertise and if they ever found out what Billy apparently has, he shudders to think what their response would be.

His mistake, he realises, was looking for the financial and business motives. From the moment he saw the smashed door, he hadn't considered the personal. If he had, it would have been Joe Vedra he'd have suspected, anyway – it was *his* wife after all. What the hell was Billy doing, getting involved in something like this over a girl he hadn't even seen since they were both kids?

But involved he is, and Matthew knows he's going to have to tread very carefully here. He suspects he's going to face a barrage of questions and his biggest problem is that he can't be sure what Billy does and doesn't know. He'll be sure to fling in the odd rogue question to which he already knows the answer, just to test how honest the responses are. He loves this sort of cat-and-mouse game.

Matthew would love to find a way to turn the tables on him, maybe even get on the front foot.

It's not an option though.

Much as he hates the idea, he's going to have to grovel.

'Am I allowed to ask you something?' he says, undoing a couple of buttons on his shirt. He's sure the temperature has climbed a few degrees while he's been out here.

'If you like.'

'Why the break-in? I mean, I know you wanted access to what was on my desktop, but why? What made you suspect me?'

Billy picks up his mobile and flicks through it until he finds what he wants. Then he passes it to Matthew who uses finger and thumb to expand the photo. Billy is in the foreground of the first one. He's laughing and turning his head away, his long hair hiding most of his face. Matthew's not sure what he's supposed to make of it.

'Where is this?' he asks.

'The Nature Reserve – Rye Harbour. Mia and I spent the morning there back in August, then had lunch at The White Vine House in town. We took that crappy old digital camera of yours and she kept trying to take photos of me when I wasn't looking.'

He remembers that day so well, recalls how much pleasure she got out of simple things like revisiting places they'd been together when he was younger. How happy she was. How alive.

'She put a little folder of them together and emailed them to me when I went back to London. It was the last thing she sent me.'

'That's all well and good,' says Matthew, watching him carefully. 'But what's it got to do with my desktop?'

Billy leaves Mia in the Nature Reserve for the time being and comes back to the matter in hand.

'When the police came round to see me the second time, they brought photos they wanted me to take a look at. Two of them were mugshots of these Albanian guys – they were wasted on me at the time, although I'm pretty sure you could have put a name to them. The other two were photos of me at Camber Sands and I must have done something to piss off whoever took them because they obviously had it in for me. They set out to make it look like I was leaving Aimi's clothes on the beach when the photos had actually been taken a couple of days before. All I was doing was fetching a bag out of her car. The police knew it was a set-up even before they showed them to me – *clumsy*, I think they called it. But what they *didn't* know was whose camera was used to take them.'

'Billy . . .'

'The photos had this hazy yellow streak in the top right-hand corner, you see? Just like this one,' he said, taking the phone back and pointing at the screen. 'And this one.'

Matthew looked closely and couldn't see anything at all.

'It's something to do with the filter or shutter speeds or white balance issues,' Billy continued. 'I've googled it and they reckon it's more likely to show up in certain lights than in others. Even then you have to look at it closely to pick it up at all and apparently not everyone can do it. Mia never could – not on any of the photos she took – and you obviously can't either, but then again we already knew that. You'd never have sent the photos otherwise.'

'Jesus!'

Matthew put his hands to his face, his fingers rubbing vigorously at his forehead as if trying to ease the pressure. This was already worse than he'd imagined. He hardly dares think how much more is going to come out. He's been trying to remember exactly what else was on the desktop. He threw it away the moment it was returned and bought a new one rather than run the risk of some sort of ongoing electronic surveillance that might have been set up, but if Billy's telling the truth about what his friends have managed to do, there's no way he can bluff his way out of this one. Somehow he's going to have to enlist Billy's sympathy, keep him onside. He hasn't the faintest idea how to go about that.

'Billy . . . look . . .'

'I don't want an apology,' says Billy. 'I think we're way past that.'

'I'm not offering one. I sent the photos because I was scared, OK? You think I'd have signed up for this if I'd known what was going to happen? I was in way over my head and Joe Vedra was crawling all over me and I knew if I could just buy a little breathing space I could sell the house, transfer all my other accounts and get the hell out of here before the roof came in. That's all I was trying to do.'

'So I was your breathing space.'

'Yes . . . but you were never in serious danger, Billy. I swear to you, I'd never have let that happen. I knew the photos would never stand up to close examination. I just needed them to buy myself a bit of time, that's all. Give them someone else to look at. Muddy the waters a bit. Aww Jesus – I don't know what I was thinking, mate. I'm so sorry. But I swear I'd never have let things go so far as to stuff you up.'

Billy raises an eyebrow, that querulous look of his that suggests he's not quite bought into something that's been said. Matthew's definition of going too far is clearly in need of a rethink.

'OK,' Billy says. 'Apology noted. So now let's start from the beginning, shall we? Forget the questions for now. I'll just sit here and listen while you tell me how this all came about, starting with when Aimi first got in touch with you. And remember – twenty-seven days at the moment. Unless you want me to keep chipping away at it, I suggest you stick to the facts and forget about trying to save face. Let's be honest – you don't really have that much left to save, do you?'

And he's right. There's only one thing for it.

A pigeon settles high above them in the branches of the cherry tree and starts cooing.

A lorry can be heard making its way down Camber Road towards the golf course.

A normal day.

Matthew starts talking. Starts with Aimi's tale of woe, designed to enlist his sympathy. About Jack Vedra's decision seven years ago to parcel up a number of properties and take them off the official books, re-routing ownership through a number of dummy corporations and offshore accounts and ultimately reinvesting in others that couldn't be touched if HMRC started to take an interest. A significant stretch of land to the north of Brighton, currently containing a couple of derelict warehouses and three properties which had been converted into flats for university students, had been put in Aimi's name under Joe's supervision. Rental income from these properties went to the two of them, as did responsibility for liaising with the lettings agency that managed them and any ongoing upkeep costs.

It was on this land that Aimi wanted to build her own dance school. According to her version of events, Jack agreed in principle to give her the financial backing she'd need to get it off the ground but explained that for various legal reasons it would be getting on for three years before they'd be able to demolish the warehouses or the rented properties. He suggested she go away, draw up plans, consult with architects and think about staff recruitment while she waited for him to give the go-ahead.

It might be her name on the lease but nothing was going to be done without his say-so.

Then Jack overextended himself in what started out as nothing more than a pissing contest with the Liri Group. The deal cost him more than he'd bargained for and although the size and diversity of the Vedra empire was more than able to cover it several times over, he found himself needing to reassess some of his portfolios quickly to resolve a temporary cash flow problem. Although Aimi's land wasn't one of several assets to be offloaded at a reduced price because of the need for a quick sale, Jack told her he now needed to keep that land on standby in case there were any further surprises. That, of course, meant plans for the dance school needed to be put on hold indefinitely.

That was the last straw for Joe. He'd argued strongly against his father's impulsive decision to take on the Liri Group when they could so easily have been bought off. All they were really after were the service contracts and a foot in the door, which his father was determined to deny them. He was convinced they were backed by Albanian Mafia money from London and that if they were given any encouragement at all they'd be changing the landscape of the whole area with drugs, prostitution, people smuggling and unprecedented levels of violence sneaking in through the back door and taking root. *Not on my watch,* he'd said, as if the moral and legal compass for the entire south-east belonged to him and him alone.

It was his error of judgement and Joe didn't see why Aimi should have to pay for it. He went through the motions of arguing on her behalf and was put firmly in his place, so he was left with three choices, as Aimi put it. He could crawl back into line and do as Daddy said or he could resign from the company and try to set up somewhere on his own, almost certainly without any financial help from his father. Or . . .

Aimi claimed she was the one who came up with the idea to sell the land and disappear. She was the ideas person, Joe was the financial whiz kid. He could set it all up and spirit the money out of the country. He also had contacts in London who would be able to arrange a new identity for her and provide documentation to match. She could disappear to Marbella, buy a property out there. He'd stay inside the Vedra tent, siphon off whatever funds he could whenever the opportunity arose – he was the Financial Director after all – and send them her way, try to steer any investigation in the wrong direction, take a few holidays during the year to meet up with her and then, when a year or so had passed and the fuss had died down, he could engineer a disagreement with his father, walk out for good and join her. His father was on borrowed time anyway. Things were about to come crashing down. Better to cash out while he could.

Matthew laughs.

'It would never have worked,' he says. 'Aimi knew it even as she was pitching the idea to him. He should have known it too but she's had him twisted round her finger ever since he saw her in that show in Cyprus, so she got to work on him, turned it into a straight choice – her or his dad.'

'So where did you come into it?' Billy asks. 'Why did she need you?'

'Because from the outset she never had any intention of sharing anything with Joe.'

Aimi's initial question about confidentiality, Matthew explained, had been prompted by one thing and one thing alone. Joe must never know what she had in mind until it was too late. She told Matthew it was ironic really, because Joe had given her the idea in the first place. They'd been discussing the drafting of the suicide note and he had come up with the idea of making it sound as if Aimi, in a fit of anger, had gone to the Liri Group and agreed to sell it to them, then decided she couldn't face him and his father when they came back from Portugal. In the end, they decided it would never work and kept the Albanians out of it, but the potential certainly wasn't lost on her. She knew how interested they'd be. For one thing, it would gain them the foothold in the area they'd been seeking. For another, it would put Jack Vedra under even more financial pressure in the short term and leave him more vulnerable to the sort of attacks they were getting ready to launch. It was win-win from their point of view.

Matthew's role was to act as middleman, broker the initial meeting with the Liri Group and then represent Aimi during all the negotiations. They worked together on the presentation, delivered it word-perfect and walked away with a provisional agreement worth three point two million plus new identities for each of them that the firm's contacts in London would be happy to guarantee as one hundred per cent effective. The land and buildings, when taken in conjunction with the site and development potential, might have been worth almost twice that much but they weren't in a position to be too greedy. Time was everything.

'It was all going so well,' says Matthew, taking a sip from a beer which he'd collected from the fridge a few moments ago. 'We'd got it all set up for her to leave sometime towards the end of September because we'd have had all the financial details tied up by that stage, but then she and Joe went to London for the weekend to celebrate their wedding anniversary.'

He lifts the bottle and looks at the label before taking another swig from it.

'They went to the theatre and bumped into some woman Aimi and I met at a charity dinner the Liri Group had invited us to after we'd been there to thrash out the deal with them. Anyway, this woman recognised her and it spooked Aimi because she didn't want Joe to get curious about it all. She was looking over her shoulder from that moment onwards, sure it was all going to come crashing down at the last hurdle. We ended up bringing it forward five or six weeks.'

He continues to talk for a few more minutes but finds he's going over ground he's already covered. When he decides there's nothing to be gained by continuing, he comes to a full stop and waits to hear what Billy has made of it all. He's been talking for almost half an hour, during which time Billy's intervened only four or five times to seek clarification on a few points. He finds it so difficult to know what he's thinking, whether in talking so openly he's managed to claw back a little of the ground he lost earlier. He knows he needs to redress the balance somehow.

'OK,' says Billy eventually. 'One or two questions.'

'OK.'

'Did you fuck her?'

'Oh Billy . . . for Christ's sake!' He knows it's not in his best interests to allow things to escalate but how on earth are you supposed to reason with someone like him? He's like a dog with a stick in his mouth – he's never going to let it go.

'This charity dinner. It was an evening do, right?'

'Right. They invited us after we'd finished the meeting and Aimi thought it would be fun.'

'Where was it?'

'Brighton.'

'And you stayed the night?'

'Yes. We were their guests.'

'Single rooms or double?'

He wants to lie but there's something about the way Billy is rattling these questions off that makes him suspect he already knows the answers.

'Look, Billy – it's not the way it looks.'

'Double, then.'

'Yes. Look, there was a mix-up earlier in the day. When the meeting had finished and we'd agreed to stay for the dinner, we were handed over to one of the PAs there and she took us to the hotel. When she was making conversation in the taxi, she asked how long we'd been married and Aimi told her six months and kept the joke going all evening with everyone we were introduced to. You know what she's like. She'll do anything to be outrageous and have a laugh.'

'So the PA booked a double room – and you didn't think to put that right?'

Matthew starts to answer but realises he's wriggling. And can't afford to.

'No.'

'So did you fuck her?'

'Yes,' he says at last with the deepest of sighs. 'I'm sorry. I know it's no excuse but we'd been drinking and I know this is going to sound crass but it didn't mean anything at all. It was just sex, you know. And it's not like it was aimed at you in any way. I mean, if you think about it, you hadn't even seen or spoken to her in twelve years. She was married to Joe and it didn't even occur to me she might still mean something to you or I'd . . . aww shit, I'd probably have still gone ahead and slept with her if I'm honest. I'd had that much to drink and we were buzzing after having pulled off the deal. But I'm sorry. I know now how much Aimi means to you.'

'I was thinking about Mia.'

There's an edge to his tone when he says this and it dawns on Matthew far too late that he's been coming at this from the wrong angle. He's not sure how he missed it.

'Where does my sister fit into all this?'

'Aww shit, Billy. You know how I felt about her.'

'I'm starting to get an idea, yes.'

'No . . . don't do this, Billy. I loved her to bits, you must know that. That night in Brighton . . . I can't tell you how much I beat myself up over it. It was just a stupid mistake and if I could undo it I would but . . . Jesus! Don't ever think I didn't love Mia. She meant everything to me, you know that. Everything.'

'So where was her ID?'

Matthew frowns, doesn't catch on at first.

'Whose ID?'

'Mia's,' says Billy in the same flat, dispassionate tone as before. 'The deal you signed with the Albanians was for three point two million plus fake IDs for you and Aimi.'

'No,' he leaps in quickly. 'No. Just Aimi.'

Billy sighs.

'You're so full of shit, Matthew. So bloody inept. You keep forgetting I copied all your emails and documents. The name *Michael Johnson* ring any bells? I'll bet you crapped yourself when the fake passport didn't come back with the rest of the stuff that was taken. Care to tell me why you needed a new ID anyway? When were you planning to leave her?'

Matthew slumps forward, his head in his hands. It's over now. There's nothing he's going to be able to say to rescue the situation. There's just this brief moment when instinct kicks in and persuades him that if he can just bring himself to track his way back through the conversation, he'll be able to find the moment where it all started to go wrong and maybe do something of a repair job on it. It doesn't last though. The weekend used up most of his emotional reserves. He'd have needed every bit of concentration and energy to get through something like this unscathed. Now there's nothing he can do and he knows it.

'What if she'd still been here two years from now? Were you planning to stick around and wait that long or would you have grabbed the fake ID and run the moment the Vedras started to turn up the pressure?'

Matthew shakes his head.

'I'd never have left her,' he mumbles, so quietly he's not even sure Billy will have heard him.

'No, of course you wouldn't.'

'I'd never have left her. I don't expect you to believe me, Billy. In fact, I don't even care anymore. I'm sick to the back teeth with this stupid game of yours and you can think what you want. But I'd never have left Mia. I loved her.'

'Yeah. So much you lied to her.'

'No. I never lied to her. Not about anything that mattered.'

'So sleeping with Aimi didn't matter, is that what you're saying?'

Matthew looks up for the first time in a while, the fatigue and strain showing in his eyes.

'I'm saying I didn't lie about Aimi.'

'Lying by omission is still lying.'

'I didn't omit anything.'

And this at least has the effect of bringing Billy up short. He hasn't been expecting this.

'She knew about what happened at the hotel?'

Matthew nods.

'I told her the next evening.'

Billy leans forward, almost eagerly.

'So how did she take it?'

Matthew forces a tired smile to the surface.

'Better than I deserved. She wasn't happy about who I slept with. She said if you ever found out about it you'd be really hurt. I couldn't see it but she was right as usual. She always knew you so well, could read you like a book. I couldn't even make a decent guess what you were thinking half the time. Still can't.'

'She wasn't mad at you for sleeping with someone else?'

'No. She was mad at Aimi, that's for sure, but she knew me. She wasn't the sort to overreact. It was a stupid mistake on my part but I'd come clean about it straight away and apologised and she was just one of those special people who manage to see the bigger picture and recognise it for what it is. She knew how I felt about her. She was just disappointed that I hadn't stuck to our agreement.'

'What agreement was that?'

'We'd talked a fair bit about the future. She said if I ever found someone I wanted to be with after she'd gone, I should do it and not worry about whether I was being unfaithful to her memory or anything like that. I should just go for it and live my own life. The only thing she wanted was for me to wait until she was gone. I couldn't even get that right.'

And now Billy knows. *At long last* . . . he knows.

He's suspected it all along but not been able to pin either of them down – mainly Mia of course, because he's had more conversations with her on the subject, but he's raised it with Matthew before now and met with the same stonewall defence. Maybe he's right about him and Mia – maybe they were a tighter unit than he'd have liked to believe. They certainly knew how to shut someone out, even if it was for the kindest of reasons.

Because back in August, when Mia had that *funny turn* and collapsed and Matthew called to ask him to come and spend the week with her while he went on business to the US – that was when she first told him what was wrong with her and admitted for the first time just how serious it was.

And when Matthew slept with Aimi and came crawling home to ask Mia to forgive him, that was in March. Five months earlier. Which meant they'd both known for at least that long, and probably a good while before then, that she was going to die. He thinks back to all those days and evenings when he was sitting in his room, hunched over his laptops or babbling about God knows what with Zak and Karun, while all that time Mia was sitting at home, bearing the burden all on her own with no one there to comfort her half the time. He could have come home more often, maybe even taken a sabbatical and spent a few months with her, taken her away somewhere. Where was it she always said she'd like to visit? The Aurora Borealis – that was it. She'd always wanted to see the Northern Lights. He could have taken her there and anywhere else she'd have liked to go and *why didn't she tell me?*

He snatches up his phone and finds the email he was composing earlier. Not the one with the delayed schedule – that was just a ploy to get Matthew's attention and guarantee he thought about his answers before lying. This one may lack some of the more extraneous detail but there's enough in it to ensure that anyone reading it will be able to identify Matthew as someone with all the answers. He checks the name – TJ – and his finger hovers over *Send*.

He looks across at Matthew, still slumped forward on the lounger, defeated. Exhausted. He hasn't moved for the past minute or so. He's staring straight ahead, resigned to his fate. Billy remembers the times in the past that he's looked at this man and wondered what the hell Mia ever saw in him. Why she allowed him to come between the two of them. What it was that persuaded her all those years ago to move out and turn their own relationship into the emotional equivalent of some distance-learning project. He tries again now and still can't see it. It's a complete mystery. A bit like the camera, really. Some people can see the hazy yellow defect in the top right-hand corner. Some people can look all their lives and never pick it out. Mia, though . . . she could see the good in Matthew – and that's maybe the one constant in all this sorry mess, it occurs to him now. The only thing that really matters.

'I don't want to see you again,' he says to the top of Matthew's head. 'Ever. You get me?'

Matthew nods without looking up.

'You get a free ride on this one because you backed Mia once and took me in when a thirteen-year-old smart-arse was probably the last thing you needed and certainly wasn't what you signed up for. I've never liked you and I know the feeling's mutual and it's not like we need to pretend anymore for Mia's sake. But you get to walk away from this because if she was standing here right now that's what she'd have wanted. But I mean it – this is payback. Debt settled. I can't imagine you'd ever want to but if you ever make any attempt to get in touch with me again, I'll make sure the Vedras know everything.'

He goes back to the phone message, swipes and deletes it.

Gets to his feet and picks up his lounger, ready to take it back to the summer house.

Turns to face him.

'Sell the house now, Matthew,' he says. 'Drop the asking price, sell it and get the hell away from here before someone else susses you out.'

And leaves.

29

FRIDAY 22ND APRIL 2016

Peaks Island and the City of Portland, Maine, USA

One week earlier

'Jesus!' she hisses, one hand pressed to her breast as if hoping that might bring her breathing back to something resembling normality. 'What the hell are you doing here?'

Billy smiles, then puts on an exaggerated frown of dismay.

'I was hoping you'd be pleased to see me,' he says. Gets up from the Adirondack chair and comes over to her. Wraps his arms around her and she reciprocates reluctantly because her mind is working overtime. This is not at all what she expected. . . and certainly not part of the plan.

'How did you get in?'

'You left a window open at the back. I knew you wouldn't mind.'

She's running through the possibilities, trying to work out the best way to handle this. In the past year or so she's imagined any number of different scenarios and played them out to their logical conclusion in her head, but this isn't one of them. She's going to have to fall back on her instincts this time. They've served her well so far. And if there's any good news, at least it's just Billy. She's legislated for so much worse.

'Of course, I'm pleased to see you,' she says. 'It's just . . . such a shock. How did you manage to find me?'

Subtext: if you have, who else will? Has anyone else been clinging onto your shirt-tails? She hopes to God he's been careful.

Billy disengages himself from the embrace and sits on the sofa, patting it with one hand, inviting her to join him. He looks pleased with the question. Has always enjoyed having his ego massaged. *So clever of you, Billy – how on earth?* That's the best way for now . . . at least until she knows exactly what she's dealing with here.

She walks over to join him, shaking her head in disbelief that may be exaggerated but is certainly not feigned.

'This is amazing,' she says, both hands on her cheeks. 'God, I can't tell you what a relief it is to see you again.'

'Me too.'

'If you only knew how many times I've nearly got in touch. I keep thinking maybe now's a good time but honestly – you can't begin to imagine what it's been like. Every time I think I've come up with a safe way to contact you, something comes up to put that little doubt in my mind again.'

She pauses and offers a rueful smile, hoping to recognise in his expression some suggestion that he understands what she's been going through. She's not sure what it is she sees there but she's far from reassured.

'I keep thinking,' she continues. 'What if they're monitoring your email somehow or your phone or maybe they've got people following you, waiting for me to get in touch because they know if I'm going to turn to anyone, it'll be you. When you're looking over your shoulder every second of every day, you get a bit paranoid, you know? Start seeing bogeymen round every corner. If I'd had you here . . .'

She takes his hand and gives it a squeeze. Then strokes it absent-mindedly as she leans back and squints at him.

'I like the hair. Suits you. Makes you look older, you know? Not *old* as in old but . . . you know what I mean. When I turned the light on and saw you sitting there, for just a brief second . . .'

'You thought I was Matthew?'

'Yeah. Sort of. Which is ridiculous, I know, but . . . I quite liked the long hair, the messy look. What brought this on?'

'I wanted to look like my brother-in-law.'

'Yeah. Right.'

She laughs uncertainly. Realises he's not smiling.

'You serious?'

'Absolutely.'

'Why would you want to do that?'

'So I could use his fake passport.'

Another tripwire. What the hell is this? She's been pausing after each of his responses, hoping he'll elaborate but he seems determined to stick to a series of one-liners and leave her to do all the hard work.

'He's got a fake passport?'

'Yep. Found it in amongst some of his papers.'

'But . . . I don't understand. Why would he have one of those?'

Billy shrugs his shoulders.

'Dunno. Bit of a mystery, isn't it?'

'Did you ask him?'

'Nope. Didn't want him to know I'd found it.'

A thought occurs to her suddenly.

'Tell me you didn't travel out here on it.'

He laughs.

'With all the security alerts and facial-recognition software? You must be joking. No – it's a shame. It would have been handy to do that but I know for a fact Matthew's already used it to travel out here at least once. If I'd tried to use it, there's no way I'd have got through. I didn't dare risk it, so unfortunately I had to use my own as far as Boston. But I've been using the fake one at the place I'm staying.'

'You say Matthew's already used it?'

Billy nodded.

'To come out to the US?'

'Yep.'

'But why, Billy? What's going on?'

'Plenty of time for that,' he says, stretching out arms and legs simultaneously, making himself at home. 'Any chance of a drink? Didn't like to help myself.'

'Of course.'

She's not at all happy about this. Why the hell is he here? And how the hell did he manage to track her down? Is he the same guy who was looking for her yesterday? Bit of a coincidence if he's not, but Tennis Lady said it was some English guy with an accent, and that automatically made her think of Matthew, who's more than capable of turning up out of the blue when she least wants to see him. But why would Billy be going around pretending to be his brother-in-law – and doing a pretty good job of it too? The resemblance has never occurred to her before but it's definitely there.

She heads into the kitchen to get them both a drink. She's still got a couple of beers in the fridge that Hobie never got around to having. She offers him one of those but he asks if she's got any orange juice instead. She pours a glass for each of them, still thinking, thinking – scrambling in search of a strategy that might work. This is Billy, she reminds herself. He doesn't pose any sort of problem as long as his puppy dog habit of traipsing after her doesn't draw the attention of others who certainly *do*. She decides she'll handle him the way she always has and then . . . then she'll have to start all over again somewhere else. And just as she was beginning to feel this could become a permanent base for her, or at least as permanent as she's ever likely to find. *Damn!* If she'd known things were going to get this complicated . . .

She brings the drinks back in and Billy apologises, asks if she's got any snacks at all. He hasn't eaten in a while and is starving. She offers to cook for him, maybe heat up something from the freezer, but he says he'll be happy with some crackers or a bag of crisps, if she has any.

'Chips,' she corrects him, smiling. She goes back into the kitchen and brings in a family-size pack they can both dip into. Not that she's feeling very peckish herself.

'I'm not sure I'm following all this,' she says. 'Does Matthew know you've got this fake passport of his?'

Billy shakes his head, waits till he's swallowed the first mouthful of crisps he's taken.

'He'll know he can't find it. Won't know for a few days yet who took it . . . along with a few of his other things. He's on his way to New York, by the way. Should be in the air about now.'

More alarm bells.

'New York? What's he doing there?'

Billy laughs.

'Not a lot. He's going to stay in a hotel room for the entire weekend, then fly home again.'

She sits back, confusion writ large across her face with more than a little concern added to the mix.

'Billy – you're not making a lot of sense.'

'We'll get there,' he says. *Crunch, crunch.* 'Give it time.'

Aimi doesn't want to leave this hanging the way it is but there's another more pressing concern she needs to address. He hasn't answered her earlier question and it's not gone unnoticed.

'You still haven't told me how you managed to find me,' she says.

'No. I haven't.'

His voice is flat – a little off, it seems to her.

'Are you OK, Billy?'

He doesn't answer immediately. When he does, there's something in his expression that evokes sympathy in her. Some sort of underlying pain he looks as if he's trying to reconcile. She's not sure what to make of it.

'No,' he says. 'Not really.'

She waits, confident he's going to go on and explain himself. She wonders if this is about his sister. She knows all about that – Matthew explained it to her the last time they were in contact with each other. She's ready with a sympathetic shoulder. Might be able to put it to good use here.

'I was here yesterday,' he says. 'Came to see you.'

'I was at work. At the Dance Academy in Portland.'

'I saw you get off the ferry.'

Oh shit.

'What . . . this side or on the mainland?'

'This side.'

Shit!

She goes for the disingenuous look.

'Oh my God, I didn't see you. Where were you? Why on earth didn't you say something?'

'You looked like you were busy.'

'Busy?'

Toss head back and laugh as realisation dawns on you.

'Oh, Hobie, you mean? He's just one of the dancers. I bumped into him on the ferry – he was coming here to see Mikey, his *partner*.' She puts inverted commas around the word. 'You should have let me know you were here and I'd have introduced you.'

'I found out where you were from Matthew,' he says, so suddenly and apropos of nothing that it takes her a while to work out what he's saying. And what the implications are. 'I stole his desktop and laptop. I've seen all the files in there.'

He looks pointedly at her.

'All the emails as well.'

He takes a sip from his glass and puts it very deliberately back on the coffee table.

'I know everything.'

Ah . . . shit! she thinks.

Change of plan.

He waits until two a.m. – thinks that should be long enough. There are no immediate neighbours to peer out of windows because they can't sleep and he can't believe anyone is going to be wandering the streets or the shoreline at this time of night. Even so, he's careful where he treads, anxious not to make any unnecessary noise and attract unwanted attention.

He's wearing gloves, not because it's cold – although God knows it's not exactly balmy down here by the water's edge at this time of night – but because you can't be too careful. They're skintight gloves which he bought earlier in Portland, the kind surgeons peel off after operations. He doesn't want his fingers to feel hampered in any way.

He walks to the end of the garden, opens the little wooden gate and leaves it ajar. Then he steps onto the rocky part of the beach and makes his way across to where the rowing boat is moored against the short wooden jetty. He checks that the oars are still there, loose in the bottom of the boat, and looks around to make sure no one is watching. It's so easy to imagine a curtain being pulled back, some insomniac taking a walk along the shore to try to burn off energy, a jogger picking the one time of the day when the island isn't invaded by tourists. Better safe than sorry – you can do everything right and still be undone by sheer misfortune.

He picks his way back across the rocks, remembers to leave the gate open again and disappears inside the house. Goes to the kitchen and collects the small portable fridge which he emptied earlier. Icebox, he corrects himself. Is that right? Whatever. He carries it through to the back door and picks up the thick blue nylon rope that he liberated earlier from a garden on an unoccupied property on the eastern shore. Threads the rope through the grille on the back, wraps it twice round the fridge itself in such a way that the strands pull tight against each other, then ties it off in a stopper knot.

He picks up the fridge and retraces his steps down to the boat, again checking carefully to make sure his movements go unnoticed.

His arms ache by the time he gets there and he struggles to let it down gently in the bottom of the boat to avoid causing a disturbance. He stands up straight, shaking his arms, then heads back to the house.

One more trip.

'I know what you're thinking,' she says.

Bet you don't, is the first thought that flashes through his mind.

He was watching her closely when he told her about the emails and he saw the alarm in her eyes, replaced almost immediately by a calculating look. Funny what the mind can do. If anyone had called Aimi devious or manipulative, even a couple of weeks ago, he'd have laughed. Not in her nature. Nobody's fool, mind. Certainly not a soft touch and if you were stupid enough to get on the wrong side of her you'd probably get what you deserved, but he'd have argued till the cows came home that she was different with him. Always had been.

He supposes it's all a matter of what you look for and how badly you want to find it.

'I can guess what a kick in the teeth it must have been for you,' she says now. 'I know it looks bad. But will you at least let me tell my side of it before you judge me? Will you do that, please?'

She reaches out for his hand again and he pulls it away. Moves back to the Adirondack chair to put a bit of distance between them. He can see her more clearly from over here.

'You must have thought I was pretty stupid,' he says. 'That afternoon on Camber Sands. The sob story – the fake bruises. They were pretty impressive by the way. Someone at your dance school, I suppose?'

She nods. Her eyes haven't left him and he warns himself to be wary. It would be so easy to drown in them.

'I didn't think you were stupid, Billy. God knows, you've never been that. I thought you were sweet and sensitive and just about the most loyal person I've ever met and I should have been straight with you from the start and just asked for your help because you didn't deserve to be lied to. But I was running out of time and so scared you'd say no. I couldn't afford to tell anyone what was happening unless they were one hundred per cent with me, you know?'

He takes another few sips from his glass, more to clear the throat than anything else. Watches as she does the same.

'When have I ever been anything else?' he asks.

'I know, I know. But we hadn't seen each other for so long. Hadn't even been in contact. You might have changed completely.'

'Like you, you mean?'

'Yes.' She hangs her head and he wants to get out of the chair and put his arm round her. Just for the briefest of moments. Old habits. 'Yes – like me. I had no way of knowing for sure. And then we had that walk along the beach and I was already selling you the fake version and it wasn't until I got home that I realised how unfair it was because you hadn't changed, Billy. You were still the same, sweet, trusting kid I knew when we were at school together.'

Billy thinks back to that day he came home to find both his parents lying side by side on the bed. Remembers the strange effect that had on him at the time, the total absence of grief, the weird fascination with the make-up that he's never managed to explain to himself or any of the therapists who've tried to get in there. Punching his father when he twitched. That too.

Then he thinks about Mia and the numbness he felt when he got the phone call from Matthew to say she'd collapsed again and wasn't going to make it this time. Calling for the taxi, not quite believing what he was saying. Taxi home all the way from London. Getting there just in time to argue the toss over whether she should be allowed to stay with him for just a bit longer. Watching her drift away and knowing there was no way he could hold onto her or go with her. Finally understanding what his father might have gone through when he decided to go with his wife rather than stay and look after his kids.

He remembers all this.

And she thinks he's still the same fifteen-year-old she knew before.

'I could tell when we were in the supermarket together – even then,' she continues, blithely unaware. So sure of herself. 'That's why I gave you my number and asked you to get in touch. I was going through such a crap time. It was all so stressful, trying to put the deal together, having to juggle so many versions at the same time –'

'So many lies.'

'Yes. I know. So many lies. And then suddenly, there you were. Out of the blue. When we bumped into each other like that, I –'

He shakes his head.

'More lies.'

She pauses. Frowns.

'We didn't bump into each other, Aimi. The police –' He laughs as he remembers them hammering away at him, hoping to get him to own up to something he wasn't even aware of. 'You know, they were so sure we'd arranged to meet there that morning and I kept saying, how could we? I didn't even know about

Tenterden. Hadn't a clue that was where Mia and I were going. I thought they were the ones being stupid. But *Matthew* knew, didn't he?'

She blinks.

'*Matthew* knew,' he continues, 'because Mia had probably told him what her plans were for the morning and even though he couldn't be sure I'd necessarily agree to go with her, he'd have known there was a pretty good chance I wouldn't let Mia go on her own. All he had to do was give you a call on his mobile before we set off.'

Aimi looks as if she's about to protest but seems to think better of it.

'Don't try to pass this off as something magical, Aimi. This wasn't fate bringing us together just when you needed an old friend to come to the rescue. You knew all along that I'd be coming home for a week. Probably knew before I did. If I hadn't been so worried about Mia, it would have dawned on me that Matthew didn't need me to come back that early. I was there for nearly five days before he left for the US . . . and we all know why he had to go there, don't we? Important business, yeah? So don't try to make it sound as if I stumbled into all this sordid little mess. You set the bait and I came skipping in like some lovesick Bambi.'

Aimi says nothing. She picks up her glass and drains it completely. She holds it in front of her face for a moment, rubbing it across her forehead. Thinking. Then she puts it back down on the table. When she lifts her gaze to meet his, it's almost a different person looking back at him.

'OK, Billy,' she says with a sigh of resignation. 'I can see you've made up your mind about me and I'm assuming you haven't come all this way and gone to so much trouble just for the pleasure of telling me what a bitch I am, so how about you get to the point, eh? What is it you want from me?'

He senses he's meant to be thrown by this. There's a sharper edge to her tone and he's clearly managed to piss her off. The Billy of old wouldn't want that and would now soften his stance, try to find a way to get things back on an even keel. The minor arguments they'd had when they were younger had all ended in the same way – with him backing down. But that was then.

'Why Matthew?' he asks. 'Why him of all people?'

She sighs, flops back in her seat.

'Why not? I needed a lawyer. He was there.'

'But why did it have to be Mia's husband?'

'Like I said, why not? I didn't owe your sister anything. She never really liked me anyway – don't pretend she did. Back when we were going out with each other, she made it pretty obvious she didn't think I was good enough for you. If you'd been around when I really needed you, it might have been different. I'd have come to you first and tried to find someone else to do all the legal work, but you weren't there so it was a case of any port in a storm. Don't make a big deal out of it.'

Don't make a big deal out of it.

He takes a deep breath. Refuses to allow himself to be side-tracked by issues that no longer matter. He looks at his watch – it's been ten minutes. Shouldn't be long now.

'You want to know why Matthew's in New York?' he asks, working hard to keep any emotion out of his voice. 'He's there because he thinks you need to talk with him face-to-face. He probably thinks you've had a change of heart.'

She frowns, shakes her head. She can make no sense of this.

'Why in God's name would he think that?'

'Because you sent him a disposable phone with a message on it saying so.'

'Billy – what the hell are you talking about? It's taken me ages to shake him off and get him to understand this is as far as it goes. He's been well paid and has got nothing at all to complain about. Now he needs to back off – I'm not interested. I had to threaten to send anonymous notes to Joe explaining his role in all of this before he'd listen. The last thing I want is him getting mixed messages.'

'You don't need to worry,' says Billy with a half-smile. 'He won't do anything. He's just going to sit there in a hotel room, waiting for you, then go back to England after you don't show. And he's had to use his own passport so there'll be a record of his flight over here when they start to investigate.'

'When who starts to investigate? Billy, I swear you're making no sense at all. And why New York? Why not Boston?'

'Because New York makes it look more as if he has something to hide. And besides, I didn't want to run the risk of him coming here from Boston airport and crashing our little chat.'

'I don't understand. I'll be honest, you're starting to scare me a little. I thought I meant something to you. Why are you doing this?'

Thought is the only word that really strikes home. The implied doubt says it all. She clearly has no idea of how he feels. How he's always felt.

'The photos,' he says. 'The ones of me carrying your clothes from the car park to the beach. Matthew told you about those?'

'Yes. Stupid idea. Just one of many he came up with. Why?'

'You knew what he intended to do with them? That he was hoping the police would think I'd either helped you or maybe even killed you? You knew that?'

'No, Billy, for Christ's sake. I didn't know about it. Not beforehand. He only told me afterwards. The idiot was spooked because he thought Joe was looking a bit too closely at him and wanted to add another scent for him to sniff at instead. You can blame me for a lot of things but not that, OK? If I'd known what he was going to do, I'd have put a stop to it.'

'But how did he know, Aimi?'

'How did he know what? That you were going to be meeting me at Camber Sands? How do you think? We were working together, remember. He knew where you were going long before you left the house.'

'It's the photo though,' he insists. 'He knew we were going to meet at the beach and he could have tracked us along there, somewhere high up in the dunes, without any risk at all of being seen by me.'

'So?'

She picks up the glass again, puts it to her mouth. Realises it's empty. Looks at it. Goes to put it back on the table but it slides away from her and onto the floor. He reaches forward and picks it up while she looks at her fingers, frowning.

'But he didn't. He ignored the safe option and chose to take it from the Oasis car park,' he continues, as if nothing has happened. 'Not much cover there. He'd told me before I left the house that he was going to be in his office working while Mia took a nap. If I'd seen him down at the car park five minutes later, even without that crappy camera in his hand, he'd have had a job explaining what he was doing. That was some risk he was taking when he really didn't need to.'

Aimi flops back on the sofa, one hand shading her eyes, the other gripping the arm of the sofa. Back rigid.

'Billy . . . I . . .'

'You'll probably tell me it was because he thought it was worth taking a chance if he could get a photo of me carrying the clothes because that would leave me with some explaining to do and that's exactly what happened. But that's not the point, is it? Are you going to ask me what the point is, Aimi?'

'Billy . . . what . . .'

She slumps forward and he catches her before she falls to the floor. He lays her down on the sofa with her legs curled up behind her. Then he lifts her head and sits down, allowing it to fall back into his lap. Her eyes are closed and her breathing is irregular as if she's having some sort of minor panic attack so he strokes her forehead, gently, the way he always did with Mia. Easing the pain away. In spite of everything she's done, he doesn't like to think that Aimi's in any sort of discomfort. He wants to look after her.

'Always take your drink with you when you go to fetch a bag of crisps,' he says, in a much softer, soothing voice, as if lulling a child to sleep. 'Didn't anyone ever tell you?'

He looks down and decides this angle is no good. She's upside down and he can't make out her features as easily as he'd like. So he slides out from under her and rests her head gently on one of the cushions. Then he kneels down next to her and carries on caressing her forehead.

'Now . . . where were we?' he continues. 'Oh yes – the point. The point is, it couldn't have happened the way you say because he'd have had to know I was going to go to your car, Aimi. Don't you see? Even if he was prepared to take all those risks just to get a photo of me carrying your clothes from the car park to the beach, how did he know you were going to forget the bag with your dog's ball launcher in it, not to mention the cardigan you wanted to take with you and never wore once because it was too hot? How could he know that, Aimi? Eh?'

Her breathing's calmer now. She still mutters the odd word every so often but it's more like she's mumbling in her sleep. It's not in response to anything in particular.

'I didn't want you to go,' he says. 'Back then, I mean. I didn't want you to go to London. We'd have been OK if you'd stayed here, don't you think? Eh? Nod your head if you think we'd have been OK.'

He puts one hand on each side of her face and moves her head forward and then back again.

'That's right. If you think about it, all your problems started from that moment. You never used to lie and cheat and steal and fuck everything that moved if it would get you what you wanted. You already had it, didn't you?'

Another nod.

'That's right. We had each other. And if I'd been there next to you all those years, I could have told you what was happening, made sure you stayed true to the old Aimi because the way people talk about you nowadays . . . you really wouldn't want to hear it.'

He leans forward and places a gentle kiss on her lips and meets with no response at all, just the gentle rhythmic sound of her breathing.

'You know what Jack Vedra said about you when I went to see him? He said, *it's who she is, Billy – it's what she does.* Like it defines you. Like he knows you. Everyone thinks they know you, they all feel they can pass an opinion on you, but they don't. Not the real you. I'm the only one who's ever seen that side of you. But you're drifting further and further away from that person and I can't let that happen anymore, Aimi. You do understand that, right? I just can't.'

She nods again.

He takes his hands away from her head.

And forgives her.

If it was a bit nippy down on the shore, it's a lot worse out here. He's been rowing for about ten minutes and has worked up quite a sweat, otherwise he'd have needed a couple of thick jumpers to cope with it. He's not sure how far out he needs to go but guesses this will probably be about right – apart from anything else, he can't ignore the fact that he'll still have to row back again afterwards.

All the way out here, he's been talking to her. Telling her about the money which isn't in her account anymore. Zak will have removed it by now, the moment he got the go-ahead. Two-thirds of it will find its way into the company via a number of dummy corporations and offshore accounts. The other third will enable Billy to leave for good and start up somewhere else. It's going to happen at last. Eurostar . . . from St. Pancras. That magical moment when the train will pull into Ashford – Ashford International – and instead of getting to his feet and stepping down onto the platform, he'll stay exactly where he is and follow that journey through to whichever destination he decides to pick out for himself.

He's pretty sure she can't hear any of it and wouldn't make much sense of it if she could, but he knows he'll feel a lot better if he says these things to her before she goes. At least this time she'll be doing so with his blessing, not sneaking off without giving him a chance to explain how he feels.

He decides this will do and stops rowing. Pulls the oars inside the boat. Turns to look at her. He's draped a blanket over her. When he undressed her just now, it was the first time he'd ever seen her naked.

She's beautiful, lying there in the moonlight. Stunning. He can see now what all the fuss was about, why she's been able to make so many men act completely out of character, although his own reasons for loving her have always gone much, much deeper than that. He felt funny about undressing her earlier. Didn't want to do it and felt dirty when his fingers started to fumble at the buttons of her blouse, but he didn't really have any choice. If he's going to leave a pile of clothes on the beach, he can hardly have her go into the water fully clothed, can he?

It's time, he thinks. He can't afford to stay out here any longer than he has to. He's no idea what time the early-morning fishing boats come out, but he wants to be back long before then. He reaches across and picks up the unsecured end of the rope, then holds up her left wrist. The one that should have been wearing the bracelet he gave her all those years ago but which she lost. Or his own, which he then gave to her as a replacement when she got out of the car at Heathrow. He doesn't believe she lost either of them. She's just fussy about what she wears. She's probably got expensive bracelets by the dozen, more than she needs. Why would she want his?

He ties the rope around her wrist, then again around her waist and fastens it in a secure knot. He lifts the mini-fridge onto the bar that runs across the back of the boat and leaves it there for now. Then he picks up the daisy chain, the one he made this afternoon while he was waiting for her to come home and then stored in the boat. He slips it over her forehead like a headband and sits back to take one last look before kissing her goodbye.

He's had this dream the last couple of days of her floating in the water on her back, totally relaxed – at peace at last. No more lies. No more cheating. No more having to look over her shoulder. He lifts her now and lowers her as carefully as possible over the side, hoping to watch her float off for as far as the rope will allow, the moonlight glistening on her body, but she starts to slip under the water which is not how it's meant to be, so he pulls her back towards him so that he can lift her head up above the surface, only the effort means the boat starts to rock and he has to let go for a second and grab the side to steady it, but that means letting go of Aimi and she's slipping under again so he leans right over in an attempt to grab her under the armpits and that's enough to tilt the boat still further and send the fridge sliding along the shelf. He realises what's happening and knows he can't get to it in time so he watches in horror as it slips off the edge and plummets into the water.

Immediately he's aware of the sheer weight that's tugging now at Aimi. Not just the mini-fridge but the water too. He's managed to grab her free arm with both hands but it's difficult to get good purchase because both his hands and her arm are soaking wet and he keeps sliding up towards her wrist. He needs desperately to untie the knot and let the fridge go on its own but he hasn't got a free hand and probably wouldn't be able to undo the knot anyway.

And he knows he can't hold on for much longer. It's hopeless. It wasn't meant to be as sudden as this. All he can do is tell her he loves her and apologise as he lets go and watches her disappear so much faster than he'd been expecting.

The last bit he can't be one hundred per cent certain about because it all happened so quickly, in the blink of an eye really, and it's not the sort of thing he'll ever get to talk to anyone about. But even though the thought appals him, even though he tries everything he can think of to persuade himself that it couldn't have happened that way, he can't shake the conviction that as she disappeared below the surface for that final time, she opened her eyes.

EPILOGUE

30

WEDNESDAY 15TH JUNE 2016

Portland, Maine, USA

BODY CONFIRMED AS THAT OF MISSING TEACHER

Police sources today confirmed that the body which washed up two days ago on the western coast of Cushing Island is that of choreographer and dance teacher Kellie Moore (27), who went missing nearly two months ago. Concerns were first raised when she failed to report for work at the Portland Academy of Dance and Performing Arts on Monday 25th April and her clothing was subsequently discovered on the shore at the end of the property she was renting on Peaks Island. Her whereabouts since then have been the subject of much speculation, with persistent rumours that she might have staged her own disappearance. Investigators will now be seeking to determine whether her death resulted from a swimming accident or from something more sinister.

A police spokesman said that he was not prepared at this moment in time to speculate on how long her body might have been in the water. An autopsy has been scheduled for later today and it is hoped that more details will be available then.

In the meantime police have repeated their request for any information regarding the movements of the deceased during the weeks leading up to her disappearance.

Jeanie Alvares lowers the newspaper for a moment and walks over to the window to let some air in. It's going to be a hot one today – they're talking about temperatures in the low eighties by mid-afternoon and this rest area gets so stuffy when the sun shines directly into it. No harm in giving it a bit of an airing now, even though she suspects most of her guests will be out and about this afternoon anyway. In weather like this, she's sure they'll want to make the most of the scenery. She always recommends the Eastern Promenade and the Bayside Trail to anyone who asks for suggestions – well, whether they ask or not, to be honest. Some people don't like to because they're afraid they'll be bothering you but it's no trouble really.

Peaks Island too, she thinks as she settles back into her armchair. That's a real favourite with everyone who comes to Portland. *Like stepping back in time*, they tell her. So nice to be able to stroll around the island and not have to negotiate a constant stream of traffic. Some of her guests aren't satisfied with just the one visit – they feel drawn back to it for a second time if the length of their stay permits it.

She remembers that odd young man a while ago who couldn't get enough of the place. Hard work, he was. Rarely took any of her recommendations other than where to eat in the evenings. Not one of her big successes, she thinks as she picks up the paper and resumes reading where she left off.

She suspects it's the article that's made her think of him. He would have been here around the time that poor girl disappeared. Jeanie's a great believer in the interconnected nature of the universe, wonders if their paths ever crossed before they went their separate ways. On the ferry maybe or during those walks he took around the island. He might have stopped her to ask her the way or check what time the next ferry was due to leave, although he should have known the entire schedule off by heart, the number of times he'd gone back and forth. Or she might have sat next to him on one of the crossings and dropped something on the floor – a lace handkerchief maybe – and he could have stooped to rescue it before the wind got up and whipped it away. They could have sat next to each other, watching the docking area draw nearer with every second, she wondering whether he was going to say something, he desperately trying to come up with something that wouldn't be too forward, fearing that anything he says will be dismissed as a cheap pick-up line. And the boat will dock and they'll get off together and she'll smile in one last, desperate attempt to encourage him, but he'll be reaching down for his rucksack and not see it and the moment will be gone. He'll trudge back to The Old Theater Guest House, kicking himself for another opportunity missed and she'll . . .

Jeanie ends it there. Doesn't like to think what's happened to that poor girl. Such terrible things you hear about nowadays. Never used to be like that – or maybe it did but so much more gets reported nowadays and in such graphic detail. It's really not necessary. She puts the paper to one side again, her thoughts still engaged with the romantic story she's just dreamt up. There's something in there that needs to be shaken loose and she realises what it is. Her sentimental little film couldn't have worked like that because didn't he have a girlfriend anyway? She's sure he did, although she can't remember the details. She remembers thinking the girlfriend, whoever she is, must really like the silent, brooding type.

Curious, she goes into reception and takes her big blue notebook out of the drawer, checking first to make sure Richie isn't around to see it. She flicks back through the weeks, checking the names. She can't remember his but she knows she'll recognise it when she sees it and sure enough – there it is. Michael Johnson. That's the one. Easy to pick out anyway, even if she hadn't managed to recall it, because most of her guests have about half a page each to their name, some of them even more. *Michael Johnson* has two lines and she'd had to go against her principles to get even that much. She remembers how she sneaked into his room when he'd gone out to dinner and rummaged through his wardrobe and chest of drawers, hoping to find something she could put in her notebook.

And she's pleased to see she was right. He did have a girl-friend – or at least, that's how she imagines it. The first note refers to a photo she found, not on his bedside table oddly enough – although she's not sure how you define *odd* when it comes to Mr Johnson – but alongside his underwear and socks in the drawer of the bedside table. You'd have thought he'd have had it on display where he could see it when he came in but there you go – strange. She remembers it was in a battered wooden frame and that the girl was a pretty little thing, maybe late teens, certainly a fair bit younger than he was. The frame suggested it might have been an old photo but you'd have to wonder why he wouldn't carry a more recent one around with him. Scope there for another romantic storyline, she decides.

The second note is born of desperation more than anything else. She couldn't just leave it as one line in the book so she was ready to include anything at all that was out of the ordinary and when she picked up the two novels by his bedside and looked inside the front cover, both had similar inscriptions – the name *Billy Orr* followed by a date, presumably when the books were first purchased. She'd thought it odd at the time that Michael Johnson had borrowed two books at once from the same person and was already noting it in the notebook when the obvious occurred to her – he'd probably picked them up at a garage sale or used bookstore. It went in the notebook anyway for want of anything else.

As she's closing it, she notices the dates he was here and gives a silent cheer. Unless she's mistaken, they match almost exactly the time when that poor girl disappeared. She goes back to the newspaper and lo and behold she's right. The girl failed to report for work on Monday 25th April and he was here for two nights, the Wednesday and Thursday of the week before. She smiles to herself, pleased that she can now embroider her little romance with a touch of added piquancy. This time, she tells herself, he can finally pluck up the courage to say a few words to her, just before they disembark. They'll discover they're heading in more or less the same direction – maybe he'll tell a little white lie about that so that he can prolong his time with her. And when the time comes to say goodbye, he'll finally ask and she'll agree to meet him for dinner. That single meeting will change the course of history because she'll be with him rather than taking late-night swims and . . .

And . . .

Jeanie leans back in her chair and closes her eyes. She's not sure where she'll go with this but she's already decided one thing.

There will be a happy ending somehow.

She just loves a happy ending.

ACKNOWLEDGEMENTS

This novel is set primarily in and around Rye, Camber Sands and Winchelsea, areas I had the pleasure of visiting for a few days while researching the book. Anyone living there will recognise a few liberties taken with precise geographical locations, but for the most part I've tried to stay as faithful to the area as possible. It is quite charming and I'd like to offer my apologies to the people of Ashford and assure them that Billy's rather warped feelings about the town in no way reflect my own!

As for the other location, Peaks Island, off the coast of Portland, Maine, I again had to take a few liberties for the sake of the plot, but it really is as delightful as described within these pages. The day my wife and I spent there in August 2016 was a major highlight of a fantastic tour of New England, and I hope others are fortunate enough to have the chance to visit some day.

So many people to thank.

So little space in which to do so.

Absolutely no chance that I'll compile a list without forgetting somebody.

For that reason, please forgive me if some of the thanks tend towards the general rather than the specific. If your name's not there, just pick the category that best fits you and remember this – if you're still with me, I'm immensely grateful for the interest and support! I might conceivably write without an audience, but having one is so much more gratifying.

So . . . thanks to:

- Elaine
- The Cotswolds network of family and friends
- The South Coast contingent who go out of their way to offer so much encouragement
- The staff at The Angmering School for not contacting me to say how much better the timetable is since Laura took over from me
- Everyone at Bonnier Zaffre, but especially Katherine Armstrong and Bec Farrell for taking me on after Joel so cruelly abandoned us all, and for making the transition as near to seamless as possible
- My agent, Adam Gauntlett of Peters, Fraser and Dunlop for the enthusiasm and the sense of excitement he brings to the whole business and for his faith in my potential
- The bloggers and reviewers who have picked me up at a very early stage and carried me through these first two years, making sure I came to the attention of a wider audience. So grateful . . . you know who you are
- Special mention to the incomparable Katherine Sunderland and the series of book panels she organises at The Harpenden Arms. The panel event earlier this year which I shared with Chris Whitaker, Alex Caan and Simon Booker, was outstanding
- Elaine

- The book clubs who have chosen either *The Hidden Legacy* or *Lie In Wait* and then invited me to talk to them about my writing. I love those visits
- Individual readers who have got in touch to say how much they enjoyed the books and written reviews for Amazon and Goodreads. Much appreciated
  - DS Chris Curtis, now retired from Norfolk Constabulary, for helping me to fill a number of plot holes. I'm sure he'll wince at a few liberties I've taken, but he's hopefully made it all the more convincing for the readers
- My fellow authors at Bonnier Zaffre who offer levels of support any writer could only dream of, but especially:
  - Gayle Curtis for the phone calls and constant reassurance
  - Lesley Allen for introducing Elaine and me to Bangor, N. Ireland
  - Chris Whitaker for boosting my street cred, although the DEA are proving to be a bit of a nuisance
- Gemma, Alex and Leah – so proud of you all
- Elaine

Read on for an exclusive letter from
G. J. Minett and a chance to join
his Readers' Club . . .

Dear Reader,

Many thanks for taking the time to read *Anything for Her*. If you have read my previous two novels, *The Hidden Legacy* and *Lie in Wait*, I'd love to hear your thoughts on this latest offering – feedback is always appreciated. If you haven't come across them yet, I hope you found enough here to persuade you to give them a go as well. Your support will always be valued.

Anything for Her was written during a fifteen-week period between mid-December 2016 and early April 2017, but the actual writing represents just a small part of the overall picture. I was planning the novel as early as May 2016, sifting through ideas and working hard to settle on a central character I knew I would be carrying around with me for the best part of a year. This is always the starting point, and the story emerges from putting this character's weaknesses to the test.

Once I had Billy Orr firmly fixed in my mind, I still had to come up with a detailed plan for the novel before I could start writing. This is a crucial part of the process for me. I know several novelists never work from a plan – they start with a scene that comes into their head and then set out with no real knowledge of where the story is going to take them. I sometimes think it might be fun to try that approach. I also know it's never going to happen. I'm not ambitious enough to strike out blindly – I need the safety net of a detailed structure to fall back on.

Even when that's in place, I'm still not ready to start the actual writing because the question of the setting has to be resolved. Whenever I visit book clubs or give talks, I'm frequently asked why I chose a particular location, and for my first two novels there wasn't a great deal I could say because I hadn't needed to do much in the way of research. I was brought up in the Cotswolds and moved to the West Sussex coast over 45 years ago, so I knew both of those areas like the back of my hand.

Maybe that's why I felt *Anything for Her* represented a chance to branch out a little. I know I could have simply invented a place, but I was reluctant to go down that road because it felt like a wasted opportunity. Many readers have commented on how much they enjoyed recognising certain locations and pinpointing the characters' exact movements. So I was always going to choose a genuine location, no matter how much I might tweak a few geographical features – it is fiction after all.

So why Rye, Camber Sands and Winchelsea? The answer may sound prosaic – and it's tempting to come up with something outlandish just for the wow factor – but the honest truth is that I owe it all to *Mapp and Lucia*. I had never even driven through that corner of the East Sussex/Kent border, but I happened to watch a TV adaptation of EF Benson's classic, which prompted me to spend a few days in Rye to see if it had potential. With Camber Sands on the doorstep, I had the perfect backdrop for Billy and Aimi's escape plan. Winchelsea was just a touch of self-indulgence on my part as I knew that Spike Milligan was buried in the churchyard there and I wanted to see for myself whether his gravestone really does say: *I told you I was ill* (and it does, albeit in Gaelic).

As for Peak's island – again, genuine location – I knew I needed to find a setting in the US, and as we were due to take a family holiday in New England, I vowed to keep my eyes open throughout the journey for anything that might fit the bill. When we spent a couple of nights in Portland, Maine, the lady who runs the guest house (and resembles Jeanie Alvares in only the most positive ways) suggested we take the ferry across to Peak's Island. The moment we stepped off the boat I knew I'd found the right place. If you ever get the chance to visit, please say hello from a grateful author. And urge everyone there to buy the book, of course!

If you are interested in hearing more from me about *The Hidden Legacy, Lie In Wait, Anything for Her* and any future books, you can visit **www.bit.ly/GJMinettClub** where you can join the G. J. Minett Readers' Club. It only takes a moment, there is no catch and new members will automatically receive a copy of a deleted scene from *Lie In Wait*. I've often been asked what happened to Danny (the misguided lad who pulls the jewellery store scam) as it's deliberately left unclear at the end of the book. Some readers, it appears, were quite taken with him, even though they accepted he was morally and legally compromised, and would like to know whether he came out of it OK. The outtake will enable you to discover what my original intentions were at least.

If you do join my Readers' Club, your data will be kept private and confidential and will never be passed on to a third party, and I promise that I will only be in touch now and again with book news. If you want to unsubscribe, you can of course do that at any time.

If you would like to be involved and spread the word about my books, you can review them on Amazon, GoodReads, any other e-store, your own blog and social media accounts or, of course, by actually spreading the word to friends and family! Reviews are so important to all novelists, not just in terms of the boost a good review will give to our spirit and self-belief, but also by boosting the marketing of the book . . . even unflattering reviews can be helpful if constructive! And we always read reviews – trust me.

For now, thanks again for reading and for your interest. I look forward to meeting as many of you as possible, either by visiting your book group or giving a talk at a bookshop, library or event somewhere near you.

With my best wishes,

G. J. Minett

If you enjoyed *Anything for Her*, why not try G. J. Minett's dark and gripping crime thriller

LIE IN WAIT

A man is dead. A woman is missing. And the police have already found their prime suspect . . .

Owen Hall drives into a petrol station to let his passenger use the facilities. She never comes back – what's more, it seems she never even made it inside.

When Owen raises a fuss, the police are called – and soon identify Owen himself as a possible culprit – not least because they already have him in the frame for another more sinister crime.

Owen's always been a little different, and before long others in the community are baying for his blood. But this is a case where nothing is as it seems – least of all Owen Hall . . .

AVAILABLE NOW IN PAPERBACK AND EBOOK

PROLOGUE

NOW: WEDNESDAY, 1ST OCTOBER

OWEN

'How long now, would you say?' she asks.

Out of the roundabout, up into third and accelerating away, engine screaming like a harpy till he manages to slam the mule of a gear stick into fourth. Gently doesn't seem to cut it anymore. Gearbox nearly shot to pieces. Probably got another five, ten thousand miles left in it, according to Vic at the garage. Then he's going to have to start looking for a replacement. New truck altogether would be nice but a couple of years away at least. Even stumping up for a reconditioned gearbox is going to leave him a bit stretched.

Willie says it's his own fault for never showing any ambition. *Brain the size of a planet – why the fuck are you pissing around with lawnmowers for a living?* Swears a lot, does Willie. You can pick him up on it as much as you like but it never does any good. Straight back at you – effing this, sodding that.

'Twenty minutes,' he mumbles. 'M-maybe less.'

'What . . . Worthing or the hotel?'

'Don't know the hotel.' He's told her this already, wishes she'd listen. Like he's got nothing better to do than answer stupid questions.

Engine starts to shudder as the needle creeps up to fifty. In the headlights he can make out the number plate of the car in front: GR02 ZMM. Total = 79, the calculation automatic, the irritation instantaneous. *Prime number*, he thinks to himself. So . . . overtake or drop back, one or the other. Anything as long as he doesn't stay too close. Quick check to see what's coming the other way and it's non-stop headlights, so he eases his foot back on the accelerator and watches as the car in front starts to pull away despite itself.

Stupid, he thinks. You wouldn't drive a car with faulty brakes or with tyres that were almost down to the rim. Why is it that people will happily pour their faith into so many leaky vessels in life – looks, dress code, personality – and yet ignore the certainty of numbers? People lie – they lie all the time. Only numbers are constant.

'OK,' Julie says, holding up her iPhone. 'Just shout when we get anywhere near Worthing and I'll switch on Google Maps.'

They're heading out into open countryside now, Yapton and Barnham away to their left. Street lights racing off into the distance in his rear-view mirror. He risks a quick sideways glance. Can't really see her face – not clearly. There's the glow from the dashboard and the oncoming headlights that strafe across her features, causing the lenses of her spectacles to flash for an instant. Otherwise, nothing. Darkness.

Not pretty exactly, he thinks to himself. Wrong word altogether. Pretty is Abi. Always has been. And he can accept it's maybe not ideal to be using her as a yardstick even now but there you go – you don't get to choose these things. No, Julie's not *pretty*. Pretty suggests petite and she's a good few inches too tall for that. Loose-limbed, athletic. Something of a swagger in the way she holds herself, he's noticed, as if she's ready for a scrap if it comes to it. At least she's here. It's not like people are queuing round the block to help him right now.

Fuckable is Willie's assessment of her. Tells you all you need to know about Willie.

Past the Climping turn-off. Away to the right, Littlehampton golf course and the seaside resort itself huddled down beyond it, dimmer switch turned right down and a strange, murky haze hanging over the lamps which have reappeared at the roadside.

'We getting near yet?' she asks again. Another stupid question.

'Quarter of an hour or so.'

She sighs, wriggles around in her seat. 'Look, I'm really sorry about this but do you think we could stop somewhere for a few minutes? I'm bursting for the loo.'

Tesco has just flashed past on the other side of the dual carriageway. He maps the next couple of miles in his head. Picks out the Body Shop roundabout. Zeroes in on the Shell station on the opposite side of the road.

'About two or three minutes,' he says.

'That's great. Sorry about this,' she giggles. 'Small bladder.' He blushes, hoping she can't see his face any more clearly than he can see hers.

New traffic lights up ahead, turning amber. He brakes and rams the truck into neutral. Glances in the rear-view mirror again as they roll to a standstill and sees the headlights of the car immediately behind, which seems to be taking an eternity to close the gap. There's a blast on the horn from further back and as the lights turn to green, the car stutters forward as if the driver has been woken from a daydream.

HK12 RCA: total = 53. *Prime number*. His heart skips a beat as he moves through the gears and pulls away once more. *Same car*. He trawls back through the journey so far, pinpoints the locations exactly. Traffic lights near the Martlets roundabout. Then just after they left Bognor seafront, as they went past the beach entrance to Butlins. Now here.

And here comes the rocking – he's moving back and forth, back and forth in his seat, mumbling the number plate to himself, over and over.

> *Oi, how many times d'you have to be told? Cut it out.*
> *Owen, dear . . .*
> *You gonna sort him out or you want me to?*
> *Owen, don't do that, there's a good boy.*
> *Like living with a bloody half-wit.*

Out of the corner of his eye he can see Julie's watching him closely, puzzled rather than alarmed. 'You OK?' she asks, and she reaches forward, placing a hand on his knee. He recoils as if she's holding a taser, forces himself to calm down, concentrate. Pushes himself back in the seat, shoulders taut, neck muscles braced against the headrest. Needs to ride this out.

'What is it?' she asks again.

'Car behind – no, don't turn round,' he says, catching her arm as she twists in her seat.

'What about it?'

'I think it's been following us.'

She pauses before replying, allowing time for this to sink in. 'Why?'

'It's been there since we left. Keeps letting other cars get in between, then closes the gap when there's no choice.'

She shakes her head. 'No, I mean why would it be following us?'

No answer to this. He's told no one about Worthing or the Burlington. Unless she's let something slip, no way anyone can know about it.

'Dunno,' he says.

She laughs, tells him he's been watching too many films.

'Let him go past if he's bothering you.'

Hand on his knee again. Slight reduction in voltage this time but he wishes she wouldn't do that. He doesn't know her well enough for that level of intimacy. Says nothing. Takes three deep breaths. One . . . two . . . three. The frantic impulse to rock back and forth is still there but it's starting to ease off a bit and he's able to relax his shoulders a little. Runs a finger across his damp forehead. Evenings starting to get cooler now but he can feel a trickle of sweat working its way down his neck and into his T-shirt. More deep breaths. Perhaps she's right. Maybe he's imagining it. All the same, he's not about to take his eyes off the rear-view mirror, watching every manoeuvre made by the car behind.

New housing estate coming up on the left, tucked away in the shadow of the sprawling Body Shop complex. One more roundabout and he'll know for sure. She's seen the petrol station up ahead and waves a finger at it.

'That any use?' she asks. 'They're bound to have a loo there, aren't they?' He nods and realises as he does so that he'd rather they went somewhere else. In his mind's eye he can still see Callum filling the car while his fancy woman disappears inside to pay. Doesn't see how he can say no though, not with her squirming around on the seat next to him.

'You need any petrol?' she asks. He shakes his head. 'Do you mind popping in and getting me some mints or something while you're waiting? I could do with something to freshen my mouth up a bit.'

He nods but in truth he's only half listening. His eyes are on the mirror the whole time, staring a hole in it. There's thirty metres between the two vehicles when he signals right and pulls across into the outside lane. Two seconds later, he winces as he sees the other driver do the same. Huge Norbert Dentressangle lorry coming from the right. Just time to get out ahead of it and accelerate into the roundabout; then *no* to the Body shop entrance, *no* to the A259, *yes* to the third exit. Copycat has to wait for the lorry and a couple of cars to pass and his headlights are no longer in the mirror as Owen turns left again almost immediately to pick up the access road to the Shell station. He slows for a second or two, half-turning in his seat to get a better look. Watches with some satisfaction as a large estate car drives straight over the top of the mini-roundabout, heading off towards Rustington. He can't see the number plate from here but he's pretty sure it's the same one that was following them. He relaxes, his heart beating a little less insistently.

'Can you let me out here?' she asks. As he pulls over towards the rear of the building, she points out of her window. 'That tyre-pressure thingy – if you park over there I'll just go and find the loo. I'll only be a second, I promise.'

AVAILABLE NOW IN PAPERBACK AND EBOOK